What Critics and Reviewers are saying about Guardian Into the Light of Day:

The Bookfest's Silver Medal Winner for Superhero Fiction 2022
"Guardian into the Light of Day, by J L Meredith, provides readers with a great story, a great protagonist, and some nail-biting moments. This action and adventure superhero novel will keep readers engaged from the start and even give them a bit of romance without going over the top."

– 5 Stars Literary Titan, Gold Award 2023

"...Guardian: Into the Light of Day is a creatively written superhero novel that is full of contrasting characters. JL Meredith packs this novel with thrilling fight scenes, witty dialogue, and steamy romance. If you love comics or superhero movies, this is right up your alley!"

- 5 Stars Reader's Favorite Book Reviews & Award Contest

"Meredith's fully fleshed-out characters, convincing situations, and fluid prose will have readers anticipating her next one. Entertaining and lighthearted, the book makes for a winner."

- The Prairies Book Review September 2022

GUARDIAN

INTO THE LIGHT OF DAY

J L MEREDITH

Dedication: To my parents, for encouraging my love of reading.

J L MEREDITH

ACKNOWLEDGMENTS

Many thanks to:

Editors: Clark Chamberlain, Catherine Rupke, Christine Hayton

Cover: Art: Jose Augusto, Design: Bobooks

Interior Art: Aleks Chansky, Rene Micheletti, Sebastião Nicolau,

Expert Advice: Dr. Brian Abraham, Dr. Najma Ahmed,
Dr Mohammed Bourouh, Dr. Jamie Coleman, Dr. Gerry Cooper,
Nick Corcodilos, Dr. Dana Fleming, Lee Harris, Kari Hummer,
Dr. Henry Miecz, Dr. Andrew Petrosoniak, Robert Ryan

"The hero is one who kindles a great light in the world, who sets up blazing torches in the dark streets of life for men to see by." -Felix Adler

Prologue...

June, 1194, County of Cornwall, England

The little blue planet looked so beautiful, so wondrous...

Stars became streaks—.

Flattened out like a puddle of golden light, the entity sheepishly rose from the hollow to reform and illuminate the Bodmin Moor like a tiny sun. Filled with excitement, it began to explore.

It crested a hill to float over a granite outcropping before descending to round the hill's green foot and probe into a valley. Under its brilliance, the white flowers, of a cluster of hawthorn trees, resembled new fallen snow. It paused to greet a toad, resting on a rock. The night's breeze carried sounds of distress. Concerned, the entity sought it out.

Beside a dirt path, two figures lay in the wind-swept grass. One stared unseeing at the night sky. The other kicked and squalled, desperately crying for its mother.

Filled with pity, the entity drew closer. It anxiously circled the scene, struggling for a solution. Rising up, it looked for other solids that might be nearby. Finding none, it wavered for a moment. To do nothing and allow it to suffer and die was unconscionable. There was only one decision...

The entity flew straight for the empty vessel. In a burst of light it permeated its flesh, filling up the space left by its previous essence. The body convulsed once, bending at the waist then flattening out again. Wounds healed, teeth straightened, hands calloused by tools and scarred by cooking fires became soft and supple. Skin tanned from a lifetime of working in the sun became as porcelain. Bones lengthened, becoming harder than diamonds while sinews became tougher than titanium.

Memories flooded in; memories of childhood, of parents and siblings, of marriage and children, memories of working the land and keeping a home.

The sharp intake of breath that followed rivaled the volume of the infant's wails. The recently deceased Elizabeth sat up, a wide-eyed look of shock upon her face. A downward glance at the infant brought instant recognition and overwhelming feelings of love and joy.

"Don't cry," she soothed, lifting and gently cradling the newborn. A strange instinct overtook her. She stood and with a swipe of her fingers, shredded the front of her kirtle and began to nurse.

"*Child?*" A voice filled with concern entered Elizabeth's mind. "*What have you done?*"

Elizabeth reflexively glanced about before looking up into the brilliant light of a second star-like being. "*Isn't she beautiful?*" she gushed, beaming at her mother.

The elder being regarded her patiently. "*The vessel—*"

"*She is called Elizabeth.*"

"*You are Elizabeth so long as you remain in that form. I sense its memories and instincts are affecting you.*"

Elizabeth looked down at the infant and smiled unabashedly. "*She's a wonder. So full of life—with so much potential! I never conceived of something so ... Mother, we spend so much time among the stars when we could be experiencing this!*"

"*The stars are where we belong.*"

"*But we fail to appreciate the beauty of a single planet or a single being. If you could know this love—*"

"*I do know it.*"

"Then you know why I must help her."

"Your compassion is admirable but these creatures are short-lived, they live and die in an instant. I would spare you this pain."

"That does not make them any less wondrous." Elizabeth glanced down at the baby affectionately. *"I'm going to stay and care for her."*

"Are you so sure? I cannot linger. You would be alone."

"I will have her and she will have me."

"But you are a child yourself, you have no experience parenting another," the elder said gently.

"I have her mother's memories—and I could teach her—and them, so much!"

"You cannot and must not," the elder admonished.

Elizabeth regarded her mother, blinking in disbelief. *"But why? I can see from her memories that they suffer needlessly. I could help them."*

"For you to reveal yourself—who you are, and what you are, would interrupt their development. It would be disastrous. You don't wish to harm them do you?"

"No."

"And you must keep your nature hidden, a secret—unknown to them," her mother said.

"If that is what I must do—."

"It is."

"Then I still choose to remain."

"Very well, but I fear it is you who will be learning—and the lessons will be difficult." The elder's voice carried an air of sadness.

"I don't care, I want to help her."

"Then I will provide you with something to assist you."

As Elizabeth cooed and rocked the infant, a gray, melon-sized ball shimmered into existence, appearing at her feet.

"What is this?" she asked.

"These creatures cover themselves for protection and ornamentation. This life-form will assist you to live among them without drawing attention to yourself. It will respond to your thoughts and assume whatever appearance you command."

Elizabeth tore the remainder of the bloodied and soiled clothing from her body. The symbiote streamed up her feet and over her body to replace the kirtle with one resembling it from memory.

"I will leave you now to learn. Mind what I have told you."

"I will, Mother. I won't harm them."

"I will look in on you from time to time. Farewell, child."

"Thank you, Mother." Elizabeth watched her elder's luminescent form quickly rise into the heavens and become lost among the stars. Looking down at the baby, she began to beam. "You are called Catherine and I will love you forever!"

Present Day, Saturday, 5 PM Local Time, Northern Kenya

Floods, and droughts, famine and conflict, oppression and desperate medical conditions, all of them brought refugees to the gates of United Nations Refugee Camp Number Seven or as its residents called it, Sehemu Nzuri (the Good Place in Swahili.) For Elizabeth, Sehemu Nzuri was ideal for hiding from the world, where her past was not nearly as important as the good she could do in the present.

In the two years she had lived there, Sehemu Nzuri had transformed from a dusty, sunbaked refugee camp to an oasis. With funds from a granting agency, the designs of permaculturists, and the labors of its twenty-thousand inhabitants, Sehemu Nzuri had become a place where drumstick and breadfruit trees ringed the nearby hillsides like victory laurels, where every child attended a modern school, and where the hospital's care rivaled that of the university hospital in Nairobi. In that hospital's operating room, a dulcet, voice concluded the final notes of *Someone to Watch Over Me.*

Doctor Elizabeth Welkin simultaneously completed her song and the final stitches of her young patient's appendectomy. She looked up at the nursing sisters from behind her frameless spectacles, her liquid green eyes twinkling with humor and warmth. "A few days in the ward and she'll be back with her family."

"I will dress the wound for you, Doctor," Sister Ruth volunteered.

"Thank you, Sister. I'll go talk with—"

The doors leading from post-operative care flew open, slamming against the wall with a startling bang. Dr. Salvador 'Sal' D'Abbraccio, a thick-bodied Brooklyn native with the accent to prove it, burst in on them. He wore a surgical mask and a white lab coat over blue jeans and a Dodgers t-shirt. He began to croon. "I've got you under my—"

Elizabeth held up a halting hand. "Let me stop you before

you begin, Dr. Sinatra." She sighed inwardly. There was always at least one at every camp, at Sehemu Nzuri, thirty-one-year-old Salvador D'Abbraccio was this camp's would-be suitor. He was handsome enough and exuded more confidence than most. One might even call him brash.

"How you doin'? Did I miss today's surgery singalong?" The corners of his eyes crinkled smugly.

"I'm afraid so, Doctor. Would you like Dalia's history?"

"Dalia?"

"Your patient?" Elizabeth flicked a glance at the eight-year-old girl on the table.

"Any concerns?"

Elizabeth shook her head. "None."

"All charted with your usual thoroughness, Sister?"

Sister Ruth looked up from bandaging to respond. "It is, thank you, Doctor."

"Then I'll read it."

Elizabeth paused to lean down to her patient and speak to her in gentle tones. "Dalia, we took care of your appendix, when you wake up, your family will be with you and you'll be feeling much better. I'll come see you soon."

"Nice touch," Sal commented.

"If you'll excuse me, I have to—"

"I need to see you Dr. Welkin."

En garde. "Is it a patient matter?" She turned to leave.

"Yeah, just give me a sec." He stopped at the end of the gurney to speak to the nurse. "Just set her up in post-op, Sister, and keep an eye on her, I'll be around." Sal followed Elizabeth into the antiseptic-smelling scrub room.

"What is it Dr. D'Abbraccio?" Elizabeth pulled off the celadon-green surgical gown and cap to pitch them into a laundry hamper. She paused and shook her creamy tresses loose with her fingers.

He pulled off his own mask. "Sal. Come on, enough with the *Dr. D'Abbraccio.* There's no one around, call me Sal."

"Very well, Salvador." She fastened a thin band of brown leather about her neck. A tiny charm of Africa hung from its d-ring.

He pointed. "I like your necklace."

"Thank you, it's a choker." She continued her dressing, donning a broad-brimmed sunhat and tugging on a pair of butter-soft leather gloves. "Who's the patient?"

"Me. I've got a fever."

Elizabeth's features became sympathetic. "Oh! I'm so sorry, I wasn't aware you were feeling unwell. What are your symptoms?" She began to look for a thermometer amongst the drawers and cabinets. "I'll find someone to replace you in the ward and—"

"It comes and goes depending on who's around."

She caught his teasing tone. *By the stars....* She turned and saw his grin. "My therapeutic advice is to avoid whomever is eliciting your symptoms."

"Illiciting? Freudian slip?"

She folded her arms across her chest. "Hardly."

"Well, I just can't avoid her, she's like the sun. I'll shrivel up."

"Mind yourself, Icarus."

He reached up and snatched her hat away.

"Whatever are you doing?" She frowned as he fanned himself with it.

"Always with the hat...the gloves...the...." He gestured to her blouse. "Long sleeves. I've never met anyone with as much skin protection as you. What are you trying to prove? You're already the fairest of them all." His own Mediterranean complexion had become bronzed under Kenya's equatorial sun. "You should wear a dress sometime. I bet you would look really good in a dress."

"I do look good in a dress, but it's not very practical. May I have my hat back, please?"

"Don't you have at least three of these?"

"Such contingencies are necessary; one never knows when a

thief may show up." She held out an expectant hand. "My hat?"

"In a minute." He continued to fan himself.

"What part of England are you from anyway? You sound like a Shakespeare actor."

"I'm surprised you know William's work," she said with a tinge of condescension.

"Hey! I went to NYU not Don't Know U."

She stifled a giggle. "It's called RP."

"What is?"

Lightning-quick, her hand shot out to retrieve her hat and replace it on her head. "My accent."

Sal's head snapped back. "Whoa, quick reflexes. I'm impressed.

Have dinner with me."

"In the ward? How romantic."

"No, I was thinkin' on the hill top. We can pack a picnic and watch the sunset. I've got a great vintage of my grandfather's vino. We could get to know each other. When's your next night off?"

"Christmas—if there isn't an emergency."

"Christmas? That's like..." His fingers fluttered in his palm as he counted off the months. "Five months away. Come on, I'm a good guy, you know what they say—"

"Abstinence is the best policy?"

"Geez Betts, how long's it been?"

Elizabeth's chin dropped. She fixed him with a look of admonishment. "Don't be rude."

He lifted his hands in a fending gesture while wearing a playful smile. "Hey. I'm sorry."

"If you'll excuse me, the Njeri family is waiting for word—"

"The who?"

"Dalia's family? Excuse me." She pushed open the door to the outside and was instantly met with a breeze carrying the scent of warm sand.

"Hey, wait a minute." Sal followed her onto the hospital's

back porch where six members of the Njeri clan waited in the shade of the overhang.

Elizabeth exchanged smiles and embraces. "The surgery went wonderfully. I have no concerns." She turned and gestured to Sal. "And Dr. D'Abbraccio will be caring for Dalia this evening. You'll be able to see her in about an hour."

Sal was quickly surrounded by the grateful family. "Hey no problem, no problem…you're welcome…you're welcome…." He nodded and accepted thanks and handshakes from her parents while his legs were hugged tight by Dalia's younger siblings.

Elizabeth chuckled at her colleague's exasperation before noting the approach of someone from behind. She turned to see a nun, her wimple fluttering about her weathered face.

"Dr. Welkin? The lorry won't start, could you have a look? It's just here at the maintenance garage." The nun pointed across the compound to a dusty and dented, flatbed truck that had been fitted with racks and benches for passengers.

"By all means, Sister, lead the way." Elizabeth began to follow her.

"Hey! Where ya goin'?" Sal's voice boomed as he hustled to catch up.

"The sister says there is something wrong with the lorry— the truck." She translated for him.

"I could take a look; back in Brooklyn they take away your Man Card if you don't know about these things."

"Oh? So, you receive a Man Card if you're mechanically inclined? Should I expect mine in the post or is there a plumbing requirement as well?"

He scoffed. "Funny. But aren't you worried about hurting your lily-white hands?"

"I haven't yet." She set out across the compound with Sal in tow.

"Hey, have you talked to that documentary crew yet?"

She gave him a sideways glance. "No, and I have no intention to." She motioned for the nun to attempt to start the truck.

Sal raised his voice over the engine as it groaned and struggled to start. "Why not? If anyone around here looks like a movie star, it's you."

"It's not a movie. It's a story about the people here and what they've accomplished."

"The way I hear it, you're the one that wrote the grants for this whole place. The school computers, the solar panels—and there's gotta be millions of bucks of new equipment in that hospital. By the way, the internet's out."

"Money is quite easy to come by if you know where to look. As for the internet I'm sure Mrs. Owiti has contacted someone about it." She turned her attention back to the engine and regarded it contemplatively and thought aloud. "It's getting plenty of fuel and I fixed the carburetor less than a month ago..." She lifted a finger and tapped her chin in thought. "Then it must not be getting a spark. I need a multimeter."

Sal leaned against the truck. "I thought you were an uptown girl, where'd you learn to fix cars?"

"Learn?" she asked only half paying attention to him. "Here and there. Excuse me a moment."

She stepped into the shadows of the cinder block garage. The majority of the tools and equipment here were new. At the back there were table saws, drill presses, lathes, and racks of hand tools, closer to the front were vices, workbenches and bright red tool chests with each drawer labeled in Swahili, English, and with descriptive pictures. At the opposite side of the garage, stacked one atop the other, were two 1000-gallon fuel tanks that gave off the nostril-rippling scents of diesel and gasoline. In moments, she quickly found what she sought.

"Crank it please," she directed the nun and watched the front of the gauge as she touched the leads to the posts of the battery, it showed 12.4 amps. "The battery is fine." She moved the leads to the starter and solenoid, and repeated her direction to the nun. The engine protested but did not turn over. The reading came back 6.4. "Hmm."

"Got you stumped? Want me to—" Sal reached out to take the meter.

She pulled the device protectively to her chest. "No, not at all. It must be one of the cables." Removing her hat, she bent over the fender and reached deep into the engine well to the ground wire mounting.

"Looking good," Sal commented.

Feeling his eyes, she turned her face to offer a rebuke. "Hush." Touching the lead to the ground cable and the starter, the reading went back up to 12.4. She righted herself and looked at him. "It's the ground wire. It's not making a good connection."

"Tell me about it," he muttered.

"Could you get me a wire brush and a ratchet with a three-eighths-inch socket please? The brush should be in the big drawer and the— "

"Yeah, I saw, in the drawer marked ratchets."

"And the mechanic's creeper too, please?"

"You're the doctor."

He disappeared for a moment to rustle around for what she requested.

She surveyed the truck. It was thirty-five years old and could probably do with a replacement, perhaps another grant…. Her thoughts were interrupted by Sal's return. "Thank you." She accepted the tools, lay back on the creeper, and rolled under the truck's bumper.

Sal leaned over the top of the fender and grinned down through the engine compartment. "Not afraid to get down and dirty huh?"

Elizabeth ignored him and busied herself by loosening off the ground wire bolt.

"Hey, can I ask you something?"

Half listening, Elizabeth noted the buildup of rust and dirt on the fastening. "Could it wait until I'm done with this?"

"Nope."

Still only half listening, she began to use the brush to scrub the bolt's threads. "Very well…" She sighed inwardly.

"Why did you come here? I've watched you work and—"

Yes, I've felt it. "Did you learn anything?"

"Yeah, but I don't think you're hearing me."

"You may be surprised at just how well I hear." The dust and rust scrubbed free of the bolt and wire; the ratchet clicked rhythmically as she tightened it down.

"Yeah but—"

"I go where I'm needed." She pushed herself out from under the truck and stood up. "Try it now, Sister!" she shouted to the nun.

The engine rumbled to life. Sal reached up and pulled the hood closed with a 'thunk.'

The nun waited for Elizabeth to pick up the creeper before giving a friendly wave and pulling away.

Sal watched her return the tools to their proper places. "What's it gonna take to get your motor runnin'?"

She turned back to him. "Not sophomoric innuendo."

"If you're not into me, why are you still talking to me?"

"A character flaw on my part, I'm far too agreeable and polite."

"You know…" he smirked, "I've been asking the kids if they think Dr. Betty should give me a shot—"

"You've been asking the children for dating advice? You mustn't corrupt them—"

"Who's corruptin'?" he asked indignantly. "They're good kids and they know a good thing when they see it. The question is why don't you? Come by the ward tonight, we'll have coffee and you know…." He shrugged. "Talk."

"I prefer tea thank you and I'm afraid my evening is already planned, after bedtime stories and tuck-ins with the orphans, I have a stack of journals to—"

"Journals? Really? Your idea of a Saturday night is—"

"Doctor Bettyyyyy!" The delighted squeal of a six-year-old

girl interrupted them.

Barefooted, Issa and her brother, older by a year, Juma, came thundering up like a stampede of antelopes.

The pair of orphans made Elizabeth's heart smile.

"Supper! Supper! Supper!" Juma clasped his hands together and bounced in place on two good legs. A year earlier, Elizabeth had saved his life and his legs after a terrible encounter with a landmine. Following the surgery, she had cradled and comforted Issa all night by his bedside.

Elizabeth peeled off her gloves; her voice became bubbly with delight. "My darling luvs! It seems someone's quite hungry." She knelt to gather them into a warm embrace and exchange affectionate kisses.

Juma released himself and began to bounce again. "Supper! Supper! Supper!"

"You're askin' Dr. Betty on a supper date? Good luck with that kid," Sal spoke over the blonde's shoulder.

Issa erupted into peals of giggles. "Juma's going on a date!"

Her brother's chin dropped to his chest. He folded his arms and he shook his head so vigorously that his entire form swayed.

Elizabeth watched the boy flush to a shade of raspberry and kept her annoyance with Salvador hidden, instead she regarded the boy with a gentle smile. "The only dates my friend Juma is interested in..." She paused to produce a handkerchief from her pocket. "Are the sort that grow in the orchard. Where it seems...." She dampened the silk cloth at her lips before leaning forward and beginning to gently wipe and dab at the syrupy residue from around Juma's mouth. "...he's spent some time this afternoon." She replaced her handkerchief in her pocket. "Boop!" She playfully tapped the end of his nose and found his smile.

"You're gonna be a great mom one day," Sal said.

Elizabeth felt a spasm of grief but maintained her composure. She stood up and offered her hands to the pair.

"Well, we can't have you hungry. Supper then?"

"Yes!" Issa shouted and Juma agreed, each accepting a hand.

"Shall we skip?"

"And sing?" Issa asked.

"I think that's a simply marvelous idea! What shall we sing?" Elizabeth asked.

"Mwalimu Wetu?" Issa squeezed Elizabeth's hand tight.

"Our Teacher?" She leaned down to smile at Issa and elicit a giggle. "That's one of my favorites!"

"Hold on, let me lock up and I'll come with you." Sal pulled down the bay door of the garage. It rumbled shut and locked with a click.

"That would be lovely Dr. D'Abraccio, but I'm afraid you can't."

"Oh yeah? Why *can't* I?" He asked in an abysmal imitation of her accent.

"Because you have patients."

"Oh…." He glanced back at the hospital, his disappointment evident. "…yeah."

"But the children would love to have you dine with them another time." She looked down at the pair who nodded in agreement.

"Maybe tomorrow?"

"Sunday dinner? Splendid. But for now, we must tend to our busy agenda. We have to skip, and sing, and wash our hands and hope we get to supper before it's all eaten up. Now…" she looked from one child to the other "…who will start the song?"

"You!" the children shouted in succession.

"Me? All right then. Goodbye, Doctor D'Abraccio, thank you for your help." The children added their goodbyes and Elizabeth began to sing in Swahili as the trio skipped away. "Mwalimu wetu hapendi keleleee…."

Sal watched them go and threw up his hands. "You're a riddle, you know that! A sphinx!"

"Thank youuu!" Elizabeth called over her shoulder before

continuing her sing-along.

Elizabeth sat at a small table in her eight by ten cell of a room. It was a gallery of love. Scores of drawings from the camp's children spanned the walls from knee-height all the way to the ceiling. She was in many of them, always with bright yellow hair, orange skin (or white if a white crayon was available,) red lips and green—and occasionally, blue dots for eyes. Along with the table, the art and the chair, a cot and footlocker completed her furnishings.

Beneath the bright bulb of a desk lamp, she clacked away at a manual typewriter. Her machinegun pace was only interrupted by the ring of the margin bell and the ratcheting of the carriage return. She didn't need the lamp to see but it helped to keep up the illusion of being human. The truck grant application was shaping up nicely. The camp needed something easier to maintain and able to do the myriad of things trucks in camps like this required, carrying cargo and passengers, and even improvising as an ambulance.

There were seven non-governmental agencies working in Sehemu Nzuri. She wrote the grant applications for all of them. Elizabeth had the best inside connections.

The Cumberland Foundation, a private family philanthropic agency always came through on her grant requests. She always knew the right words to say, because in New York, at the Foundation's headquarters, she wasn't known to them as Dr. Elizabeth Welkin but by an alter ego, the ever elusive, jet-setting dilettante, Charlotte Cumberland. Ms. Cumberland was occasionally heard from, but had only ever been seen once. Communication always occurred through correspondence or telephone calls. An urgent rapping at her door interrupted her work.

"Dr. Welkin!" Through the door the voice of Ayana Owiti, the camp's administrator, called, and then called again.

Elizabeth yanked open the door. "Ayana? Is there an emergency?" She began to reach for her medical bag.

"It isn't medical." Ayana puffed; her hand came to her throat.

"Please...." Elizabeth gestured to her chair. "Come in and sit down. It isn't that French documentary crew prowling around again, is it? I don't do interviews."

Ayana waved off the offer of a seat. "I just found out a rock...." She paused to swallow. "A giant asteroid is going to hit the Earth. How do we tell everyone? Should we?"

Feeling her heart seize, Elizabeth kept her emotions from her face. "One moment, Ayana. The internet is filled with all sorts of nonsense. Allow me to have a look." *Silly thing, I hope it still has a charge.* Elizabeth fished her mobile device from her pocket and surfed to the BBC's site.

'US Launches Missiles to Divert Asteroid Collision' read the headline.

"The American president has sent rockets—missiles to stop it. Should we tell them?" Ayana gestured towards the camp. "Will it do any good?"

Elizabeth read the first paragraph of the BBC's article. She blinked, doing some rough mental calculations. "That was ten hours ago. The missiles should be about a quarter of a million miles into space by now."

"What do you think we should do?"

"Who else knows about this?"

"Just us but it is so horrible, how can we tell the camp?" Ayana looked at Elizabeth.

Elizabeth's jaw tightened; her slender eyebrows knitted pensively. She took a deep breath. Her fists clenching as she stalked about the room for a few seconds. The blonde paused to stare, unfocused, at the crayon drawings pinned to the wall.

Ayana's expression changed to one of surprise as she watched the young woman. Elizabeth's usual relaxed posture now resembled a spring that had been coiled too tight.

Her fists unclenching, she turned back towards Ayana, "Please listen to me," she said in a soft yet serious tone, "we don't need a panic on our hands; the refugees have enough to worry about without this. I suggest informing the other staff and calling your family in Nairobi. I'm sure they will solve this; people can be very innovative when they are motivated." She wished her confidence matched her words.

"Are you sure?" Mrs. Otiwi asked, her eyes becoming glassy.

"Yes." She handed Ayana her spectacles and mobile device, "Please take care of these for me. I have something to attend to."

"Where are you going?" Mrs. Otiwi began to pursue her but quickly fell behind.

"Remember we don't need a panic on our hands!" Elizabeth called over her shoulder as she disappeared around the corner of the staff quarters.

How the hell did I miss this? Elizabeth ran for the camp's perimeter. The sun had set. The faint light of the gloaming was against her back as she ran east into the purple night. Kicking up plumes of dust and nearing the speed of sound, it was still a plodding pace. She wanted to be over the ocean before taking flight. Someone would certainly take notice of an object suddenly moving at hypersonic speeds into space and she couldn't have it traced back to the camp.

Space, near Earth

Hundreds of miles above the Earth, Elizabeth grimly studied the asteroid as she would a trauma patient. Craggy and gray, it was mountainous in size. On the near side, a gash-like crater pulsed a brilliant ruby red. Vapor trailed from the hole like the tail of a comet. She traced its wake back towards the sun.

The blonde gnashed her teeth in self-recrimination. Somehow she had missed the asteroid's approach in her weekly survey for extraterrestrial threats. Setting aside her feelings, she turned her attention back to the matter at hand.

Salvos of nuclear missiles flew to intercept the marauding rock. Their trajectory suggested a sound strategy. Rather than attempting to explode the asteroid, the missiles were set to explode alongside it in an effort to divert it.

Watching a dozen of the weapons explode near the crater she realized it would not be enough. The strategy was sound but the distance from the hurtling body to the Earth was less than half the distance to the moon. There was too little time to achieve the necessary deflection.

It needed more.

Trusting the calculations of the scientists on the ground, Elizabeth nestled herself Atlas-like into the reddened area and began to push. Her teeth on edge, she felt its glassy surface against the side of her face. She leaned in, grunting with exertion.

She grimaced as the shock wave and gamma rays of another nuclear salvo struck her.

The asteroid shuddered. Veiny cracks spider-webbed through the crystalline surface. The gaseous discharge became a pea-soup fog. A fissure opened right next to her face. A spoke of red light spotlighted her. More spokes appeared, jutting out like the quills of a sea urchin. The asteroid quaked.

Her eyes widened with alarm.

An explosion of red lit up the heavens. Then all was dark.

###

"Slow down!" Cheryl Johnson shouted to her oldest son.

"It must be the asteroid!" The teen crashed through the tall emerald stalks of corn. They rustled and cracked as he cut across the rows. "This is going on the front page of the paper."

"You're going to be on the front page of the paper as the boy who broke his neck running through the corn. Now slow down, Cal! Gerry can't keep up!" Cheryl Johnson pressed the thick stalks apart for her youngest to scamper through.

The teen burst through the corn stalks and skidded to a halt at the sight before him. "Mom!"

"What's wrong!" Cheryl picked up her pace, thrashing through the forest of maize.

"It's a lady!"

The sound of voices and stench of scorched Earth began to rouse Elizabeth from her stupor. Her eyes flew open. It was daylight and she was splayed out, deep in a blackened crater. Sitting up, she examined her surroundings. A teenager, American judging by his accent, stood at the edge of the hole with his mobile phone's camera pointed at her. She glanced down, for a split second to ensure the symbiote was intact. To her relief the life-form had even cleaned itself to the point her outfit looked like it had been freshly laundered and pressed.

"What!" Cheryl emerged from the corn near her eldest son.

Elizabeth extended the palm of her hand toward the teenager in an attempt to block her face. "Could you please stop taking my picture?"

Cheryl looked down into the charred pit. "Hey hon! Just hold still. We'll call the paramedics. They'll be here in no time." She glanced momentarily at her son. "Cal, stop that and go get the ladder in the shed. We've got to get down there."

"It's okay ma'am I just want to ask you a few questions. I'm a reporter for the Oak Leaf—that's my school's paper. What happened? Where'd you come from?" Cal looked up to the sky and then back at her. "How did you get here?"

"Cal make yourself useful and get her an ambulance!" The brunette looked for an easy way to descend into the crater. "Just hold on hon and we'll be down to help you in a minute."

Touched by her concern, Elizabeth gracefully rose to her feet. "I'm all right." She paused to brush bits of scorched corn leaf from her hair.

"We thought you were an asteroid. Hey…did you come down with the asteroid?" Cal halted his call and looked up and then back at the blonde.

"Where am I?" Elizabeth asked, looking up into the sky and then back at Cheryl.

"Earth!" Cal interrupted.

"Where on Earth—" Elizabeth struggled to keep her tone even.

The youth cackled. "You sound just like my mom—'Cal, where on Earth'—"

Cheryl rolled her eyes and waved a hand at her son. "Calvin Elroy Johnson stop pestering her and CALL…*AN…AMBULANCE*." She looked back at Elizabeth. "Are you sure you're all right?"

"Yes." Elizabeth leapt to the top of the crater in one bound. "Whoa!" The teen shouted, bringing his phone up again to record. "Are you English—"

"Please, where am I? And what time is it?"

"Did you fall out of a plane?" Cheryl sheltered her eyes with her hand and glanced at the sky before looking back at Elizabeth.

Elizabeth's tone became more emphatic. "Please, I must know."

Cheryl checked her watch. "It's almost twenty past noon and we're about five miles south of Red Oak in Iowa. You just take it easy. I think you took a bump on the head."

Elizabeth did the time difference in her head and estimated she had lost a few minutes.

A wide-eyed kindergartener peeked out from behind his

mother's leg. "Are you an angel?"

Elizabeth's expression softened and she shook her head. "No sweetheart. I'm not, but that's kind of you to say."

"I'm Cheryl Johnson and these are my boys, Cal, and Gerry." She paused to affectionately tousle Gerry's hair. "My husband's at the State Fair in Des Moines with our daughter. But do you know who—"

"I'm terribly sorry for any distress I may have caused you. I'll see that you are compensated for the damage." Her eyes narrowed as she looked up and saw the asteroid through the blue canopy of the midday sky, it was in pieces, most of which were still speeding towards the planet. "Do you have a cellar to retreat to? The asteroid is still coming and I must leave."

"Leave? We have plenty of room. I think you may have amnesia, hon. You'd better stay with us until we can get you looked at. Do you know who you are?"

Impressed by the woman's compassion, she considered her response for a split second then offered a reassuring smile. "A friend." Glancing upwards, the blonde arrived at a decision. *In for a penny, in for a pound.* Elizabeth began to quickly rise into the air. "Again, I am sorry for the trouble. Please hurry to your cellar." She turned her face to the sky.

"She's flying! Like a superhero!" Cal lifted his phone to record it. "Puthergoin'!" he hollered.

Gerry tugged as his mother's pocket. "*Is* she a superhero mom?"

Her mouth agape, Cheryl stared up at Elizabeth's rapidly disappearing form. "I...I don't know...." Her expression of wonder changed to a flinch at the whip crack of the sound barrier being broken.

Elizabeth's whole being clenched with vexation, eight hundred years of obscurity was gone in an instant. Grumbling inwardly, she wondered how she missed entire oceans in her crash. Even a volcano would have been preferable but there was nothing for it now—and there was still an asteroid to contend with. Her mother's reaction—if she was even aware of what happened, would have to wait.

Space, Near Earth

The mysteries of the universe never ceased to amaze Elizabeth. High above the Earth, she stared, confounded by what she beheld. The explosion that knocked her senseless and threw her back to Earth had not sent pieces of asteroid careening in every direction. Instead, a glittering starscape of blood-red gems surrounded the planet in an ever-tightening sphere. Fist-sized and larger, they swarmed downward in a broad band at a terrifying velocity. There was no time to contemplate the meteorites' strange behavior. Her expression hardened. Like a tigress protecting her cub, she took off, fists extended, to intercept them.

Flying at near light speeds, she resembled a silver ribbon spooling itself around the planet. Round and round she flew, crashing through the shower of crystals, blasting them into dust. As the threat drew closer and closer to the Earth, she became aware of another complication.

###

Perspiration glistened on the mission director's forehead and streaked the back of his dress shirt. "Station this is Houston, stand by for final evacuation decision."

"Roger that Houston," the International Space Station commander said. "We are suited up and ready to evacuate." There were three of them crammed cheek to jowl in the Soyuz escape capsule, two astronauts, and a cosmonaut. A sense of doom upon their faces, the other three members of the International Space Station crew were waiting just as anxiously in a nearby capsule.

"Roger Station, we are monitoring the asteroid shards and will have an answer for you shortly."

"Roger Houston," the commander responded before toggling his microphone to speak to his crew. "How's it looking out there?"

"We're gonna get bombed. There's no way those things are going to miss us, whether we're up here or running for home in the lifeboat." The mission specialist's features were blanched white.

"Have we thought of everything we can do?" the commander asked. He glanced about; it was his fifth time asking the question.

The station suddenly lurched. The astronauts shouted in alarm and grabbed at their, now flying, checklists.

"Have we been hit? Damage report!" the commander demanded as the five other members of the crew checked and rechecked monitors and diagnostic indicators.

"What is that?" The cosmonaut, pointed out the porthole.

"It's a girl." The American specialist leaned forward and pointed outside in disbelief.

"Woman," the cosmonaut corrected him. She double-checked using the capsule's periscope.

Elizabeth gripped the truss that ran the entire length of the station and began to push. It lurched and accelerated rapidly. She glanced over to see the stunned faces of the crew peering through portholes in disbelief. She gave them a friendly nod of acknowledgement as she moved the station to the high Arctic and out of the path of the crystalline fusillade. Giving the crew a brief wave, she was gone.

Standing in mission control, among a collection of desks and monitors, the flight director addressed the astronauts. "Station, this is Houston, We may have a malfunction of instrumentation, what is your position? Over."

"Houston, we're all right! We are passing over the Arctic Ocean at ninety degrees north, one hundred thirty-five degrees west. It's going to miss us! Over."

"Station, what is going on up there? How did you get there? Over."

"I don't know, a woman showed up outside the station and

pushed us here. Over."

Brows raised, the flight surgeon glanced at the flight director before asking his question. "Station what are your oxygen levels?"

"Oxygen levels are optimal Houston," the commander responded after a quick check.

"Station, do you believe you observed an extra-terrestrial entity? Over," the director asked. He glanced at the other members of mission control before the camera feed from the space station came up on one of the screens, eliciting a chorus of shock.

"That's affirmative Houston, over."

"Post-Detection-Protocols are hereby ordered. This encounter is classified," the flight director declared. His eyes became stern as he surveyed the faces of mission control staff for comprehension and acknowledgement before relaying the message to the space station's crew.

The shards Elizabeth missed continued onward, unrelenting in their path. Like tin cans set up for target practice, satellites along with thousands of pieces of space junk—were suddenly part of an interstellar shooting gallery. The burning remnants rained down, along with any remaining meteorites.

Elizabeth pursued their vapor trails into the blue skies of Earth. Opening her mouth, she loosed a formidable sonic scream. Turning her face, left and right in a wide arc, crystals and space junk shattered to dust as if struck by a sledge.

In a last-ditch defense, the Earth's militaries blazed away with every weapon they could bring to bear. The few meteorites that leaked through finished their flights in explosions of flame or hissing geysers of water.

8:40 PM, Local Time, Strasbourg France

In her more than one hundred years of practicing medicine, Elizabeth learned in critical care cases the why something occurred often needed to be set aside in favor of what to do about it. Her immediate concern was saving the 'patient' in front of her, which happened to be in Strasbourg, France.

The hotel, La Maison du Vicomte was ablaze. Its flames licked at the night sky. Thick black smoke poured from the windows of the elegant seventeenth century manor, darkening its ivory facade. Elizabeth dove from the clouds and into the inferno via a hole in the château's roof. In the periphery of her vision, she saw television crews interviewing a fire chief at the fire cordon.

"At this time, we have confirmed one dead and thirty-one injured," the chief explained to an AFP tele-journalist as she held the microphone for him. "The injured are being evacuated to the university hospitals for treatment. We are still attempting to evacuate the hotel. When that is completed, we will attack the fire."

The interview was interrupted by the shouts of surprise by onlookers at Elizabeth's dramatic arrival.

"Hello!" Elizabeth bellowed in French. Striding through the acrid smoke and crackling flames of an interior corridor she listened for a response. She began to reach out with her cosmic sense for signs of life when sounds of coughing and cries for help in Dutch, drew her attention.

She switched languages. "I'm coming!"

The door frame splintered with a crack. As the fire roared behind her, she beheld an elderly couple on the floor, the wife cradling her husband's head in her lap.

"Please, help my husband!" a slight, elderly woman pleaded between coughs.

Elizabeth knelt by his side. His complexion was gray and his breaths, rapid and shallow. Believing he had a heart attack, she pressed her fingers to his carotid artery to take his pulse. It was thready. Quickly arriving at a decision, her fingers lingered at his neck for a few seconds more. The elder's breathing eased and his color improved.

"I have him," Elizabeth said in Dutch. She scooped him from the floor and over her shoulder. A sharp kick pushed out the wall below the window sill and sent debris tumbling to the abandoned café below. "I'm going to get you out of here. Put your arms around my neck." Elizabeth waved her into her free arm and gathered the woman to her side. The matron cried out at the height and squirmed.

"Are you crazy!" she demanded.

"Don't worry, I've got you." She gave the woman a reassuring smile and quickly floated down to the rear of an ambulance where a pair of paramedics stood by.

"Smoke inhalation, start them on ten liters of oxygen and get them to a hospital," she directed.

The pair stared at her with bewildered expressions.

"Quickly!" Her exclamation snapped them into action.

Looking for the scene commander amongst the crisscross of yellow fire hoses and flashing blue lights of fire trucks, she found him. "Chief, are there anymore in there?" she asked in perfect Parisian French.

"I have no more time for reporters." A scowl of annoyance creased his Gallic features. The fire chief glanced about for a gendarme as droplets of water beaded on his white helmet and bunker coat.

"I'm not a reporter. Are there anymore that need evacuating?" Elizabeth glanced up at the blazing hotel as cameras focused on the pair. "Chief?" She looked at him expectantly.

"I don't know who you are or how you got behind the line, but I am busy! Police!" He shouted, waving for officers stationed along the police cordon.

He turned back to see her leap back into the flames in a

single bound.

Elizabeth delved into the most inaccessible part of the hotel, its center. Walking through showers of glowing red embers and sheets of roaring flame, her hair and face became smudged black with ash. She made her rescues bashing down doors and breaking through walls. After her third of nine evacuations, the gendarmes gave up trying to arrest her and stood back gesturing to the startled fire chief in admiration.

Conveying the last of her rescues onto waiting stretchers, she was gone, roaming over the Earth to continue what she had begun.

In Pakistan, she stopped to aid rescuers at a collapsed apartment building, lifting slabs of concrete over her head like they were sheets of cardboard. In Siberia, she burrowed through the earth to evacuate a family buried alive in their cellar. In Chicago, she used a dumpster to draw water from its river and douse a foundry fire.

On it went, hour after hour without rest. Her heart broke when some rescues became recoveries. It soared when she reunited victims with anxious families. After an entire day, and it became apparent anyone who could be saved, had been saved.

She withdrew, turning her attention to the question that had nagged her continuously since Ayana had burst into her room; the asteroid. Where had it come from and what was the cause of its odd behavior?

She circled the Earth, and the solar system before turning her gaze outwards to the Oort cloud a bubble-like shell comprised of billions of pieces of rock and ice more than two light years distant from the Earth. She found nothing. Frustrated, she turned for home, a place she had long ago dubbed, Avalon.

Tuesday, 4 AM, Local Time, Avalon, Maine

On October 4th, 1957, the Soviet Union launched the first satellite, Sputnik. Elizabeth countered the new technology's surveillance capabilities by creating an underwater tunnel to her home and further added to her precautions by splashing down at random locations hundreds of miles from its entrance before swimming the remainder of the journey. Hours before the first rays of dawn, she arrived home, popping up through a trapdoor concealed behind a stack of straw bales in Avalon's little red barn.

In an earlier time, the barn housed horses, a few chickens, and a carriage, now it was home to her wood working shop, a tarp-covered 1956 Jaguar Roadster, and her welcoming committee. A series of whines and waffles signaled Delilah and Butler were awake.

"You're home!" Delilah, a wiry black Labrador retriever, happily whined while her tail and hind end wagged incessantly.

"Yes darling, I always come home." *And I think I'll be here for quite some time.* She smiled wistfully, feeling Delilah's pink tongue affectionately bathe her cheek.

"Hello," Butler waffled and huffed. He pressed his whole body into the blonde's flank.

"Hello, my fellow." She corralled his neck in her arm, scritching the top of his velvety head.

The tawny Great Dane snuffled Elizabeth's dripping locks before sneezing. "Stink," he declared.

"Nice to see you too." She regarded her old friend with amusement. She had rescued him from being euthanized. A victim of a dog fighting ring with severe trust issues, he had been considered unadoptable. The shelter's staff was stunned at how he transformed when Elizabeth stepped to his cage to meet him. In her care, the enormous dog had become so gentle that even the rabbits that lived in the meadow and thickets trusted him.

"I clean," Delilah barked and renewed her enthusiastic lapping at Elizabeth's ear and cheek.

"Delilah…" Elizabeth's face scrunched into an amused cringe. "I suppose I do need a bath."

"Bath?" Butler backed away.

"Bath! Bath! Bath!" Delilah barked and doubled down on her affection.

Elizabeth chuckled and rose. "A bath for me, not you two."

Unconvinced, Butler kept his distance while Delilah stayed at Elizabeth's side.

She checked their food and water, the dispenser she had constructed for times of enforced absence still held several days of provisions. Satisfied, she stepped out into the moonlight and onto a path of fragrant, red thyme that stretched out like a carpet to the porch of her home. Flanked by a meadow of crimson poppies, blue cornflowers and white daisies, the swaying flowers seemed to wave in greeting as she made her way to the wraparound porch.

The enormous farmhouse's white clapboards and cheery red shutters concealed granite walls better suited to a medieval keep. Roses vined around the covered porch's lattice work, filling the air with their sweet scent. Beyond the clearing, a forest of oak and chestnut, pine and spruce, surrounded the house for miles.

Tails wagged and nails clicked on the porch's whitewashed floorboards, as the dogs followed her around to the mudroom at the backdoor.

Delilah forced her way to the doorjamb, ready to push her way inside. Elizabeth had rescued her from a puppy mill. After six forced litters, Delilah's maternal instincts were set. On one occasion, Elizabeth had found her protecting a fledging dove that had fallen from its nest from a hungry bobcat.

Kneeling down again she embraced the pair in another lopsided hug. "I'm sorry I was away for so long."

"Too long." Butler panted softly. Beneath her hand, his eyes had become contented slits.

"Too long," Delilah agreed with yap. Her eyes shone with affection.

Elizabeth stood up.

"Play?" Delilah barked and stretched into a bow of invitation.

"Sorry luvie, I need a bath and a rest. Perhaps tomorrow."

"Sad?" Delilah asked.

"A little."

The pair of dogs yowled softly in sympathy.

"I help," Delilah volunteered giving Elizabeth a single, gentle lick on the back of her hand.

"I help." Butler leaned his enormous form against her hip.

"You're both so sweet." Elizabeth bent to hug them again.

"Mudroom?" Butler asked, hoping to be let inside the back door.

"Not this morning. Go play."

"Play!" Delilah bounded through the moonlit meadow like a dolphin leaping through the ocean's waves.

Butler shuffled after her, his broad chest blazing an easily discernible trail through the grasses and wildflowers.

Elizabeth watched them go and thought of Kenya.

6 AM, Local Time, The office of Senator Rupert Longstreet The Russell Senate Office Building, Washington DC

The ice wallowing in Rupert Longstreet's last trickle of bourbon clacked together like chattering teeth. The sound drew him from his ruminations long enough to notice his white-knuckle grip on the glass. Downing the remainder of his drink, he felt its burn and set the tumbler on his coffee table. Unlike most of his colleagues in the Congress, Longstreet did not flee for home, he stayed to work the phones, keeping abreast of developments and greasing the wheels of the emergency management agency. He turned his attention back to his office's television screen. She was on every channel. He would doze off and wake up to see the endless loop of her.

HER.

It had been nearly forty years since Beirut but after seeing her from every angle, he was absolutely certain that it was Dr. Bridgette Sheehan—at least that was what she was called herself back then. It was a lie. She was not human. She was a liar and a threat.

According to the news, she was known by dozens of names. Some believed her to be a doctor others thought she was an engineer. He knew what she really was, a protector of terrorists, and a goddamned alien to boot. He left the office sofa to go to his desk and pick up the photos there. In one frame was a picture of his long-deceased wife, the other was the last picture of his platoon. Studying their faces his scowl deepened, there was nothing he could have done then but now...now there was only one option. She had to be destroyed and he would use every means at his disposal to do it.

Around him, on the walls, were the culmination of forty years of accomplishments; plaques and awards, photos with celebrities he had appeared in movies with, honorary doctorates hung next to his actual degrees in political science and business administration, the head of a twelve-point buck, and a sweater from Louisiana State's football team. It was a personal hall of fame but none of it mattered if he failed them.

He turned it over in his mind again and again. She was an alien, who, if the interviews on the TV were to be believed, had been here for at least fifty years. What had she *really* being doing all this time? The classified folders on his desk, compiled by an alphabet soup of agencies both civilian and military, were of no help. None of the data pointed to anyone who looked like her, could fly, walk through fire, and toss aside slabs of concrete with ease.

His mobile phone vibrated on the coffee table, he looked and saw it was his chief of staff, Chuck White. He pressed the device to his ear and answered. "About time, Chuck."

"I'm on my way in, sir."

"Have you made the calls?"

"You'll have everything they have before they print it or it goes on air."

"And?"

"You'll be their first call."

Longstreet looked over at the discarded wrappers and half-eaten sandwiches on his coffee table. "Bring me something to eat. I don't care if it's a goddamned waffle. And while you're at it, find out who stocks the vending machines. I want them gone."

"I'll take care of it. What are we going to do, sir?"

Longstreet looked back at the television where someone from a refugee camp claimed to have been treated by her. "I have a plan."

9:12 AM Avalon, Maine

Three hours past dawn Elizabeth's eyes opened. Her mind crackled with thoughts about her self-imposed exile and what she might do with the time. Her first thought was to inquire around the interstellar neighborhood about the asteroid, one filled with gemstones wasn't unusual, but this one was. Someone had to know something about it.

Wearing a fluffy white robe, Elizabeth fixed a breakfast of yogurt, croissant, and fruit and carried it, along with a fresh pot of tea, to Avalon's expansive subbasement. Much of her home's living space was dedicated to art and beauty, the subbasement was dedicated to medicine, science, and engineering. If she needed to make a repair, a modification, or to mill a part, the equipment was here to do it. She kept a well-equipped laboratory that often assisted in diagnosis of patient diseases from far flung parts of the world. There was a thick-walled vault for her cache of bullion, multiple denominations of currency as well as a cabinet full of identities to assume when it became time to move on from one place to the next. The final aspect of the workshop was the information center.

Taking a seat in her plush, leather executive chair, she waited for the six screens, arranged three across and two high, to begin to yield images of the news. The destruction of so many satellites blacked out some of the news networks and left others pixilated and interrupted. Rather than endure micro-sound bites conveying bits of images and reports, she muted the televisions and concentrated on the three computer screens. The internet provided uninterrupted news and the headlines were as diverse as the nationalities that created them.

"A 'Friend' Drops In On Iowa Family" read a headline. A Red Oak Iowa farm family were startled by the crash of a young woman into their cornfield Sunday morning... Elizabeth scanned the rest of the article.

There was an enlarged picture of her from the shoulders up, and another of the Johnson family. Apparently, the military had taken over the crash site and was thoroughly investigating it. There was even a link to Cal's digital recording. Clicking on it brought Elizabeth's hands to her cheeks with a self-conscious groan. She saw and heard herself beginning with her unconscious state in the smoking crater before transitioning to her engagement with the family and finishing with her disappearing into the sky. The video had already been viewed over 400 million times.

"Oh no," she moaned, feeling her heart sink. "I should have taken the phone. I could have sent him ten phones or even a car."

"Crashing Jet Given a Soft Landing" read another headline.

Tabloid headlines were sensational to the point of being cringe inducing; *"Blond Bombshell Extinguishes Foundry Fire"* from a Chicago paper, and from a British Tabloid: *"Buxom Beauty Buzzes Britain." "Who's that Girl?"* wondered a New York paper's website. Established news sources speculated as to her origins and motives: *"Not Alone Anymore?" "An Alien on Earth?"* A second read: *"Aliens Among Us?"* A third read: *"President Sanderson grateful to 'Celestial Guardian Angel'"*. The wider fallout included stock markets tumbling, speculation about being attacked, and religious adherents expressed confusion, outrage, or renewed faith.

Elizabeth sighed deeply and began to talk to herself, a habit she acquired from hundreds of years of traveling alone. "Sorry, this show was one night only. I'm retired for three or four decades." Experiencing a wave of grief, she thought of Sehemu Nzuri and the children. Living a lie was difficult enough, letting down the children hurt most of all. She wondered how she could make amends—or if it was even possible.

BREAKING NEWS appeared on the three screens of American news networks, pulling her from her melancholy. Attention grabbing headlines followed on the ticker at the bottom of each broadcast.

ALIEN IN CHICAGO?

POLICE HOSTAGE SITUATION IN CHICAGO

CHICAGO POLICE OFFICER HOSTAGE

Elizabeth decided to pay attention to the network mentioning an alien and turned up the volume. The camera focused on a well-coifed field reporter at a police line, far in the background was the burned-out shell of the foundry that she helped firefighters to douse.

"We're coming to you from the edge of the parking lot of Windy City Steel Foundry in Chicago where a Chicago police officer has been taken hostage. The foundry was the site of—"

There was a sudden loud bang followed by shouts of alarm. The camera dipped and ducked before slowly coming up again and panning out onto the parking lot. The newsman's voice narrated as the camera zoomed in on the source of the disturbance.

"Ladies and gentlemen it seems an ingot of steel has just landed on a police car. We don't know if anyone was hurt but we're being—"

Elizabeth was out of the workshop and running for the barn. Her mind raced through the species that could lift a steel ingot. There weren't many and they didn't take hostages. The symbiote shimmered as it changed from the robe to her customary work clothes from the refugee camp, a white blouse, khaki slacks, and brown field boots.

8:40 AM Local Time, Chicago

Looking down from the clouds, Elizabeth observed a mixture of vehicles around the burned out foundry. Police and media helicopters hovered overhead while at the scene's edges, blue and white police cars and tactical trucks, were intermingled with black JLTVs, Joint Light Tactical Vehicles, from the military.

She floated downwards, bypassing the crowd of gawking onlookers to alight in front of the armored police command post. Her eyebrows rose at the jagged, fist-sized holes in the truck's rear section. Two officers, the police scene commander and the military scene commander were arguing.

"When the tanks get here, we're going in," the military commander said.

"Like hell! He's got two little kids and another on the way." The police commander jabbed a finger at his opposite number.

"You want it out here? Who's the one serving and protecting?" The military man waved an arm in the general direction of the assembled onlookers.

"We're not going in until—"

"You just aren't getting this. Your chief's on the way and once he gets here—"

Elizabeth was about to call out to them when a hand forcefully encircled her upper arm.

"Where do you think you're going other than jail?" A black-clad tactical officer began to demand as she easily slipped through his grip. "Hey!" He double-timed it to get in front of her. "No media. Get your butt back behind the line."

Elizabeth patiently regarded the square-jawed cop. "I apologize constable—erm, officer. But I must speak with your superiors."

"You're gonna' need to be speaking to a lawyer because you're going in." He reached for his handcuffs with one hand and for her with the other.

She evaded his grasp by rising into the air above him. Issuing a word of apology to the officer, she looked to the commanders. "Gentlemen, may I help?"

Shouts of 'Freeze' and 'Get on the ground' came from all sides as guns pointed upward. In the distance, the crowd came alive with shouts and cheers.

"Commander?" She gestured to the officers with their guns pointed at her.

The senior cop nodded and spoke a terse order into his shoulder radio.

After the guns were lowered and officers turned away, Elizabeth floated down and stepped up to the commanders.

A sheepish smile appeared beneath the police commander's mustache. "Sorry about that."

"Don't trouble yourself, Commander. It's a rather tense situation. What can you tell me about it?"

He motioned her forward and turned back to a table with a map of the streets with the foundry to scale at its center. "When you were here, did you see anything strange? Because I've got two fire inspectors and a twenty-year detective claiming they saw—"

"That's classified." The military man scowled. Tall, his red hair was styled in a crew cut. He wore a hazmat suit with the mask off and hood pushed back.

"Classified my ass, Colonel," the police commander shot back. "No one is putting one of our guys in danger for a bug hunt."

Elizabeth interrupted. "What did they see?"

"They claim something big and gray came out from behind a stack of ingots and attacked them."

Big and gray? Small and gray she knew. "Has anyone talked with it? Where was the last known location of your officer?"

"You're not going in there." The Air Force officer shouldered his way forward.

Elizabeth sized him up. She had met thousands of soldiers in hundreds of wars. She was not impressed.

She spoke to the soldier in even tones. "Not until I have more information, Colonel."

The policeman cut off the colonel's retort. "There's been no communication." He paused to point to the map. "At last report, the infrared cameras showed two heat signatures, here and here." His fingers traced an area on the map closer to the front of the structure. He keyed his shoulder radio to confirm it with the overhead helicopter.

"Have the paramedics standing by." She turned to go.

"Do you want backup?" the cop asked.

"I think it would be best if I went alone."

"You go in there and I'll arrest you." The military man's hand came to rest on the butt of his pistol.

"Barnes! You try and stop her and I'll arrest you," the police captain countered.

"I'll have your officer out in a moment and then I'll find out who or what is in there with him. Excuse me." Elizabeth turned her face to the foundry, took a half step back, and leapt in a high arc to drop through a hole in the foundry's roof.

The blackened interior was as quiet as a tomb. The acrid scent of ozone lingered in the air. Debris and stony puddles of slag made walking treacherous. Elizabeth floated down the foundry's rail line calling out to the missing detective. The sound of his breath brought a surge of relief.

She found his unconscious form in the shadow of a stack of ingots, his scalp was bloodied and his ankle fastened to the floor by a loop of steel. A quick yank snapped the bond. She checked his pulse, it was quick but strong. One of her fingers began to glow like a penlight. She carefully lifted his eyelids to check his pupils. One contracted, the other was blown. *Subdural hematoma.* His brain was bleeding inside his skull. She spoke softly to him. "Detective, I'm a doctor. I'm going to get you out of here."

Preparing to lift him, she scanned the gloom for whatever

attacked him, and did a double take as the stack of ingots seemed to animate. "By the stars…." She looked on with astonishment.

A blackened spire began to rise from the top of the pile. Limbs and features began to morph and take shape. Its mouth opened, glowing like molten iron. In a blast-furnace voice it roared, "Get out!"

Elizabeth stood, placing herself between the fallen officer and the metallic being. "This man is injured." She half-turned to gesture to the detective's form. "I'm going to take him away from here and—" Elizabeth's head swiveled to the left when she heard scuffling outside a nearby door. "No!" she shouted.

A deafening explosion shook the building, gray smoke and debris filled the air. Booted feet pounded against the floor. Air Force commandos dressed in orange biohazard suits charged in brandishing assault rifles. They advanced in columns of four, their weapons raised and ready to fire. Colonel Barnes appeared behind them, pointing a pistol. "Surrender or we will open fire—"

"Get…OUT!" The gray metal being belched forth a gout of flame and a fusillade of molten steel slugs.

There was a whooshing sound as Elizabeth's form became a blur. She stopped short of a trooper and braced her body. Red-hot projectiles ricocheted off her chest. She glanced at the colonel. "Get your people out of here!"

"Look out!" An airman dove for the floor.

Elizabeth turned to see an ingot hurdling directly for them. Her fist met it. The screech of rending steel filled the foundry as the ingot peeled back like a banana and flew across the building. A second ingot tumbled through the air towards another airman. She stopped short of him, and caught it across her body. She paused, looking for a safe place to toss it. The ingot jolted. She grunted. Her shoulders reared back.

An impossibly thick arm rose from the steel of the floor attached to the ingot. It became searing hot, folding around her in the shape of a fist, trussing her arms to her body.

The metallic figure seemed to surf on the hardened puddles of steel towards her.

Barnes gave the order to fire. A storm of bullets rang off the alien's body and bounced against the blonde.

"Stop shooting!" Elizabeth began to levitate off the floor, lifting her attacker with her.

The police appeared on the heels of the military.

"What the hell!" The police commander shouted and ducked for cover from the ricochets.

"Get your detective to a hospital!" she shouted.

"Where are you going?" Barnes demanded.

"To cool him off!"

KATHOOM

Elizabeth took off, dragging the metal man through the remains of the roof. Outside, the assembled onlookers cringed, ducking towards the ground and crying out in alarm. Elizabeth flew for the Chicago River with news and police helicopters in dogged pursuit.

Still held firmly in her assailant's grip, Elizabeth plunged the two of them into the center of the river, sending up a geyser of water and a cloud of steam. A yellow water taxi gunned its engine and nearly heeled over as its pilot violently spun the wheel to avoid the danger. Startled passengers rushed to the stern to see what the commotion was about.

Muddy brown water swirled and bubbled about the pair. The sounds of squeaking and crunching rang through the water. The metal man sank quickly, kicking up a plume of mud as he hit bottom. Flash-boiled fish bobbed to the surface. Elizabeth could not see him through the cloudy water. She attempted the use of her aura, it was no help.

"Let go!" Elizabeth's voice became a shrill gurgle. She shrugged once and felt the hand crack. Giving a muted shout, she threw her arms out from her sides and shattered the fist from within. Erupting from the water, she hovered, dripping and watching for signs of movement.

A muddy subsurface trail made its way towards the bank. Guardrails lined the sidewalks and parklands along the river. Traffic screeched to a halt and sirens could be heard approaching in the distance. A flat steel hook splashed out of the water, knocking down a railing. The hook scraped across the sidewalk before digging in. A second hook joined it as the metal man hauled himself out of the river.

Droplets of water boiled off of the dull-grey surface of his form with a hiss. His footfalls cracked the sidewalk. A head and face that could have been sculpted by a master artisan appeared atop the humanoid form.

Catching sight of Elizabeth, he pulled a lamp post from the ground in a shower of sparks. He raised it like a club and glared at her with pupilless steel eyes.

Hovering several yards above the ground, Elizabeth studied him and raised her hands in a gesture of neutrality. "Please, I only want to help you."

A compact red car, its horn blaring, hopped the curb, swerved to one side, then skidded down the slope of the riverbank. A young woman of Mediterranean complexion exited the car and sprinted towards them.

"Rudy!" she shouted.

"Josie?" The metal man lowered the lamp post.

"Is it you?" she asked.

"It's me, baby," the metal man responded in a roaring voice.

"I thought I'd never see you again!" she sobbed tears streaming down her cheeks

"Wait!" Elizabeth landed halfway between them, noting the engagement ring on the woman's finger. "Don't get too close, he's as hot as an oven."

The young woman slowed her pace to a tentative creep. "When I saw the fire, I thought you were dead." Her hand came to her mouth.

"I'm here baby, don't cry."

"What...what happened to you?"

"I don't know," a garbled reply bubbled up. "I was taking a nap and I woke to this flash and then everything was on fire—"

"You fell asleep at work again? How many times..." She stepped towards him.

"I'm sorry Joes, if I'd a known..." He dropped the lamp post, took a step and then halted himself.

Elizabeth interrupted. "You were working at the foundry when the meteorite struck?"

"Meteorite?" he asked.

"I called you so many times...what are we going to do?" Josie asked plaintively.

Rudy's voice rumbled. "Don't worry baby, it's going to be all right. I've been thinking about it, we'll find the best doctor we can."

Elizabeth interrupted them. "May I try something? I would like to take your pulse. Don't worry, you can't burn me." *Let's see if this works.*

"My pulse? How come I didn't burn you?" he rumbled.

"She's from outer space..." Josephine looked at Elizabeth. "Right?"

"Yes, but—" Elizabeth began to say.

"Outer space? So can you do something?" He gestured to his predicament.

Elizabeth took his wrist and allowed some of her life force to flow through her finger tips. Her eyes fluttered with surprise as she detected a pulse. She watched his complexion, filled with hope. She had saved so many lives this way. There was no change, his condition remained.

Keeping the confusion from her face she looked up him. "You have a pulse, it's strong and steady. To answer your question, I think what first is needed is a complete medical workup before we can diagnose—"

The sounds of screaming sirens and screeching tires interrupted them.

"The police say you attacked one of them?" Josephine asked.

"I asked for help and they pulled their guns. I didn't want to get shot."

Josephine looked at Elizabeth intensely. "Listen…I saw on the news you help people, right? You won't let them take him, will you?"

Elizabeth glanced up the bank. She heard conversations on police radios. There were more police on the way.

"I'll speak with them, but you mustn't attack anyone." She gave Rudy a penetrating look.

"Not unless—" Rudy began to say.

"He won't!" Josephine cut her fiancée off. "Just tell them it was a mistake; that he didn't mean it!" she exclaimed.

Guns drawn, police officers were now advancing down the slope.

Elizabeth rose into the air, attempting to cut them off. She stretched out her arms before her. "Please, for everyone's safety, don't do this."

"Out of the way ma'am, we've got to—" A sergeant waved for her to move aside as other officers assumed firing positions, pointing their guns at Rudy.

The roar of powerful engines and the thump of tires bouncing over the curb announced the arrival of the Air Force in their JLTVs. Machine gunners in the vehicles' copulas took aim as the vehicles halted and disgorged their troops.

"The army? What are we going to do?" Josephine glanced at the growing numbers of armed men and then back to her fiancée.

"If they try and hurt you. I'll—" Rudy moved forward.

Elizabeth shot Rudy a stern glance. "No. Stay there."

Colonel Barnes assumed jurisdiction and ordered the Chicago Police back before advancing down the bank. "Why are you defending this thing? Is he one of yours?"

"He's not a thing, he's a man. His name is Rudy. Moreover, I'm defending something all soldiers love, peace."

A second officer strode up behind Barnes. Slim, middle aged and tanned, Elizabeth noted his grave expression through the transparent shield of his hazmat suit.

"Sir, I suggest you remain back until we have the situation under control," Barnes said.

"You're in command?" Elizabeth looked at the second officer while trying to keep an eye on the assortment of police officers and Air Force commandos.

"Yes, I am, ma'am." The microphone in the suit gave his voice a metallic tone. "You're the woman from the cornfield?"

"Yes. And who are all of you?" Elizabeth landed to meet him on an equal footing.

"I'm Colonel Ferguson of the Army Medical Research Institute of Infectious Diseases and this is Lieutenant Colonel Barnes of the Air Force Office of Special Investigations."

She knew about the Air Force OSI. It was a kind of law enforcement branch tasked to investigate crimes and incidents in sensitive areas including extra-terrestrials. It seemed they had leapfrogged over the National Public Health Commission and the Center for Disease Control and went straight to the army with this matter. She noted the OSI officer's hostile glare.

"You're an epidemiologist Colonel Ferguson?" Elizabeth asked, receiving a nod of confirmation.

"That's correct."

"Could you help me de-escalate this situation? We would all be safer for it." She glanced at the airmen forming a crescent on the riverbank. "The guns?"

Ferguson turned his whole body to see Barnes. "Colonel Barnes give the order."

"Sir, I strongly advise against this."

"Noted, now dial it back a notch."

Barnes waved over his radio operator to issue the order.

"I'm a physician; may we have a word?" Elizabeth motioned for him to follow her away from the couple and all of the troops.

"How the hell are you a doctor?" Barnes snarled.

Elizabeth turned to look Barnes in the eye. "I've been here longer than you think."

"How much longer?" He demanded.

"There are far more pressing matters at hand than my resume."

"I'm coming with you." Barnes kept his gun by his side.

"Colonel, keep your station, and only fire if you're attacked. There are civilians all over the place and…" He glanced up at the news helicopters beating the air before turning back to Elizabeth to walk a few steps.

"So, you're from out there?" Ferguson asked.

"I am, but first can you tell me how everyone from the foundry incident are? The detective? The police? The soldiers?"

"I believe they are flying the detective to a trauma center. As for the rest, no one else needed an ambulance, thanks to you."

Her face and shoulders relaxed. "I'm quite relieved to hear that, Doctor."

"Have you ever seen anything like this?" Ferguson cast a glance in Rudy's direction.

"I haven't, not here or anyplace else."

"So you believe he is—or was human. Could there be more?"

"I was about to ask you if there were more reports of similar cases."

"Not that I'm aware of. And it seems you have established a rapport with him?"

"I think he calmed down because of his fiancée but they asked me to speak for them."

"You know he's got to go into quarantine, we can't have someone that can toss hunks of steel around like footballs out in public."

Well I can too but we won't bring that up. "This isn't a hot agent, I'm sure of it." She referred to a level four viral hazard, contagions that were both lethal and had no known treatment or cure.

"Then what?"

"A mutagen, whether it's a one off or this has happened elsewhere—"

"Mutations..." He looked at her with alarm.

"Yes, I know, the body normally destroys them or they're cancerous, and they take some time to develop."

"We got to get him into a clinical setting. Do you think he'll go peacefully?"

"I'll talk with them but I don't recommend the slammer." She referred to a forced quarantine of thirty days.

"You don't think we can contain him?"

"I don't. He's been traumatized and is in great distress, threatening him could set him off. His fiancée seems to have some sway—"

"Then we'll bring her along—"

"And pair them off with your most cordial officer. They're very frightened and need compassion not accusations." She glanced at Barnes.

Ferguson shook his head. "It won't be Colonel Barnes, ma'am."

They turned back towards the vehicles. "Colonel Barnes have the quarantine vehicle ready to be brought up, we're going to try to take him and his fiancé with us."

"Begging your pardon, Colonel, we have orders to move both the specimens to a secure location for quarantine."

Elizabeth squared her shoulders and fixed Barnes with a stare that would cow a samurai. "Neither he nor I are *specimens*. We are people and you *will* speak to us and about us, as people. Moreover, I will not be going with you."

"They'll get the VIP treatment. Are you sure you won't come with us? You seem to have some insights that would be very useful with this patient," Ferguson asked in diplomatic tones.

Elizabeth shook her head. "If there are more out there like him, I might need to intervene and prevent other rash actions."

Barnes scowled.

Ferguson nodded. "I understand."

"I'll go speak with them." She began to turn away before turning back. "Oh, while I'm thinking of it, are you taking them to Fort Detrick in Maryland? I only ask because if something does go wrong, I'll know where to go and help."

"That's classified information," Barnes said curtly.

"Very well." She floated off to speak to Josephine and Rudy.

"How long will we be there?" Josephine asked. Her eyes darted to a large black bus with yellow biohazard trilliums painted on its side. It eased down the slope towards them.

"I don't know," Elizabeth said.

"He hasn't done anything wrong and it was self-defense with that cop."

"You're not being arrested," Elizabeth explained patiently. "These doctors are some of the very best in the world and they have access to top equipment."

"Do you think they can find a cure?" Rudy asked.

"I think you have a better chance with them than without them."

"What do you think, Josie?" Rudy asked.

The young woman looked at her fiancée, then at Elizabeth, and finally at the windowless bus. "We have to try."

Elizabeth regarded the pair sympathetically. "And I'll try and do what I can for you too."

"Thank you." Josephine impulsively flung her arms around Elizabeth.

Elizabeth briefly returned the embrace before she turned back to where Ferguson stood with a group of his officers and nodded emphatically.

A hatch at the back of the bus lifted and a ramp lowered to the ground. A young, cherub-cheeked lieutenant strode down the ramp to them.

"I'm Lieutenant Brooks. I'll be your nurse." She gave the couple a pleasant smile but gave Rudy a look of particular caution.

Elizabeth exchanged goodbyes with the pair and watched the bus's ramp bow and rear sag as Rudy stepped up and in. She waved to the growing crowd before taking to the air. Deciding to conduct her own investigation, the blonde made a quick return trip to the refinery to stealthily find and collect the slugs Rudy had struck her with.

9:45 AM, Local Time, The Russell Senate Office Building, Washington DC

After two hours of sleep and a change of clothes, Longstreet better resembled his unofficial moniker of 'Senator Hollywood.' His silver pompadour was in place, his pale blue cravat was perfectly tied and fluffed and gray suit was pressed and neat. He sat on the edge of the sofa watching the latest news from Chicago with a renewed sense of alarm.

The door to the outer office swung inward. His scheduling secretary, Shannon Kerr strode in bearing a tray. "Here you are, sir." She carried a tray of aromatic breakfast selections from the cafeteria.

"What's this?" Longstreet sat up, craning his neck to see the tray's contents.

"A healthy breakfast; my mama always said breakfast is the most important meal of the day."

His frown didn't cease. *Well, your mama's got cancer.* "Thank you. Just set it on my desk." He glanced at the tray's contents then watched her hips as she turned to follow his directive.

Blonde, Shannon had soap and water good looks. Dressed in a gray pencil skirt and a white blouse, she wore her hair pinned up. Her pumps thumped softly in the blue pile carpet. Longstreet took a second to enjoy the shape of her figure. He had to admit she was doing all right pulling double duty while his regular secretary was struggling to make it back from a south-seas anniversary cruise with her husband.

Shannon set the tray down with a rattle. "Sir? Was the list of her locations all right?"

"It was fine. You did just fine."

She set a file folder of news articles on the coffee table in front of him.

"It's hard to believe all the places she's been reported to have lived—and kind of scary."

"Don't you worry. We're going to take care of it."

"That's a relief, sir. Can I get you a refill?" She bent to reach for his college mug.

"Thank you." He gestured to the television. "And find out which hospital they took that Chicago cop to. I want to send him some get-well flowers."

"That's very thoughtful, sir. I'll take care of it." She moved to leave and nearly bumped into his chief of staff, Chuck White. She smiled apologetically and slipped past him.

Chuck was a tall drink of water with slicked-back hair and piercing, ice-blue eyes. Rakish, the shape of his full lips gave the impression of a perpetual sneer. He carried a banker's box with a manila file folder laid on top.

"Are those the files from State?"

He set the box down on the coffee table. "State Department, USAID, and the CDC, sir. There are few other things too, sir. I took care of that Veterans Administration issue with that sailor. He's going to get his prosthetic replaced. The Department of Transportation came through on the extra repair funds for I-49 and there's this photograph from Baton Rouge..." He pulled a black and white photograph from the folder. "It was taken last Friday."

Longstreet's eyes became flinty as he looked over the picture of women in niqabs and men wearing taqiyahs gathered around a casket. He looked up at his aide, "And?"

"Bashir Darbi a sixteen-year-old refugee murdered last Wednesday on his way home from soccer practice. His cousin is Abdi Darbi, a wanted member of the terrorist group, Daesh. Look who's at the funeral sir...." White tapped a corner of the photograph.

Rupe saw his rival, the National Party's most likely Senate nominee in the next election. A triumphant smirk curled his lips. "Tanner Jenkins, that boy's bleeding heart is gonna be the political death of him," he drawled.

"The Triple S are suspected—"

"Well, that's too bad, isn't it? If ole'…Babi? Rabi? Dabi? Whatever his name is had steered clear of 'em, he'd still be alive. But his loss is our gain." He held up his hands as if to frame a headline. "I can see it now, 'Jenkins Associates With Known Terrorists.' Put a pin in this Chuck, we can use it in the next election."

Chuck slipped the photo back into the file folder.

"It writes itself sir. How's Shannon doing—other than massaging our eyes?" He smirked.

"She's no Madeline, but she's eager."

"Eager enough to be a team player?"

"We'll see after next month's convention in Vegas." Longstreet gave his aide a wink. He allowed himself to entertain a three-second fantasy of Shannon mimicking her predecessors' 'service.'

"I've got something new to help with that." Chuck produced a pen from his breast pocket. "From our friends at G&S…. Lens here…." He pointed to the pen's tip. "The clip is a microphone and you just give it a twist to turn it on. It uses Bluetooth directly to your mobile."

"Set it up, and I'll bring her onboard." Longstreet handed over his mobile device and turned his attention back to the news. "But for right now, this is the priority." He looked to the images of the Chicago incident. "Anyone that comes to my office that isn't here about this, direct them to their congressman."

"I'll let Shannon know."

He pointed to the screen. "Is there anyone at your old stomping grounds who might know something?"

White went to the side of the TV and tapped the image of Colonel Barnes with the camera-pen. "He might. Ike Barnes was my roommate at the academy. We got our commissions together and worked out of the same office for a time."

Longstreet managed a smile. "That's the best news I've had in three days."

"I'll arrange to have him debrief you—"

"I want him here tomorrow. A complete report. Everything they have."

"Consider it done, sir." White handed the spy-pen and mobile device back to his boss.

Longstreet tucked the pen into his suit's inner pocket and sat back, motioning to his aide to take a seat. "Typhoid Mary...what do you know about her Chuck?"

White shrugged. "Not a lot beyond someone who spreads a disease."

"The original Mary was a cook that was asymptomatic but spread typhoid to over fifty people, even killed a few of them. Now look here..." Longstreet spread a handwritten page out on the coffee table. "All these people claim she was helping at these pandemic sites. What if she was patient zero—the spreader of disease?" Longstreet smiled sadistically.

White's eyes gleamed. "Typhoid Blondie."

"We'll have to sell it, of course."

"There are enough conspiracy nuts out there that it will go viral in no time—pardon the pun."

"She'll be wishing for a pardon when we're done."

"This will hurt her." White smirked.

"You're damn right it will. That's what I intend to do, hurt her, and keep hurting her."

"But you've seen what she can do though, sir. She's not a gray or a reptilian, we can't match her."

"Not yet. We need to stay asymmetrical...harass her until we find a weakness we can exploit. We need information, Chuck."

"Some people are already claiming to know her or things about her."

"I know, I've been watching the news. Let's find a way to accelerate it."

Chuck stroked his chin for a moment. "What if we had The Spoiler do something? Some donor money for stories, sightings, anything we can use."

"Now you're talking, they get their readers to do the legwork, while we get the good stuff. Find some money, Chuck, and make sure it can't be traced back to us."

"Done, sir."

A soft chime from the Senator's desk phone followed by Shannon's voice on its speaker interrupted them. "Sir, I have the New York station manager for IBN on line one."

Longstreet motioned to his chief of staff, "Let's find out what they have to say..."

10:15, Local Time, Avalon, Maine

In her basement laboratory, with the television news chattering in the background, Elizabeth waved a Geiger counter over each of the recovered slugs. The instrument clicked a static warning, indicating the presence of beta and gamma radiation.

Frowning with concern, she used a fingernail to cut a razor-thin sliver from one of them to examine with her electron microscope. Placing it on the instrument's stage, she adjusted the focus on the monitor and gasped. Her hand rose to her chin.

"How is this even possible?"

Staring at the screen, she came to a conclusion: she needed a metallurgist *and* a geneticist. They needed to be discrete, trustworthy, and have some theory to explain what she saw.

In another life, she knew an aspiring metallurgist. He was a college freshman in the US Peace Corps when they met. A nudge of her toe rolled her chair across the floor to the communications center for an internet search.

Dr. Bernard Roper was in Boston, teaching at MIT. There was a picture of him.

It always struck her how quickly time passed for humans. When they worked on that aid project, Bernard's hair was sandy blond and thick, his face, fresh and youthful. In the decades since, his hair had become thin and silvered. His face was now covered in a charcoal-gray beard. The eyes looking back at her through the black frames of his glasses were definitely his. She was certain he would remember her, but whether he would receive her in lieu of the past few days' events was another matter.

Looking up, she paused to watch the televisions. News of her Chicago escapade was on every channel. She groaned as talking head experts speculated about everything that could be picked apart, over-analyzed, and sensationalized.

"Were We Invaded?" was the subject-line ticker of one broadcast. Another read "Alien Above the Law?" There was a picture of her hovering over the Chicago cop who attempted to arrest her. A blustering expert claimed she had broken the law and put lives in danger. She chafed with annoyance as another panel speculated about her clothing, hair and makeup. The ticker read "Super Camper?" She was not the only one being put under the media microscope.

Some particularly resourceful producer had dug up Rudy's picture and some of his coworkers were being probed for their thoughts about him. Others speculated that there might be others like Rudy at every impact site. Her frown grew deeper. There was much to do. The first thing she needed was a uniform. There would be no more cases of mistaken identity. *'Super Camper' indeed!* In seconds, Elizabeth stood before her bedroom's dressing mirror.

In the 1950s, she discovered comic books and spent a rainy Sunday afternoon reading stacks of them before giving into an impulse of silly fun. She created her own super uniform. With a mental command, the symbiote began to morph and change, becoming thicker and longer in some places, sheer and tighter in others. It was white, the color of peace and of medicine. Swashbuckler gloves and boots seemed heroic to her, a calf-length cape, a leotard emblazoned with a haloed four-point yellow star. Suntan tights gave her legs some color and broke up the uniform's monochromatic nature. Placing her fists on her hips, she pivoted left, then right, examining her profile in the mirror while resisting the urge to laugh. The figure flattering uniform certainly did things for her.

No one would mistake her for a reporter, an interloper, or anyone else than who she was. But was this her now? No, she had interfered enough. This foray would last just long enough to solve this mystery. She was certain people were out of danger for now. Directing the symbiote to create a slender pocket at the small of the suit's back she tucked a pair of cosmetic spectacles into it and sighed in recollection that she needed to retrieve her mobile device.

Returning to her lab, she placed some of Rudy's improvised bullets in a lead pig, a heavy, lead-lined jar, and left for Boston.

10:45, the Campus of MIT, Boston, Massachusetts

The symbiote was a remarkable creature, over the years it had provided clothing for any culture or setting she needed, but one thing it could not do was sub-divide itself. In Boston's morning heat, shorts and sandals would blend in best but she made do, disguising herself as an MIT graduate student, in leggings and a school t-shirt. She completed her ensemble by transforming her cape into a school backpack with the lead pig inside.

MIT impressed Elizabeth. Standing outside Bernard's office, she mused that if he could make sense of the sample, he might join the school's long list of Nobel Prize winners. Like Sal, Bernard was another would-be suitor that had to be gently steered away. Commanding the symbiote back to her uniform, she hesitated for a moment before rapping on his door.

A muffled voice came through the wooden door. "It's open."

Elizabeth poked her head inside. "Bernard?" She bit her lip.

Wearing a pale yellow, short-sleeve, dress shirt, Doctor Bernard Roper sat in a veritable nest of books, above him ball and stick molecular models of various alloys hung from the ceiling.

Slack-jawed, he began to stand pausing only to confirm he was wearing his glasses. "Claire?"

Elizabeth sighed inwardly with relief as he called her by the name she had used when they worked together on an aide project in the 1970s. "Bernard!" She beamed, crossing the short space to hug him into an embrace. "It's so good to see you!"

He stiffened then hugged her tight. "I never thought I'd see you again, and then you were on the TV and now you're here…I never would have guessed you were a superhero!"

"Neither would I!" She laughed.

Still holding her elbows, he retreated a half-step and looked her over. "I knew it was you the second you said my name, no one else has ever said my name in quite that way."

She could feel the heat of the torch he still carried; it singed her heart. "I'm so glad you're here."

"I'm still here, thirty-five years this past May. I must say you look really nice."

"Oh…." Aware of the intensity of his gaze, she glanced down at her uniform. "Thank you."

Bernard flushed red. "You know when I was in New Zealand, I looked for you, in Auckland and in Wellington…but your accent has changed."

"I'm so sorry, Bernard. My circumstances have required a change of identity every few years—"

"Like a spy? Are you a spy for another planet?"

"No." She smiled with good-natured amusement. "Nothing like that—"

"You can trust me," he said.

"I'm not a spy but your discretion is appreciated. Bernard, I've come a long way to see you. I need your help."

"From outer space?" He released her and looked out the window in wonder.

She smiled again. "Not quite that far. Did you happen to tell anyone you knew me?"

"If I did, they'd say I'd gone completely around the bend and that it was time for me to retire."

Well, that's a small relief. "I wanted to talk with you about Chicago, about what happened there earlier today."

Bernard broke his gaze to gesture to a small TV tuned to the news. "What is he made of? Did he hurt you?"

"Just a bit of a squeeze."

"Is he an alien, like…?"

She decided to save him. "Like me?" She hefted the lead jar onto his desk. It landed with a thud. "He's human—or was. I came to ask your help in finding out what happened and if possible, to cure him. This is a tissue sample." She opened the top of the jar to allow him to peer inside. "I did a quick examination and discovered it is emitting detectable levels of beta and gamma radiation but what is strangest of all is its structure. The metal closely resembles human cells."

"Organic steel?" His brows came together, "Fascinating...."

"I thought if anyone would know where to begin with this, it would be you." She pointed at him.

"Well, I could...I could have a look." His gaze became intense. "We could get one of the smaller, more secluded labs and—"

"Do you know a good geneticist? Discretion and trust are key—that's why I came to you, I trust you, Bernard."

"I appreciate your confidence." He stroked his chin. "I think I know just the person. She came to us as a fourteen-year-old undergrad. She completed her PhD at Stanford. I'll could call her office and see if we can meet with her."

By the stars. "She sounds extraordinary. By all means." She gestured to his desk telephone.

He lifted the phone, punching in an extension. His eyes shone. "It's so good to see you again, Claire."

###

Under the hum of the florescent lights of a secluded biology lab, Elizabeth perched on a lab stool speaking to a rapt audience of two about the asteroid and her adventures since. She was forced to pause when it became apparent Bernard was having difficulty with his sight, constantly adjusting his glasses. Draping her cape across her lap seemed to remedy his impairment.

"This is the coolest thing ever! Ever-ever-ever! I have so many questions!" Dr. Jennifer Novak squirmed on her stool. Petite, she wore a white lab smock over a blouse and jeans. Her crimped, copper hair was pulled back in a bun. Pink, tortoise-shell glasses framed her sapphire-blue eyes.

"I appreciate your enthusiasm Dr. Novak, but you mustn't tell anyone." Elizabeth leaned forward to hold her attention.

"We get to do ultra-secret astrobiology with a superhero? Mum's the word." Jennifer made a zipper motion across her lips.

There's that term again.

"The image is coming up now." Bernard directed their attention to the electron microscope's screen.

"These look like muscle cells not flower shaped dendrites." Jennifer left her stool to increase the magnification of the image.

"Do you think you can take a genetic sample from this?" Elizabeth bit her lower lip.

"I'll attempt to do a PCR DNA sequence." Jennifer tapped the screen.

"Do you have a hypothesis?" Bernard asked.

"I think the piece of the asteroid that struck the foundry acted as a mutagen of some sort. I tested these samples and got readings of five to ten millirems of beta and gamma radiation. The neutron levels are negligible." She gestured to the heavy lead pig on the counter.

"Radiation can alter DNA. I've just never seen or even heard of anything like this...."Jennifer touched a finger to her lips, continuing to stare at the screen before turning back to Elizabeth. "Have you? I mean since you're from...out there."

Elizabeth shook her head. "Nothing like this."

Jennifer frowned. "It's fascinating but so awful. That poor man."

"Do you have a sample of the asteroid?" Bernard asked.

"Not yet, I'm going to see about that later today. If I can obtain one, I'll bring it to you."

"My colleagues and I have speculated about its make-up and from what you've told me about the appearance and behavior of the pieces, they could be a ferrosilicon compound. This is just a hypothesis but if these asteroid crystals you described are silicon based, they could have combined with the iron ore of the foundry and the carbon of his body. I'll run a spectral analysis and see what's there," Bernard said.

Jennifer gestured to the screen. "Silicon bonds aren't usually as stable as carbon bonds but who's to say there isn't an unknown element bonding them together."

"I can see I've come to the right two people because this is the hardest steel I've ever come across."

"Maybe this new alloy has greater tensile and yield strengths. If we can find more asteroid pieces and his biological processes could be reproduced, the possibilities for deep sea and space exploration could be immense," Bernard mused aloud.

"This isn't just a curious scientific anomaly, Bernard. This is about a man's future—about his family's future." Elizabeth stood up and looked at the pair gravely. "Do you understand? This man is suffering, he wants to be cured."

"Isn't the government helping him?" Bernard asked.

"They're trying but I don't think they'll be very forthcoming with their information."

"What if there are others who don't want to be cured? Are we doing this to find a weakness to exploit?" Bernard leaned on a counter to regard Elizabeth.

"I'm a physician, this is about healing. As for others, I dread the idea of it."

"What would happen if someone…what if someone who was affected tried to reproduce? Do you think a pregnancy could be carried to term?"

Elizabeth's lips pinched with consternation. "I don't know. I do hope that you can help me find some answers."

"Don't worry; team science is on the case!" Jennifer exclaimed.

Elizabeth's eyebrows rose at the interjection.

Jennifer blushed. "I mean we'll do everything we can, won't we Bernie?"

Bernard nodded in agreement. "Everything."

"Thank you. I'll check in as often as I can but remember, discretion is absolutely key not even your spouses can know." Elizabeth looked at them, one to the other.

"Oh, I don't have one of those but I now have a new superhero friend." Jennifer beamed at Elizabeth.

Elizabeth found the woman's optimism uplifting. "Well, the friend part sounds lovely." Her eyes flared with warmth.

Jennifer's voice became hushed and mystified. "My superhero friend...."

"I'm sorry I can't stay to discuss this further, but I must go."

"Do you have to," Jennifer made a swooping motion with her hand, "go save someone?"

If it were only something that simple. "Something like that." She stood to leave.

"Before you go...." Bernard caught up to Elizabeth at the door. "Will you have dinner with me? Now that we're reunited? I mean, if you're not married. I forgot to ask. You're wearing gloves so I didn't see a ring and—"

Elizabeth saw the hope in his eyes and her heart broke for him. "I'm not. How about a celebration dinner? Once we have some answers?"

"Just the two of us?"

She smoothed his sleeve and felt his heart. "Well, we do have a lot to catch up on, so yes, just the two of us."

"I'll get to work—it's so good to see you again Cl—" He caught himself. "Secret identity, sorry, I almost forgot." His shoulders hunched, he gave her a sheepish smile.

"Thank you again—both of you." She gave them a smile before departing.

11:25 AM, New York City

Bernard and Jennifer's reception contrasted with the distress presented in the media around the events in Chicago. As she flew, a thought struck her. She halted in mid-air to ponder it. Looking south to New York with as much enthusiasm as someone needing to see the dentist for a toothache, she flew for the spires of The Big Apple. A conversation with NASA about the asteroid would have to wait a little longer. She needed to grant an interview.

Over the Bronx, above the din of trains and cars, telephones and industry, murderous words sliced through Elizabeth's anxious anticipation and chilled her heart.

"Let's see what this monkey's brain looks like…"

"Bet it's peanut sized!" Another derided.

"Grab him!" a third, barked.

Seeking the source of the threat, Elizabeth changed course. She streaked into the borough's backstreets and found a trio of musclebound skinheads dressed in black jeans and white tank tops charging a homeless man like a pack of hyenas.

Their bedraggled victim turned to run and stumbled into his overstuffed shopping cart, tipping it over and spilling its contents of bulging, garbage bags onto the asphalt. He staggered, struggling to stand. The hoods were upon him. A crow bar rose, and viciously fell.

WHUMP.

The steel rod smacked against Elizabeth's gloved hand. Its wielder shouted a curse and gripped his wrist in pain.

She pinched the tool, snapping it in half. The pieces fell to the asphalt with a clang.

Wide-eyed, the trio retreated a few steps.

Elizabeth's hands rose to her hips with swagger and defiance. Her eyes narrowed at the sight of Nazi tattoos and jewelry mixed with another group she detested, the stylized triple 'S' lightning bolts of the Society of Southern Sons. "Well, who do we have here? History's collection of losers…Himmler, Gobbles, and Höss?"

The leader had a face like a bulldog chewing on a wasp. "Get the fuck out of the way! We're takin' the streets back."

"Then you can start by removing me."

One of the skinheads pointed. "Race traitor!"

Ugh. Elizabeth's face creased with distaste. "There's no such thing as race—"

"Lies!" The other minion snarled.

"Fuck her up." The leader waved his partners forward.

"This is gonna be fun!" One of the pair taunted, smacking his fist into his palm.

"Bloody steroids…." she muttered.

Hunched over like boxers, the pair edged forward.

As they neared, they reached for her.

Elizabeth's own hands shot out to seize them by their shirts and lift them from their feet. Ignoring their protests, she swept them together like a pair of cymbals catching their leader betwixt them. They thudded to the street in a neat pile of crumpled unconsciousness.

Elizabeth clapped her hands together like she was brushing dust from them. She frowned. "And I was going to give you the opportunity to confess your crime to the police."

She turned to their victim.

He was dirty, unshaven and smelled like he had not showered in weeks. His army boots were sole-worn and badly scuffed. There was a scar on the side of his head. What struck her most were his eyes. The nut-brown skin around them was creased like dried leather and there was a dark and profound sadness to them. They were the eyes of the injured, the eyes of the traumatized.

Crouching down next to him, her expression softened with sympathy. "Are you all right?"

"Am I dead?" he asked.

Elizabeth shook her head with gentle humor. "No luv; you're

very much alive. But are you all right, Mister...?" She offered him a hand up.

"Mannie." His expression became one of surprise as she pulled him to his feet. "Whoa!"

"Mr. Mannie?"

"Just Mannie." He looked her over and then up the street. "Where'd you come from?"

"I happened to be nearby. Have you had lunch?"

He stared at her blankly for a moment. "I could eat."

"Splendid. Let's gather your things." She saw a police car slowly round the corner a few blocks away. *No time to talk with them* "Are you frightened by heights?"

"Hell no—I" He gave her an apologetic look. "Heck no, ma'am, I was in the paratroopers, the 173rd."

She chuckled. "We'll fly then, it's much faster."

"Fly?" He swore with surprise as she lifted off carrying both him and his cart.

Passing low over the rooftops of apartments and businesses, Elizabeth quickly learned the name of her companion, Manuel Sanchez. She was struck by the conundrum of what to call herself while in costume, she decided that Doctor would do for now.

Flying several blocks, she spied a chrome diner on a corner and set them down at the steps of a weathered brownstone on a quiet street.

"Level with me...am I drunk?"

She turned her face to him and regarded him thoughtfully. "You don't seem to be."

"I gotta be hallucinating then."

She played a hunch. "Do you ever hear voices—I mean other than from people who are nearby?"

"All the Goddamned time! I wish they would shut the hell up." He wore an expression of sheer exasperation.

"Do you have any medications?"

"Yeah, I've got the bottles right here." He rummaged through a black garbage bag for a few moments before producing a handful of empty bottles.

Elizabeth looked at them, four different medications from four different doctors. She grimaced sympathetically. "First, we'll dine and then we'll see what can be done about this."

"Where do you keep your wallet?" He scrutinized her for a moment.

"Not to worry. What can I get you?"

"Anything, but I like milk. Good for the teeth."

"I'll be back shortly." She moved down the street and walked into the narrow alley behind the restaurant to emerge out the other side, wearing jeans, a t-shirt and her cosmetic glasses.

When she rejoined him, she was back in uniform and bearing a stack of white take-out trays, they sat on the brownstone's steps as Elizabeth briefly told him her story before listening to his as Mannie polished off his club sandwich, half of hers and all of their sides of coleslaw and French fries.

Medically discharged after suffering a brain injury from a roadside explosive in the Afghan War, he came home to find his home foreclosed and his girlfriend, Charlene, and their daughter, Lindsey, gone.

"Then I came looking here, this is where Charlene's family's from. I ran out of money, I lived in my car for a while but then that got stolen. My headaches got worse, sometimes I can't think straight. I'm trying to get up but every time I do, something kicks my feet out."

Elizabeth listened with a soft, sympathetic expression. "I miss my family too. It can be very difficult. However, you still have a chance. Manuel—Mannie, I know a place that can help you get back on your feet and back on your journey."

"A shelter? Nah." He shook his head. "People steal. Thanks anyway, ma'am."

"What if you could have your own room with a lock? And they have social workers who could help you find Charlene and

Lindsey. This could be a wonderful opportunity for you."

He shrugged.

She tilted her head and gave him a reassuring smile. "Shall we have a look?"

"Are we flying?"

Her eyes twinkled. "Door to door service, Manuel."

He stood up. "Sorry I smell so bad," he said as she wrapped her arm around his waist.

"You're not so terrible, I lived through the Middle Ages," she quipped before lifting off.

Built in 1900 as seven stories of brown bricks, Ark of Hope was originally the Regency Hotel. The changing fortunes of the Bronx led to its decline before a coalition of social agencies purchased it with grants from the Cumberland Foundation. It was revamped to be a place where the formerly homeless could access safe housing and the services they needed to get a fresh start. Elizabeth set them down atop its roof.

Accessing the stairwell, they descended to the seventh floor to ride the elevator to the lobby. Elizabeth puzzled over the scuffed, threadbare, carpet, chipped and cracked paint of the walls, and judging by the stifling temperature, the lack of air conditioning. Boarding the elevator, she added one more task to her list.

The lobby was a mixture of tasteful late nineteenth century walnut molding and modern utility. The wrap-around check-in desk and molding around the doors, baseboards and ceilings had survived the remodel but the tiled floor that was ivory when new had faded and scuffed to beige.

"Nice and cool down here," Manuel observed.

"Let's see if there's room at the inn." She led the way to the repurposed check-in desk where a willowy blonde in a leopard print blouse and gold bangles stood staring at the screen of her mobile device.

Elizabeth resisted the urge to tap the bell on the counter and cleared her throat.

The blonde looked up. "Oh, hey." She looked her over. "Are you new?"

"New?" Elizabeth glanced back at Manuel who pushed his rattling shopping cart up behind her. "I, no, I'm not new. I'm here to help Manuel—Mannie, to obtain a space."

"Then why are you dressed like that?" The blonde pointed a pink lacquered nail.

"It helps me stand out."

"I'll say."

"About a room?"

"Yeah, one second, I'll get Sly." She turned, giving them one more glance before knocking on the door located behind the desk.

"What!" came the bellowed reply.

Elizabeth could hear a sports broadcast, by the excited banter of the commentator, it sounded like soccer.

The blonde slipped through the door and pushed it shut behind her.

Elizabeth cocked an ear.

"Did you bring in another girl?" the blonde asked.

"What? No. Why?"

"There's a blonde outside in a leotard. She's got a homeless guy with her."

"What's she look like?"

"Oh, you'd like her."

"Well get her in here then."

The door opened and the blonde stepped out. She smiled and tilted her head towards the open door. "Go on in."

Elizabeth led the way around the end of the desk and through the office door. The office contents were not what she expected, ox blood leather furniture, a big screen television, and a bar refrigerator were the most prominent parts of the office. Behind a paper strewn desk, sat Sly. Thick-browed and thick-armed, she guessed him to be about thirty. He was in the middle of a lunch of steak and potatoes though she could barely detect the smell of his meal over the nose-wrinkling musk of his cologne.

Keeping her sense of wariness from her face, Elizabeth smiled congenially. "Hello there."

He pulled a paper bib from around his neck to wipe his lips. "Hey…"

Elizabeth noted his gold watch and an ashtray filled with cigarette butts imprinted with lipstick.

"I'm Sly." He looked her over and offered his hand.

Not as sly as you think. She had met hustlers from Bangkok to Bogotá and he matched them in look and feel. "And I'm looking for a place—I"

"Sure, Beautiful, we can set you up on two."

"For my friend, Manuel." She placed a hand on his shoulder.

"And who might you be, lovely lady?"

"His friend."

"Hello, friend." He fiddled with his gold pinkie ring, twisting and spinning it around his finger.

Elizabeth noted the dollar sign on his ring and chuckled affectedly. *I didn't say your friend.* "I have a rather busy itinerary planned for today, may we get started?"

"Well, we wouldn't want to get in the way of that." He smirked. "We've got some space open up on seven."

"It's quite warm up there."

He shrugged and smiled gregariously. "Not much I can do; the AC is out."

"I'm sure you're doing your best to restore it."

"Absolutely. Have a seat." Returning to his chair, he shoved some papers aside to find the computer's mouse.

"Before we get started any…you know…mental problems?"

How rude! Elizabeth spoke up. "Why do you ask?"

"Works out best if there isn't. We're not really set up for it." Sly flicked a glance at Manuel.

Knowing that the situation was supposed to be otherwise, Elizabeth struggled not to rebuke him. "Well, that's to be determined. I'm a medical doctor. I could—"

"You don't look like any doctor I've ever met."

"We come in all shapes and sizes."

"I like your sh—"

"You don't recognize me, do you?"

"Only from a dream."

Elizabeth resisted the urge to groan and instead she leaned forward in her chair to pinch the edge of the desk and lift it from the floor.

Sly's face screwed up with annoyance. "How the hell are you...?" leaning sideways in his chair his head dipped low towards the floor. "Holy shit! You're—"

"Yes. Quite."

"I didn't know you were English."

"I'm not, but I am a doctor. And now, with Manuel's permission, I will conduct an assessment."

Sly's head bobbed. "Whatever you want."

She looked at her companion. "Will that be all right?"

"Will there be any needles?"

Elizabeth's stern expression softened. "No needles, I promise."

Mannie shrugged. "Okay then."

"You may go, Sly." She waited for him to leave before turning her chair to face Mannie and begin.

Holding up a finger she asked him to follow it with his eyes while she pondered her options on what to do about Sly and what she suspected he was up to. She could tip the police but involving them would place every resident under the stress of police scrutiny, something they did not need or deserve. She could take Manuel out of the place and put him in a hotel but that would not solve the problem and it might tip Sly to her suspicions. She decided on a third option but it would require her to work quickly.

For several moments she ran a battery of tests, from coordination to orientation to time and place. She detected coordination difficulties from his brain injury. She also believed he was showing signs of schizophrenia and decided to eliminate all of his health concerns on the spot. "Could you watch the clock on the wall behind me and tell me every ten seconds while I take your pulse, Manuel?"

Removing a glove, she pressed two fingers to the flesh where his thumb joined his wrist and feigned taking his pulse. When he reached forty, their point of contact warmed. She watched his face. His eyes cleared, the lines around them disappeared, the rattle in his lungs ceased.

After he got to sixty and she released him, Mannie looked at her. "What's wrong? Am I sick?"

Elizabeth cocked an eyebrow. "Do you feel sick?"

"No, I feel good, even my headache's gone. Did you do some kind of hypnotism on me?"

"No hypnotism. Perhaps you were just hungry and your lunch is finally catching up with you?"

"Then that's the best lunch I've ever had."

"Manuel, now that you're feeling better, I must say that something very wrong is taking place here and I don't feel comfortable about you remaining."

Manuel frowned. "Yeah, he's dirty."

"You noticed that."

"'Lived too long on the street not to."

"I thought we could find you a place here and some help but—"

"I'll be fine." Manuel waved a hand at her.

"What?"

"I've been to war. That seedy sonofabitch doesn't even rate."

"But—"

"If I keep my head down and don't make a fuss, he won't even notice me."

She looked at him with doubt. "You're certain?"

"It beats sleeping on a sidewalk—especially when it rains."

"I still have reservations but I'll let Sly know you're fit." She laid a hand on his shoulder. "I'm going to sort this out, Manuel. In the meantime, take very good care of yourself. I know you'll find your family."

Mannie reflexively reached towards his scar. "Thanks—" Unable to find the injury, he felt around before giving up. He stared at her back as she exited the office. "For everything...."

12:40 PM, Arc of Hope, New York

Outside Sly's office, a small crowd of his associates startled her with an explosion of cheers and squeals of delight. Their comportment and racy apparel only added mounting evidence Sly had injected a bawdy house into *her* aid project. Keeping her growing fury in check, she lingered only long enough to confirm Mannie's fitness before blowing past them with an apology about needing to 'help some people'. A fast trip to Avalon to obtain items for her disguise and she was back in Manhattan and atop the Boise Building, home to the Cumberland Foundation.

The foundation grew out of Elizabeth's first experience working at an aid camp. A funding cut and the subsequent fallout demonstrated the need for consistent and robust financial backing. Tapping into her personal fortune, she created the identity of debutante and heiress, Abigail Cumberland.

In the years that followed, the foundation grew in its breadth and scope, helping desperate causes that required immediate intervention to first save lives, then to rebuild them. All the while, she remained hidden from the world, working as a humble doctor in the very projects the foundation funded.

Seven years previously, after the first executive director of the foundation retired, a new executive director, Kate Tekakwitha, came on board. Elizabeth carried on the fiction, posing as Abigail Cumberland's granddaughter, college-bound Charlotte Cumberland. She met Kate briefly before 'Charlotte' disappeared first to school and then into the life of the idle rich. In the time since, Kate had led the foundation with compassion and aplomb.

In the restroom of the top floor, Elizabeth transformed her appearance. The white uniform became a navy-blue sailor dress with white piping. Her pumps, hose, bag, and wide-brimmed sunhat matched her dress. She pinned her hair into a tight bun and donned a pair of Garbo sunglasses big enough to be a domino mask. Balancing the bag in the crook of her elbow she gave herself one last look and nervously hoped no one would see through her ruse.

Assuming an air of disinterest, she pushed the foundation's door open and stepped onto the short pile carpet of the reception area. Her eyes came to rest on the receptionist, her placard read Elaine Stewart. She recalled the woman and hoped the recollection was not mutual.

Elaine was heavy set and had cotton-white hair. She looked up through her glasses, "May I help you?"

Elizabeth changed her speech to American standard tinged with Mid-Atlantic. "Charlotte Cumberland to see Kate Tekakwitha."

The revelation had the receptionist on her feet. "I'm sorry, Ms. Cumberland, I didn't recognize you. But did you hear the news?" Elaine gushed. "She was spotted at one of our projects."

Elizabeth froze. "She?"

"I don't know what to call her but the superhero. She was seen at Ark of Hope."

By the stars, news travels quickly. "How nice. Is Kate in?"

"I'll show you to her office. Is there anything I can get for you? Coffee?"

Elizabeth wrinkled her nose like she'd been offered a stole made of live skunks. "No, thank you. I would just like to speak with Kate."

The pair walked under a television mounted over the door to the all-news broadcast station of INB. The volume was down low. Talking heads chattered and speculated about the superhero and the implications of the early morning incident in Chicago. "...this video of the Battle in Chicago, as some are calling it, already has twenty-two million hits on Youtube...."

Battle of Chicago? Elizabeth cringed inwardly at the title.

"Isn't it incredible about her? Social media is practically on fire—and I think she's wonderful."

Despite the heartwarming compliment, Elizabeth gave the

other woman a penetrating look. "Social media? You don't allow that nonsense to distract you from your work, do you?"

"No, I'm—I'm too busy. I was just saying, Ms. Cumberland, she's everywhere." Elaine led her along a line of office doors where senior staff managed grants and applications for them.

Elizabeth frowned dismissively. "A nine days' wonder, I'm sure."

Elaine led her to the door of a corner office and knocked. A voice from within bade them to enter.

Kate met Elizabeth halfway across the floor. An elder in the Iroquois Confederacy, Kate wore a red business dress and black pumps. A barrette kept her straight, iron gray hair from her face. She greeted Elizabeth warmly and ushered her in.

"It's been a long time." Kate smiled and retook her seat behind the desk.

"Yes, it has. I was in the city I wanted to check on my family's foundation and our projects. I hope that none were affected by recent events."

"I haven't heard any bad news."

"Well, that's comforting. How are your daughters?"

"High school and junior high school in three weeks, they're excited."

Elizabeth allowed herself a smile. "I'm glad that you're all right. Elaine mentioned that the superhero was reported to have been at the Ark of Hope project."

"I don't know if it's true but if it is, that's very exciting."

"How is their board to work with?"

"I haven't had any reason to be concerned."

"Contact them, please. Suggest a floor-by-floor inspection. If a project associated with the foundation is about to come under media scrutiny, I want it to be exemplary."

"I'll do it as soon as we're done here. But I wonder if she knows about us? This has potential. If we could get her to speak at a fundraising dinner, we could fill the largest ballroom in the city." Kate gestured excitedly.

Elizabeth kept her demeanor serious. "Is there some project that requires additional budgeting. So much so that a fundraiser would be necessary?"

Kate shook her head. "I get the impression you don't approve?"

"I don't. The Cumberland Foundation isn't about publicity. This isn't an exercise in public relations, that's why we have no communications director or publicist. Quiet dignity is my preference." *Says the lady in the cape and tights.*

Suddenly subdued, Kate's mouth clapped shut. "I just thought it would be a way to draw attention to all the good things we do here."

"You and the staff should be proud of those things, but in a way less pronounced than some gauche media spectacle." Elizabeth waved her hand dismissively.

Kate's fingers rose to her mouth. "I suppose, yes."

Elizabeth leaned forward, "However I have been remiss. I really should make a point of making an appearance here more frequently if for no other reason than to express my gratitude to all of you. What do you think of an appreciation dinner? You could arrange for the rental of a small ballroom and perhaps some form of entertainment."

"I think the staff would appreciate it. Will you be able to attend?"

"I lead a very busy life, despite what some in this office might believe, it isn't always Monaco, Bali, and Aspen."

"Well, we'll hope for the best." Kate smiled optimistically.

"The real heroes are the people working on the aide projects, the people out there in the office facilitating those projects and you, Kate."

"Thank you. That means a lot coming from you."

Elizabeth shifted in her seat and sniffed. "As for this superhero business—if indeed it turns out to be true, I want you to remind the staff about their confidentiality agreements when it comes to our sponsorships and for you to handle all media inquiries."

"Is there anything you want me to say or not say, in particular?"

"Say nothing unless someone comes to ask for an official comment and if they do, tell them there is no affiliation, official or unofficial with her."

"I understand." Kate nodded.

Elizabeth rose and smoothed her dress. "There's no need for publicity Kate; you're already a star." Elizabeth shook the other woman's hand before moving to depart.

"Will you be in New York long, Ms. Cumberland?" Kate walked with her towards the door.

"That remains to be seen," Elizabeth answered cryptically.

1:10 PM, Manhattan, New York City

Elizabeth left the Cumberland Foundation and flew to the ultra-modern, glass and steel studio of INB, Independent News Broadcasting, near Times Square. Tourists and New York natives prowling the site for the slightest glimpse of a celebrity, gaped as she landed in their midst. Gasps became laughs as they pointed, waved or applauded. Some scrambled to record her appearance on their mobile phones. *So far so good.* She smiled and acknowledged the throngs of well-wishers before hastily disappearing inside the building.

The crowd pursued, prompting gray-uniformed security guards to scramble to lock the doors behind her. As the latches clacked tight, she glanced back finding she was effectively trapped inside. Giving the crowd a final wave, she turned her attention to a conversation that seemed to be concluding at the reception counter.

A good-looking Hispanic man wearing a leather messenger's bag across his body pled his case to a smartly dressed Asian-American woman. She frowned at him from behind her round glasses.

"Ms. Cho, I think your viewers would find what I've uncovered very interesting—" he said.

"This is a news network, not a tabloid. Go back to The Spoiler to tell your Elvis stories," she said tersely.

"I've been investigating aliens for—"

"We're not interested in tall tales from the trailer-park."

The sudden commotion at the lobby's plate glass windows distracted them away from their dispute.

The reporter's face brightened. "Speak of the...." He pulled a mobile phone from his bag and advanced towards Elizabeth. "Hello there, I'd like to interview you, Ms...?"

Elizabeth smiled pleasantly. "Are you employed here?"

"He's not." Cho stepped up and gave him a look of annoyance. "Good afternoon, Mr. Ramos."

Elizabeth looked at Ramos apologetically. "I'm terribly sorry but I only wish to do one—"

Ignoring the other woman, Ramos smiled disarmingly at Elizabeth. "Hey, no problem, I can wait and then we—"

"You can wait outside on the sidewalk." Ms. Cho motioned for one of the security guards and pointed to Ramos.

"Hey, Ms. Cho, reporting on aliens is my shtick." He looked back at Elizabeth, "No offense."

"It's quite all right," Elizabeth said, watching a security guard take Ramos' arm. "Please don't hurt him."

Cho's demeanor shifted from annoyance to something far more affable. "He'll be fine. I'm sorry he bothered you. Welcome to IBN. I'm the news editor, Lisa Cho."

Elizabeth shook her hand. "I'd like to talk to someone about doing an interview?"

"You've found her. We'll get you into the studio with our evening anchor right away."

"Evening? Should I come back?" She looked back at the glass doors and the eager faces pressed to it.

Cho's expression became anxious. "No-no-not at all, you're prime time. We'll dedicate a whole hour to this interview. If you'll just come this way." Cho extended a guiding arm towards the elevators.

"I envisioned an interview that was more...compact."

"We'll work out the details once we're upstairs—and...." She glanced at Ramos as he was being directed out to the street. "If you want to take off from the helipad after the interview, we would be happy to oblige you."

###

After spending some time in hair and makeup, and meeting several executives and producers, Elizabeth sat in the studio's plush cupola chair as primly and congenially as an English lady serving tea at a garden party. Seemingly every person who worked at the station was shoe-horned into the grand studio. The impromptu audience stood behind the cameras whispering and laughing softly, murmuring with speculation and wonder. The pageant-queen smile she wore belied her racing thoughts. *Remember you're doing this for them…*she reminded herself as Bill Boothman arrived.

Boothman was nearing retirement. His thinning pompadour was almost white. He had crow's feet at the corners of his eyes and wisdom lines across his forehead. The seasoned news anchor carried a list of suggested questions from his producer. He set them aside on a short table abutting their chairs, paused to consider her posture and began to speak in his famous shoe-leather voice. "Relax, there's no need to be nervous."

"I'll try my best." She tossed her head and tilted it to one side to expose her neck.

Bill's eyes flicked across her lap and leisurely travelled back to her face, lingering on her lips before meeting her gaze again. "That's good for ratings. Now, if I ask a question that you don't understand what I'm asking, just let me know and I'll ask it another way."

Indeed. "That's very nice of you, Mr. Boothman." Elizabeth cooed while struggling to keep her eyes from rolling like slot machine reels.

"After we're done, I'll take you out for a drink. Have you ever had a drink?"

"Oh? You're allowed to do that at work?" Elizabeth asked innocently.

Bill puffed out his chest. "I'm the Big Wheel around here. Play your cards right and you'll go places." He gave her a wink.

Oh, do tell! She struggled to keep the disdain from her face and turned to smile sweetly at the approaching producer who announced they were ready.

"Relax, and I'll take care of you." Bill reached out to pat her hand.

"I'll do my best, Bill." *En garde.*

Hair and makeup artists darted in to provide touch-ups to their features. The studio lights blazed down upon them resembling the unblinking intensity of the sun. The camera operators framed their shots. Bill began to speak.

"Superhero who saved the Earth, blonde bombshell, celestial angel from on high. Her arrival has shaken the world to its core. I'm a very lucky man to be sitting down with her for an exclusive IBN interview." He turned from the camera to his guest. "We are pleased to have you here, welcome."

"It is my pleasure, Mr. Boothman."

"What should I call you? Do you have a name?"

She considered her response for a second. "President Sanderson called me a Celestial Guardian Angel—which is quite a mouthful. How about just...Guardian?" *Now if I can remember to answer to it.*

"All right. Let's start with something easy, Guardian. Are you married?"

"I'm not."

"So, you're saying you play the field? You have a lot of admirers?"

Guardian resisted the urge to cock an eyebrow at the question instead her nose scrunched up playfully. She pointed to his left hand. "As I can see that you're married, are you asking for a friend?" She tilted her head, giving him a crooked, tight-lipped smile.

"Happily, for forty years." Bill smirked. "Let's talk about your costume for a moment, can you stand up and give us a twirl?" His eyes glittered.

Guardian burst into a soft laugh. "Oh Bill...." She gave him a dainty, dismissive wave of her hand. "I think that 70s television program was wonderful—but I don't spin in place to change into my uniform."

"Wouldn't you say that that your costume is deliberately provocative? It doesn't leave a lot to the imagination."

Your imagination. "My uniform is eminently practical. It's comfortable and easy to move in—just as a gymnast or a wrestler's clothing is—and I do call it a uniform because just as you recognize a police officer or nurse by what they wear, so too will people see me and know that I've come to help." Her eyes twinkled with challenge.

"What planet are you from?"

"I was born in space but I truly feel human."

"All right, let's talk about something related to that." Bill turned his face to a large monitor positioned behind them. An image of her eating lunch with Manny appeared on the screen, his face had been pixilated out. "What's happening here?"

Guardian's face softened. "Lunch with a new friend."

"That was nice of you."

"I hope not."

Boothman's brow furrowed. "I'm not sure I understand."

"To be nice is to say to someone in his situation, I hope things get better for you. It's a platitude. To be kind is to work to make his situation better."

"I see. So, did you pay for this lunch?"

"I was happy to."

"So, you're saying you have been here long enough to earn money?"

She took a sip of water before responding. "Longer than three days."

"So, you're saying you've lived here all this time and didn't tell any of your coworkers. Wouldn't you say that's dishonest to lie about who you are?"

"I'd say it isn't the sort of thing that normally comes up in the course of conversation without one's mental health coming into question."

"But you're saying you did lie about who you are."

"No, Bill, I'm saying it never came up in conversation."

His dark eyes narrowed and he pointed to the blonde. "But you're saying you would lie to people if they asked."

Twit. "Let's not talk in hypotheticals."

"What did you eat when you were having lunch with this homeless man?"

"He's just a man, not—"

"Just a man? What I'm hearing is you think we're less than you?"

Perplexed, Guardian's brow creased. "No, I'm not saying that at all. I'm saying to label him homeless diminishes all that he is. You're all wonders in my eyes—every one of you. And to finish my answer to your question, we had club sandwiches."

"So, you're saying you eat flesh?"

"That's a rather provocative way of phrasing it, Bill. I eat what the USDA would deem acceptable proteins as part of a balanced diet."

"Let's talk about what happened this morning in Chicago. You feel you're above the law?" A new image, one her hovering above a Chicago cop appeared on the screen.

Her lips trembled as she struggled to suppress a smile. "Well, despite what's happening in this picture, no I don't."

Boothman frowned. "You find this funny?"

"I'm sorry, Bill. I promise I won't laugh until you say something else that's funny."

"You're saying that breaking the law is fun?"

"No, I didn't say that at all. This was merely a brief misunderstanding during a tense situation. That's why I decided to adopt a uniform, to prevent future confusion."

"But you are saying that it's acceptable to insert yourself into military operations unlawfully?"

Wondering why he was being so adversarial, Guardian resisted the urge to confront him. "If I said I was the best person to handle that situation I would sound like I was boasting, but if I said I wasn't I would be lying. I knew I could resolve it peacefully."

"By breaking the law."

"No, Bill. By saving lives and protecting the peace."

Bill bobbed a pen at her like a pointer. "So, you're saying this alien is lethal."

"I don't believe he's an alien, I believe he's human and was afflicted by exposure to the asteroid shard and the circumstances—" She cringed inwardly as the words passed her lips.

"So, you're saying he has a disease that was brought to Earth by the asteroid just as some believe Ebola and HIV-AIDS were?" His expression became panicked.

Guardian shook her head. "No, if that were the case there would be metal men popping up all over the place but I haven't seen anything in the news to indicate that—and I know how thorough you try to be when it comes to finding and reporting the stories that matter."

"So, to put it another way, we've only seen patient zero and that anyone exposed to a piece of the asteroid could be potentially dangerous?"

She struggled to keep exasperation from her voice. "I'm not saying any of that, Bill. This man is in a secure medical facility where some of the very best doctors in the world are working to determine what happened and hopefully restore him to his former state of health and well-being."

"In other words, anyone exposed to a piece of the asteroid should be in quarantine and you were exposed to it the most. Shouldn't you be in quarantine too?"

"I don't ever get sick Bill and I don't carry diseases; my metabolism knocks them out. And as I said there haven't been any other reports of anything like what happened this morning." Guardian looked over Bill's shoulder, the assembled studio staff seemed disconcerted by the implications of his remarks. *Bloody wonderful.*

Bill was looking a little pale, he fidgeted in his chair. "I think that's all we have time for. Thank you for coming in, Guardian." He turned his face towards the camera. "IBN will continue to report the latest on this breaking news story."

The camera panned backwards. The lights faded down low. The producer shouted, "'We're clear.'" Bill was out of his seat, breathing heavily and struggled to free himself from his microphone.

Guardian stood up and reached to help him.

He flinched and retreated. "Don't touch me. I don't feel well."

"Mr. Boothman—Bill, you're having a panic attack. Just sit down, take a few deep breaths and sip some water."

He looked at her wide-eyed. "Just stay back." He retreated off the raised dais. He began to fuss and struggle with his microphone wires. "Somebody get this goddamned thing off me!"

Guardian's hands fell to her sides.

A production assistant appeared and helped Bill free himself. Now flushed and breathless, he demanded to be taken to a hospital.

Guardian's lips pinched with annoyance. She commanded the symbiote to release the microphone and its body pack into her hands. She turned to see Lisa Cho approaching. "You cannot air this."

"Of course we're going to air this. We've already done the promotions."

"Then you must cut the final segment, it is alarmist and would be spreading falsehoods that might cause real harm."

Aileen shook her head. "It's better to err on the side of caution when it comes to public safety."

Guardian reached out her hands turned upward in supplication. "But this could induce a panic."

"Relax," Aileen soothed, "we'll send a team over to the CDC's office for comment and run it right after your segment."

Guardian regarded her skeptically. "That will not be enough."

"I have no doubt that with the reassurance you gave, it will be. People love you!" She gushed and reached out to smooth Guardian's arm.

"The purpose of this interview was to put people at ease. He seemed to go out of his way to do the opposite."

Cho's expression became serious. "Look, I'm sorry but you

do know this is about ratings, right? What did you think he was going to ask you? Your favorite color? What your hobbies are? This isn't Young & Fresh." She named a music network's channel directed toward tweens. "Now, can I show you up to the roof or would you prefer the front door?"

Guardian looked at the other woman with disbelief. "Your intentions to air this go beyond unethical, it's immoral. You must reconsider—"

"It's not my decision to make."

"Well, I can be very persuasive. Who should I speak with?"

"This is a network decision, if you try and stop it, you'll only come off looking badly."

Guardian scowled. "Show me the way to the roof." *And be happy I don't create my own exit.*

4:30 PM Goddard Space Flight Center, Greenbelt, Maryland

Guardian sat in front of Robert Brown's broad executive desk. A doctor of astrophysics, Brown was the director of NASA's Goddard Space Flight Center in Maryland. In addition to his personal work area, his spacious office contained a long boardroom table, a lounge area with sofas and comfortable cushioned chairs. Deeply tanned, his eyes shone with intelligence. The director wore a dark navy-blue suit and a tie that was distinctly NASA blue. He beamed at her as he leaned against the front of his desk and gripped its edge. She wondered if Brown's elation matched her level of anxiety. She needed to find a sample of that asteroid and NASA seemed to be her best option.

"...what puzzles me most about the asteroid is its behavior. The manner in which after breaking apart, the pieces continued towards the Earth anyway," Guardian said.

"Some of it might be gravity and a failure to achieve escape velocity, but we're puzzled by its behavior as well."

"I would like to follow its trajectory back to its point of origin but before we do that, a piece or sample of some sort could provide some initial answers."

Brown's eyebrows rose. "That could be quite a distance."

"Yes," Guardian gestured, wondering how many light years it might entail, "But for now a single meteorite would be a good start."

"We're looking into it but so far we've found only craters, the impactors seem to explode or vaporize as soon as they make landfall. We are trying, and welcome your assistance. I have one of our top people in satellite image interpretation coming to work with you. He should be here shortly."

A knock at the door halted his speech. He bade them to enter.

Guardian watched Brown draw himself up to full height. Directly behind her, the door swung shut with a soft thud. Guardian listened to footfalls of a military cadence against the slate-blue floor. The director greeted Jackson cordially. The sudden scent of citrus and sandalwood beckoned her to turn and rise.

Brown ushered the newcomer forward with a sweep of his arm. "Guardian, this is my friend and colleague, Dr. Mark Jackson."

The blonde needed to look up to see more than the bottom of Jackson's neck. Her gaze rose to lock eyes with a man whose countenance shone with intelligence and, possibly, mirth. Her hand rose reflexively to her throat as her breath left her.

Mark Jackson was taller and broader shouldered than her first husband, Tom. He had the regal bearing and a deep ebony complexion that reminded of her second husband, Musa. Jackson wore a jet-black tailored suit and handmade Italian oxfords, polished to a glass shine. She caught herself glancing at his hands searching for the golden gleam of a ring and found only a silver Marine Corps ring on his right hand.

She felt his eyes trace her face. An amused smile played upon his lips and she had second thoughts about wearing her uniform.

She took a second to find her voice. "Erm…" She stammered, "How do you do, Dr. Jackson." Instinctively, she offered her hand and watched him envelope it with his own.

He gazed down at her. A silky, baritone voice rumbled from his throat to caress her ears and leave her soul quaking. "Enchanted."

She struggled to keep from melting and, judging by the way her knees felt, she was failing in the effort. The implication was disconcerting.

"We call him 'Magic.'" Brown stood between them. She was grateful for the interruption. "Magic?"

Brown stepped closer; his chest puffed out. "It's like he has a magic wand. When we need something found, presto, he finds it." He clapped Mark on the big man's bicep, its curve visible through the material of his suit. "He's just the man you need."

Guardian looked up through feathery lashes despite herself. "Well then, I can't wait to see your act."

Mark chuckled.

Brown looked at the blonde and then to Mark. "It's the least we can do. Not only did she save the Space Station's crew—and the station, but she's offered to fly replacement satellites into orbit."

Guardian held up a halting finger. "Well, the non-military ones."

Mark rumbled, "It sounds like I've been upstaged."

"Not at all Dr. Jackson, this is your theater," she said.

Brown glanced from one to the other. "I have a feeling this is going to be a great partnership."

Jackson turned back to Guardian. "I have a car waiting."

"I'm anxious to get started," she said.

"Now, if there are any problems—if you need anything at all, the full resources of my office are at your disposal," Brown offered.

Jackson's eyes had never left Guardian's. "I think we can work out the details."

Yes, and you can read the telephone directory to me while we do that. Guardian pulled herself away from Jackson's gaze. "I'm so very grateful, Dr. Brown." She shook his hand before allowing Jackson to usher her out of the office to a bank of polished elevators, one was waiting open for them.

"Deputy director of suborbital and special orbital projects, that's quite a mouthful." She said over her shoulder as Mark allowed her to step in first.

Mark pushed the 'G' for the ground floor. "You'll get used to it, ma'am."

Guardian laughed incredulously. "You must be joking."

"What a beautiful laugh."

She flushed a dusty rose. Her eyes dropped demurely and she scolded herself inwardly for making the archaic gesture. "Thank you." She took a deep breath. "Is there something I may call you instead of...that lengthy moniker?"

"Sir."

"Sir? Really? How about Magic?"

"You have to earn that, ma'am."

Earn it? "Please don't call me ma'am."

"Yes, ma'am."

She groaned inwardly. "How about Guardian?"

"Guardian." He murmured it a second time as if swishing it around his mouth like a sommelier with a sample of wine. "Well, it fits the outfit."

She gripped the edges of her cape and swayed in demonstration. "You don't think it's too ostentatious, do you?"

He looked her over appraisingly. "That's as good a word as any."

Guardian's jaw dropped open.

"Like a dime among pennies."

Her heart bounced. "Thank you, then.*"*

"Wasn't so hard, was it?"

Guardian's eyes narrowed. Her tongue touched the cupid's bow of her upper lip. *Oh En Garde.* "I was—you expect—" the elevator's bell cut off her sputtering retort.

Mark turned his face back towards the doors and chuckled. "There's a crowd waiting to see you in the lobby."

The elevator doors slid open and a crowd of NASA staff and contractors burst into applause.

Her hand rose to her throat. "By the stars!"

"Better get used to this," Mark murmured.

"I don't know if I ever will."

"NASA knows heroes, so they spotted you right away— but...if you're uncomfortable, I can have security move them back."

She turned her face towards him and spoke out of the corner of her mouth, "Certainly not! That would be rude. Always acknowledge your audience—especially a grateful one." *And besides...* She thought of the interview in Chicago, *I'm going to need all the support I can get.*

They stepped forward into the crowd. Mark stayed half a step back to one side. She heard a chorus of whispers.

"It's her."

"Check out, Jacks. Magic's cast his spell on her."

"Oh geez—"

"Don't be dissin' the Jacks."

"Did you just say 'dissin'? You're from Vermont."

Jacks? Hmmm. She shook several hands and slowly pressed forward.

"Her planet is the first one we need to visit."

"Mark's been abducted."

"I volunteer to be next."

"The line starts behind me."

Silly. She rolled her eyes inwardly.

"Miss Ann can't take our Mark away."

"I would kill to have her hips and thighs."

"She must be queen of her gym."

"Yeah, a gym where they lift jumbo jets."

"I need to get a picture."

Guardian mentally doubled checked that she was indeed smiling.

"She smiled at us. Did you see that?"

"I might have to stop by Dr. Jackson's office later to drop off some files."

"Like she'd ever talk to you."

How rude!

"I can't wait to tell the kids when I get home."

"You can fall in love with an NTI, can't you?"

"Are those breasts even real?"

Guardian struggled to keep from laughing at the notion. *Of course, they're real—really fabulous.*

"I'm going to see if I can shake her hand."

Under the steady strobe of camera flashes, she shook every hand that was extended, met everyone and addressed them by name, and even hugged a few that were overwrought. The fear of how the interview would be received prompted her to take extra care with each of them.

"You have no idea how surreal that was for me," Guardian said to Mark as they were finally in the backseat of the car.

"For you?" Mark chuckled and shook his head.

"I can understand how my sudden appearance could be—"

"World changing?"

"Until three days ago, no one thought twice about me."

"Somehow, I doubt that."

It suddenly seemed awfully warm in the air-conditioned car. "Erm, thank you."

"We're going to work out of my office, it'll be quieter...fewer distractions."

Speak for yourself.

5:10 PM, Mark Jackson's office, Goddard Space Flight Center, Maryland

"We've lost a few satellites," Mark said.

"Whatever images you can provide will be of help." Guardian's cape fluttered behind her as they walked. "And, if it wouldn't be too much trouble, could we check the internet for any breaking news?"

"That can be arranged." Mark pushed open the varnished wooden door to his outer office. The trailing security detail remained outside.

Guardian paused to meet Jackson's assistant, Katie, before he showed her into his compact office.

The room was as neat as a barracks readied for inspection. One side of his desk displayed a picture frame and on the other she recognized a maquette of the Bussa Emancipation statue. Behind the desk, were shelves filled with books and manuals organized by subject. Polished frames contained his academic degrees. There was a Marine officer's sword and a shadow box containing his medals, ribbons, dog tags, captain's bars and a picture of him in his dress blues. Every card and paper on a bulletin board was neatly spaced as were several team pictures on the wall. *Ain't No Mountain High Enough* played softly on his computer's speakers.

Her head began to slowly bob. "I love this song." She looked up at him as she recalled a performance at the Apollo theatre.

"Gaye and Terrell, ain't nothing like the real thing."

"I love that song, too." She continued her survey of his office.

"Take a chair, I'll check the news." He patted one of the padded chairs in front of his desk.

Her hand traced the back of the seat but she was drawn to the photographs. Little league football team photos, spanning back ten years, along with a plaque for coach of the year, Mark's name appeared on it more than once.

He turned from his computer. "Nothing jumping out as a news alert."

She pointed to the photographs and cooed, "They're adorable."

"Those are my teams." Mark moved to stand beside her.

"So, you're a footballer?" she asked.

He chuckled. "I *played* football, including a year in college. That's where I got my nickname, not from finding things on a map."

"Oh, you gave it up?"

Mark grimaced and shrugged.

"Oh, I'm sorry. You're not comfortable with discussing it."

"Nah, it's all right. Freshman year… bowl game. I got my chance. Quarterback threw a perfect spiral. It was beautiful. I snatched it out of that blue sky only a yard from the goal line. I turned and that son of a bitch cut me off at the knees. I fell into a touchdown and a blown ACL. We won the game but I was done. No chance of a pro-career after that."

Guardian looked at him sympathetically. "I'm so sorry."

"Don't be. A different school, a different scholarship, and I met my wife—"

Wife? She kept her annoyance from her face.

"—And got a good education. I couldn't run forty yards in 4.3 anymore but I could still move. I still got to be a Marine like my dad, I work at NASA and I'm talking with the only confirmed extra—sorry, off-worlder that we've ever encountered."

"You were going to say extra-terrestrial, weren't you?"

"No offense."

"It's all right, I am."

"But you're not brown, short, squat, and blue eyed. You've got green eyes."

"Yes." And *you're married so stop it.*

"So, you've seen that movie?"

"I make a point to see everything on the subject of extra-terrestrials," she said, happy to be off the subject of her eyes. "Shall we look at those satellite images? That way I can be out of—"

"Out of my hair?" He smirked, running a hand over the smooth surface of his shaved pate.

"Sorry!" She flushed a deep shade of pink.

"It's all right. I can grow it back but I like the look."

"Could we look at those images please?"

"Sure, just let me pull a chair around for you."

"I can stand." Guardian extended a digit to a photograph at the far corner of his desk, tucked next to his monitor. "Is that your wife and son?"

Mark picked up the picture and thoughtfully examined it for a moment before handing it across the desk to her. "Yeah, the love of my life and my little man. Tyson was eight when that picture was taken. He'd be starting his sophomore year in a few weeks...."

Her expression softened. "Oh...did something happen?" She shook her head at her question. "I'm sorry, never mind, it's none of my affair."

"It's all right. It happened when I was deployed in Afghanistan, a Friday night in July. Melissa—my wife, was bringing him home from his game. We used to go for ice cream after his games, Ty's favorite was chocolate. A drunk ran the light and took them both from me." He took a deep breath and let it out slowly.

Guardian's hand rose to her chest as she felt her heart squeezed. "I'm so sorry. I didn't mean to..."

"It's all good. It's nice to talk to someone about them, it's like they're still around."

She stepped around the desk, blinking rapidly to clear her vision. "Mark—and I can say this with all certainty. Love has no age, no limit and no death. When we love someone, we give them a piece of our heart, and if they go away, they take that piece with them, that's the emptiness we feel. But, if they loved us, they gave us a piece of them to hold onto. Over time...our hearts become this beautiful mosaic. Melissa and Tyson's pieces are the most beautiful in your mosaic—and they are very much *still around*."

Mark brought his tongue to his upper lip and nodded. "Yeah, they are." He took a deep breath. "Are you sure you don't want a chair?" He lifted one by its back.

"A chair would be lovely."

"Just let me move the desk forward and make some space for us—." He reached to push it and his speech stopped short as the desk lifted off the floor and moved away from the wall several inches.

She had pinched the lip of the desk between her thumb and index finger and lifted it from the floor. "Is that far enough?"

"I'll bet that comes in handy when it's time to vacuum."

"It does but I wish they would make a more powerful appliance, even after rewiring it, it still takes five minutes to clean the house." She sighed and shook her head in mock disappointment.

"Five whole minutes? Do you live in a phone booth?"

She simpered. "No, and I don't change clothes in one either, but on the subject of housekeeping, dishes take the longest, they're so very fragile."

"So, you eat?" he asked.

"Yes; I love to eat!" She laughed, it seemed silly that anyone would assume otherwise. "And I love to cook. Eating is one of the five great joys of life."

"And what are the other four?" He stroked his chin while wearing an expression of amusement.

She counted them off with her fingers. "Love, art, music, and dance."

"But not wine?"

She shrugged and smiled. "It doesn't really affect me."

"You can't get drunk?" Jackson chuckled.

"Not even tipsy and I don't fall ill." *Which only makes these butterflies more alarming.*

"That's funky."

"It is likely for the best, flying around while inebriated—or worse, bumping into things. I could do a lot of damage."

"You're probably right." He chuckled again and held her gaze.

The door's knob rattled and then swung inward. A bespectacled teen burst into the office, his arms laden with three thick binders. "Hey, Dr. Jackson! "Did you hear that she's herrrrre!" Tripping on the door jamb, he yelped and pitched forward. The manuals and his glasses flew through the air.

A sudden wind roared through the office. The papers on Mark's bulletin board fluttered and snapped like flags in a gale. One, two, then three binders, clattered into a neat pile on Jackson's desk. The teen's glasses were plucked from the air and he fell into her arms.

"Damn!" Mark exclaimed.

"I've got you!" Guardian laughed at the intern's bewildered expression.

Harold Warner flushed tomato red. "You're...you're here!"

She stood him up and carefully fit his glasses back onto his face. "And you're right there." She gave him a playful wink.

His hand came to his chest. A gasp became a wheeze. The color quickly left his face.

"By the stars, are you all right?"

"Asthma attack," Mark said. He swiftly strode around the desk. "Where's your inhaler, Harold?"

"Let's sit you down." Guardian helped him into a chair.

Harold struggled to speak, wheezing as he attempted to get his hand into the pocket of his chinos to find the device before fumbling and dropping it.

Guardian caught it mid-fall. "I've got it." Kneeling beside his chair, she scanned the prescription before shaking it. "Take one puff and hold it for a count of ten and then take a second puff." She handed it to the youth as he wheezed and nodded anxiously.

"I'll get a nurse up from the clinic." Mark picked up his

telephone's receiver.

"It's all right, Dr. Jackson, I'm a physician," Guardian said, not taking her eyes from the youth.

"That's right." Mark nodded and put the handset down. He watched and listened as she spoke soft reassurances to the intern. His gaze strayed to a picture framed in the far corner of his desk and then back to the pair.

"You're going to be fine." She smiled, sat back on her heels, and turned her face to look up at Mark. "He's going to be fine."

Jackson crouched down. "You feeling better, man?"

Guardian watched the black of Harold's pupils nearly eclipsed the blue of his irises. "Oh, I think he's feeling much better." She rolled her eyes in amusement.

"Looks like you're good." Mark clapped the youth on the shoulder.

"Harold...I like that name." She watched him light up and felt her heart warm. "Are you feeling well enough to stand?"

"You're here."

Mark straightened up. "I think your secret's out."

Harold launched himself out of the chair. "This is—this is so cool! Can I—Could we—would you—"

She glanced at Mark and looked back to Harold. "What is it luv?"

"Selfie!" He managed to finally blurt out.

Guardian's expression became serious, her voice a mystified whisper, "Well, Harold, that's a very special thing to ask of me. You'd be the first person I have ever agreed to pose for a picture with."

His voice filled with awe. "The first ever?"

"Yes." She nodded, keeping her expression solemn for a moment longer before breaking into a congenial smile. "I'd be happy to, but perhaps Dr. Jackson could..." She gestured for Harold to hand over his mobile phone.

Harold showed his boss how to work the camera application before moving to stand next to Guardian, his complexion red, his posture rigid.

"Just put your arm around my waist." She felt his arm across her back. It was stiff as a board. "Go ahead and squeeze, I won't break."

"Really?" He grinned unabashedly and relaxed.

"I promise." She smiled as two pictures were snapped.

"Do you want one too, Dr. Jackson?" Harold offered.

Guardian raised her hand to her chin in consideration, "Well…if you'll vouch for him Harold, I suppose it would be all right."

"Dr. Jackson? You can trust him."

"It's good to have connections." Mark replaced Harold at her side, slipping a hand around her waist to it rest on the curve of her hip.

She felt a tingling and licked her lips to concentrate. "My you're tall, I should have worn boots with heels."

Leaning down to her ear, Mark murmured, "I like your boots."

"I beg your pardon?" A fiery scarlet flush rose up her neck and colored her cheeks. "You like my…." Guardian replayed Mark's words in her mind. She placed a steadying hand on Mark's chest as peals of laughter escaped her throat. "I'm such a silly goose."

Harold was wide-eyed. "Did you—did you say—"

"Boots Harold! He said boots!" *What would Sigmund say?*

"Yeah, what did you think I said?" Mark's eyes gleamed with mischief.

"Boots."

"Uh-huh." Mark continued to smile for a second picture.

Guardian blushed a deeper shade of red and groaned inwardly. *Wonderful.*

"I'll email it to you, Dr. Jackson," Harold said, tapping icons on his phone display before a soft reggae tone was heard coming from Jackson's jacket pocket.

"Got it. Thanks, man. Why don't you take these binders to

the main group and work there today?"

Harold's face fell. "Y-you don't need me to stay and help?"

"We're going over impact sites from those asteroid pieces."

"I could help with that."

"I got this, man. Thanks for the offer though. I'll see you around."

"Alright." Harold cast a longing glance at Guardian.

"It was lovely meeting you, Harold. I'm sure we'll talk again."

Harold lingered at the door, his heart clearly beating against the fabric of his shirt. "Can I email you the pictures?"

"Oh, I don't have email but if you can print one for me, I'll put it in my scrapbook of memories." She smiled at him gently and exchanged goodbyes. She waited for the door to close before turning back to Mark. "He's really sweet."

Mark spun his executive chair around and patted it. "Have a seat."

The soft leather squeaked as she sat back. She watched as he pulled the other chair in front of her. She noted the warmth in his eyes had been replaced by something more penetrating. "Is everything all right?"

"Harold's a good kid, he's smart, loyal, eager to help, and I try to look out for him. You got him pretty flustered. You're not going to do that to anyone else around here are you?" Mark regarded her with reproach.

"I'm sorry. Is it the uniform?" She looked down and smoothed it to her hips, anxious to hear what he would say.

"That's part of it."

"What's the other part?"

"All the other parts." Mark's eyes shone with mischief.

She felt her skin flush. "By the stars, I'm blushing."

He leaned in. "Speaking of the stars...any more like you kicking around?"

"More like me?"

"Off-worlders?"

She shook her head, "I've done my best to see off any other

off-worlder visitors."

"Talk to me."

"I know, Dr. Brown, you, and likely everyone else here have questions."

"Intellectual curiosity comes with the job."

"You have neighbors, Dr. Jackson. Most have gotten the message, and keep their distance but there are always a few renegades." She frowned in recollection.

"Renegades?"

"Yes. They complicate things."

"And you don't like complications."

"In medicine, complications mean suffering."

"Complications are part of life and sometimes they turn out all right." He winked.

She smiled with hope. "We'll see."

"I want to hear more about these other off-worlders, but it's time to put you to work."

Her hand came to her throat. "Me?"

He nodded. "Let's have some fun."

You mean more fun. She vacated his chair and watched him as he sat down to 'play.'

Mark changed the screen and with a few clicks of his mouse, began to pull up data. "Impact sites...." He gestured to a contoured map of North America as one by one, tiny red stars began to appear all over it and in the coastal areas.

She glanced over the screen. "583?"

"It isn't accurate. We lost a lot of birds. The Russians even more."

"These were taken with Terra and Landsat?" She leaned in, trying to focus past his cologne.

"You know about our satellites?" He looked at her sideways.

"I've examined them—when the space station was over the horizon of course." She turned her face to him. They were almost nose to nose. With a furtive glance at his lips, she drew her face back. "Erm, sorry." A drop of perspiration trickled down the back of her neck.

"What did you think?"

"Well, all the parts seem to be in the right places." She glanced at him sideways.

Jackson chuckled. "I'll print off the locations."

"It's all right, I've memorized them."

"You have an eidetic memory?" he asked.

"It's quite useful for remembering birthdays. About the asteroid though…has there been any analysis of it? I found its behavior…." She grimaced. "Odd."

"Well, it's not my usual area, but I'll tell you what, I could find some things out and we could compare notes. What kinds of things did you see?"

"Thank you, I appreciate that. As for the asteroid, its makeup and behaviors are different than anything I've ever seen. First, its entire internal structure resembled a gem or a crystal, as such, the friction of the Earth's atmosphere should have burned it up. And to add to its strangeness, it was off-gassing, both in space where the nuclear arms were striking it and the pieces as they reached the Earth's atmosphere. Finally, when the asteroid exploded, it did not scatter in a conventional manner, it formed a ring around the planet."

"How the pieces survived entry, we'll have to wait to get a sample. As for the off-gassing, heat will do that with some compounds and elements. But the third part has us stumped too. Gravity is only a partial expRuthtion."

"Well, if we can find one, or the residue, maybe we can get some answers."

"That's what I'm hoping. And on that note…." She began to push her chair back. "At least one of these sites must have something worth examining and as such, I should get cracking. And again, I'm so very grateful for your help."

He turned in his chair. "You'll probably have company."

"Why do you say that?"

"Besides the military, there's a whole alphabet soup of

agencies out there looking at sites."

Guardian paused to consider the information. "I suppose that's to be expected. Do you know if they found anything?"

"I can find out if NASA picked something up."

"What about the others?"

"The Air Force has a special unit that would take charge of anything else."

Her face soured. "Yes, I had dealings with one of their officers this morning."

"It didn't go well?"

"Incompetent is the word I would use. Where would the Air Force take anything they found?"

"Probably some kind of Area 51 facility. Incidentally, do you know if Roswell was real?"

"Very real. Renegades from Zeta-Reticuli."

"The gray ones?"

"Yes. It was so badly handled. If I would have caught them first...I believe it would have saved some headaches."

"We're going to have to talk about this some more."

"Perhaps, but I have a question that you might be able to answer about the asteroid."

He spun the seat of his chair completely around to face her. "All right, go ahead."

"When did NASA detect it? I'm up there every week and I'm very thorough."

"Well...." His stomach gurgled. He chuckled, sheepishly patting his abdomen. "Pardon that, it seems like I've got an alien inside me."

"And I've kept you from your dinner, I'm sorry."

"Do you like Italian? It's Italian night in the cafeteria."

"Oh...." Her eyes fluttered at the invite. "Thank you, but I don't normally—"

"Today has been anything but normal." He rose from his chair.

"Dr. Jackson—"

"Mark."

She smiled nervously. "Or Sir?"

"You know it. Come on."

She fidgeted beneath his gaze. "I couldn't possibly. People would think—"

"As far as eating together, the only opinions that matter are ours, but if you don't like Italian—"

"Il cibo italiano è meraviglioso. That means—"

"I agree, it is wonderful."

"You speak Italian," she said, beginning to follow him.

"And you speak it like a native. Speak any others?"

"I doubt you'll believe me."

"Try me."

"All of them."

5:40 PM Goddard Space Flight Center, Cafeteria

Mark and Guardian's appearance in the Flight Centre's hanger-sized cafeteria began with excited murmurs and ended with a standing ovation. It was the experience of the lobby magnified twenty times. Mark continued to speak to her in Italian and the room seemed more intimate, the unexpected adulation, more manageable.

After standing in line for their meals, and acknowledging well-wishers while they waited, Mark found them a place at a refectory table near its glass wall. It looked south onto the patio where curious diners peered through the glass.

Guardian dabbed some salad dressing from her lips with a napkin. "Perhaps you can answer a question for me."

"Okay? Shoot." Mark reached for his breast pocket.

"Does everyone dine with their telephones in hand? It seems rather rude." She glanced around. Mark paused, chuckled and withdrew his hand from his jacket. "No, not everyone."

She stabbed a leaf of lettuce. "I do need to retrieve mine though. I left it with a friend when all of this kerfuffle began."

"Does he know about...." He made a swooping gesture with his hand.

Guardian squelched an amused smile with the tip of her tongue. *That was subtle.* "I imagine *she* does now."

Through the murmur and clatter of the dining hall, her ears detected a particular conversation behind her.

"Now that's a heavenly body." She heard a male voice declare.

"I'd like to lie between those thighs," a second said in a low growl.

"I wonder if she spits or swallows the watermelon seeds."

"Dessert?" Mark asked.

"What are my choices?" Guardian continued to listen.

"But you know what she likes..."

"Stupid bimbo, what a waste."

Guardian's eyes closed with disgust.

"I've never seen anyone make a face like that over chocolate cake," Mark said.

"No, I love chocolate cake, I just need to…" She turned in her seat, looking for the source of the comment and spied the speaker almost immediately. He quickly lowered his face and tried to hide behind the diners at the tables between them. His partner spun around and hunched over.

"Excuse me a moment," Guardian said, taking her napkin from her lap and setting it beside her plate.

"Everything all right?" Mark, along with the security detail sitting across the aisle, began to rise.

"I won't be a moment." She assumed a saccharin smile and strutted to the pair's table. Her voice became a sultry purr as her hips swayed seductively. "Well, hello there."

Wide-eyed, they grinned up at her. One of them stammered out. "H-hey."

She moistened her lips. "I heard what you said. I don't think you know about my ears…they're amazing." She brushed her curls back to expose a lobe.

They looked at each other and then up at her, their grins suddenly far less certain.

"And who are you?" She looked from left to right.

A lanky twenty-something with a Frankenstein forehead and jug handles for ears spoke up. "I'm Rusty and this is my buddy, Carl."

"Hey there." Carl's blue eyes slithered over her.

She leaned deep over the table until she was resting on her elbows. She looked at one to the other, "How long have you two been playing this joke? Is your name really Rusty?" She lifted Rusty's ID lanyard with her finger tips. "It says you're Carl."

Carl looked at the laminated plastic card and then at his own. He was wearing Rusty's lanyard. "How?" His eyes bulged.

Guardian's smile vanished; her voice changed from sultry to philosophic and finished cold and sharp. "It's quite maddening, isn't it? The inequalities of life? For example, I'm jealous of all the people who've never had the displeasure of your acquaintance—whatever your names are." Her eyes narrowed. "You're a disgrace to your employers. I wonder how I would contact them. I'm sure someone around here knows...." She lifted her head to look around to see congenial expressions in her direction.

They paled, squirming beneath her gaze. Panic filled eyes refused to meet hers and instead looked for an escape route.

Guardian straightened up, assuming the sultry voice again. "Goodbye, boys."

Turning on her heel, Guardian found her way back to Mark to retake her seat.

"What happened? Did they say something to you?" Scowling, Mark began to rise out of his chair.

"Please, don't trouble yourself."

"It's not me who's gonna have trouble."

"Your concern is appreciated, but I don't need a knight to come charging to my rescue." She gestured to his chair. "Please?"

"This is about treating people with courtesy and respect." Mark glowered at the pair for a moment more before resuming his seat.

She knew that protective look. She wasn't sure how she felt about it when it concerned her. "I think they've already received more attention than they deserve." She took a sip of her water. "Can you tell me what time and date the asteroids were discovered?"

"The Swift and GRAVITY telescopes spotted it. We got the call to move the Hubble last Friday a little after Seven PM. The president didn't have a lot of time to make his decision about what to do."

"Near Earth Objects didn't spot it?" She nibbled her bottom lip in thought.

"That's a touchy subject around here, but no."

"I missed it too. Last Monday I was up looking for threats

and I didn't see it. I didn't see any disturbance in the Oort Cloud when I was up looking this morning either."

"The Oort cloud? That's like two billion miles away," he marveled.

"Indeed, it is." She smiled.

"That's...we definitely need to do some question-and-answer sessions."

"Perhaps a few, but can you tell me if the Chandra telescope was pointed in its direction before it was spotted?"

"I can find—"

"Excuse me? I don't mean to interrupt but I have to say that your aid work just makes me admire you even more." Visibly quivering a young brunette shifted from foot to foot while she smiled apologetically. She had a round face and wore horn-rimmed glasses.

Guardian's eyes fluttered as a pit of fear yawned open in her stomach. "My aid work?"

"I think that is so neat you've been here helping people for so long, could I possibly get a picture with you?"

"Of course." She forced a smile while her mind raced back to Kenya.

The staffer handed her camera to Mark before she crouched down for the snapshot.

Mark chuckled as he handed it back and their visitor departed. "I'm surprised she's the only one so far."

The blonde rose from the table. "I'm...I'm sorry but I need to retrieve my telephone. Would you mind too terribly if we continue our conversation in your office after I return?"

Mark stood up in response. "Is everything all right?"

"I'm going to find out. Thank you for dinner." She placed her visitor badge on the table and strode out the nearby patio door.

A human wave surged forward to bubble and froth against the glass, babbling with enthusiasm and speculation.

Guardian looked to the sky. Her body seemed to coil like a spring. FFFFBOOM. She was airborne and quickly gaining altitude. The crowd pointed with delight, cheering as she disappeared into the coming night.

Wearing an expression of concern, Mark stood behind them and watched her soar east.

1:30 AM Local Time, Sehemu Nzuri, Kenya

Floating over the camp, Elizabeth detected no signs of journalists or unfamiliar vehicles. Heart aching, she paused to look longingly first at the orphans' dormitory and then at the hospital. Exhaling a sigh that reached all the way to her toes, she descended into the shadowy space behind the administrative building that doubled as Ayana's quarters.

Attired all in black, she silently glided around to the front and let herself into the reception area. She knew where the extra key to the office was hidden and quickly used it.

Her mobile phone was tucked inside the center drawer of the desk, slipping it into the pocket at the small of her back. She looked at the door leading to Ayana's apartments and bit her bottom lip. Settling on what was to her mind a poor alternative to speaking to her friend directly, she took a sheet of paper from the office's printer and a pen from the desk to write a note.

Ayana,

I apologize for my lack of forthrightness. I hope that we might speak together soon.

All of my love,

E

PS: I have my mobile

She frowned at the note and considered writing another but what needed to be said had to be done in person. Folding the paper once and putting her friend's name on the outside, she set it on the center of the desk for it to be found before slipping away as quietly as she had arrived.

###

Guardian arrived at the security shack of the employees' gate, to find Mark waiting for her. He wore an anxious expression.

"What is it, Dr. Jackson?" she asked, forgetting her sorrows.

"We got the call from the Canadians. There's an emergency at the impact site near the Columbia River involving three of our people."

Guardian flew to him. "What happened?"

"The Mounties reported they got a 911 call, there was some screaming and then the call cut out."

"I'm leaving right now." She prepared to launch herself into the air.

"Do you remember—"

"The site near the British Columbia-Washington border?" she asked.

"That's it—"

"Tell them I'm on the way."

###

Her departure marked by a gust of wind, Guardian rocketed to space where, moving at speeds beyond light, she was instantly looking down at the jade ribbon of the Columbia River. It languidly meandered through the Kootenay Mountains, continuing south of the border into Washington State. Parked on the shoulder of the highway that ran alongside it was a red, white and blue NASA van and a boat trailer. Police road blocks halted traffic miles from the van in both directions.

On the opposite bank, an aluminum boat, covered in glistening mucous, lay crushed in the center of a deep furrow. Scientific equipment was strewn about it in an equally mangled state.

Her sense of worry building, Guardian's eyes quickly traced the furrow up to the tree line to an enormous mound of earth. Atop the mound was a hole large enough to allow the passage of a train. Perplexed, her face pinched with question. Snakes did not leave slime trails, worms did but worms dieted largely on dead plant matter.

Swooping into the scene, the scent of petrichor, touched her nostrils. She called out to the missing scientists while quickly traversing the distance to the mound's summit.

Reaching the lip of the inky, black hole, she cautiously peered into the darkness. It smelled of chalk and seemed to stretch all the way to the abyss. About to delve into the blackness, she startled at the sound of a telephone ringing behind her.

She traced the ringing to a slime-covered mobile phone hidden among the debris. Crouching down in the channel, she plucked it from a puddle of cold, sticky goop. Wiping its face clear, she touched the screen to answer.

An ear-splitting screech filled the valley.

Guardian's hair stood on end. Instinctively, she spun to find its origin. A wave of icy water struck her face, temporarily blinding her. Something cold and slimy slapped over the top of her skull.

Heart in her throat and her vision obscured, a gurgling slurp filled her ears. Feeling the fleshy cap, stretching over her face and neck, she clawed at it in desperation. Teeth on edge, she grunted, struggling to resist as the cap quickly became a sleeve sliding over her shoulders and down her body.

Arms trussed to her sides, she was yanked from her feet. A shrill cry echoed in her throat. The tube of flesh slipped over her hips. She kicked and wriggled, slowly disappearing inside.

The gurgling sound of a drain emptying rattled in her slime filled ears. The stench of fish and mud filled her nostrils. There was a pause. She could hear the pounding of her own pulse. A slurp that sounded like a wet sponge being stomped on jerked her body onward.

She began to fly against the pull of the appendage, trying to free herself. Muscles strained, then spasmed, stabbing her brain in searing protest. Yet she resisted. It was a tug of war with her body as the rope.

Another grating screech pierced her ears. Guardian felt her sinews begin to tear. She was being pulled apart. With pain radiating throughout her body, she relented.

Like a sculpture molded in wet clay, Guardian's writhing formed a glistening bulge that dimpled the tongue's maroon membrane. Against the worm's slime coated flesh, her horrified expression of protest appeared as a Melpomene mask of the damned.

The lips of the worm's monster tongue softly squealed, squishing out a frothy dollop of mucous as Guardian's fluttering feet disappeared inside and the orifice sealed shut. With that, the tongue snapped back into the beast's maw. Six, fat, stubby lips puckered together, and the worm slipped back into the chilly waters of the river.

Slathered in clammy mucous, and encased like stuffing in a sausage, Guardian fought to keep what remained of her senses as the undulations and stinking goop pulled her inward.

Reaching the end of the worm's esophagus, she slipped free. Her relief was short lived. Wiping the slime from her eyes she found herself sloshing about in the worm's crop, a gurgling cavity filled to its top in churning, digestive fluids and mud slurry, one stage shy of the grinding rocks and spasms of its all-consuming gizzard.

Barely able to see her hand in front of her face, she allowed her light to shine forth. The effect was negligible, adding only inches to the depth of her perception.

Something bumped her. She turned and startled at the gray, shovel-like snout of a deceased river sturgeon. Shoving it aside Guardian began to frantically swim through the cold stew, swishing her outstretched arms through the mixture, pushing aside fish carcasses, in the hopes of finding the NASA scientists.

After many moments, her fingers brushed up against fabric. A little more exploration revealed it was a sleeve. The woman was cold and without a pulse.

To a doctor, a drowning victim was not dead until they were warm and dead. Guardian gave her symbiote a mental command to cocoon the victim in her cape and pull her along. She rapidly felt about for other victims. After many anxious minutes, she found none.

Resigned that any others were beyond help or were safely elsewhere, Guardian set upon extricating the both of them from their predicament.

Needing to put the worm and them on solid ground, Guardian burrowed through the upper layer of mucous lining the cavity to find the fleshy inner wall of the animal's digestive tract. Steeling herself for the reaction, she jammed in her hands like the mandibles of a tick and quickly began to lift.

The effect was immediate. She felt the worm twist, and buck, and convulse. Grimly determined to get them to land, she lifted and pushed for several seconds before the mutant animal's thrashing shook her free.

A sense of vertigo took her as the animal's spiraling contortions tumbled the two of them like dice in a cup. She grunted as they struck something hard, bouncing them off the bottom of the worm's gullet.

The muffled sounds of explosions resounded around them. Brilliant orange flames and daylight poured through gaping holes in the worm's body. The contents of the crop began to pour out. The stench of searing flesh and burning gasoline assaulted the blonde's nostrils. Her efforts to lift the animal onto the river's bank had been successful but with unforeseen complications.

Tearing through the animal's sinews, a sheet of roaring flames enveloped her. Protectively cradling her cocooned patient into her arms, she soared clear of the smoke and burning fuel to witness a squadron of attack jets turn for a second pass. They screamed in, dropping another load of ordinance.

Amid the burning hellscape of blackened trees and the

melted highway, the giant mutation writhed, its acrid scent competing with the stench of burning gasoline and asphalt.

Getting clear of the smoke and flames, Guardian's cape receded to expose her charge. "We'll have you back in the pink in short order." The palm of Guardian's glove parted. She pressed her hand to the NASA scientist's limp wrist. Blue lips flushed with color. Her patient began to cough and sputter, becoming wide-eyed with the realization of her airborne situation.

"Don't worry," Guardian soothed, "I've got you."

Guardian flew for an ambulance parked at the distant police line, startling both emergency workers and bystanders. They began to cheer.

She carried the woman to the back of the red and white truck and laid her on the gurney for assessment. "Hypothermia and near drowning, start her on fifteen liters of oxygen and get her to hospital."

As the paramedics began to work, a police sergeant appeared at the back of the ambulance. "Ma'am, when you're done, we could use your help getting the other two out."

She paused to finish covering her patient with a blanket and offering a moment's reassurance before emerging from the back of the truck. She resisted the urge to demand who had requested the jets and made a different demand instead. "Show me."

"On the side of the mountain." He pointed to the edge of the inferno as it chewed its way up the mountain's slope.

"I'll take them straight to hospital."

"It's just up the highway in the town of Trail," the cop pointed north, "It's the white building, big blue and white H on the roof."

"Right." She took to the sky, resolved to halt the growing list of complications brought by the asteroid.

7:30 PM, MIT, Boston Massachusetts

In the corner of a secluded MIT laboratory, under the hum of the fluorescent lights, Guardian sat on a stool. She was wrapped in a clear plastic sheet that served as a substitute salon cape. With great care, Jennifer slowly drew a comb through the blonde's hair, depositing crumbled bits of charred worm into the emesis basin she held. The long gentle strokes reminded Guardian of the children brushing her hair while she told them stories.

"Thank you for doing this. Obtaining a specimen was an afterthought that came too late."

"They were lucky you got there when you did." Jennifer watched the fragments of worm tissue drop into the kidney-shaped tray.

"By the time I got the other two to the hospital, they already had Dr. Nakahara in quarantine and under armed guard. I couldn't even obtain a swatch of her coveralls. I'm sorry to complain, but it's so bloody frustrating."

"I think you have every right to be irked."

"If I could find the person that ordered that airstrike, I'd give them a good dressing down." She sighed and her gaze fell upon Jennifer's mobile device on the nearby counter. "I do hate to be a bother but could you check…"

"On it." Jennifer set the comb and tray down and retrieved her mobile to scan the 'breaking news' feed.

Guardian watched her manipulate the device for several seconds. "Anything?"

"No word of giant worms or anything like that, but this is interesting…Canada requests help of US Air Force…."

Guardian's hand formed into a fist. "Blast."

Jennifer looked up from the screen. "It probably wouldn't be the best PR move to dress down a head of state."

"Not the Queen. It would be their head of government, the prime minister," she said, absent-mindedly. "That's twice today that it's gone the military route instead of giving any chance to negotiation.”

“Well there is not a lot of reasoning with a worm—or nematode, that’s probably what it was. Some are very carnivorous...”

Guardian gave her a mild look of reproach.

“Right...not helping.” Jennifer set down her mobile device and went back to her combing. “Anyway, you need to get the word out that you’re around to help so maybe they’ll not do that as a first response. You need a PR agent.”

“Public relations?” Guardian raised an incredulous brow.

“Seems like anyone in the public eye has one. You know? Someone to coach you? Manage the message —”

“I could have used one of those this afternoon in New York.”

“It’s something to consider.”

“Are you finding anything?”

“It’s not looking good.”

“Crumbs,” the blonde cursed.

“That’s what they look like, burnt cookie crumbs.” Jennifer finished her task and presented the tray speckled and dotted with bits of charred worm.

Guardian grimaced at the site. “I must say you’re quite good with hair.”

“It was just a comb through.”

“You have a gentle hand.”

“Years of practice trying to look as old as my classmates. But all the hair and makeup work really didn’t help. They never invited me out anyway.”

“I’m sorry.”

Jennifer shrugged. “It’s not like my parents would have let me go.”

“Bernard mentioned you were the youngest in his class. That must have been challenging for you.”

“It was, but if biology doesn’t work out at least I have a fallback.” Jennifer laughed.

Guardian shared the moment of mirth, then spied lettering

on Jennifer's wrist. "And you have a tattoo."

"Three." The scientist pulled up her sleeve to show the periodic table notations for Thorium, Iodine, Nitrogen and Potassium spelling ThINK. "Then I have this one on the back of my neck." She turned to lift her hair for another group of periodic table notations spelling 'science,' albeit with the notation for Neon inverted. "And one at the base of my spine." She began to remove her lab smock before Guardian extended a hand to stop her.

"What does that one say?"

"It's a double helix—an act of rebellion for my eighteenth birthday."

"I'm not surprised, if you were kept cloistered away."

She shrugged. "My parents meant well and I don't think I'm too weird for it—but more importantly do you have any tattoos?" Jennifer's head bobbed around looking at what little flesh she could see.

Guardian shook her head with amusement. "Needles won't make it through my skin."

"Well, take it from me, you need a tattoo."

Guardian looked at her with mirth. "Do I, now?"

"If only to give that perfect skin some character. Do you even have pores?" She drew even closer to the blonde's face and neck.

Guardian looked at the other woman with amusement. "Yes, and all of the other anatomical correctness as well."

Jennifer straightened up. "Well, I'm going to make you some press-ons. They're completely organic and they only last a week or two."

"I wouldn't even begin to know what I would want or where to put it."

"Well think about it." Jennifer poked her in the ribs.

Guardian chuckled. "I'll do that!"

"If you're needle proof, why don't you feel like a statue?" Jennifer poked the blonde again.

"That will be quite enough of that!" Guardian complained in mock protest.

"Well then, spill it. Why don't you? Inquiring biologists want to know!" Jennifer leaned in, an expectant look on her face.

"From what I can tell, my cells—like yours have cytoplasm but the fluid is non-Newtonian in nature. A little prod or a hug and I feel like you, do but a punch, or a hydrogen bomb, and I'm as tough as old boots."

"Would you ever consent to any kind of study?"

Guardian imagined all the alien species she'd kept from studying humans, it was all she could do from laughing at the irony. "I'd rather not."

"I guess that was kind of rude."

"I would have expected some kind of scientific curiosity on your part, Dr. Novak."

"Jennifer, or Jen, but not Jenny."

"Very good. Well Jennifer, I promise I will obtain something viable for you to work with."

"If you can find someone who's willing to part with a blood sample or a cheek—"

"Cheek swab." Guardian matched her words.

"Jinx." Jennifer held up a pair of crossed fingers and grinned.

Guardian smiled. "Perhaps NASA has found something. I was there earlier today. In fact, I rather rudely left dinner with the engineer assigned to help me."

"Dinner? Is he hot?" Jennifer teased.

"Hah!" Guardian scoffed and rolled her eyes.

"He is!"

"He's...charming. Most assuredly, charming. And he has the most gorgeous voice. Chills...." She shivered in emphasis.

"So please explain to me why you're still sitting here?"

"I doubt I'll see him again after tonight—*if* I decide to fly over there."

Jennifer grinned. "Fly! Fly! But first wash your hair, you smell like worm guts and gasoline. He'll think you're a dirty girl."

Guardian felt a sudden warm tug in her lower abdomen at the notion.

"Well, if only to obtain a tip on a sample."

"Whatever you want to tell yourself." The redhead mugged.

"You're not going to let this rest, are you?"

"And I want details. It's the least you can do for making me deal with charred worm guts."

"Maybe he'll think I'm being too forward."

"Go!" Jennifer gave her a playful push.

Spurred by the scientist's enthusiasm, Guardian slid off the lab stool while suppressing a giggle. "All right! After I wash my hair."

8:45 PM Mark Jackson's Office, Goddard Space Flight Center, Maryland

Accompanied by a security escort, Guardian walked towards Mark's office. The officers were polite but were otherwise silent. The building was likewise quiet, with much of the staff having gone home for the day.

As their footfalls echoed off the tiles of the corridor, she re-did her mental checklist: *Hair? Done. Makeup? Done. Boot heels? Four inches high, totally impractical, and therefore perfect.* Butler and Delilah had both sniffed her hair, proclaiming it smelled like 'flowers' before sneezing in succession.

Reaching his office, she knocked on the outer door and waited.

She heard him finish a telephone call and hang up the receiver. Through the frosted glass that bore his name, she saw the shadow of the inner door open and Mark's form backlit by his office's light.

He opened the door. "Come in." He stepped aside and motioned her inward.

She stepped in and waited for the door to click shut behind her. "I'm so glad you're here, Dr Jackson—"

"Sir." He growled.

Guardian's brows rose and her mouth fell open. "Sir...?"

He winked.

Her shoulders dropped. She shook her head. *En garde.* "Cheeky man. I just came by to apologize for leaving so abruptly."

He gestured her forward into his office. Mark's face creased impatiently. "Don't worry about it. We didn't get a lot of details about your rescue other than it was successful."

"It was that, but I would rather talk about other things."

"Fair enough. What about why you took off? Is everything all right? Did you get your phone? How's your friend?"

"It is, I did, and she was asleep."

He pulled a chair away from his desk and offered it to her. "We watched your interview on the auditorium's screen."

She winced. "How bad was I?"

"You didn't watch?"

"I didn't want to relive the experience."

"I think he was out of his league."

"What league is that?" she touched her upper lip with her tongue to stifle a smile.

"His league or yours?"

She shrugged good-naturedly. "His?"

"He's strictly bush league."

"And that's bad?"

"Amateur hour."

"Then what league am I in?"

"We'll have to line up some tryouts and then we'll know." He gave her a crooked smile.

"Tryouts? Is that like an audition?"

"Something like that."

She smiled. "I'd better be on my best behavior then."

"I hope not."

She sputtered out a chortle and waggled a finger at him. "Cheeky man. Cheeky-cheeky man."

"You seem to have a cheek-thing goin' on."

Guardian pressed herself back into her chair. "I do not." She looked away and looked back and found his gaze fixed upon her. She straightened up. "I thought you could help me with something."

"Whatever you want."

"That fellow in Chicago this morning...he has a fiancée and wants to have a family. He—they, need a cure."

Mark took the chair opposite her and leaned in. "So, what can I do?"

"First, thank you. Second, did anyone recover anything from the searches that were being conducted? A soil sample? A DNA sample would be particularly helpful."

"DNA? You think some sort of pathogen came in with those meteorites?"

"Possibly, but if they encounter someone who has suffered a mutation and wishes to provide a sample...." She pressed her lips together, deciding to keep her own rule about her tiny cadre's existence secret.

"I hear you. Well, it's a little late to ask now, but I'll make some calls in the morning. And you'll be glad to know that, barring a few hold outs like North Korea, I'll have a nearly complete map of impact sites tomorrow."

"Thank you, I'm so very grateful."

"You're welcome." He leaned back to look at her. "I have a question for you."

"All right?"

"That turkey that interviewed you isn't the only one on the news who's talking about you."

"Yes," her eyes fell, "I know."

"Nah, it's not bad, just I'm trying to get my head around it. People are showing up in interviews saying they know you from like the 60s, the 70s, the 80s. But that would make you—"

"Eight hundred and—"

Mark's expression became incredulous. "Say what?"

"And a bit, yes...." She bit her bottom lip, wondering what he was going to say next.

He licked his upper lip, his eyes dancing with mischief. "Well, if I'd known that earlier, I would have asked for the senior's discount at the cafeteria."

Guardian doubled over in her chair with peals of laughter. A knock on the outer office door brought her back upright. She touched the corner of her eye with a knuckle and took a deep breath to settle herself.

"Give me a second." Mark excused himself, leaving the office.

She smiled, and took a few more steadying breaths. The laughter felt good and his reaction to her age brought a sense of relief.

The door opened and a white-clad kitchen steward pushed a rattling serving cart into their midst. He gaped at Guardian, then, after receiving a congenial hello, he grinned and began transferring his tray of confections from the cart to Mark's desk, a pair of frosted cakes, one chocolate, one vanilla, a silver tea service, a champagne bucket containing a carafe of chocolate milk and pints of both chocolate and vanilla ice cream. He added glasses, cups, cambric napkins, silver utensils, and two gold-trimmed china plates.

Before he departed, Guardian personalized an autograph for him in flowing Edwardian script and penned a thank you note to the cafeteria staff for the steward to deliver.

With the click of a mouse, Otis Redding began to softly croon from the computer's speakers. "They don't normally cater this far from the cafeteria but I told them who it was for."

She admired the spread and the thought behind it. "This is lovely, thank you."

He came around the desk. "They don't serve rum or Shiraz at the cafeteria. Tea? Or are you feeling a little adventurous?" He touched the neck of the carafe of chocolate milk.

Her eyes twinkled. "I'm feeling very adventurous."

"Chocolate milk and chocolate cake?"

"Chocolate everything!"

Mark chuckled, fixing her a plate and one for himself.

Spreading a napkin across her lap, she waited for him to serve them. She shared a toast with chocolate milk before settling into her snack and questions about his travels. She listened as he told her about being a Marine brat and his family's travels first to the Philippines and then to Italy before returning to America. She told him about saving Galileo from being executed for heresy by passing enough gold to the right people to keep the father of physics under house arrest instead of him receiving a far more tragic and unjust punishment.

Half-finished his slice, Mark paused and set his plate on the desk and pointed. "You changed your boots."

"Yes, I got tired of straining to see you." She lifted a foot to show-off the boot's heel.

He caught her ankle in his hand and traced a line up her leg with his eyes. "I do like your boots."

"They come as a set." She lifted the other foot in demonstration.

He caught it and crossed it over the other.

"Very nice." Mark cradled them for a moment, before folding them together across his knee. "When you took off, you brought an entire room of rocketeers to their feet."

"Were you standing up as well?" She burst into giggles.

Mark bobbed his head as if listening to a song. "I knew then that I wanted to fly with you."

"It took that long?"

"Nah, not really. So, you enjoy...flying?"

Her eyes twinkled. "Did you have a particular destination in mind?"

"Everywhere, around the world, over the moon."

She felt her pulse quicken. "Over the moon as well?"

His eyes gleamed. "I'd love to fly over the moon with you."

"You're a very confident man, Dr. Jack—Mark—sir..."

"Very competent."

"I said confident."

"That too." He grinned.

 She burst into laughter. "By the stars."

"Do you ever dream about flying?"

She held up a finger. "I know what that means."

"Oh yeah? What does it mean?" He squeezed her ankles.

"You know...."

"I'd like to."

She shook her head and took a sip of her drink. "This is not what I pictured when I decided to come here."

"What did you picture? Flying?"

"What? No!" She doubled over, gripping the arms of her chair.

"Need to catch your breath?"

"What? No—yes. It would be nice to do that." Her heart jumped then jumped again at the sound of the elevator in the hall opening and a murmur of an approaching crowd. "Someone's coming!" She hissed and frantically pulled her feet from Mark's lap and cocked her head to listen.

"I think they're in there," one male voice said.

"Do you have a pen I could borrow? I want to get her autograph," a second said.

"I wonder if they're canoodling?" A female voice speculated with a giggle.

"Who's coming?" Mark asked, straightening up.

"A group...a crowd—more than one."

Mark chuckled and sat up. "Word travels fast."

"I should probably go talk with them," Guardian began to lift herself from her chair.

He was already on his feet. "You just relax. You've had a long day. I got this." He gently pressed one of his enormous hands to her shoulder in reassurance.

Guardian looked up at him with a relieved smile as he swaggered past, pulling the door closed behind him. The latch failed to catch, leaving a tiny crack of space allowing her to see the outer office. She turned in her chair, resting her cheek in her hand to watch and listen.

"Hey folks. I know you want to see Guardian but she's had a very long day and we're still working. She'll be back tomorrow," he said before fending off petitions to see her anyway.

Guardian's hand slipped down from her cheek, a silly smile spreading over her face.

Mark reappeared in the door and looked down at her. "All taken care of—probably for the best, with that dirt on your face."

Guardian's eyes widened, she flushed with embarrassment. "This whole time I've been walking around with mud on my face?" Her hand rose, frantically brushing at her cheek and then other. "But I checked—never mind."

"Nah, I'm just playing with you. It's a crumb." He lifted a napkin from the desk. "Can I get it for you?"

"Erm..." Her breath caught. She watched him take a knee next to her chair. "All right."

"They probably knew you were here from the steward." Holding a napkin wrapped over two fingers, he moved slowly towards her face. "Now hold still."

Feeling the heat coming off of him, she straightened up and stared straight ahead. "All right. Just...hurry." She was trembling again.

"Are you cold?" he asked softly, his cheek almost next to hers as he gently brushed her skin with the napkin.

She fidgeted, beginning to cross her arms before halting herself. Her cheeks flushed. "I don't get cold."

He chuckled. "Let me check the other side." He tilted his head to look.

Elizabeth gazed at his lips; they were so close. Her heart thumped. He smelled so good.

"Are you all right?"

She turned her face... *Is he...?* "I just thought that you were about to—"

The kiss came quickly. Her eyes popped before sliding shut. Sultry, sweet, and dizzying, his kiss melted her into her boots and sent her shooting through the stars in the same instant. She huffed and then just as suddenly his lips were gone, leaving her tingling and befuddled.

"You kissed me."

He fixed her with a penetrating gaze. "You got a man?"

"I...no." She resisted the urge to touch her lips and realized he was holding her hand in her lap.

He kneaded her palm. "Friday night, dinner and dancing in Baltimore."

Her hand tingled. Her thighs tingled. A warmth began to

well in her tummy. "I...Dr. Jackson—"

"Or sir." He smirked, only two hand spans from her face.

"I...I have reservations."

"Cancel them, we're stepping out."

Her instinct was to stand and escape but she would have to knock him over to do it and instead stayed in place, glancing at their hands in her lap and looking back up at him. "No, what I mean is. I have reservations about going out—"

"Don't want to be seen with me?"

She shook her head. "No, that's not it at all."

"Then it's nothing."

She licked her lips, forcing the words out. "I don't want to put you in any sort of danger."

He regarded her sternly. "Look here. I'm a grown man and a Marine. I'll make my own decisions about what's dangerous."

Seeing his resolve, she nibbled her bottom lip and gave a tentative nod.

He cupped a hand to his ear. "What was that?"

She smiled in feigned exasperation. "Yes."

He brushed her hair back from her face and kissed her again, longer this time.

The blonde felt his fingers maddeningly tugging her mane at the base of her skull. The fingers of his other hand wove their way between hers. A giddy-shivery effervescence like newly-opened champagne had her sighing uncontrollably. *All man....*

Mark softly and sweetly pulled his lips from hers. "Wear a cute dress and shoes you can dance in. I'm taking you someplace nice."

Feeling breathless and light, she could have floated away with just a puff of wind. "What time?"

Mark smiled and kissed her again, this time quickly. "Seven o'clock at La Carroza Ristorante, but you better give me your number." He produced his mobile telephone, opened the contacts and after putting in 'Guardian' as a name, he handed it to her.

She looked at the phone speculatively. "Do you encrypt?"

He looked at her suspiciously. "What are you planning on sending me?"

She flushed with confusion. "What? I-no, I'm just a very private person."

"Just playin' with you. If you use Signal then we're good." He named a popular encryption application.

"I do." *One more thing in common.* Resisting the urge to tell him she hadn't given her number out in decades she added the number to her mobile and handed it back. "I guess I haven't told you my real name yet."

"I figured you get around to it when you were comfortable, besides going on a date with a mystery woman is an adventure."

"Mystery woman." She scoffed in amusement.

Taking her hands, he drew her out of her chair to kiss her again. "Buona note, bella."

"Buona note, signore," she whispered.

###

In the outer office, Guardian's hand first rose to her throat. She took and released a steadying breath. Struggling not to smile, she gave up. Looking back at his door, she heard him stacking dishes. Taking another steadying breath, her eyes began to flutter in realization at what she had agreed to do.

She stared at his door for a long moment. What was she doing? She knew how this would go. It would not be fair to him or to her.

Her hand rose to knock. She hesitated, dropping it back to her side. She reached for the doorknob. Again, her hand fell back to her side. Her mind a jumble, she decided to talk to him in the morning, after she had time to regain her feet and think about how to break their date.

9:10 PM, Senator Rupert Longstreet's Office, The Russell Building, Washington DC

The scent of barbecue sauce lingered in Longstreet's office. A pile of chicken bones and a smear of mashed potatoes were all that remained of Longstreet's dinner. He leaned forward on the sofa, grinning and watching the commercial break following Guardian's interview.

Thirty seconds in length the production company had worked quickly, using a combination of scenes from the foundry incident in Chicago, stock footage of terrorism, and an ominous voice-over to ram its point home.

"It's been a terrifying few days with more likely to come as we enter into a new era for our planet and for our country," the male narrator said in grave tones, "but you can help. You can help do your part to help get things back to normal. If you see something odd, see someone acting in a manner that is just beyond what is possible, pick up the phone and contact your local FBI field office or Department of Homeland Security. Do your part to keep yourself, your family, and your community safe. Make the call and let the professionals investigate. We're better when we work together." The commercial ended by naming its sponsor, The Committee for American Safety.

Chuck White stood next to his boss's desk, his features illuminated by the television's flickering light. The chief of staff gave a prideful nod and turned his attention back to the desk telephone.

"Good job on the interview, and that was a nice touch with the extra drama at the end," Chuck spoke into the telephone's microphone.

"Spare me the soft soap job," Bill Boothman snarled from the other end of the line.

Wearing a frown, Longstreet rose to stand next to White. "Now don't you get snippy with my chief of staff—especially when he's giving you a compliment."

"People will think I'm a bastard."

The Senator rested his knuckles on the edge of the desk and leaned over the phone. "Cut the bullshit Bill, you're pissed because you thought you had a chance. We helped you dodge a bullet, who knows what the hell's she's got down there."

"Are you going to send what we agreed upon or not?" Boothman asked.

"You should have it by mid-afternoon tomorrow," Chuck said.

"This is the end of it," Boothman said.

"Now Bill, don't be like that. You're a national treasure, even if the herd doesn't know it," Chuck soothed.

"I feel like a goddamned ninny."

Longstreet glared down at the speaker. "Yes, but you're my goddamned ninny—until I say you aren't."

"I'll expect that package tomorrow." The phone clicked as Bill hung up.

Chuck snickered and punched the orange hang-up button on the telephone's console.

Longstreet grinned as he watched the office television. "How bad do you think he was squirmin'?"

"I could hear it, sir."

"Poor fool shouldn't have his worm visiting other holes."

Chuck laughed. "Even if he hadn't, his boss would be calling his tune."

"Alarming lack of character in folks these days," Longstreet lamented, "infidelity, secret abortions, drug use and drunkenness, tax evasion, all manner of debauchery and vice, it's terrible, just terrible."

Chuck guffawed at his boss's mock disappointment. "Terribly useful, sir."

Longstreet turned from his television. "How many sets of pictures do we have on him anyway?"

"Four or five, sir."

"Well, which is it? Is it four or is it five?"

The smile left White's face. "Five, sir."

"Send him a set—no make it two. That kind of performance at the end deserves acknowledgement—and we don't want to seem ungrateful." Longstreet chuckled and took a sip of his bourbon.

Chuck chuckled in response. "Yes, sir."

"If he gets uppity just remind him that he's saving his marriage one favor at a time."

"He should be thanking you, sir, with your help, he'll be married at least fifty years."

"I don't know Chuck, have you seen his wife? I've seen smaller jowls on hound dogs."

"That's probably why he..." Chuck ceased talking when the doorknob rattled and the door swung open.

"All finished, gentlemen?" Shannon asked as she breezed into the room.

"It was good, Shannon. You must have flirted with that delivery boy to get it here so hot." Longstreet grinned as the blonde moved to clear the men's dishes.

"Oh, I don't know about that, sir." Shannon's eyes twinkled.

"Leave those for a minute." Rupe waved her away from the supper dishes. "You've been working since eight this morning. Fix yourself a drink and have a seat." He motioned to the sofa.

"Oh, I couldn't sir, I have to drive."

"Nonsense, book yourself a room and stay over." He watched her as she took a seat at the far end of the couch.

Shannon expressed a murmur of physical relief and turned to look at her boss. "I have to be home for mama."

Longstreet pointed at her. "That's very responsible of you, you're a good daughter. Didn't I say that just the other day, how responsible Shannon is?" Longstreet turned his face towards White.

"That's right, sir, you did. He thinks very highly of you—we both do...for all the extra duties you've been handling while we're short-staffed."

"Just doing my best, sir." Shannon glowed beneath the

praise.

"Well next month you'll be packing your bags for the party convention in Las Vegas."

"Wow! Thank you sir, but I wouldn't feel right taking Madeline's place." Shannon shifted in her seat.

"It's settled, you've earned a weekend in Vegas. Now how is the cross-matching of stories coming along?" He slid closer to regard her in the light of the TV.

"I still can't believe she's been here this long—"

"Pretty damn scary, isn't it?"

"But all of these reports can't be right. They're coming in from all over the world."

"You know what they say, where there's smoke there's fire. Who knows how many diseases she's been spreading by duping terrorists into spreading them for her."

"But what about the reports of her being a doctor, sir?" Shannon asked.

"What wouldn't be a better camouflage for experimenting on humans and spreading diseases—this one in Chicago is the worst one yet." He studied the contours of her face and neck as she spoke. She looked so good, so fresh, so...ripe.

"Which is why I should get back to work." She began to rise.

"Shannon, your country owes you a great debt of gratitude."

"Thank you, sir, but I really should finish up."

"No more tonight, you go take care of your mama."

"I'll just clear these up before I go." Shannon gathered up the plates and cutlery and exited.

"She'll come around, sir," White murmured.

"They always do." Longstreet sipped his whiskey and went back to watching the news.

Wednesday, 8:10 AM, Offices of The Spoiler Tabloid, New York City

The morning sun shone under the half-closed blinds of The Spoiler's *'bullpen,'* a labyrinth of half-cubicles where the majority of the writing staff crafted their tall tales and half-truths for the world's largest tabloid. Sean Ramos made a habit of arriving an hour ahead of his colleagues. The quiet cut down on interruptions and allowed him to hold onto his thoughts as he worked.

He listened patiently as the telephone line clicked and crackled. "Connected, please talk," the heavily accented voice of the operator directed.

"Ms. Amudee, it's Sean Ramos calling you back. Were you able to learn anything about Guardian working there?"

"Hello Mr. Ramos, we don't have any pictures but our records say she worked Khao I Dang from 1990 and finished in 1993 under the name Jillian Graham."

"Was there any indication of what she was?" Sean's pen pressed to his notepad.

"I was only thirteen years old at the time but there is nothing mentioned in any of the logs of her being able to fly," Amudee said, her accent coming through the staticky connection.

Sean added a hint of gentle humor to his voice. "I suppose that would be something they would note. Do you have a list of agencies that sponsored the camp that I could follow up with?"

He listened intently as she began listing various United Nations agencies and non-governmental agencies involved with the camp at the time. He stopped her and asked her to repeat them a few times as their names were often lengthy and her Thai accent made clarification necessary.

Thanking her he concluded the call and looked at the list, flipping back and forth between it and the page from another call to another refugee camp where Guardian had been purported to have worked at in Liberia. So far, he had many of the same United Nations agencies and some of the same agencies from Western governments and three of the same non-governmental organizations.

"What'cha working on, early bird?" A woman's voice lifted his head from his work.

"Probably a whole lot of nothing other than eliminating things about Guardian," Sean lied and glanced at the clock. It was a quarter past eight. Most of the staff would not arrive for another thirty minutes.

Always wary when she was around, he watched Lulu L'Amore, whose real name was Louise Lamont, sashay her way through the desk farm. The pretty blonde's dress and heels were color-coordinated to her magenta nails and lipstick. If The Spoiler was the realm of quidnuncs, she was its queen.

"Nothing is plenty to work with; let's us get creative filling in the blanks." Lulu smirked. "So, what have you got?" She leaned in to look at the contents of his notebook.

Ramos purposely kept his eyes from her proffered décolletage. "I can confirm that records indicate she did work in two of the places people are saying she worked."

"Meh, that's nothing." Lulu straightened up and gave him a dismissive wave. "You should tune into my webcast for something really juicy. My sources have given me some really fun stuff. Did you know she's left a string of babies all over the world?"

Sean thought about challenging her about her 'sources' but wanted to be rid of her as quickly as possible, and besides, he wasn't her editor or producer.

Ramos flipped his note book shut and stuffed it into his bag. "Babies, huh? I'm going to run over to the UN and talk to some of the agencies and get some background on these places."

"You take this reporting thing too seriously. This is The Spoiler, not the Times."

If I get this story, it will be the Times. "Just the facts, ma'am." He nodded to her, slung his bag over his shoulder, and headed for the elevator.

"Oh, be a pet and bring me back a soy latte grande?" she called after him.

8:30 AM, Avalon, Maine

Barefoot, Elizabeth padded into her basement laboratory carrying her tray of breakfast. Pouring a cup of Irish breakfast tea, she tore off a piece of buttery croissant and nibbled it in trepidation, wondering what the morning news would bring. A tap of the mouse blinked the computer monitors awake. The morning headlines were, by her estimation, an unwarranted slap.

The New York Advocate: *"Superduped: Would The Real Guardian Please Stand Up?"* The lead began by reporting on her multiple identities over the decades. She shook her head in disbelief. She owed them nothing. Her work and the reasons for her subterfuge seemed self-evident.

The Chicago Standard: *"Pandora's Pandemic: Has a Plague Been Released Upon The World?"* She was certain the answer was no. She just needed proof.

The Washington Banner: *"See Something Say Something Campaign Busily Taking Calls"* She scanned the story and regarded the accompanying photo and quote of support from Rupert Longstreet with pity and annoyance. *Still as suspicious and mistrustful as ever, eh Rupert?* She would need to talk with him before this campaign took on a paranoid life of its own.

The Spoiler: *"Who's Bed Have These Boots Been Under? Who is Her Latest Love Connection?"* Mortified, her eyes pressed shut in disgust at the picture of her boots surrounded by a frame of men's faces—three of which were telling the truth. She could not believe that the Spoiler reporter would ever think he would get an interview—especially after this. She checked the byline; Sean Ramos' name wasn't attached. The image of suspending the editor in chief out a window by his ankle sprang to her mind. What would Mark think? The thought jarred her back to her plan for the morning. It was just one more reason to break their date. In the meantime, she needed to make an example of the journalistic rag.

She needed a lawyer, she needed a publicist, and she needed

facts about the asteroid. Scarfing down the remainder of her breakfast, she hastily finished her morning rituals and was away to the Flight Centre.

###

Walking up to the door of Mark's office, she was filled with sadness and dread. Whether it was courage or pride that prompted his declaration about personal safety, she would have to be the sensible one. Given the salacious nature of The Spoiler article, breaking things off was the prudent choice. If he refused to accept her decision, she would have to ask Dr. Brown for another partner to work with. She might have to do that anyway, just to protect him from any association. Parting ways with the security detail, she stepped into the outer office to exchange cordial greetings with Mark's secretary.

"Your boyfriend is waiting for you inside." She smiled, scrunching up her nose.

Her face contorted with question and distress. "I beg your pardon?"

Katie laughed. "Harold is in there waiting with some files from Dr. Jackson. He posted the picture of the two of you on the Center's internal message board." She turned her computer monitor to allow Guardian to see it.

Guardian's expression became one of relief. "You surprised me."

"Sorry to tease you, but I think you have a fan."

"I like him too." She brushed a strand of hair from her face and tried to sound nonchalant. "Is Dr. Jackson in?"

"I'm sorry; he had a department head meeting to attend this morning. But is it something urgent?" Katie began to reach for her telephone. "I could call him?"

Guardian considered the offer. This wasn't the sort of thing you discussed on the telephone. She shook her head. "It can wait."

"Alright. I have to say, the picture of the two of you turned out really well."

"Of Dr. Jackson and me?"

"Yes." Katie clicked her mouse to fill the screen with their picture.

Guardian's hand came to her mouth in astonishment. Harold had captured her in mid-laugh. "By the stars, I look like a silly goose."

"I think it's a cute picture, and it's nice to see him smile like that."

She felt a sudden twinge of pity. "He doesn't normally smile?"

"He does, but let's just say he's very dedicated to his work."

"I had better go see what Mar-Dr. Jackson left for me." She excused herself.

"Good morning, Harold, lovely to see you." Guardian closed the door to Mark's office.

"Oh hey, hi. You look really great today." Harold's eyes shone as he rose from the desk. He fidgeted for a moment before his arms fell limp to his sides.

"Thank you. Katie said there were some files for me?"

"Umm, yup." He slurred his speech through his braces in an excited gush. "Right here and I got your pictures for you." He opened a file folder, his hands trembling and his face flushing.

She spread them out on the desk experiencing a fluttery thrill and a sudden warmth at the sight of them. The way he was beaming at her and perhaps the way she was looking up at him in mid-laugh. *Crumbs.* "These...these are wonderful, Harold."

Producing her phone, she took a picture of each before returning them to the folder. "I have a lot of traveling to do today, would you hold onto them for me?"

"Sure. Would you autograph the one of us?"

"Of course, but I must say I find your request a little odd."

He blushed. "Sorry did I—I didn't mean to—"

"Harold. I'm not offended, I just find it odd that one friend would ask another friend for their autograph."

"We're friends?" His grin renewed.

"Of course, we are!" She reached out and gave his arm a gentle squeeze.

"Cool! I made you something," he said eagerly, "want to see it?"

"Certainly, I just need a moment to read this file." She fluttered through the pages and looked up pensively. A sample of the asteroid remained elusive and soil analysis would take some time.

Harold gestured to the file. "Wow, you read it that fast?"

"Librarians love me—I always bring my books back on time." She winked at him. "You had something to show me?"

"Do you want to sit down?" He offered Mark's chair, sneaking a glance at her legs as she stepped around the desk beside him.

A flicker of a smile momentarily creased the corners of her lips. *It's better to be looked over than be overlooked.* "I'll stand thank you. What is it?"

"Remember yesterday when Dr. Jackson said you were working on finding other people like that guy in Chicago? I modified a web crawler program to search for anything that might be related to the asteroid and mutations. It searches lists, message boards, social media and the news. It will help you find people. See...?" He held up his mobile phone where a stream of information scrolled down the page.

"This is brilliant. How long did it take you to put this together?"

He shrugged. "A few hours."

She imagined judging by the dark circles under his eyes, it was more than that. "How do I install it?" She held up her phone.

"I can do it, if you want?"

She handed him her mobile and watched him as he gripped it, tapping and swiping with his thumbs. "I'm going to have to pay you back for this, Harold. Coffee or lunch, or something else we can do as friends?"

He looked up and stared at her. "Umm, wow! That sounds awesome."

"It will be, but my eyes are up here." The pads of her fingers lifted his chin.

"I didn't—"

"Of course, you didn't."

He handed her smart phone back to her. "All done, just tap the picture of the ruby called Asteroid."

She tested it, read a few entries and looked up at him. "Smashing, thank you."

"Umm, I thought of something for our date—"

"As friends." She looked at him pointedly.

"Sure but..." he paused, trembling before his words poured forth in a torrent, "W-would you go out with Dr. J instead? I mean if he asks you. He really needs someone awesome in his life and...." He stopped to take a gulp of air as perspiration appeared on his brow.

Guardian looked at him with concern. "Are you having an asthma attack?"

He shook his head. "Would you just—"

Her expression softened. "Harold, that's very noble of you, but I don't think Dr. Jackson needs any help getting dates."

"Dr. J is my best friend, and yes he does need it," he said solemnly.

"He must have lots of women that want to date him."

"He's too smart for them. But you're a doctor... a...a surgeon," he said, his voice filled with admiration.

"I am but—"

"He's the most interesting guy you'll ever meet. He takes me fishing and we talk about all kinds of things and he gives me advice—"

"What sort of things does he give you advice on?"

"Everything you can think of. He always tells me to follow

my dreams, to live up to my potential, to make the most of every opportunity, and to not be afraid of failure or what people say."

She reached out to touch his shoulder. "That's some very good advice."

"See? You already have some things in common."

Guardian laughed softly. "Harold, dating me could bring dangerous complications into his life. Which reminds me, could you take our pictures down? I don't want any harm coming to you or Dr. Jackson—"

A transformation came over Harold, his puppy dog eyes became defiant. "Dr. J isn't afraid of anything. He's the toughest guy I know. See that bronze star?" He directed her gaze to the shadow box. "He got that for saving a little girl in Afghanistan."

"Harold, I'm sorry I didn't mean to imply…." She turned to face the protective case on the wall. "Did he tell you about it?"

"No, one of his friends was here one time and told me about it. I guess there was a big fight and he covered her with his body and carried her out of there."

Her heart warmed. "I'm impressed."

"He's the best guy."

"I was talking about what a good friend you are."

"Thanks, but will you? If he asks you out, will you go out with him?"

"Shouldn't that be something between Dr. Jackson and me?"

"I know but if he asks, just give him a chance. Please?"

She studied his face. He was guileless, completely in earnest. *What am I doing?* She sighed, defeated. "All right, Harold, if he asks me—"

"You will? That's awesome!"

"I'll consider it—"

"That's all I ask." He waved his hands about.

"Now about taking down those pictures?"

Harold nodded emphatically. "Sure, whatever you want. I'll do it right now." He plopped himself into Mark's seat to fulfill her request.

She watched him work and spoke over his shoulder. "I still want to have lunch with you, Harold Warner. Something tells me you're a very interesting person. For now, I'm off to put your late-night project to work." She lifted her mobile for emphasis before exchanging smiles and goodbyes.

9:10 AM Goddard Space Flight Center, Maryland

Floating high above Goddard, Guardian scanned Harold's application while trying to push the youth's advocacy for romance from her mind. There were a number of mentions of incidents and unconfirmed rumours about metahumans, the closest one she could see was not too far away. A man named Charlie Hill in Kanesatake, near the New York-Quebec border, was reported to have been affected by a meteorite. The pictures in the feed included one of a crater and another of a crumpled door knob. She flew north with a sense of hope.

A churned-up hole in the ground, downed tree branches, an orange safety fence and a small crowd of curious children on bicycles confirmed she was in the right place. The asteroid shard impacted near the end of the Hill's laneway. Situated on a heavily-treed residential lot, the single-story house was painted brown, with a satellite dish jutting from its side. An older blue sedan was parked in the dirt driveway. Guardian noted the presence of a middle-aged woman hanging laundry in a sunlit clearing of the backyard. It was Sally Hill, if the picture from the CBC news report was correct.

Not wishing to startle the woman, Guardian landed and called out a friendly greeting. Not sensing any more alarm than what one would normally expect on her sudden appearance, she ambled across the lawn at an angle. "Would you like some help?"

Sally Hill chuckled. "Sure, but you're here to see Charlie, aren't you?" The woman spoke in mild tones and briefly made eye contact before returning to her chore.

Guardian lifted a sheet from the basket and carefully hung it over the clothesline. "I'm here to speak with all of you about what happened." She selected a handful of clothespins from Mrs. Hill's clothespin sack and fastened the damp sheet securely.

"The kids are up in Alberta planting trees for the summer and Charlie's gone to work."

"Do your children know?"

"Not sure how to tell them." Sally began pinning up another sheet.

"I know it's worrying but start with the truth and tell them what you know."

"That's the problem, I don't know. Nobody seems to."

"You can tell them I've come to help." She gave the other woman a hopeful smile.

"I'll try calling them tonight when they're done working."

"How is he feeling?" Guardian lifted another sheet from the basket and began to hang it.

"I want to show you something. Be back in a minute." Sally retreated into the house.

Guardian kept at her task, carefully hanging the sheets. She used her own clothesline for sheets, the symbiote took care of most of her clothes, save for hats, wraps, and a few pairs of sandals.

Sally reappeared carrying a lump of glittering metal that had been a doorknob, she handed it to the blonde. "He's gotten really strong."

Guardian took a moment to examine the handle. The hollow knob was squeezed flat like a crushed soda can. "Can you tell me any other symptoms he's exhibited? Has he been seen by a doctor?"

"Charlie hates doctors. Bad experiences with them when he was a kid at school." She glanced in Guardian's direction, lifting a sheet from the basket.

Guardian frowned and nodded sympathetically. "How some could ignore their oaths and conduct themselves in such a manner...I can understand his wariness." She exchanged a knowing look with the other woman.

"Good. Remember that."

"I will. But to the matter at hand, did he express any pain or distress?"

"He says he feels like a teenager but I'm worried about him. It's not natural for someone to be like that."

"I'll try to find you some answers. Do you think Charlie would talk with me?"

"Talk? Probably. But can you cure him?" She looked at Guardian hopefully.

The heroine glanced away for a moment and spoke quietly, "If I learn how and if he wants that."

"I want that." Sally clutched the edge of the sheet tightly.

"When will he be home from work?"

"He's an ironworker in New York so not until Friday night."

"Do you think it would be all right if I went to see him today?"

Sally dropped the sheet into the plastic laundry basket and reached for her hip pocket to produce a mobile phone. "He's working at the 400 Block of Park Avenue on a high-rise condo project. I can call him for the address."

Guardian waved her off. "I'm sure I can find it."

"Please help us."

"I promise I'll do all I can." Guardian smoothed the other woman's arm. "Try not to worry." She stepped back to get ready to fly.

"Thanks!" Sally shouted as Guardian slowly took to the air, rising and turning south-east for New York City.

Guardian gave a friendly wave before turning her face skyward. *Now all I have to do is something worthy of that thank you.*

###

Guardian cruised through a maze of office towers and skyscrapers, occasionally surprising someone who happened to be gazing out their window at just the right moment. She liked this city. There were millions of people here, each with an interesting story to tell.

She quickly found Charlie's Manhattan worksite. A portly

security guard along with a police officer kept a considerable media contingent from penetrating the gate. Charlie's presence was causing a stir.

"I'll bet you're here to see Charlie too?" a swarthy foreman in a white hard hat asked as Guardian landed to the whistles and catcalls of some of the laborers on the ground.

She raised her voice to carry over the clanging of steel and rumble of truck and crane engines. "Can you spare him for a few minutes?"

"Why not?" The foreman shrugged. "The place has become a circus. One more act won't make any difference."

"Has there been trouble?" Guardian asked with concern.

"With Charlie?" he asked, glancing at the beams high above them. "Not at all. He's one of the best workers we've got. Now he can do the work of six men and can carry beams without a crane. I don't know how much money the union is going to ask to pay him. The damn media keeps hanging around though," the foreman said with a frown.

"Hey baby won't you bring those muchachas over and keep the sun off me?" A worker hooted.

"Look at that bitch, sheeit! Hey?" Another joined in.

The pair turned to regard eight men who were laughing and hollering some distance away.

Guardian glanced first at the woman working in the catering truck and then to the women standing at the gate. She scowled. Her jaw tightened. She held up her index finger to the foreman in a gesture of pause. "Excuse me." Ignoring the foreman's enjoiners to stop, she marched towards the gang.

"The stripper's here! Let's get the party started!" A yellow hard-hatted worker guffawed uproariously while his belly shook.

"Her boots are under my bed next!" Another of them shouted as a cement truck passed between her and them.

Stepping through a cloud of dust, she spat out a retort. "What an asinine thing to say!"

"And what an ass! It's freakin' perfect!" A worker cackled and reached from behind to touch.

Guardian's eyes bulged as she felt a calloused hand grab her bottom. Lightning-quick, the masher's wrist was captured. Lifting his dusty paw high overhead, she glared at the pack of catcallers. "Is anyone missing a hand? I seem to have found an extra."

They fell silent.

Dragging her stumbling captive behind her, she walked the work gang's line, and repeated her query.

Red-face with his arm stretched out above his head, the lout protested, "Hey! Lemme go!"

Reaching the end of the line she turned to scowl at the lot. "No takers?" When none spoke, she flung the cad's hand back down to his side and spoke to them in terse tones. "Are those your best lines? Am I supposed to swoon?"

She glared at them, suddenly aware that work on the ground had ceased. Some of the work gang's faces had lost their color others were rubbing their necks and were unwilling to make eye contact.

"If you wouldn't want it said to your mother or daughter, don't say it to *this* mother and daughter!"

Some clapping and higher-pitched hoots of support came from the direction of the gate.

"I'll bet you don't even have any of those, you're an alien!" One particularly brave workman scoffed.

"Hush!" Guardian hissed. She held up a hand snapping her fingers and thumb together like a closing trap.

"Hey whoa...whoa, we're sorry." A bearded worker held up his hands in a gesture of neutrality.

Her expression remained flinty. "Then stop acting like a troop of baboons."

"I think it's time you guys got back to work." The foreman approached, allowing the bunch to retreat.

Glowering, she watched them go before turning back to the

foreman.

"Sorry about that," the foreman said.

"These men could cost this company a lot of money."

"You're right," he nodded, "I'll take care of it. Charlie's up on forty-seven." He pointed to a figure against the skyline.

She spotted him and then glancing over at the television crews pointing their cameras in her direction. "That's going to play well on the evening news I'm sure," she murmured to herself and sighed.

"Thanks, I've always wanted to say that to them," the catering truck operator said as she provided Guardian with a complimentary tea and a coffee for Charlie.

"I'm sorry it needed to be—and thank you for these." She accepted the two beverages and slowly lifted off to her destination.

I'll probably have to pee after this. Guardian grumbled inwardly as she landed on a newly emplaced beam.

Above the fracas and gray of the urban jungle, up in the blue sky where the wind whistled about the new building's rust brown skeleton. She found Charlie Hill. He was wiry and deeply tanned from a lifetime of working in the outdoors. He wore his sticker spackled hardhead backwards for a clear line of sight in the ironworker fashion. A Mohawk ironworker, he worked with the diligence, intelligence, and fearlessness, they were noted for.

Not wanting to startle him, she approached cautiously, calling out as he tightened fastening bolts with newly strengthened fingers that worked as efficiently as a torque gun. "She:kon," she said over the wind.

Charlie looked up, "You speak Kanien'kéha."

"I do. How do you feel about speaking with me? I brought you a coffee." She held it up as an offering.

He eyed the cup with curiosity. "Double-double?"

"Two creamers and two packets of sugar—the caterer said this was your favorite."

He walked with uncanny balance along the windswept beam to accept the beverage. "Thanks." Taking a sip, he murmured in approval and took a seat to dangle his feet into the four hundred feet of empty space between them and the ground. He gestured for her to join him.

Guardian spread her cape out beneath her as she sat down next to him as casually as if they were chatting on a park bench. "I just came from talking with Sally...."

"I thought you came to see the show, like them." He looked down to the cameras far below and gave them a wave.

"She's quite concerned about you."

"She just wants me to retire and take a job closer to the ground—and I am. I'm going to play running back for the Jets, be the MVP, and get us a championship."

Guardian kept the volume of her voice raised over the whistling wind. "You've taken a position with a sports team?"

"Not yet, but they'll take me. I can get a touchdown every time." He thumped his chest with his free hand.

She had reservations about the fairness of that plan but chose not to voice them. "I'm not here to discuss your vocational choices...your work, or your... home life."

"Good." He took a long pull of his coffee and gazed out over the cityscape.

"I'd like to talk with you about the changes you've gone through."

"Go ahead." He took another drink.

"What happened to you at the time the asteroid piece landed in front of your home?" She brushed her hair from her face to look at him.

"Not much to tell. I was going out to bring Sally's mother to our place. There was a flash and a boom." He shrugged. "I woke up with Sally crying and the paramedics looking at me."

"But you didn't go to the hospital?"

He gave a brief shake of his head. "Didn't need to, nothing a couple of aspirin and a good night's sleep couldn't fix. Besides, nothing much can hurt me now."

Guardian's eyes filled with concern. "What do you mean?"

"We did some competitions before work today. You know? Boards, crowbars, sledge hammers, a nail gun."

She was aghast. "You let people hit you with these things?"

"Well, the nail gun I did myself, but I only got a little red dot, see?" He switched his coffee and held up his hand for examination.

She examined it with a clinical eye. "I don't see anything."

Charlie checked his palm, smiled and shrugged. "I guess it healed."

"Well, it seems you're not easily hurt. That's very curious. That fellow in Chicago—"

"The metal man?"

"Yes. He wants to get better…to return to who he was so that he can marry his fiancée and start a family. You might be able to help him?"

"How? I'm not a doctor."

Guardian reached for the pocket at the small of her back to produce a buccal swab and test tube. "Would you mind too terribly if I obtained a few cells from the inside of your cheek to—"

Charlie eyed the cotton swab with sudden anger. "Yeah, I mind." He gulped down the remainder of his coffee before flinging out the final few drops.

"It won't hurt."

"I know it won't because I'm not doing it. I'm nobody's lab rat." He stood up.

"You could help Rudy, and others who also may not want this change. You could be a real hero."

"You're the one in the cape."

"Won't you please reconsider—"

"No."

Guardian pressed her lips together halting her entreaties. "I don't agree with your decision but I will respect it."

"Good. Thanks for the coffee. I've got to get back to work." Stone faced, he turned away, crushing the cup and tucking it into his bag of bolts before returning to his labors.

Sighing, she watched his back for a moment in the hopes he might change his mind. Standing up, she consulted Harold's program again. It was only her first request, there had to be someone out there that would be amenable to helping her.

7:10 AM Local Time, the Foothills of Northern California

Disappointed by Charlie's refusal, Guardian rose high above the metropolis, studying the news feed from Harold's program for another who might be more receptive to her request. She immediately noted a report of a missing camper at the site of an impact in Northern California. Recalling the location from Mark's computer screen, she set aside her search and hastily departed for the Golden State.

Reaching the foothills described in the report, her brow wrinkled with confusion. The dry grasses showed matting and crisscrossing by multiple vehicles. Large flattened out circles indicated the use of helicopters. Yellow police tape surrounded a square of bare earth half the size of a football field. The sod had been removed and the soil excavated to at least waist deep. At the edge of the yellow tape a single National Forest Service SUV guarded the scene. She landed and began to stride towards the truck.

The door opened, a fit middle-aged officer stepped out and donned a tan Stetson over his graying crew cut. He smiled. "Good morning, ma'am."

"Good morning, officer. It looks like I missed all of the excitement," she gestured to the yellow tape as she approached him, "how long do you have to guard this hole in the ground?"

The officer chuckled and spoke with an Oklahoma accent. "I'll be relieved at seven o'clock tonight but I never expected to see you here."

"I've heard that before."

"I'll bet."

She smiled and caught the boom-chicka-boom beat of Johnny Cash emanating from the truck's interior.

"Johnny's keeping you company though?"

"Uh…" the officer began, glancing back at his truck, "yeah, I guess he is. Why are you here, ma'am?"

"Do you have a favorite song?"

"I Walk the Line," he said without hesitation.

"Or watch the line." Her eyes twinkled playfully.

"I reckon," he conceded good-naturedly and stepped closer. "Now, how can I help you, ma'am?"

"Well," she said, putting her hands on her hips and looking all around her at the trampled-down grass. "I heard about the missing camper. It looks like they were thorough in their investigation."

"They came in and took everything in a thirty by thirty square and three feet down into the sod, including the flowers and the gray pines that were standing there."

Aware of his eyes upon her, she twisted her body in a half-turn to examine the olive-brown clay. The impact site itself had been dug down to the gray bedrock. There was nothing worth examining. She would have to try to get some answers from him.

"What about the camper?"

He shook his head and scoffed. "Something to tell the media to explain all the commotion. But don't tell anyone alright?"

Lying to the media...lovely. Another annoying thought sprang to mind. There had been no mention of the worm in the morning headlines either. Unable to process it further, she gave a curt nod and passed her fingers over her lips in a zipper motion. "Mum's the word officer. But can you tell me...." She licked her lips. "Did they find a shard—a piece of the asteroid?"

"Uh, no ma'am, just a hole and some downed tree boughs."

"You also said there were flowers. But all I see around here are dried out, dying grasses."

"I wasn't here for the initial investigation but I suppose that is suspicious."

"Who did the initial investigation?"

"I think the sheriff's department called the Highway Patrol and they called in the military." He shrugged.

"And they didn't include you in all of the excitement?" she teased.

"I'm just fine catching poachers and arsonists. I'll leave the weird stuff to somebody else."

"Is that all they found? No animal tracks or signs of people?"

"Well...I suppose since you're trying to figure this out too...they found a few small items. A used packet of pepper and couple of butts—blunts, but it's been so dry they could have been there for days or even weeks."

She looked at him quizzically. "What are blunts?"

"Roll your own marijuana cigarettes. Lots of hippies out here in California."

"Hmmm..." she mused.

She noted his gaze she lifted her hand to her chin in consideration. "Let's try another perspective." She lifted off, beginning to slowly fly upright around the perimeter of the tape.

"What are you looking for!" he shouted as she cruised around the farthest corner in her lap around the excavation.

Her keen eyes spotted signs of the grass being parted all the way to a parcel of thick pines. "Signs of someone walking away. Tell me, would there be any reason for someone to walk into those woods?" She pointed.

"Excuse me, ma'am." He keyed his shoulder microphone and began requesting backup officers from the sheriff's department and California Highway Patrol.

"I'd rather you hadn't done that..." Guardian murmured with disappointment. "It could be nothing, I'll have a look." She waved to the officer who called for her to come back.

###

Guardian followed the walker's trail, into the darkness of the forest. Eyes that could read a match book from the moon found signs of passage, a partial sandal print, a bent bough, and disturbances in the pine litter. Silent as a ghost she followed for miles, weaving between the trees, shaking branches like a gale with the speed of her passage.

Drawing close to the forest edge, the scent of rain mixed

with pine caressed her nostrils. She beheld a perplexing scene. Beyond the edge of the tree line, a shower drenched the clear-cut landscape, every tree was now a stump. In a sign of persistence bordering on defiance, shoulder-high saplings grew from the center of the stumps closest to the forest. They stretched all the way up the hill. Seeking the source of the astonishing sight, she rose through the tree tops and above the rainclouds to spy a lone female figure rambling along, just steps ahead of the shower. She watched as the woman would pause at a stump, pat its center and within seconds a sapling would rise sturdy and tall. Guardian flew around to be north of the ragged gray clouds and got a better look.

She was young, not more than twenty and carried a well-worn canvas rucksack. As she walked, her legs pressed against the folds of a long, flowing skirt. She wore a poet blouse and a floppy sunhat. Tight ringlets of copper-colored hair escaped from beneath it and bounced with each step she took. Guardian landed a few dozen yards ahead of the woman's path, and began to walk towards her. It was some time before her presence was noticed. When it was, the response was unexpected.

"Hey!" the redhead exclaimed. She looked around with an expression of amusement. "Sorry I didn't see you sooner." The young woman pointed without missing a beat. "That outfit is the bomb."

Guardian's shoulders shook with a chortle of amusement. "You're very chic yourself." She continued her greetings with an introduction learning that although her name was Melanie Lopez, she preferred to be called Sierra 'like the mountains', before asking about the asteroid impact.

"I was meditating on my blanket," she patted her rucksack, "and I heard a roar, then there was a flash. I woke up dusty and now I can do this." The college coed placed her palm flat on a tree stump and within seconds the smell of pine sap and the squeak of wood expanding filled the air. A young sapling as tall as either of them shot up and began to green before their very eyes. "Pretty cool, huh?"

"It is quite…cool." Guardian smiled, unable to resist the other woman's enthusiasm.

"Not only that, but I just thought that it could use some rain and it started to fall." She turned and gestured to the shower's edge which was only feet from where they were standing.

"So, you just touch a plant and it grows?"

"Kinda, I have to think it too." She looked down to her bare feet and a thick cluster of yellow poppies sprouted and opened in full bloom. She bent down, plucked one and offered it. "For you."

"Thank you." Guardian lifted the cup-shaped flower to her nose to enjoy the fragrance and noticed Sierra's gaze.

"You have the most gorgeous hair."

"Thank you, I was just admiring yours."

Sierra lifted her sunhat from her head and dramatically shook out her ringlets.

Something about them caught Guardian's eye "Melanie—Sierra…were you aware you have green roots?"

"What? Really?" The young woman fished a compact from a side pocket of her backpack and spent a moment angling the mirror and lifting her hair to check. "Wow, that's different."

"I must say that you' re taking this quite well."

Sierra shrugged. "Well, you just gotta take life as it comes and do your best with what you've got. Now I've got a lot more so I can do a lot more."

"Sierra, not everyone shares your acceptance about these sorts of things."

She shrugged. "Well, that's their problem."

"I wondered if we might go elsewhere and talk." Guardian looked over the hills for emphasis.

"I'm sorry if I made you think something else and I am totally flattered chica, but I have a girlfriend. Besides, I've got enough supplies to last another two days and I want to fix this whole clear cut by then."

Guardian sighed in frustration. "Sierra, no. I mean—you see, I'm sorry but I inadvertently mucked things up. The authorities are looking for you. They're on their way."

"Well, I *really* can't go then."

Guardian tilted her head in disbelief. "I'm sorry?"

"I have to regenerate as much of this forest as I can, but we can talk while I work."

"Sierra, I support your efforts but this is urgent."

"Then you'd better talk fast." She giggled.

Keeping a frown of frustration from her face, Guardian quickly explained what occurred in Chicago and the need for a DNA sample to begin helping Rudy and Josephine.

"That's really awful. But I can't do that, sorry."

"But why not?"

"Because if you can reverse what happened to him, you or someone else could do it to me and the planet needs my gifts. Look what I've done so far." She gestured to the hundreds of new saplings.

"We don't know what the long-term effects are."

"I know what they'll be if I don't keep these powers."

"Sierra, I would never force anything on you. But I—"

"Good. I mean...if it was just about anything else, I'd roll up my sleeve and donate but I can't. Sorry."

"It's not even a blood donation it's just a cheek swab." Guardian produced the tube and swab.

Sierra gave her a tight-lipped smiled of apology and shrugged. "Sorry."

Guardian's head turned at the sound of helicopter rotors chopping the air. "They're here."

"I'd better get as much done as I can then." Sierra's pace picked up, she trotted between tree stumps, swatting their centers to smell the scent of fresh pine oil and hear the squeal of wood stretching into a sapling. The clouds overhead began to roil and expand, turning from battleship gray to slate. The steady shower became a hammering deluge. Sierra pulled on a jacket as the gray curtain enveloped them. She gestured to the sky and grinned impishly. "That should slow them down a bit, huh?"

Guardian commanded the symbiote to expand and form a deep hood. As the rain spattered off their backs and shoulders, she drew it over her head and pulled the cape over her shoulders like a traveling cloak. "Sierra, please…"

"No." She shook her head. "I've still got trees to grow." She turned to continue her efforts.

Guardian trailed after her like a phantom. "You know I could stop them from taking you."

"No violence, not by me, and not *for* me, do you understand?" Sierra shouted over the sudden crash of thunder.

Guardian glanced skyward and then back at her. "Did you do that?"

"I think so…maybe—sorry, but no violence, okay?"

"Here they come," Guardian said as a black and white sheriff SUV crested the hill with a roar. It was quickly followed by a pair of similar vehicles from the Highway Patrol.

"I wonder if I covered the ground with weed if that would make them a little crazy?" Sierra laughed and turned to face the approaching vehicles.

"Don't joke about that," Guardian snapped.

"Amiga, you worry too much. Five hundred bucks and I'll be out again—"

The driver's door of the sheriff truck flew open and a young deputy in a khaki uniform and peaked cap emerged pointing a pistol. "Don't move! Face down on the ground! Now!"

"Please put your gun away before someone gets hurt," Guardian said, stepping in front of Sierra whose easy-going demeanor quickly vanished.

"I'm not resisting!" Sierra thrust her hands into the air.

"This isn't Chicago. You're not above the law here, lady." The deputy snarled as the Highway Patrol drew and pointed their guns.

Yes, and sometimes the law is an ass.

"Why does he have his gun out?" Sierra asked with alarm.

Guardian kept her eyes on the police officers as she spoke. "Because he's frightened."

"Of what?"

"Of what he doesn't understand."

"I said, get on the ground, now!" the deputy ordered.

Seeing his bulging eyes and reddened face, Guardian kept her voice and expression calm. "Deputy, it's been a very stressful time these past few days, the asteroid, my sudden appearance, what happened yesterday in Chicago—"

"Don't try and handle me, now get the fuck down—"

"No violence! I'll go with you!" Holding her hands in the air, Sierra darted out from behind Guardian.

A pistol barked. A bullet emerged from a gout of flame and smoke. There was a sound like linen being torn asunder.

Standing between Sierra and the deputy, her expression resolute, Guardian held the bullet tightly between her thumb and index finger. She fixed the cop with a steely glare. "That was both irresponsible and reprehensible."

"Get out of the way. She's a threat and she's going in." He took a step forward.

Guardian stepped in front of Sierra again. "How? How is she a threat?"

"These dope smoking hippies come up from Berkley and Davis and try to put men around here out of work. They take food off the plates of the children in this county. They don't care who they hurt."

"And that justifies guns?"

His eyes narrowed to mere slits. "For you."

His words stung like a slap. Guardian took a breath, regarding him with momentary sadness. She recalled some of the more sensationalized headlines, wondering how many others felt as he did, and what she could do about it.

"It'll be okay, chica. I'll go with them. After I call my dad, I'll be out before lunch. I just don't want anyone getting hurt, please?"

"No one will be harmed, Sierra, but you have done nothing wrong."

"I'm sure the judge will think so too." She smiled mischievously before turning her attention to the highway patrolmen. "I'm ready to go!" she shouted over the rain that continued to beat down on the clear cut.

Their weapons holstered, the pair of patrolmen quickly handcuffed Sierra's outstretched wrists while eyeing Guardian warily.

Guardian watched with frustration as the young woman was led away and called after her. "Don't say anything, Sierra. I'll ensure you'll have the best representation available." She turned to coolly regard the deputy who still had his gun out. "The only threat here today was your fear, Deputy. You have much to learn about keeping the peace." She dropped the bullet at his feet, and took to the sky before he could offer a rebuttal.

She didn't know very many lawyers but she did know a few top ones.

10:45 AM New York City

A trip home to Avalon allowed for the securing of funds for a retainer and for the placing of Sierra's gift in a tiny crystal vase of water. Guardian returned to Manhattan to the offices of Atkinson, Marble, and Woolfolk, the law firm that represented the Cumberland Foundation.

As she landed atop the steel and glass skyscraper, Guardian reflected on how she had made more trips to the borough in the last two days than she had in years. The stairwell made for a faster and quieter trip to the twenty-fifth floor than the elevators. A startled receptionist quickly verified that Ruth Atkinson could see her immediately.

Ruth was middle-aged and slight of build. She wore a black skirt suit with a silver broach shaped like a fern leaf and kept her chestnut hair in a conservative bob. Guardian had met the lawyer in the persona of Charlotte Cumberland five years previously. She was relieved she showed no signs of recognizing her. She watched the lawyer unspool the red thread fastening the manila envelope containing her retainer.

Atkinson held up a thick sheaf of certificates intricately embossed in green ink and denominated in ten-thousand-dollar units. "Bearer bonds?"

"I wish to retain your firm." Guardian settled back into her chair.

"We don't normally take payments of this kind." She set the stack down and smiled patiently. "But I suppose, given the circumstances—secret identities and all, I think it will be all right. What can we do for you?"

"Thank you. I'll start with my most pressing need." Guardian began her recount of the events in California as Ruth scribbled notes on a yellow legal pad.

The lawyer lifted her pen as Guardian concluded her story. "You're lucky that you weren't arrested for obstruction.

"I recognize that I walk a tight rope whenever I involve myself."

"Like this morning?"

"After centuries of gazes in my direction, I've grown accustomed to it—but I will not be pawed at. As to the matter at hand, can you assist Melanie?"

"We have someone in the office licensed to practice in California, I'll have him on a plane this afternoon."

"I'm grateful. But there are other things that I require your assistance with."

"Of course." Ruth flipped to a fresh page on her tablet.

"I need to be seen in the best light possible and if you're paying attention to the news this morning, my name has been coming up in a most unsavory manner. I want to launch a defamation suit against the tabloid, The Spoiler."

"They've printed something untoward?"

"I would call it character assassination for profit and entertainment." She went on to explain the cover of the tabloid and stories contained therein.

"I'm sorry," Ruth said softly.

"I'm a damn good surgeon and I will not have my reputation dragged through the mud."

"You're not being attacked because you're a doctor, if you were, we could do something about it."

"What!" Guardian sat up, her face a mask of bewilderment and outrage.

Ruth explained in sympathetic tones. "You're not just a doctor anymore, you're a celebrity now and as such," she sighed, "we would have to prove what is termed, *actual malice*—and that's very difficult to do with a tabloid."

"The Spoiler has me on their cover with twenty-four men— twenty-four!"

"Not to be indelicate, but is any of it true?"

Guardian took a deep breath and looked at the portrait at the corner of Ruth's desk. "Is that your husband with you in the picture?"

"Yes."

"How long have you been married?" Guardian asked.

"Twenty-two years, this past May."

"Twenty-two years? That's wonderful."

"Thank you, but we've had to work at it," Ruth said.

"When you don't age, someone would notice long before twenty-two years came to pass."

Ruth's features became sympathetic. "I'm sorry, that must be lonely."

"You make friends where you can, and find a kind of love—even if it is only a passing resemblance, where you can."

"Were any of the men in the tabloid, a *passing resemblance?*"

Guardian sighed with dejection. "Three, but I never imagined they would do something like this."

Ruth set her pen down and folded her hands together on her desk. "Well, we can go after them with everything we've got but—"

"Good."

"Please hear me out. But we're talking about years of litigation, hundreds of thousands of dollars in costs for likely very little result."

"Yes, and in the meantime my reputation is destroyed. Can you do anything?"

"We can send a cease-and-desist letter but it will probably be ignored and if we pursued it, they could have legal cause to investigate you, delve into your past, even bringing you in for a deposition under oath on video. The questions could get very personal. Basically, it's the Scorpion's Defence."

Guardian's frown deepened. "Which is?"

"Essentially, you don't attack a scorpion because you'll get stung."

"There has to be something..." Guardian's finger rose to her chin in thought. "What about money?"

"Catch and kill?"

"What is that?"

"Basically, it's greenmail, you pay someone with the

exclusive rights to some embarrassing incident and they never publish it. You catch the story then kill it."

"That sounds like extortion."

"All right, then you could change the narrative, manage it, go on the attack."

"How does one go about doing that?"

"You need a publicist. Someone to build you up to the point that attacking you would be like attacking Santa Claus, motherhood, and apple pie."

"Do you know someone? I'm rather busy and don't have a great deal of time to interview candidates."

"If you can leave it with me, I can contact you with what I come up with."

"Are your calls encrypted?"

"Of course."

"This is my number." Guardian recited it and watched the lawyer type it into her mobile phone.

"I should have something by tomorrow."

"Thank you." Guardian rose and offered her hand.

Ruth came around her desk to shake it in parting. "I'll get to work on the cease-and-desist letter and a publicist—and don't worry about Melanie; we'll have her out and at home in time for dinner."

Departing the lawyer's office, Guardian allowed the other woman's optimism to rub off on her.

Atop the high rise she consulted Harold's program and found a promising candidate for a DNA donation, this one wanted to be a superhero. Taking to the sky, Guardian departed for Texas.

6:35 PM, local time, Plano, Texas

The trip from New York to Texas held many emergency diversions. In West Virginia on a bridge over the Ohio River, she pushed a teetering bus back to safety after its driver had a heart attack that sent the vehicle through a guardrail. In Kentucky, she gently intervened in a suicide attempt from the roof of a high rise. In Tennessee, she trussed up a would-be carjacker by stuffing him in a garbage barrel and squeezing its lip shut around him. In Arkansas, she broke through the wall of a burning fertilizer factory to rescue trapped workers and then stayed to assist the firefighters. By the time she reached Plano, Texas, the sun was already dipping below the horizon.

Guardian found the Spellman home quite easily. The suburban street was a veritable zoo. A pair of police officers kept a gaggle of over-groomed TV journalists and their bored camera operators at the foot of the driveway. She saw the backyard had been dug up in a manner similar to what had occurred in California. The front of the home was splattered with dried eggs and the words DIE FREAK was spray painted in neon green across the double garage door.

From what Guardian could deduce, Ray-Anne Spellman's celebrity was self-inflicted. The college student had recorded and posted her new abilities on social media and the internet trolls had pounced. The presence of the TV media probably wasn't making it any easier, they had effectively doxxed her with their news coverage.

Guardian's appearance overhead snapped the mob from their doldrums and drew the blaze of their cameras' lights. She landed and was immediately beset by a cacophony of questions. Saying nothing, she raised her hands for silence and waited patiently for several moments until the reporters began to settle themselves. Once their clamor abated, she spoke, "I'll answer one question each—" Her words were cut off by a renewed fracas.

She waited in silence for several minutes, waiting for them

to fall silent once more. "But not here, find a neutral public location." She gestured to the subdivision. "Somewhere away from these people's homes."

"The Saver-Mart is three blocks from here just off the highway, we could use a corner of their parking lot," one journalist offered.

"Splendid, I'll meet you there." Triggering a stampede, Guardian turned on her heel and began to walk up the Spellman driveway.

One of the officers chuckled. "Why didn't y'all come down here when this all started? It would have saved a whole lotta trouble."

"I'll try to be more timely in the future but what about this?" She pointed to the vandalism.

"There's been an investigation launched ma'am," The other officer supplied.

As news teams quickly packed up their equipment to speed away, Guardian rang the doorbell. She saw the door's peep hole darken for an instant before a barrel-chested man in a plaid shirt and wearing a Texas-sized belt buckle opened the door. There were dark circles under his eyes and he wore a nickel-plated revolver on his right hip. "Well boy, howdy! Look who's here!" He thrust out a catcher's mitt-sized hand to shake the blonde's. "I'm Bill Spellman, I'm more glad to meet you than you can possibly know."

"I'm very happy to make your acquaintance, sir."

He looked past her shoulder. "You scare those buzzards off for us?"

Guardian glanced at the street as news vans revved and squealed down the street. She turned back to smile at him mirthlessly. "I offered them a bigger spectacle."

"Well good. It'll give me a chance to get Ray-Anne up to my brother's ranch."

"Oh? You're leaving?"

"I planned on sneaking her out at 3 AM but we'll get while

the getting's good."

"Before you go, could I ask you and your daughter a few questions?"

Bill hooked a thumb into his belt. "Maybe, if you can do something for me?"

"How may I help?"

"Anything my daughter sets her mind to, she gets. Pageants, lead in the school play, the dean's list. She cheers on the Dallas squad, made it on the first try-out. She planned to go to dance in the Paris Ballet but now she wants to be a superhero—"

Guardian's shoulders slumped. "I read that...you have my sympathies."

"Even changed her hair to look like yours. All her life she had beautiful auburn hair like her late mother's. Sometime yesterday she snuck off and got it done. You've got to talk her out of this fool-headed notion."

"The asteroid changed her that much?"

"I could take you in the garage and she could show you how she can lift my truck off the floor-without even touching it. She just looked at it, and lifted it two feet! All four tires!"

"Has she been examined by a doctor?"

"Paramedics came and checked her out. She's as fit as a fiddle. Just needed a good night's rest." His expression became worried. "Why? Is she sick?"

"Not that I'm aware of, but I would like to ask her for a genetic sample—a swab of her inner cheek." She produced the kit for him to examine.

"I'm not sure how I feel about that."

"I promise it won't be given to anyone else."

"Everyone else has been coming to see us. Public Health, State Health, Texas Rangers, the FBI, the damn army dug my yard up and wouldn't even talk about fixing it."

"I'm so sorry, that must be very frustrating."

"You can ask her after you convince her not to be a superhero."

Bill didn't give her a chance to agree before he turned and shouted for his daughter.

Athletic and comely, Ray-Anne appeared in the doorway. She was barefoot, wearing a t-shirt and shorts and had hair styled almost exactly as Guardian's. She used both hands to smother a surprised squeal, turning away in shock before throwing her arms around her idol. "Omigosh, I imagined meeting you but I never thought—" The young woman burst into tears, needing the use of her father's handkerchief to dry her eyes.

Guardian basked in the warmth. "That's the nicest hello I've had all day."

"Well, I'll let you two talk. Once I get the truck packed, we're leaving for your uncle's so talk quick." Bill gave Guardian a nod and disappeared into the house.

"This is so amazing. You're so amazing!" Ray-Anne beamed.

"Thank you. Your father informed me you want to be a hero?"

"Not just a hero, but a superhero."

"I'd rather you be safe, Ray-Anne."

Ray-Lee's expression rapidly changed from stunned surprise to a defiant pout. "What? No."

"Did you see what happened this morning in New York?" So much had happened since; she could hardly believe it was still the same day.

"Yeah, they got what they deserved."

Guardian gently slipped her arm around the young woman's shoulders and directed her attention to the garage door. "I appreciate your support but do you see that?"

"Assholes," she spat.

"What would you have done if you caught them?"

Ray-Anne jutted her chin out. "They wouldn't have liked it."

"What I did in New York was not about punishment, it was about changing things and that is why you should go to your uncle's with your father."

"I don't believe this! I'm offering you help and you're saying no?" Petulant and red-faced, Ray-Anne crossed her arms and glowered at Guardian.

"You want to be a hero?"

Her pout evaporated. "I'll do anything!"

"That man in Chicago? The one turned to metal? He needs your help"

"What can I do?"

"He needs a cure."

"But I'm not a doctor."

Guardian reached to the small of her back to produce the kit. "A genetic sample to effect a cure. It will only take a moment and it's painless."

Ray-Anne's eyes flashed with anger she began to retreat towards the garage. "You don't want to cure him. You want to take my powers away because you don't want anyone else to have powers...just you!"

Guardian's brows knit with consternation. "Ray-Anne—"

"You're just a jealous bitch, who can't keep her legs closed."

Guardian's gasp became a grunt of discomfort. An invisible force jolted her backwards and through the crown of the family's oak tree. Snapping branches and an explosion of leaves marked her trajectory.

The officers at the end of the lane straightened up and started up the driveway.

Floating on the opposite side of the tree, Guardian extended her hand to wave them off. "It's all right officers, just a little demonstration."

Brushing debris from her shoulders and hair, Guardian floated back to her original position, her face a mask of anger and disbelief.

Ray-Anne stood tense with both of her hands clasped over her mouth.

Guardian's eyes flashed with displeasure. "If I was a normal person, you could have killed me, Ray-Anne."

"Oh my God! I am so sorry!" She wept.

"I accept your apology. Now go with your father to your uncle's and remain there."

The rumble of the garage door opening and the crank of the truck's engine interrupted them. Bill backed his truck out of the garage.

Guardian watched the girl sprint to the passenger side of the truck and get in.

Bill powered down his window and dropped his hand below the sill to give Guardian a clandestine thumbs up.

Hurt by the allegation, Guardian stood watching as the Spellmans departed. She grimaced at the bewildered officers on the curb and took off into the sky.

The young woman's accusations echoed in her ears. She considered others might force reversion onto the changed and it frightened her. Moreover, what if someone wanted powers? Could geneticists inject new material into a volunteer to create more mutations? She had a lot of work to do.

Consulting Harold's program she was determined more than ever to obtain a sample. About to leave, she recalled her promise to the journalists. Sighing with frustration she looked over the landscape and spotted the blue and red Saver Mart sign.

From her vantage she could see the assembled pack of reporters, with their boom microphones they resembled an ancient Greek phalanx ready to attack.

Despite her sense of foreboding, the blonde assumed a congenial smile and reminded herself to *'manage the narrative,'* as she floated down towards them. Cameras focused on reporters as they set up their viewers for what was coming. Her white uniform stood out against the rapidly approaching night and they quickly spotted her.

As the cameras' lights flooded the space, she was forced to

speak over the chorus of questions. "To make this simple I'll receive questions from left to right, there will be no two-part or follow-up questions." Her declaration netted some protests even as she turned her face to the first journalist.

An Hispanic reporter in a rose-colored dress was first. "Maria Sanchez, Channel 22 WT News. Why were you visiting the Spellman home?"

"I was there to assess her health and well-being. I am pleased to report she is in excellent health."

"Keith Thompson, Channel 3 Dallas. Earlier today you were involved in an incident in New York. What do you say to those who say you attacked a defenseless workman?"

What nonsense. She looked directly into the camera. "Earlier today at a New York construction site, I was accosted by eight men. I was quite careful to leave an impression without leaving an injury." She turned to the next reporter in line.

"Erin Bush, Observer Satellite Radio. How can normal people protect themselves from these metahuman mutations?"

"I have found no evidence of a threat. These are regular people with families and friends and jobs and dreams, their bodies may have changed but their characters haven't."

"Emilio Williams, Channel 77 Houston. What are your thoughts on the immigration bill proposed by Senator Rupert Longstreet to include people with mutations?"

Longstreet. She growled internally. "My politics are kindness; my policies are to help those in need. Part of being kind is not discriminating based on arbitrary criteria."

"Bob Bradley, LNN. It's been reported that three decades ago you worked in United Nations Refugee Camp Twelve in the Kingdom of Jordan, placing you there at the same time as notorious terrorist Imad Atwae. This man is accused of plotting and carrying out operations that have killed dozens, why didn't you attempt to stop him?" He lifted a stylized 'LNN' microphone to her face for a response.

Well, that's not leading at all! "I don't comment about

specific patients but he would have been a child at that time, and although I can do many things, my ability to predict the future is as limited as yours." She turned to the next reporter. "Savannah Stone, Plano Chronicle." A brunette reporter held up a mobile device, "There are reports in social media that you were at NASA, what is your involvement with them?" Guardian licked her lips. "I will confirm that I have been working with NASA to determine the origins of the asteroid which has not netted any results other than what is already known, that the asteroid's trajectory was obscured by the sun." Seeing her answer was accepted without skepticism, she sighed inwardly with relief and turned to the next journalist.

"Michelle Ling IBN Dallas. Reports are coming in from all over the world that you have lived a kind of vagabond lifestyle, assuming an identity and staying in a new place every two or three years. How do you feel that affects the people you leave behind?"

Ugh, why did I pick that network? "It's always difficult to say goodbye to people you care about. I do my very best to improve a place before I go."

"But you still lied to people for years."

"Next question, please?"

"Ryan Rose, Manstream News. We polled our online viewers and had them vote for what question they wanted us to ask you."

She had never heard of the internet news network. "Yes?"

"Our viewers want to know, what's your favorite position?" The reporter grinned lasciviously through the groans and whispered condemnation of the group.

By the stars.... She regarded him thoughtfully. "Well, Mr. Rose, when you've been in as many ten, or twelve, or even sixteen-hour sessions as I have...." She paused as he leered and his colleagues' eyes bugged out. "I would have to say chief of surgery but dean of medicine does hold some intrigue as well."

"So, you like to play doctor?"

"You're being deliberately provocative and I said I was only going to answer one question each but to make it perfectly clear. I practice medicine, I don't play at it and I'm very, very good at it."

"Is that a euphemism?" He persisted.

"You have much to learn about boundaries, impulsiveness, and courtesy Mr. Rose."

Rose took a step forward. "Or else?"

"You will reap what you sow."

"Is that a threat?"

"An observation." Guardian regarded him like a principal disappointed by a failing student. "You can do better."

"Excuse me, ma'am?" Someone asked in a sweet, high-pitched voice.

Guardian looked for the source of the interruption and found it. An African-American girl of about six had managed to circumvent the gang of reporters and come around from behind her. Behind the girl, an African-American boy held a digital home camera. They reminded her of Issa and Juma.

"Hello there," Guardian beamed as she sank to one knee, "What's your name and what network are you from?"

"Umm..." The little girl took a deep breath and looked up to the sky. "Kya, Kitchen Table News." She turned back to her cameraman.

"That's Nathaniel—"

"Nate. I'm *older*," he said self-importantly.

"He's my brother."

"Hello Kya and Nate, what is your question?"

Nate interrupted his sister. "Did you ever fight a hippopotamus?"

Guardian tilted her head and smiled with gentle good humor. "Is there one in your bathtub that you need me to talk to?"

"No, no, no." Kya giggled and shook her head

"Well Nate." She looked at him directly. "Hippopotami are

very protective of their families and their homes, everyone should feel safe in their homes and not be...do you know what the word accosted means?"

"No," Nate said.

"People should respect hippopotami homes and leave them alone."

"They're one of the most dangerous animals," he said sagely.

"I've only ever talked with hippos, Nate but yes, like humans, they are very protective of their homes and families. What was your question Kya?"

"Umm, what..." She took a deep breath and checked the piece of paper in her hand. "What do you like best about the Earth?"

"What do I like best about the Earth?"

"Yes," Kya said with an emphatic nod.

"I think what I like best about the Earth is meeting people like you and your brother." Her eyes twinkled as she gave the girl a playful, giggle-inducing poke in the tummy. Feeling her spirits buoyed the blonde scrunched up her nose and lingered a moment longer before standing up. "Thank you, children but I'm sorry I must leave." She stepped back gave them one final smile, and a wave, before taking to the air.

"Have a safe trip!" Kya yelled after her.

A check of Harold's program pointed to China and someone the internet had dubbed 'The Stone Tiger,' but there was something she needed first, chocolate.

8:15 AM, Local Time, Guanlizhen, South-West China

Elizabeth entered the ancient village of Guanlizhen posing as a backpacking coed. She wore a cherry-red t-shirt, navy blue leggings and a seemingly beaten up rucksack. Making her way to the village's postal outlet, a smile and a few pleasantries were all that were needed to obtain The Stone Tiger's real name, Li Huan. The clerk went on to answer every question she posed, including where she could find him. Bidding him adieu, she stepped back out onto the road's muddy shoulder.

It was monsoon season in South-West China. The early morning air carried the intermingling scents of congee and coming rain. Pausing to contemplate what the clerk told her, her expression became pensive.

Scarcely eight miles from the border with Burma, the tiny village was a natural base of operations for a criminal syndicate. It kept its population in fear and its local authorities on its payroll. The previous evening, Li put an end to the operation and she could hardly begrudge his actions.

According to the postal clerk, the local gang's list of crimes was lengthy, including extortion, and the trafficking of guns, drugs, and human beings. Li had set upon them like a tiger, overturning their vehicles, wrecking their base, and scattering the gang's small army of hoods. It was laudable behavior but thinking of Ray-Anne, she wondered about his future ambitions, would he continue to use violence to bypass legality? It was something she needed to find out—while attempting to convince him to part with some genetic material.

The box of fine chocolates she carried in her cape-turned-rucksack was part of her plan. Even the red paper and gold ribbon that bound it were specifically chosen to create a favorable impression.

In the West, social niceties were kept to a minimum, but in China protocol was far more involved. Following the clerk's directions, she followed the mud-puddled road until Li's siheyuan came into sight. Like most of the homes in the village, it was medieval. Its walls, buildings, and curved roofs were weathered ash-gray from centuries of exposure. What set it apart from its neighbors was a water-filled crater at its front and the two statues flanking its gate, one of a tiger, the other of a dragon.

Hoping Li knew of her alter ego, Elizabeth glanced around for signs of observers before beginning her transformation back to her uniform. She completed the change by plucking her spectacles from her face and pulling the rope next to the siheyuan's gate to ring the bell.

A gray-haired elder soon appeared at the entrance. He wore the dusty, black clothing of a laborer. His broad smile quickly transformed to an open-mouthed expression of surprise and delight. "I heard someone was coming to visit. But he didn't say it was you."

She stifled a chuckle and maintained her smile. "I heard Guanlizhen has a tiger prowling its streets."

"You mustn't give credence to idle gossip." His eyes danced with good-natured humor.

"The way your friend at the post office describes you, I don't think there's anything idle about you, Mr. Li."

"Not so! I enjoy a nap every afternoon." He smiled playfully.

She tittered in response. "I do apologize for calling upon you at such an early hour. Won't you please accept this token of friendship?" Gripping the edge of her gift with both hands, she offered it to him.

He held his hands up in good-natured refusal. "No token is needed."

"Please…." She held it up again. "I will be sad if you do not accept."

"I would never wish to be the cause of a new friend's sadness. Thank you." He accepted the gift and stepped back to hold the door open. He motioned her inward. "Can I offer you some breakfast or tea?"

Guardian smelled congee. "I apologize. I have interrupted

your morning meal."

"Breakfast was two hours ago."

"Perhaps just tea?"

His eyes continued to dance. "This way." He stepped back and stretched out his arm in a gesture to enter.

She followed him inward, accepting a string of flattering compliments that to the uninitiated might seem insincere, but in his culture were customary. He led her to the entrance of a courtyard where she detected the sweet smell of citrus from a pair of mandarin trees at the entrance to the main house. The brilliant orange fruit hung like ornaments against the trees' lush foliage. The courtyard's bricks fit neatly together and bore the green hue of moss. A table and chair sheltered beneath the eves. It seemed Huan was playing a game of Go against himself. She stifled a pang of sympathy and kept her expression bright. Choosing to turn their attention to the courtyard's most striking feature, the statues.

Around the perimeter of the courtyard, five statues made up the remainder of the décor. Evenly spaced, and life-sized, four were of fighters striking fearsome kung fu stances. The fifth, carved in pink granite was of a comely Chinese woman. She balanced a parasol over one shoulder and bore a sweet, serene smile.

"These are wonderful," she praised.

"Thank you. Four of them were my greatest competition, the lady was my wife."

"You're so very skilled." She turned to face him. "And I understand that you are a master of kung fu, I have studied it as well," she said, seeking to strike some common ground.

"Oh yes, what school?"

"The monastery in Henan."

Huan clapped his hands together, a pleased expression upon his face. "Really? You must know my old friend, Sifu Zhang."

"I haven't had the pleasure. My teacher was Sifu Ng Mui."

Huan gave her a quizzical look before bursting into laughter and shaking a finger at her. "You're teasing an old man."

A smiled played upon her lips as she shook her head. "No."

He murmured in astonishment before composing himself to regard her for a moment.

"I'm not teasing you, Sifu Li."

He tilted his head and stroked his chin for a moment. "Show me." He motioned her to follow him across the courtyard up a step and paused at the door to bow.

She immediately knew where she was, a kwoon. Placing the flat of her left hand over her right fist, she copied his bow and stepped inside.

The training hall was nearly three times as long as it was wide. Hand sewn tapestries bearing the axioms of the philosopher Sun-Tzu hung on the walls. At one end, incense smoldered at a Sun-Toi, an ancestral altar. The plank floor was clean but showed signs of decades of wear.

"You wish a demonstration of my kung fu?"

"No." His eyes twinkled. "I wish to spar you."

She looked at him sideways her nose crinkling with amusement. "Now you're teasing me."

"After three hundred years you must be magnificent, I would regret it the rest of my days if I did not seize this chance."

She glanced back towards the courtyard. "Wouldn't you rather a nice game of Go? I'm quite proficient."

"Perhaps another time. Now for stakes...."

"Stakes?"

"An incentive." He smiled simply.

"Such as?"

"A statue."

By the stars... "I see...."

"And what will you fight for?" he asked.

She tapped her chin with her index finger contemplating what sort of man he was. If she defeated him quickly would his pride get in the way of her prize? If she gave him a fight and allowed him to win, would he be agreeable to her request? The latter option ruffled her pride.

"Have you decided?" he interrupted.

She came to a decision. "Yes, I have. A boon."

"What favor?"

"I'll tell you when I win. Shall we begin?"

"A moment, please. I don't want to ruin my shirt." Stepping from his slippers, his fingers plucked at the fastenings along the center of his breast.

She looked on with a sense of alarm. "Sifu?"

"A moment."

She watched with astonishment as he turned away from her shrugging the garment from his shoulders, his skin and form began to metamorphize before her eyes. He was growing in height and span. His hair disappeared completely into tiger-orange granite striped with black. His shoulders grew wide enough to fill the kwoon's door. When he turned, she was no longer looking into the liquid eyes of a human but at eyes that resembled those of a statue.

"Are you ready?" His voice had become a low guttural growl. His smile revealed a set of stone fangs.

In her travels through the galaxy, she had met more exotic looking species but the transformation was astonishing nonetheless. She nodded stepping to the center of the kwoon's floor. She dropped her hips into a half-crouch, with all of the weight on her forward foot while using her back foot to keep her balance. Her hands clenched into fists, one high to guard her head, the other low, to protect her body.

"Ah, dragon." He growled, crouching low, his hands opening to resemble the bared claws of the great cat he resembled.

Her eyes glittered as she decided on an attack. "En garde."

His brows knitted quizzically. "I beg your pardon?"

"An expression from a teacher of another art—but I promise to only use kung fu."

"You will have to tell me about this art, after. Begin."

A thought struck her. She held up her hands. "One moment Sifu. I'm sorry." She reached to the small of her back to retrieve her glasses, mobile device, and the specimen kit. "I wouldn't want these damaged." She held them up for him to see.

"Of course."

Carrying the items to the corner, she paused to check Harold's program and felt her blood run cold. "I'm so sorry, Sifu Li. Our match will have to wait."

"What is it?" he asked, advancing upon her.

She started towards the door. "I must go."

"Why?

"Someone is killing soldiers and police in Mumbai."

 "I'll come with you."

"Sifu, with respect, this is no match."

His countenance became grim. "No, it seems it will be a street fight—perhaps to the death and two are better than one when dealing with a murderous enemy."

She hesitated a second, after what happened with the worm, it might be useful to have someone watching her back.

"For me to turn away would be shameful," he added.

"Then we must go right now, and you must remain in your current form."

"Time is wasting."

Wrapping her arm around his waist, they were out the door and airborne in the blink of an eye.

7:30 AM, Local Time, Mumbai, India

An iron dome of security sealed the peninsula of southern Mumbai. One of the megalopolis' oldest and poshest neighborhoods, the colonial district, resembled a warzone. Fighter jets streaked through the air, naval patrol boats crept along the peninsula's shoreline while larger vessels turned their guns and missiles inland in search of a target. In the city itself, soldiers, police, and a regiment of tanks lined a security cordon.

Clutching Huan to her hip, Guardian grimly followed a tendril of greasy, black smoke to the scene of a massacre. "Keep your eyes open," she murmured.

Scorched and shell-pocked, the shattered avenue resembled the worst parts of a battlefield. The stench of burning kerosene, mixed with the coppery tang of blood and the cloying scent of flowering landscapes. In the center of the carnage, a lamppost protruded like a spear from the side of a burning helicopter. The chopper's crew, still strapped into their seats, was charred beyond recognition. Nearby, a broken fire hydrant impotently sprayed water into the air.

Huan released himself from Guardian's grip to drop down onto the shattered pavement. He landed beside the broken hulk of a seventy-ton tank; its hull was rent in half like it was made of foil. Agilely stepping around chunks of heaved-up asphalt, he encountered the broken and twisted bodies of young soldiers. Moving from one to the next, he crouched down to check for signs of life. He looked to her and shook his head sorrowfully. "Some of them aren't even old enough to shave."

Nearing the ground, Guardian reached out with her cosmic sense and felt emptiness. "He took them all. They've all ascended," she lamented.

"All of them? Are you sure?" Huan checked another young man and grunted with anger. His bones shattered, the young man flopped over like a sopping ragdoll.

Guardian regarded her companion sorrowfully. "I'm sorry."

Huan picked up a fist-sized piece of concrete and squeezed it to dust. "This wasn't a fight! This was butchery for fun! Where is the bastard?" He looked left, then right in search of a foe to fight.

Guardian shared his sentiment. She pointed to a sign, seemingly finger painted in blood on the sidewalk. "He left that." She translated from Sanskrit for him.

I AM RAVANA

"Ravana? That's his name?" Huan asked.

"Ravana is also a demonic figure in the Hindu faith."

"A demon?" Huan asked, stunned.

She crouched beside the gory message. "More likely someone with a grandiose opinion of himself. And by the size of those finger prints...." She pointed to the letters. "He's enormous."

"That will make him easier to hit."

"Be careful, he might still be about." She stood up and looked around for emphasis.

"I hope that he is."

"For the moment, please try to put out the fire while I go up and look around."

Giving the fallen a final look, Stone Tiger trudged across the asphalt to the damaged hydrant to press his hands over the gushing water and redirect it onto the burning helicopter. The fire hissed and belched clouds of gray smoke before going out.

The task completed, Huan hopped up onto a garden wall to aid in the search. His nose began to twitch then bounce in the air. He shouted up to her, "I can smell his stench!"

"How close? Can you tell?" She looked around warily.

Huan jumped down and jogged past the wreck to where the air was clearer. His tongue lolled out to rest on his lower lip. His nose wrinkled with disgust. "This way!" Huan began to follow his nose, picking up speed. "He stinks of blood, and sweat, and shit," he growled.

Guardian swooped down to pick him up. "We must be careful. He's not going to be easy to subdue."

"Subdue?" Huan questioned between sniffs, "There's only one way to deal with a mad dog."

She regarded him patiently. "I share your anger, but there will be enough mothers crying tonight, I won't be responsible for one more."

Huan scowled. "Do you have the fortitude for this?"

"Master Li, I'm grateful for your help, but the Earth is under my protection. This is my task and my responsibility. We will subdue him."

Huan scoffed. "And then what?"

"We are not executioners."

"I'd like to hear your solution."

"I'm considering a few options. Some of them are off-planet."

"Punching him into space is acceptable."

It was not what she envisioned but she decided not to elaborate. "Let's go—but no killing."

Huan's sense of smell led them through a neighborhood of elegant, whitewashed Victorian manors and to the front of a majestic Italianate mansion. It virtually gleamed in the dawn sun. Georgian windows draped in diaphanous sheers looked out over broad porches, expansive terraces and showcase gardens.

In the gateway, beneath the gently swaying palms, the engine of a luxury sedan smoldered. The entire front of the car was crushed to the pavement. Its roof had been peeled back like a sardine can. The pair grimaced at the sight in the driver's seat. The chauffer's head was turned backwards. Nearby, one of the car's rear doors lay atop a jasmine shrub, crushing the delicate, white blooms beneath its weight.

Huan extended and curled his fingers like claws. "We've got the bastard."

"One moment, Master Li." She paused, extending her senses to determine if there were hostages and how many. "He's in there. There's someone with him…likely the passenger."

Huan sniffed the air repeatedly. "I smell tobacco and drink, mixed with perfume and…sex." He looked at her.

Guardian's heart froze. "Oh no…" she moaned. The revelation brought back fearful memories from Elizabeth before the joining.

"Let's take him."

Taking a breath, she set her feelings aside. "We must be intelligent about this. Her safety must come first."

"I'll distract him, you fly her out." He began to stalk across the lawn.

She darted ahead of him and stood in his path. "Wait." She held up a hand. "I can hear the television news from inside. The military has the area sealed and the media doesn't seem to know we're here. I'd wager he doesn't either." She paused to listen some more. "His name is Ravana Doshi. He escaped a prison in Kolkata when it was struck by one of the meteorites."

"It seems a demon truly was created."

"And a hero as well." She squeezed his shoulder and gave him a nod of encouragement.

"Well, if we are not expected then he is unprepared. We have the advantage, let's use it." Huan took a step for the house.

"Please…wait."

He turned back to her. "Why? The sooner we solve this, the better."

"Give me a moment to find out where they are—for her safety."

Huan folded his arms across his chest. "All right. How long?"

"A moment or two."

"I'll be waiting."

Guardian circled the house twice, noting the entrances before forcing open an upper story window and slipping inside. The plaster moldings, elegant furnishings, and tasteful artwork resembled her own home's décor. Reaching out with her cosmic sense she quickly determined her quarry was on the main floor below her.

She floated ghost-like through the house and down the staircase. Midflight she beheld the splintered remains of the front door strewn about the entryway. Down the central corridor that led into the depths of the house, the television blared.

She paused in the foyer to examine the remains of shattered portraits and scattered mail. She was familiar with the faces in the smashed picture frames and names on the correspondence from the entertainment pages, Shivani and Rajesh Mehta. They were a Bollywood power couple; she, a movie star and he, a noted producer.

Grim-faced, she hugged the wall of the home's central corridor and floated towards the sounds of soft sobs intermingled with the blaring TV.

A rank odor, reminiscent of the worst parts of the Middle Ages, assaulted Guardian's nostrils. Her face twisted in disgust.

From her perspective she could see the living room's fine décor was in shambles. The intricately patterned rug was littered with the shattered bits of champagne bottles. A cigar butt smoldered in a porcelain bowl from the Ming dynasty, and much of the once-elegant furniture was smashed to sticks, bits of fabric, and leather. Halting at the archway, the blonde cautiously leaned out to peek inwards. Seeing Shivani Mehta, she had to fight the urge to charge to the rescue.

The woman's eyes were closed in a grimace of pain. Her red sari was in tatters. Angry bruises and the streaks of tears marred her rich brown complexion. Her lips were turning blue with shock. An enormous brown hand completely surrounded her neck.

"See what lying gets you?" A rumbling male voice sneered in English. The enormous hand gave her head a shake eliciting a whine. "Are you listening, whore?"

Guardian's anger nearly bubbled over as she listened.

"I'm sorry," Shivani sobbed.

"You've only begun to be sorry," the voice growled.

Debating inwardly whether Shivani could be left for a few moments more with her captor, Guardian caught the news anchor's report on the television.

"Once again, the prime minister has ordered the military to surround Mumbai's colonial neighborhood where it is believed this man, convicted rapist Ravana Doshi, is trapped—"

"You dog fucker." There was the sound of a bottle shattering against the wall and a frightened wail from Shivani, "There is no such thing as rape, and you cannot trap a god. I'm here to punish a liar and temptress!" His hand shook again, eliciting another tormented cry.

Fists clenched and teeth set, Guardian listened to the news report for whatever she could glean before flying back to Huan.

Huan crouched behind a copse of laburnum trees. "What's the plan?" he stood up as she alighted next to him.

She quickly recounted what she had seen.

"You said that there was a side door on the porch?"

"French doors, small glass panes in wooden frames, yes."

"We could strike where he least expects it, from two sides, the inside and the outside, confuse him."

Guardian folded her arms across her chest and shook her head. "We don't know how he will react. I don't want to risk panicking or inciting him. I think..."

"Yes?"

Her mind raced and reeled. "I think I might be able to distract him away from her long enough for you to come through the side door and get her out of there."

"I could distract him. After all, you can fly her out."

"But I think he would attack you on sight."

"But not you?" He looked at her skeptically.

"My impression of the man is he wouldn't consider me a threat." She noted his expression, "I know you want to spare me the risk. I know that you want to exact some justice for his crimes. I commend you for your gallantry, but our success must be measured by saving her, and this would seem the best way to achieve it."

Huan pressed his lips together, nodding and murmuring as he did. "Appear weak when you are strong. A sound strategy. "

"Thank you. Now...." She turned and pointed in the direction of the side yard. "I want you to take Shivani there and I will circle around and lift both of you out."

"All right, but do you know if he can fly?"

"I don't, but we don't have the time or means to determine it. If all goes well, this will be over in seconds. Sifu Li, are you ready?"

"Give me a moment to get around the side."

She glanced at his stone feet. "I'd better set you down on the porch."

Mirroring her downward look, he gave a nod. "Quieter that way."

Gently setting The Stone Tiger down on the porch, she whispered to him, "See you in a few seconds." She gave him an optimistic smile that belied her inner feeling of dread and flew around the house to halt short of the entryway of the living room.

Steeling herself with a deep breath, she set her shoulders back and stepped into view.

"Fancy yourself a god, do you?"

Ravana uttered a curse and turned to find the source of the interruption. His eyes widened for a split second then narrowed. "The British slut."

Her jaw set defiantly. "Neither."

The floor cracked beneath his cinder block-sized feet as he jumped up to confront her.

Her mind reeled. He was enormous. A greasy, foul smelling, grossly over-muscled, built-like-a-bus, ogre of a man. What struck her most were his eyes; they were not the wild-eyes of a man who held a tenuous grip on reality. They were cold, and black, and glittering with sadistic glee. He reminded her of a lion leisurely dining on a kill and she needed to avoid becoming dessert. She rose off from the floor to look him in the eye.

"Welcome to my temple…." he stretched out his arms in a grandiose manner. "You'll be my next worshipper."

"Really?" she asked, her tone dubious and defiant.

"I'm feeling very generous." He turned his face towards his victim and smirked. "I gave her something her husband never has and I'll bet you've never had—"

Seeing his attention divided, an impulse seized Guardian. She darted for Shivani.

In the same instant, he shuffled into her path.

Bouncing off his bulk, she grunted like she had flown into the side of a mountain. She backed away, shaking her head to clear it.

"Clumsy *and* stupid. But stupid makes things easier." His eyes gleamed.

Her expression sharpened to one of defiance. "You'll find I'm one of those difficult women."

"Get on your knees and worship or I'll pop her head off like a cork." He smiled sadistically, reaching to run his thumb along Shivani's jaw to elicit a whine from her.

In seconds, Guardian's expression rapidly cycled from flinty defiance to sympathy and then to disgust as she caught sight of the filthy curtain he wore tied about his waist in a langot, shift and stir.

"Here! Now!" He pointed to the floor at his feet.

Guardian considered the demand for a split second. One hard punch to the pelvic floor and he would be on his knees coughing and retching. Resisting the urge to taunt him, she kept her expression one of trepidation she landed and took a tentative step towards him.

"Get over here, slut!" he bellowed.

Stone feet drummed on wood in quick time. The French doors exploded inward in a hail of wood and broken glass. Huan sailed through the air, his leg extended in a flying sidekick.

Ravana winced, grunting as Huan's foot connected with his ribs.

Guardian darted for Shivani pausing to gently gather the woman into her arms. "I've got you!—" Her words of reassurance became a squawk as heavy fingers seized her neck, jerking her backwards and upwards.

Legs kicking for purchase, Guardian pried at the entrapping hand, managing to gurgle out one word to the other woman, "Run!"

Shivani stared at her for split second, struggling to rise before rolling onto the floor and beginning to crawl for the front foyer.

Huan leapt up from the floor, striking and clawing.

Bloody stripes appeared across Ravana's face.

THWACK!

The back of Ravana's fist swatted Huan, sending the fighter crashing through the house's wall in a cloud of dust and debris.

"Tiger!" Guardian kicked and groaned, feeling Ravana's fingers press painfully into her neck.

"Tiger?" the brute scoffed, "more like a kitten." Still clutching Guardian in his hand, Ravana languidly followed after Huan, crossing the porch and stepping down onto the lawn in two strides. "Have you ever heard the sound a cat makes when it's skinned?"

Her mind recoiled. She grasped at his hand, noting where his thumb was and that each step took them further from Shivani.

He sneered, "And when I'm done with him, I'll pluck your petals for the whole world to watch."

Not bloody likely! Guardian seized Ravana's thumb and yanked it back from her neck to fly free. Not waiting for a reaction, she seized his greasy locks at the scalp and flung him across the yard and through the garden wall before turning to fly to the old master's side. "Huan!"

Stone Tiger sat slumped against the garden wall, a trail of broken trees marking his path.

He lifted his head sluggishly. "He is formidable."

Guardian tamped down her urge to admonish him and quickly began an assessment. She suspected a concussion. A trace of her hands found cracks along his shoulders and flanks. An attempt to surreptitiously heal him failed just as it had with Rudy.

"I can fight," he said defiantly. He gripped her shoulder trying to force himself up.

"I'll have to make the fight for both of us." She anxiously glanced over her shoulder for Ravana.

Huan's jaw set stubbornly. "I'm not leaving."

An idea struck her, "Sifu, Shivani needs help. You must get her to safety." The ground began to shake. Her head snapped around to see Ravana bounding towards them. "Now go!" She lifted him to his feet.

"Remember your Sun-Tzu. Fall on him like a thunderbolt," he groaned holding his ribs and staggering away.

"I broke your friend and now I'm going to break you!" Ravana laughed, flexing his bulging muscles. "But I'm going to take my time, little kitten, centimeter by centimeter."

"Then it should be quick." Guardian grabbed a fallen tree at her feet and threw it at him like a javelin.

He held up an arm defensively, exploding it into splinters. "I'm going to enjoy your prayers."

"Not today!" She flew at him to land a left hook to his jaw, the impact sounded like a rifle crack as bone struck bone. She followed the hook with a socking right that staggered him. Her knee shot up under his chin, snapping his head back.

Ravana shook his head to regain his senses. He roared indignantly and grabbed the blonde's narrow waist in a bear hug, heaving her from side to side in a horrid waltz of pain.

Guardian yelped, feeling her vertebrae pop.

"Music to my ears!" he crowed.

"Get ready for the greatest hits," she growled through gritted teeth, boxing his ears then jamming the pads of her thumbs against his cringing eyelids.

Ears ringing from the double-clap, he bellowed, wincing in pain.

Slipping free, she darted back and away. Grimacing, her hand snaked around her back. An ancient memory assailed her, pain, real pain. She clenched a hand into a fist to keep from crying out.

"You smell nice!" he taunted.

She spoke through gritted teeth. "And just imagine how good you'll smell when you're back in chocky, showered, and in a fresh uniform."

"Then we couldn't play." He sneered. He seized a marble statue of a lion and chucked it at her. "Catch!"

Guardian met the incoming missile with a punch, turning the lawn ornament into a cloud of white dust. "I'm not here to play." She glowered down at him.

"Well, there are other toys around." Ravana took a step towards the house.

"No, you won't!" She stretched out her arms and flew at him like a battering ram.

The brute grinned and squared his body, bracing himself.

The impact sounded like the collision of two freight trains. Guardian's arms buckled. Her head struck his breast bone. Stars exploded before her eyes. She fell to the lawn and struggled to rise on wobbly legs.

Staggered, the giant coughed, wheezed, and then coughed again. He teetered backwards before stumbling forwards, swinging wildly.

She blinked hard to clear her vision. Through the haze, Guardian saw the mass of Ravana charge. Instinctively, she raised her arms to protect herself.

Ravana seized her wrist and used it to snap her like a whip.

Guardian yowled, feeling her shoulder wrenched.

Holding fast, Ravana raised his opposite hand, drawing it back to deliver a haymaker. He smiled down at her with a demonic gleam in his eye. "I'm going to enjoy breaking you." The brute threw his head back and guffawed sadistically.

Guardian blinked hard, the pain of her shoulder combined with his crushing grip was withering. Through gritted teeth, she sucked in a deep breath before opening her mouth to release an ear-splitting scream aimed at the wrist of his ensnaring hand. His flesh rippled, turning from deep brown to purple.

Ravana howled. His hand sprang open. He slammed his good fist down upon her like a sledge pounding a stake.

Freed of his grasp, Guardian met his blow forearm to forearm. Her legs began to quiver under the crushing weight of his blow. Her mind screamed at her to stay on her feet.

Still locked in their test of strength, Ravana launched a punch beneath their crossed arms and into Guardian's quaking solar plexus.

Her eyes bulged. Her breath escaped as a croak. Folded in half, she cannoned backwards, snapping trees, exploding walls, and collapsing houses in her path. In that split second, she realized she had picked a fight with a force of nature.

Her flight ended with a collision with one final wall. She slammed into it with a bone-jarring crunch before slumping to its foot.

Covering the distance in a few bounding steps, Ravana was upon her in an instant.

Guardian felt her ankle seized then her shoulder. She made a groggy effort to struggle free.

Ravana lifted her overhead. "Now, I break you." He hurled

her back to Earth.

A cry escaped Guardian's lips before all went black.

Pain burrowed into Guardian's consciousness. She groaned. Something was poking her and clawing at her.

"Fucking clothes!" Ravana snarled.

Guardian's eyes flew open. She was on her back. Ravana had dragged her from her place at the wall and now knelt between her splayed-open legs. He tore at her uniform, attempting to rip it apart. Her symbiote faithfully followed her last command, keeping its appearance and repairing itself the second it was damaged.

"No!" Guardian scissored her legs shut and made for the sky.

"Get back here, bitch!" Ravana snarled. He seized her ankle and yanked her back to Earth. Holding fast, he scrambled to straddle her hips and pin her in place. "Back to sleep." He grabbed her throat pressing her to the ground with one hand while cocking the other into a fist to let it fly.

Guardian crooked her arms over her face to protect herself.

When his knuckle met the point of her elbow the resounding crack was quickly followed by a roar of pain that reverberated over the city.

Ravana jerked his fist back to his body and covered it protectively.

WHAP.

Guardian's cape plastered itself over his face to obscure her counter- attack. Her shin snapped into the fork of his legs. He doubled over then arched backwards. Gagging and wheezing, he grabbed at himself like he had been impaled.

She lifted her leg higher and jammed her booted foot against the giant's chest, sending him tumbling over Mumbai's rooftops.

Guardian fell back for a moment, emitting a groan that

reached all the way from the marrow of her bones. Her head throbbed. Her joints ached. A metallic taste lingered in her mouth. Everything hurt. "Bloody hell," she groaned.

Overhead, helicopter blades chopped the air. The rotor wash pelted her with dust and leaves, announcing the arrival of a pair of army medics descending on ropes.

As they hurried to kneel beside her, the cobwebs in her head were beginning to clear.

"Where are you hurt, miss?" a sergeant asked as he shrugged off a rucksack of medical supplies.

She raised herself up on an elbow. The sight of the destruction brought a stunned oath to her lips. Gritting her teeth, she rolled to one side and pushed herself to her feet. "I'll mend. But was the neighborhood evacuated?"

"Oh yes, miss. Some time ago," the younger of the two said.

"Completely?"

The pair of medics looked at each other before responding. "Yes, miss."

Guardian's shoulders sagged with relief.

"Please, if you would just allow us to assist you, miss." The sergeant gently touched her shoulder.

"No." She waved his hand away. "He'll be coming back. He's not the sort of man to let anyone get the best of him. You two must leave immediately."

"But miss—"

Her thoughts went to Huan and Shivani. "Go to the boulevard, there are two patients to see to."

"They have been evacuated. Let us help you too," the sergeant persisted.

"You can help me by getting to safety. Now go." Not bothering to wait for a reply, she was airborne and following Ravana's trajectory.

Fists clenched and snorting like an enraged bull, Ravana

charged up the broken street, each bounding stride a leap of yards.

Diving upon him from above, Guardian's fist caught the corner of his jaw mid-leap, turning his head and sending him spinning to the ground in an explosion of dust and broken asphalt.

Dazed, the giant rolled over and pressed himself up while shaking his head.

She began to fly in a circle around him, the speed of her flight forming a tornado with him in its eye. The vortex of dust and debris pelted him as he turned in place, swiping at her.

Guardian alternated between veering out of his reach and punching at his swiping hands.

"Stand still and fight me!" Ravana shook his injured hands and then lunged at her with both.

Guardian deftly captured his thumb and arm and twisted into a Judo throw that sent Ravana skipping and bouncing down the street. Not tarrying to admire the effects of her technique, she flew on ahead of him to land in his path. Watching him tumble towards her, she extended her foot like she was stopping an errant soccer ball.

His body shivered, rocked by his sudden halt.

Giving him no time to recover, the edge of her hand came down in a chop at the juncture of his neck and shoulder. In the span of a split-second, his blood pressure spiked then dropped, inducing a faint.

Guardian put her fists on her hips and frowned down at his inert form. "Never fight a doctor, we know where it hurts."

Looking around, she surveyed the damage. Her eyes softened with sorrow at the lives lost. "You've much to answer for..." She reached down to seize his thumb and take to the sky. "But first we need a place to put you until other arrangements can be made."

7:45 AM Local Time, Rural Maharashtra, North-West of Mumbai

Ravana's thumb was as big around as Guardian's wrist. She gripped it tightly, using it as a handle to tow him through the air at a high altitude while desperately hoping the low oxygen levels would keep him unconscious long enough to find a place to confine him. She noted she was not alone; fighter jets matched her flight path, while a swarm of helicopters trailed behind her at a lower altitude. When she spotted what she was looking for, she tightened her grip on her prisoner's digit and plunged for the deck.

The abandoned mine formed a scar on the landscape. The dusty yellow gravel of the site was interrupted by a few wooden structures with rusting tin roofs. Noting the lack of activity and that the gate was chained and locked, Guardian crashed through the barricade at the mouth of the mine pulling Ravana along behind her.

Down she flew, to a full hundred stories of depth. Reaching the bottom, she veered into a side shaft. At its end, she roughly deposited him on the dusty floor and waited.

After several moments he began to stir, groaning and cursing as he did. Ravana attempted to stand then fell. "What the fuck did that bitch do to me?"

"Mind your tongue," she scolded, a disembodied voice in the pitch-black darkness of the mine. "You have a touch of altitude sickness, it should pass by tomorrow."

"I'll be long out of here by then." He forced himself up and struck his head on the shaft's seven-foot ceiling, triggering a cascade of dust, a bellow of pain, and a fit of coughing. "Where the fuck am I?" He looked about, turning in place.

Guardian nervously glanced up at the ceiling, placing a hand on its surface to check its stability. "Where you'll stay until I come get you," she said, floating well away from him.

"You'll come for me right now." He sneered and began swiping the air, like a boy playing blind man's bluff.

"By the stars," she groaned. With a thought, light shone forth from her face and pores in her uniform, illuminating the passage as bright as noon.

Ravana cursed, holding up a hand before his eyes and peering through the spaces between his fingers.

"As I said, you will remain here until—"

"That's what you think." He started forward, keeping his hand out to shield himself from the brilliance of her aura.

Guardian retreated further and reached for the ceiling. "Stop right there or I will pull this place down on top of you." She hoped her bluff was the sort of vicious threat a man like him would believe.

"You don't think I can't get out of here?" He smirked but halted in place.

Seeing him pause, she felt a sense of relief. "You will remain here and the necessities will be brought to you."

"What are you going to do? Stand guard?"

"For an eternity if necessary. Now stay put." She extinguished her light and flew for the main shaft. She paused once to ensure he was not following her and noted the creative string of curses being bellowed in her direction.

Guardian flew from the mine and into the morning sunshine to behold a full military operation underway. Heavily armed commandos in battle dress sheltered under cover, their weapons trained on the mine's mouth. Helicopters hovered in a ring, some of them armed with rockets pointed towards the mine's entrance. One of them loosed ordinance the moment she was clear of the mine's opening.

Experiencing a moment of panic, Guardian caught the salvo of rockets in rapid succession, twisting her wrist and sending them flying harmlessly high into the sky to detonate. She frowned at the pilot and held up her index finger in a gesture of admonishment. Over the din of the helicopters' rotor blades, she heard someone shouting to her. Turning in place, she gave the helicopter crews one more look of warning before descending to the ground.

A fresh-faced officer bade her follow him for a few dozen yards to where a general and his staff sheltered behind a large boulder. He saluted his superior before departing.

Like the rest of the soldiers surrounding the mine, the general wore camouflage battle dress and a ballistic helmet. Paratrooper wings adorned the space over his right jacket pocket and his thick, neatly trimmed, handlebar mustache was streaked with gray. She saw something else in his gaze, more than annoyance, it was disapproval.

"You are interfering with a military operation, miss."

"And you're interfering with my mission, general."

The officer bristled. "And what mission is that, *girl*?" he demanded.

"There are already too many families that will be grieving tonight, I will not allow that numbered to be added to—and it's Doctor or Guardian.

"*He* is the source of that grief."

"And he will stand trial."

"You doubt the verdict?"

"Not the verdict. It is the sentence that concerns me."

"Which is what we are here to do. My orders are from the prime minister—"

"And I can be at his office door in seconds. I will not let you execute him, general. He's my prisoner, he will stand trial."

"There is no prison that can hold him."

"Not on this planet." She saw the general's head jerk backward. "Give me a few moments with the prime minister—"

"What would you know about it, *girl*?"

Guardian's hands rose to rest on her hips, tenting her cape outwards.

"I've lived on this planet for the past eight hundred years, General. I know a great deal."

"Are you injured, Doctor?" A mellow voice asked.

Guardian turned to see the source of the interruption. From

the caduceus of the medical corps on his beret and rank on his shoulders, she quickly deduced he was the regimental surgeon.

"I'm fine thank you, Doctor." She turned back to the general. "General, I—"

"I must say you speak excellent Hindi, Doctor." The surgeon smiled politely.

She knew what the surgeon was attempting and decided to use the opening. "Thank you, I've lived in India several times. My third husband was Indian, he was called—"

"Three husbands?" the general tutted.

She flicked a glance at the general before continuing, "Mansabdar, Jadhav Aharya. We were married five hundred years ago and I still miss him," she said, shifting her attention and demeanor between the two men. "Again, thank you for your concern, Doctor. But to the matter at hand, general, I will not allow—"

The ground shook then rumbled. A gout of coal dust shot up from the mine and swirled about them. Soldiers stumbled then ducked reflexively as their officers shouted orders.

Guardian flew into the mine's entrance to find the shaft had collapsed and the passage filled with dust and rubble.

"No!" she protested. Lifting her arms over her head she steepled her hands together and began to spin like a drill. Upended, she dove into the shaft to burrow through the tightly-packed rubble for several stories of distance.

The layers of detritus continued with no sign of air pockets. Recognizing her prisoner either intentionally or accidently committed suicide, Guardian retraced her passage, carefully levitating back through the layers of rock and soil.

The general and his staff greeted her when she re-emerged, with their scarves tied about their mouths. "It seems the problem has taken care of itself," he gloated then broke into a cheer that the rest of the commandos quickly joined in.

Ignoring their celebration, Guardian touched the army doctor's arm to gain his attention. "Do you know where they took—" She caught herself before she used Huan's name. "Mrs. Mehta and my friend?"

The jubilation on the doctor's face quickly faded. "Yes," he said, leaning in to her ear. "They were flown to Bombay Medical Centre, Doctor."

She took a moment to shake her colleague's hand and thank him before leaving the impromptu party.

8:00 AM, local time, Bombay Hospital and Medical Research Center, Mumbai

Guardian first flew to the Mehta home in an attempt to scavenge a sample of Ravana's DNA but found the house a veritable anthill of police officers. Deciding that surreptitiously obtaining a sample would be well-nigh impossible, she flew on to the hospital and entered via its rooftop heliport.

The antiseptic smell, the bustling staff, and the sheer size of the place prompted a romantic notion of returning to a center like it to obtain another medical fellowship, and to pass on her knowledge to a new crop of doctors. The reality of her situation quickly intruded to quash the fantasy. Her newly acquired fame would likely make such an initiative difficult if not impossible. With an air of sadness, she pushed the idea aside to approach the trauma ward's nursing station and inquire after Huan and Shivani.

The nurses readily provided her with the information before tactfully offering her toiletries and a towel. A glance in a mirror revealed why. From the neck up she resembled a dust mop. Using a shower in the staff change room, the dirt and bits of leaves were quickly washed away. Her hair combed slick to her scalp, she was directed to the elevators and down one floor to another surgical ward where Shivani had been rushed for emergency surgery.

The sudden influx of patients from the street battle left the ward of near pandemonium, with the staff only pausing for a second to smile or say hello. She struggled to not roll up her sleeves and dive in with an offer to assist. A young ward clerk was the only staff left at the nursing station. After the young woman's initial star struck reaction wore off, Guardian explained her reason for being there.

"Is it true?" the clerk asked, "he attacked her because she testified against him for raping that actress?"

Guardian rested her hands on the station's counter. "Today has been distressing enough, I'd rather not contemplate the dark motivations of that man's mind."

"Yes, I suppose there is no sense in adding problems is there? Speaking of which…would you like me to go in with you to see Mr. Mehta? He's very upset."

Guardian noted the reluctance in the young woman's expression. "Understandably, and thank you for your offer but this isn't the first time I've had to do this. However, before I go, can you tell me if he has been informed about the nature of the surgery?"

"I believe so, miss."

Thanking her, Guardian negotiated her way down the corridor to a waiting room door. She knocked once and not getting a response, she pushed it inward to reveal a small, dimly lit, waiting room painted in dusty pink and furnished with cushioned sofas and chairs. The only light came from a small table lamp in the corner.

She recognized Rajesh Mehta immediately from the smashed portraits at his home. He was a slim, middle-aged man. The black hair at his temples was streaked with gray. His linen suit was rumpled and his tie and shirt collar loosened. He sat alone on a short sofa, staring at the floor.

She tilted her head and regarded him sympathetically. "Mr. Mehta?"

His gaze flicked sideways for an instant in acknowledgement before returning to the floor.

"I'm so very sorry that we're meeting under these circumstances. May I sit?"

She waited a moment and after not receiving a response, took a seat on the edge of an adjacent chair. After years of practicing medicine, she found patients often coped better in times of difficult circumstance than their loved ones did. "Mr. Mehta, I know that this—"

Mehta's fists clenched as he turned to face her. "What that Dalit did…she is ruined. *I…I* am ruined." He choked out his last words.

Guardian bit back a rebuke attributing his hasty words to shock. "Mr. Mehta, you wouldn't be here if you believed that."

"She should never have testified!" he thundered.

"This is not her fault. Not only must you know and believe this but she must. And you must be the one to remind her of this every time she thinks it is her fault. What she did was very brave and very decent—heroic even. Now you must be as well."

"No!" he slammed the base of his fist into his palm and launched himself from his seat.

Guardian watched him stalk about the room in a rage. "A crime of this nature doesn't just injure the victim but also everyone who loves them. This man...this criminal, took a great deal from your wife; her choice, her sense of peace, her health. Don't allow him to take you, too."

"How can I ever? After he..." His fists white knuckled and eyes clenched tight, he turned away.

Guardian stood up. Resisting the urge to touch his shoulder, she spoke to him in gentle tones. "You couldn't have stopped him, the hospital is filled with those who tried and there are even more still lying in the street." She paused in thought. "But you can protect her now."

"How?" he demanded, "How can I? What's done is done. It cannot be taken back."

"You're right it can't, but you can be her lion. You can protect her from those who will say this is her fault. This crime was the choice of a cruel and vindictive man and you must be his opposite, you must be kind...patient...compassionate. You must do as you promised when you were married."

"Where is he now? I want him—"

"He died...by his own hand." She paused to regard him with compassion. "Mr. Mehta, if you want to avenge your wife's honor, cleave to her...support her. Helping her to heal will help you to heal as well. If you want revenge, living a long and happy life together will provide you with the satisfaction you seek." Guardian glanced at the clock on the wall. "Shivani will be in surgery for a few more hours, I trust you will be by her side when she wakes up in the recovery room? Are you strong enough to do that?"

Mehta looked down at the floor before straightening up. "I am."

"Good," she said. "There is just one more thing before I go."

"What is it?

"The word, Dalit...that word and the idea it represents does not belong in the mind or the mouth of a good man."

He nodded and sighed. "I was angry but that is no excuse."

"It's going to be a long road for the two of you and I encourage you both to seek counseling. But, if you stand by each other, I know you'll make it."

"Thank you for saving my wife."

"Please extend my best wishes to her. I should like to remain but sadly I have another visit to make."

"I understand. Be safe, and thank you." He smiled for the first time since she had met him.

She gave him an encouraging smile, and turned to depart as he re-buttoned his collar and straightened his tie.

Guardian rode an elevator down to the emergency department. The doors slid open to reveal a beehive of activity. The ward brimmed over with military casualties. The medical staff moved briskly between bedsides. Walking wounded congregated in cliques and spoke in low, serious voices about those who were in surgery and about those who had not made it.

Her sudden presence turned heads and elicited excited murmurs that quickly became applause. She smiled reflexively but balked internally at the adulation, if she had been on scene sooner, most or even none of them would be here. It was times like these she wished she could go from patient to patient and instantly remedy their ailments and injuries but she had already turned the world on its head once this week, and she had no wish to interfere with long held beliefs and cultural touchstones. It did not mean that after seeing Huan she could not lend a hand...

She began her slow wade through the throngs of staff and patients. There were pauses for pictures, and the dispensing of words of encouragement, good-natured jokes, and brief answers to questions.

It took some time to reach Huan. She wanted everyone she met along the way to feel as important as she knew them to be, giving them a moment's attention seemed to do that. The only two that did not seem to be happy to see her were from the Chinese consulate. Their dour expressions deepened as she drew nearer. They did not step up to meet her, glaring instead from a distance. Deciding there were too many people around her with real problems rather than imagined ones, Guardian carried on to Huan's bay.

Reverted back to flesh, Huan lay face down on a gurney. His face protruded through a halo pillow attached to the head of the bed. Brightly colored wire leads ran from his body back to a monitor that silently provided information about his pulse, blood pressure, and oxygen levels.

Guardian lay back and floated six inches off the floor to look up at him. "I read your chart," she said, feeling a pang of remorse, "a concussion and six fractured ribs...I'm so sorry this happened to you."

"You didn't need to come here."

"At this moment, this is the only place for me to be." She gave him a smile of encouragement.

"Someone must be waiting at home."

She felt a small spasm of loneliness but kept her expression cheerful. "That reminds me, is there someone I should contact for you?"

"An official from the consulate is calling my son and my nephew in Kunming."

"I think I saw them when I passed the nursing station, they did not seem happy."

"Probably because of their terrible haircuts," he quipped.

"Just how much morphine have you received."

"Enough to feel better. Did you remember your Sun-Tzu?"

"I was rather busy but I was reminded that if you can find a reason, you can find a way." She added quietly, "He won't be harming anyone else."

"I heard. As for his statue, I'll need a much larger slab for him than I will for you."

"Be serious, Master Li, and please don't mistake this for ingratitude, but I should not have brought you along."

"My presence was advantageous. You changed the plan and were impulsive."

"I saw an opportunity for rescue."

"But you failed and you could not have fought him and rescued her at the same time."

It was hard to deny him when he wasn't exactly wrong. "About fighting, Master Li, when you're well enough, and if you're inclined, I would like to train with you regularly."

"A weekly lesson in humility, or more frequently than that?" He smirked, laughed and then grunted, his teeth on edge.

Her giggle of disbelief ended abruptly with a wince of sympathy. "No laughter until those ribs have healed, which means no teasing me. Doctor's orders."

He coughed then groaned. "You may be right."

"What was that, young man?" she teased.

He grumbled. "I think our first lesson *will* be in humility. Standing on one foot, holding bricks with your arms extended."

"Perhaps we can have a contest. Who can hold that pose the longest. Shall we count by seasons?" Her eyes twinkled playfully.

"Perhaps I'll sculpt you in that concentration pose as a

reminder of the dangers of being impulsive."

She held her retort as the privacy curtain drew back.

A phlebotomist dressed in a white lab smock and carrying a tray of needles and tubes appeared in the opening. "Excuse me I need to get a sample of the patient's blood for testing." He knelt and worked at the awkward inverted angle of his patient.

"By all means." Guardian stood up to allow the technician to work, chatting and translating for both.

When the second vial of blood was deposited in the tray and the worker turned back to Huan to acquire a third vial, Guardian deftly filched it, tucking it into a newly created pocket at the small of her back. *Sorry Huan, but Rudy and the world need answers.*

As the blood technician left, she resumed her position hovering above the floor. "I think they'll be moving you up to a room soon. You needn't worry about paying for this, I'll see to it."

"You have money?"

"Enough." She smiled.

The curtain slid back again, this time much wider. A pair of porters, the two consular officials, and a nurse stood in the gap. The nurse leaned down to speak to Huan.

"They have a bed for you," Guardian translated, "I'll come see you once they have you settled, young man." Kissing the tips of her fingers, she pressed them to his cheek.

"No respect for my age or station," he grumbled.

"Don't be too much trouble for them."

"No more than you are for me."

Thursday, 5:30 AM, Avalon, Maine

After Huan was moved from the emergency room, Guardian looked at the backlog of patients and approached the department head to offer a hand. Upon learning she was a neurosurgeon for an eyebrow raising number of decades, a hastily called meeting with the hospital administrator occurred and she was directed to the hospital's trauma center.

A young soldier that Ravana bounced off the side of a house was not expected to walk again. She scrubbed in on the operation, surreptitiously ensuring that for at least one of Ravana's victims, the injuries would not be permanent. After the surgery, she dropped in to see Huan before returning home to Avalon. It felt good to use her medical skills and although obtaining the DNA sample was not a piece of the asteroid, she counted it as a victory.

Her feelings of happiness and accomplishment were short lived. While she was in the operating room, the world's obsession with her continued unabated. Someone had obtained a copy of her pictures with Harold and Mark and turned them into a kind of cyber carnival cutout. At seventeen million downloads and counting, their personal moments were now a mass commodity. The aftermath of her battle with Ravana was a topic of fear and speculation as some wondered aloud about how Ravana died. To top it off, Rupert Longstreet was making political hay at her expense.

Staring at the center screen and eating an early breakfast, she watched and listened as he drawled in front of a bouquet of microphones.

"Despite Ms. Guardian's assurances to the contrary, what happened in India clearly confirms the concerns of many that these metahumans are dangerous. To this end, after speaking with my colleagues in the House of Representatives and the Senate, we will, in the interests of public health and now in light of recent of events, undertake emergency sessions at the start of next week to debate a bill on the registration of metahumans here in the United States."

Elizabeth felt like she'd been struck a physical blow. Her hair prickled. He was stirring up controversy to provoke a reaction. She thought of Melanie and Charlie, Rudy and Ray-Anne. Melanie might be a pacifist but the reaction of other metahumans could turn tragic.

Her jaw set. If anyone was to react, it had to be her. Huan's words about remembering her Sun-Tzu and the philosopher's axiom about knowing an enemy rang in her ears. Seizing her stack of library cards, she left Avalon. She had a lot of old news files to read on the subject of Rupert Longstreet.

What she found was troubling.

Thursday, 7:58 AM Goddard Space Flight Center, Greenbelt, Maryland

In Boston, the windows of the laboratory were disappointingly dark. Guardian imagined Jennifer was likely still at home and beginning her day. The delivery of Huan's blood would have to wait. Overcoming a half-serious urge to blackout a few television studios, she carried on to Goddard where it seemed security was not taking its cues from the sensationalized reports in the media. She forced a smile and spoke congenially with the security detail that accompanied her to the outer door of Mark's office. Katie's desk was unoccupied and the computer was off. Having been assured that Mark was at work, she rapped on his door. It opened immediately.

Wearing a charcoal gray suit, Mark was as polished and dapper as the moment she met him but his face was filled with concern.

He reached out and gently took her arms. "How are you doing? Are you all right?"

Her recollections of the previous day and morning news vied for dominance of her emotions. "It's been a very busy twenty-four hours."

He grimaced sympathetically. "I hear that. Is there anything you need? Or anything I can do?"

She hesitated.

"Come here." His hands slid down to her wrists to tug her into his arms.

Giving way, Guardian pressed her cheek to his lapel, accepting his embrace. She felt her stress ebb. "Thank you," she murmured.

"I got you."

She snuggled into him, murmuring with relief.

"Where you scared?" he asked, quietly.

She sighed. "There were moments. But that's not all of it."

"What else?" He gently placed a peck atop her head. "What they're saying in the news? Longstreet?"

"That's part of it…." she murmured.

"Talk to me." He loosened his grip enough to look her in the eye.

"It won't change things."

"What things?"

"I think I'm having my knees taken out from under me." She grimaced at the thought.

"How?"

"When I was operating on that young man—"

"That was righteous."

"Thank you. Before I went in, I checked Harold's program for any other incidents, and luckily there weren't any."

"Well, that's good news."

"Yes, and as I was there standing at that table, I couldn't help but feel anxious that there might be another similar incident going on somewhere that might land another person on an operating table and I wouldn't be there to stop it. "

"You can't be everywhere at once."

"But can I still be a doctor?"

"Taking your knees out from under you…right." He nodded. "But good things happened to me because of the day I had my knees—or knee taken out from under me."

"I love being a doctor. The only way I can see to keep doing it is to find a cure for this metahuman condition. To do that, I have to know what I'm dealing with."

"The asteroid."

"That's why I'm here—at least one of the reasons."

He smiled down at her.

"And I'm so very grateful for your help." She laid her head on his chest and squeezed him tight.

"You're welcome."

Basking in his warmth, she murmured. "I'm sorry if I'm being a burden."

"You think you're a burden?"

"I'm sorry."

"A burden?" He asked, his voice tinged with mischief.

She looked up to see an impish gleam in his eyes. "Dr. Jackson?"

"Let's find out." The big man ducked into her waist like he was about to make a tackle and hefted her onto his shoulder. Pinning her legs to him, he stepped back into his office and began to spin in place.

"Doctor—Mark! What are you doing!" Her vision half obscured by her cape, the room began to spin. Her bleat of protest quickly became a squeal of laughter.

After several turns and a playful swat on her backside, he set her down.

"Nah, you're not a burden at all," he concluded.

"Did you just spank me!"

"Didn't you just laugh when I did?"

"It was a reflexive action." She rubbed her bottom in an attempt to assuage her injured dignity.

"I think you enjoyed it." He closed the inner office door.

"I didn't come here to be spun in the air." She felt her face heating up with embarrassment.

"You're not going to be any help to yourself or anyone else if you're too wound up to think straight."

"Still...."

"What?" He smirked while his eyes continued to gleam with playfulness.

She looked to the floor to compose herself. "Erm...did you happen to see what someone did with Harold's pictures of us? Has the media shown up here or at your home?"

"No media, and yeah I saw. It seems like Harold isn't your only boyfriend," he teased, grimly.

"Be serious, Mark. Someone knows about us and where is Harold? Does he know? Did he create this application?"

"He knows and no, it wasn't him."

"I just don't want all of this to fall on you." She saw him about to object and cut him off. "Please allow me to finish. I think..." She bit her bottom lip. "I think it would be better if we put our date off until—"

"No. Now you just hold on a minute. We've already had this discussion. If you don't want to go out with me, I'll be disappointed but I'll be okay. But don't you dare give in to worst-case hypotheticals."

"I'm just trying to keep you safe."

"And I appreciate that. Look...." He raised his hand to her chin, stroking it with his thumb. "You are beautiful, brilliant, powerful, and sexy and I'd be kicking myself for the rest of my life if I let a bunch of fools keep me from knowing you."

The blonde felt her heart flutter. She beamed at him and saw something primal looking back at her.

Mark examined her face, tilting his head to one side then the other before leaning in to heatedly meet and part her lips. His hand seized a lock of hair at the base of her neck with a steady tug.

The press of his soft lips provoked thoughts and images that left her breathless.

Breaking the kiss, Mark looked down, seeming to study her for several moments. His eyes danced. "So did you kick that guy's ass?"

Still breathless, her shoulders quivered in mirth at the sudden question. "I—yes, only to keep him from hurting anyone else. I regret that it ended with his suicide."

"A bad guy took himself off the board. Don't mourn him too long. He did a lot of damage—hurt a lot of people."

"Yes, he did."

"And who knew there was that much whoop ass in a buck twenty-five?"

Her feelings still jumbled, she tittered, happy to be off the subject of Ravana. "Ninety-five."

He squeezed her arms. "You may have pipes of steel but you ain't no buck-ninety-five."

"Ninety-five pence—and they're titanium."

"Titanium huh?"

"Yes." She flexed her arms, instantly hardening the tissue.

"Damn." He tested them with an additional squeeze. "What about this ass? Is it titanium too?" He swatted her bottom and smothered her giggling protest with kisses.

"Dr. Jack-...Mark...are... you...cat...calling...me?" she stuttered out her words between kisses.

Mark drew his face back. His eyes flashed intensely. "This lion is roaring, and from now on, you call me Marcus."

She sounded it out. "Marcus..."

"That's right. Mark and Dr. Jackson are for the people around here—"

"Or sir," She teased.

"I like the way you say that." He squeezed her bottom in the cradle of his hands.

Flustered, her voice came out breathily. "Yes, sir."

"Pardon?" He swatted her bottom playfully.

She jumped, unable to keep from smiling, enjoying the game. "What are you doing to me, Dr. Jackson?"

"Say my name." He swatted again.

"Marcus."

"How do you feel?"

"Better."

"Only better?"

"More than better."

"I do enjoy a challenge," he declared.

Guardian raised her chin. "En garde."

Marcus pulled her hips tight to him. "Touché."

She giggled. "You speak French."

"Not the way you speak it." He smirked.

She gasped and fanned herself with her hand. "By the stars...."

His smirk faded. He regarded her thoughtfully. "I learned a long time ago, when people are talking shit, what they say is more about them than about you."

"You're a wise man, Marcus."

"Thank you. Now I've got a question for you."

"Yes?"

"Everybody seems to know you by something different. What's your name—your real name?" Marcus dropped his chin to fix her with a penetrating gaze.

"My name? It's…." She took a steadying breath. "Elizabeth—or Betty, but please not Beth or Liz."

He tilted his head back, like a sommelier savoring a particularly good vintage of wine. "Queen Elizabeth…."

She struggled to keep her composure certain he knew what he was doing to her. It was both gratifying and terrifying. "I haven't been called that in centuries."

Marcus cocked an eyebrow. "Queen Elizabeth?"

"Yes."

He looked at her sideways. "Queen?"

"Yes."

"Are you messing with me?"

Guardian simpered and shook her head. "I'm not—I promise I'm not."

"Well tell me then, Queen Elizabeth." He swayed her hips with his hands.

Still pressed to him, she realized how she was affecting him. "After…."

"After what?"

"No. I mean after, I left England my travels led me to Africa and specifically, Niani, the capital of the Malian Empire."

"So, you were a queen in Africa?"

"For a few years."

"How did that happen?" He looked at her with an expression of amused disbelief.

"Well…." she smiled and absentmindedly traced his chest with her fingertips. "As you might expect, there weren't a lot of fair-skinned blondes in that part of the world. A royal official spotted me shopping in the bazaar and took me to meet the

Mansa—or emperor, Musa. We…it was…we fancied each other and after a short courtship, I became his fourth wife…his Golden Queen."

Marcus gave her a self-satisfied grin. "So, I'm taking the Golden Queen of Mali out dancing?"

Elizabeth rolled her eyes. "It was nice to have a family again."

His hands slid up to her hips. "So did you two have kids?"

"We had a palace full but…his other three wives…"

"I get you." He nodded soberly. "You know my family is from that part of Africa. I could be his direct descendent."

"Oh, Mansa Marcus is it?" she teased.

"You know it."

"And you're very cocksure, aren't you?" She groaned inwardly at her choice of words.

"The only way I know how to be. You ready to work?" He took her hand leading the way around his desk.

"Me?" She feigned shock. "I'm going to sit up on that desk and try to keep an eye on those wandering hands."

"You mean magic hands," he scoffed and lifted her by the waist onto the edge of the desk.

As he turned to take his chair, she caught one of his hands. "I do feel better, thank you."

"Don't let them dominate your thoughts."

She shifted in place. "Was there anything new on the asteroid shards?"

Marcus clicked on the computer's mouse and brought up an email to open an attachment. He leaned back to allow her to see. "As of four hours ago this is a catalogue of all the calls that just NASA has received about the asteroid."

"By the stars, there must be thousands of them!"

Marcus stared at the entries, the glow of the screen reflecting off his pate. "Yeah, a lot of people wanting to be famous, like the ones you see in The Spoiler claiming to have seen a UFO."

"I wonder if Russia has had any success, they have eleven time zones, there must be something."

Mark swiveled in his chair to face her. "How do you think that will go over—especially with Longstreet? He seems to have a personal vendetta."

"After watching him talk about a metahuman registry this morning, I spent a few hours researching him."

"Yeah? What'd you find out?"

"He's had some difficult times in his life."

"You and I have both lived long enough to know that everyone has tough times."

"He lost his wife, and two of his assistants have committed suicide."

"Well, that's not suspicious," he muttered.

"And he blames me for the loss of his platoon in the Marine Barracks Bombing in Beirut."

"What?" Marcus sputtered. "Has he lost his damn mind?" "In 1983, I was working at a refugee camp in Beirut and he was a freshly minted Marine lieutenant looking for terrorists. He believed that our camp was harboring them. It wasn't. It was elders, and orphans, and broken families. I did keep an ear out for any kind of terrorist talk and anyone engaging in it would find themselves picked up by Lebanese Police the moment they set foot outside the camp. There was no connection to the bombing and I absolutely forbade his entrance into the camp," she said, recalling their confrontation, "furthermore, the camp administration raised the issue with his commanding officer. I think tragedy has colored his vision but I must try to dissuade him from his plan."

"He's a snake, Elizabeth. He wanted to militarize us. An organization dedicated to the peaceful exploration of space and the sharing of knowledge for the benefit of all."

"And what he proposes is bloody monstrous. Presumption of guilt, guilt by association..." She gestured with her hands before stopping short.

"Yeah."

"I'm sorry." She slid a glove off to press a hand to his cheek and kiss him in apology.

"You've done nothing wrong."

"I haven't done enough, Marcus. But if some kindness can soothe—"

"Kindness? With him?" He sat back in his chair to regard her.

"Perhaps that's what is needed to cool his anger. It doesn't always work but if nothing else it will signal to him that he's not going to change me with his rhetoric or his actions."

"Well, if anyone can change him, you'd get my vote."

She smiled with gratitude. "Thank you."

"When do you plan on doing this? He's setting it all in motion next Monday."

"At the earliest opportunity, in the meantime...Russia."

Marcus swiveled in his chair to face her. "All right, are you just going to drop in on them?"

"No, in the interests of diplomacy, I thought I might call ahead and arrange a talk with their interior minister."

"Just like that?"

"Well as you know, I was a queen." She mugged. "I think a call to the Russian embassy would be a prudent first step."

Marcus picked up the telephone and glanced at the clock. "There should be someone there by now. I'll have Katie put in a call. But Senator Hollywood might use it against you."

"Weren't you the one telling me not to go imagining worst-case hypotheticals?"

"Touché." He chuckled and picked up the desk phone to speak to Katie while reaching out with his other hand to rest it on her knee.

She noted he was looking into her eyes and smiling as he spoke with his assistant and found herself smiling in response while struggling not to bite her bottom lip.

He hung the telephone up. "She's putting in a call."

"Thank you. I lived in Russia you know."

"You weren't a queen there as well, were you?"

She chuckled. "No, just a courtier."

"Do you speak perfect Russian too?"

"Da."

The electronic ring of Marcus' phone interrupted them. Chuckling and shaking his head, he picked it up only to hand it to her. "The Russian embassy."

For many moments, Guardian spoke, first in English before switching to Russian. She smiled into the receiver as the conversation progressed and was forced to use her spare hand to halt Marcus'. He had wound them around her knees and was using his fingertips to draw tiny, maddeningly distracting circles in the tender flesh behind them. It was all she could do to avoid breathing heavily into the ambassador's ear.

"Are you mad?" She asked after hanging up.

"I like what you do to those tights. Pretty, sexy, sophisticated...." He gave her a sideways smile as his hand traced halfway up the top of her thigh. "...mysterious."

She flushed with pleasure. "Do you have any notion as to how difficult it was to concentrate during that call? I mean really! There's a time and a place for...amorous advances." She stopped his hand and smiled despite herself.

"Amorous advances? Is that what I was doing?"

"It's very distracting."

"Come here." He motioned her forward.

She leaned in to oblige him, feeling his hands return to their languid massage. Pressing her lips to his, she felt dizzy as his tongue found hers. Afraid she would fall off the edge of the desk and into his lap, she steadied herself by placing her hands on his shoulders.

After a moment, she broke their kiss and caught her breath. "I don't normally do this."

"Neither do I," he said, still inches from her face.

"I have an appointment to keep." She slid off the edge of the desk.

"I know, but before you go…." He stood up to face her.
"Yes?"
"Give me some sugar." He tapped a finger to his lips.

Thursday, 8:20 AM MIT Lab, Boston, Massachusetts

Dressed like a coed taking a morning run, Elizabeth jogged through the MIT campus in a state of euphoria. Reaching the lab, she stopped outside to ensure Jennifer was alone. Through the heavy wooden door, she could hear the raspy, soulful voice of the artist Pink belting out a song. Listening with a set of ear buds, Jennifer sang along. With a thought, the running gear transformed back to her uniform and she entered the lab.

Jennifer had changed her hair to loose auburn tresses. Spotting Guardian, the scientist charged across the room to throw her arms around her and hug her tight. "I was so worried! Are you okay?"

Touched by her concern, Guardian returned the embrace. "I got him, for her, for them, for me."

"Good."

Guardian pulled back. "Enough about him. I like your hair."

"Thank you. I was thinking we could do a little R&R. You know? A girl's night? Pizza, wine, do our nails, and maybe go see the greatest movie ever at the Boxcar Theatre over on Putnam Avenue?"

"That sounds delightful, when?"

"How about tomorrow night?"

Guardian's face pinched up with the pain of regret. "I'm sorry I can't. You see…." Her expression quickly morphed to glow with enthusiasm. "I have a date!"

Jennifer clasped her friend's arms. "Who is he? What does he do? What's he like? Where is he taking you?"

"Well…his nickname is Magic but—"

Jennifer grinned and playfully rocked her shoulder into Guardian's. "Magic, huh? Are you going to let him saw you in half?"

The thought had occurred. Guardian smiled and touched her tongue to her upper lip. She turned away long enough to find her mobile phone and produce the more dignified picture of the two of them. "This is Marcus. He's a very self-assured, affectionate, and terrifying, engineer."

"Ooo," Jennifer cooed as she looked at the picture and fanned herself, "tall, dark and hunka-hunka, wunka-wunka! But you don't look very terrified in this picture."

"Terrified is a more recent development."

"What did he do?"

"He's asked me to go out for dinner and dancing—

Jennifer regarded her dubiously. "That's not very terrifying."

"It's the afterwards."

"You mean you've never...." Jennifer looked at her with astonishment.

Guardian caught the other woman's look and had to keep herself from laughing at the idea of it. "No, that—that's fun. It's the after-after. You see I haven't had a...a boyfriend, in quite some time...."

Jennifer choked. "You must be ready to swallow your legs!"

Guardian scoffed with exasperation. "My relationships with men are purposefully short with no attachments."

"Because of your unique situation."

"Precisely."

"But this guy has you twitterpated."

"Only when I'm around him, or think about him. And I think I mentioned his voice."

"Wowzers," Jennifer said softly.

"But I'm not sure if they will let this work."

"They?"

Guardian sighed. "The Paparazzi...the gossip mongers. If someone puts us together and it becomes news, it could put him in danger."

"You are going on this date and I'm going to help you. Come by my place, twenty-two and a half Tufts Street. It's a yellow townhouse, only a few blocks from the campus. I'll give you a makeover—a completely different look. And...." Jennifer smiled mischievously. "And you know... a tattoo would add to your disguise."

Guardian rested her wrists on her hips in disbelief. "You're still determined to turn me into an art project, aren't you?"

"Think about it…if people see a tattoo, they'll automatically assume it couldn't be you."

"No disrespect to you, I'd rather not have my arms decorated like a sailor's."

"Not your arms. There are lots of places for ink. I'll make something on my lunch and you can come back and tell me what you think."

"Make what? I haven't even told you what I could possibly want."

Jennifer grabbed the blonde's arm excitedly. "Well think of something! Something sexy, something meaningful."

Guardian tilted her head back in thought. After a moment a whimsical expression appeared upon her face "Well, there is something…."

"Tell me." Jennifer's eyes gleamed.

"Could you do one of Africa?" she asked before going into an expRuthtion of her conversation she had with Marcus about her second marriage and his claims about royalty.

Jennifer took a stool at the laboratory counter and began doodling sketches.

"What do you have there?" Guardian asked, straining to see.

Jennifer tucked the paper into the pocket of her lab coat, "Nothing Your Highness, just some ideas."

"It's Sultana and what have I just agreed to?"

"Sultana?" Jennifer giggled. "Sounds like a kind of cracker."

Guardian smiled in disbelief. "I suppose it does." She gave the folded sheet of paper a final wary look. "So, what is the greatest movie ever?"

"*Close Encounters of the Third Kind*, of course!"

"Close Encounters?" Guardian deadpanned. "Is that a romantic comedy?"

Jennifer's jaw dropped. "What? You can't be serious!" she shrieked. "You've never heard of *Close Encounters of the Third*

Kind! Come on! It's about first contact with an alien species. You *have* to have seen it!"

Unable to keep a straight face any longer, Guardian smirked. "I'm sorry, I'm teasing you. It is a good story—"

"But there aren't really gray aliens?"

Guardian sighed deeply, pressing her lips together pensively.

"Yes? No? What?" Jennifer asked.

"This is your favorite movie…"

"And there's something you don't want to tell me about it. Now you have to." Jennifer grasped the blonde's forearm with both of her hands.

Guardian glanced down at the woman's pawing hands. "Are you sure?"

Jennifer's expression sobered, she removed her hands and nodded her head once. "Tell me."

"There are gray aliens—Zeta-Reticulans. But they aren't the benevolent beings the movie depicted."

"They really do abduct people and do experiments?"

"Not if I can get to them first. You know about the Roswell Incident of 1947?"

Jennifer shrugged. "What Ufologist doesn't?"

"I was assisting on a surgery at the time or that incident would never have taken place. After a handful of them crashed and were taken in by the United States government, others, despite my centuries of warnings to stay away, came looking for them and for more specimens to abduct."

"What do they do when they abduct people?"

"They…they're slowly going extinct as a consequence of generations of genetic modifications. They increased their intellects and life spans at the expense of loss of emotions, and the ability to reproduce."

"They use people to reproduce?"

Guardian shook her head. "No, but they think they can use human genetic material to restore their capacity to reproduce.

To date, they have not been successful."

"We could help them, if they need genetic material, there's plenty of that to be had."

"Speaking of which, I have something for you." Guardian produced the vial Huan's blood. "From a metahuman."

Jennifer held the vial up to regard it intently. "Not a lot but it's enough to get started with. Let me put this in the refrigerator for the moment." She disappeared from sight for a moment before quickly returning.

"Be careful with it."

Jennifer took a seat on a lab stool. "I'll guard it with my life and get to work on it, as soon as you're done telling me about the Grays."

"As I was about to say, they want living specimens not just samples of genes and I will not allow it. The last two I caught I took before an interstellar adjudication board and—"

"Hold on, an interstellar adjudication board?"

"The Earth has twenty-three neighbors capable of interstellar travel, they have a loose federacy that, among other things, settles differences and prosecutes crimes by its member species. I'm an Examiner in this federacy, sort of combination prosecutor and sheriff."

"So, you're a space cop?"

An amused smile ghosted across Guardian's lips. "A version of one I suppose, but as I was saying, the last two I caught were particularly terrible in their conduct. So bad that the adjudicators were inclined to order them into the Void."

"The Void?"

"The Void is a horrible place, cold, and dark."

"Sounds like hell."

"A version of it. The condemned wander alone for an eternity as void wraiths."

"Void wraiths? Seriously?" Jennifer's eyes fluttered.

"Pure evil, and semi-corporeal. I send them back wherever and whenever I find them."

"They're here on Earth?"

"Not many at present; but over the years, I've sent thousands back."

"Thousands?" Jennifer adjusted her glasses. "What do they look like?"

"They resemble shadows. Inky, black, shadows that cackle and hiss with malice. Many of the monsters of human folklore were humans, animals, or even corpses corrupted by a void wraith. They expel the essence and take control of the vessel."

"Vessel?"

"There is more to you than stardust, Jennifer." She regarded her friend thoughtfully.

Jennifer raised a hand to her head. "You're blowing my mind here."

Guardian grimaced. "I apologize, I didn't mean to frighten you or ruin your favorite movie."

"No! This is fascinating, go on."

"Well, with regards to those two, I petitioned the adjudicators not to execute them so they were incarcerated for some decades instead."

Jennifer looked away for a moment. "Wowzers! That kind of changes things."

"I'm sorry to have ruined your favorite movie."

"I'll still watch it, especially with a friendly *off-worlder*, if you want."

"Well, I suppose I could break my date..." Guardian said half-jokingly.

"Shut-up. You're going on that date because I'm already formulating what I'm going to do."

"Be gentle with me."

"When I get done with you, he won't be able to keep his hands off you."

"He can't do that now." Guardian giggled.

"Is he a good kisser?"

"Only in the most intoxicating way."

Jennifer tapped her chin with her forefinger. "Hmm, sounds like I'll need to do all-night makeup."

"You're incorrigible!"

Jennifer waggled her brows. "Come by around five—no four, I really want to do a great job."

"I didn't say I would be spending the night."

"Not according to that flush in your cheeks, but don't worry, Aunt Jennifer will look after you." She turned to go deeper into the lab.

Guardian frantically removed a glove to pat her face. It was warm and seemed to be getting worse.

"What about you? Anyone special?"

"I workout so my relationships don't have to. What's that lipstick called?"

Guardian felt a pang of sadness for her and relented. "It's called Joie de Vivre. I'll pick you up a few tubes the next time I'm in Paris, but for now, I need to get to Russia to talk about a possible meteorite sample."

"And I have work to do, very interesting work."

"And thank you so much for doing it. If we can prevent another Ravana...well, my gratitude will be eternal."

"Heh-heh-heh." Jennifer cackled and rubbed her palms together fiendishly. "What could I do with that?"

Guardian smiled and shook her head. "The truth is out, you're a mad scientist."

"My test results aren't back yet." She grinned wickedly.

The laboratory door swung open. A breeze passed through the room. Bernard stood in the door, a sheaf of newspapers tucked under his arm and an attaché case in his opposite hand. "Good, you're here," he said with an air of urgency.

Jennifer straightened up with a perplexed expression on her face at the sudden disappearance of Guardian. "Where...where did she go?" she asked Bernard before getting up to look around, "Where are you?"

Perplexed, Bernard joined her in the search. "Who are you

looking for?"

"Guardian, she was just here…"

"Still here." The blonde stepped from a hiding place among the cupboards and counters. "Good morning, Bernard," she said brightly.

Bernard advanced on Guardian with his arms outstretched. "Are you all right?"

Guardian felt his arms surround her shoulders and allowed him a brief squeeze. "Thank you, I'm fine."

"You're sure?" He paused to look her over.

Sighing inwardly with frustration, she tried to regain his attention. "Jennifer tells me you've been quite a night owl. Be sure to get your sleep, Bernard."

"Doctor's orders?" he quipped.

"Most assuredly. But show me what's been giving you those dark circles beneath your eyes."

"I put the ingot you brought through the spectroscope. It's extraordinary. My analysis indicates the presence of chromium, nickel, and other elements like carbon and silicon but some of these elements aren't on the periodic table. And the tensile strength…" He shifted his papers to one side and snapped open the clasps on his case.

Guardian caught the headlines of the paper. "*BATTLE OF INDIA*" dominated the top of the page with a side column about Longstreet's metahuman hotline.

"As you can see…." He spread the sheets of a printout on the countertop and pointed to specific lines. "The initial data is astounding."

Guardian lifted the first page and held it so that Jennifer could read along too.

"Yield strength, tensile strength, impact strength…and the results of every other test are beyond any known alloy." He paused to tap another sheet of data. "The uses for this metal could be virtually limitless, cars, bridges and buildings, unsinkable ships, unstoppable tanks."

"I don't think Rudy would have any interest in that." Guardian set the page down.

"Why not? He'd be a billionaire, a multibillionaire with virtually no end to his wealth."

"Because he wants to be normal again, Bernie," Jennifer interjected. "He wants to start a family. Guardian brought me a blood sample from another metahuman to analyze."

"But anyone can do that, only he can do this. Does he even realize this?" Bernard looked at the pair of women almost feverishly.

"Some things are more important than material wealth." Guardian regarded her friend looking for understanding.

"I think he should hear all the facts. Who has him? The army?" The metallurgist held up the sheet and pointed to it emphatically.

"They do, but you can't talk to him."

"Why not? My information is relevant to his condition."

"Because you promised me total discretion?"

"I did." He stroked his chin. "Could you get in to see him?"

"I would rather wait and give him some news about his condition that would give him hope."

"And becoming a billionaire wouldn't do that?"

Guardian spoke in firm, even tones. "When the time is right, when we have more information and it is safe, then you can tell the world and collect a Nobel Prize. In the meantime please keep your promise. You haven't told anyone have you?"

"Just you two."

"Thank you. Please, just us." Guardian reached out a steadying hand to his shoulder. "I'll nominate you to the Nobel Committee myself."

"Maybe keep running analysis to refine your data?" Jennifer suggested.

"That's a wonderful idea, Jennifer." Guardian glanced at the clock. "I'm sorry but I must go, I have an important appointment in Russia." She started for the door.

"Okay, if I don't see you sooner, I'll see you tomorrow at four."

Bernard smiled. "What's tomorrow at four?"

"She has a date." Jennifer grinned.

Guardian's eyes slowly slid shut in a wince. Turning on her heel, she saw a look of confusion on Bernard's face.

Jennifer glanced from one friend to the other.

Bernard cleared his throat. "I didn't think you had time for a date."

"It will probably be cancelled due to some emergency." Guardian gestured and took a step closer. "But you and I are still having dinner—and I'm looking forward to it."

"Show him the picture of the two of you," Jennifer urged.

"I thought you never took pictures."

"I didn't take it but since I've been on the front of every newspaper for days, it didn't seem to matter."

"Show him," Jennifer urged.

Guardian kept her frustration at Jennifer's doggedness from her face as she presented her mobile device's screen.

Bernard adjusted his glasses. "Tall...." He looked back at Guardian. "He kind of reminds me of that doctor you dated back in Nigeria."

Guardian's lips crinkled into a sad smile. "What happened in Nigeria is the reason I don't date where I work."

"Aren't you working with this fellow?" Bernard pressed.

"Not every day, or even very much of any day. I prefer to think of it as...." She searched for a word. "A consulting relationship."

"Consulting? Is that what they're calling it now?" Jennifer needled.

You're not helping. Guardian shot Jennifer a look of reproach. "Behave."

"As long as you don't!" Jennifer giggled.

"Of course. Well, I should uh...get back to my office, there are calls to return, emails to respond to." He hastily collected his lab report and stuffed it into his case.

"Thank you for your help, Bernard, and did you think of a place for us to go to dinner?" Guardian asked hastily.

Bernard snapped his attaché case shut. "I'm still asking around. I'll see you soon—enjoy your date." He strode out of the lab.

As soon as the door clicked shut, Guardian turned back to Jennifer and sighed. "That could have gone better."

"Sorry, I didn't know, but he's a grown man, he has to know that there are others."

"Perhaps in his head, but not his heart. Unless there's an emergency, I'll see you tomorrow at four, and thank you again for your help."

Thursday, 4:50 PM, local time, The Kremlin, Moscow, Russia

Guardian arrived to red carpet fanfare at the Grand Kremlin Palace. A crowd of surprised tourists cheered as the Russian president, Ivan Petrov, greeted her. He escorted her past an honor guard from the Kremlin Regiment while a brass band played Pomp and Circumstance. She paused to wave to the onlookers who were kept well back by a velvet rope and stern-faced security officers.

"Welcome to Russia, did you have any trouble finding the Kremlin?" Petrov asked.

"It was right where I remembered it to be," she quipped good-naturedly.

"So, you've been here on vacation?"

"I lived here at one time, Mr. President."

"Oh? When was this?" he asked.

"During the reign of Alexander the Second, shortly before he emancipated the serfs."

"Really? You must have many stories to tell."

She gestured to their surroundings. "These walls have seen a great deal of history."

"And a great deal of walking."

She laughed at his jest. "But fortunately, the artisans' work is a pleasant distraction." She gestured as they walked with him down a broad corridor of tiger-eye marble floors, soaring white marble columns, and massive crystal chandeliers.

"A very pleasant distraction." He gave her a complimentary glance. "Would you ever consider living in Russia again?"

"I never left, Mr. President."

A look of confusion crossed his face. "I was not aware of this."

Guardian reached to touch his arm reassuringly. "What I

mean to say, Mr. President, is the Earth is my home and its people, my family. Russia is one expansive and beautiful room in that home. It is a room I always enjoy when I visit and miss when I am away."

Petrov's tense expression eased, he chuckled softly. "We are going to the Green Drawing Room for some pictures and a small press conference. If you don't understand a question or are confused, just look to me and I will take over."

"Thank you, Mr. President. I thought we might take some time to discuss—"

"Yes, you had a request. We will address it after the press conference, but please don't mention it to the reporters."

"Of course," she said agreeably while experiencing a sense of dread at another round with the media.

Petrov escorted Guardian into the opulence of a room out of time. Decorated in a Renaissance style, the walls were upholstered in gold brocade and rich jade green flowers. Ornate candelabras and a crystal chandelier provided light. She took a seat in a gilded chair with green silk upholstery. Remembering Marcus' encouraging words, she sat with regal grace, her chin up, shoulders back, ankles crossed and with her hands folded primly in her lap.

Under the glare and flash of the media's lights, Petrov made some remarks of thanks, mentioning her role in saving the International Space Station before inviting questions.

A pale reporter waved a pen at her like a conductor's baton. "You intervened in Mumbai without official authorization. Some are calling you a vigilante. What is your response to that label?"

"I understand this concern. It is my hope and intention to be a good Samaritan rather than an avenger of wrongs."

A second reporter fed off her remark. "The good Samaritan is a parable about being kind, but in this case a man died."

"I sense the light of life in everyone I meet…" She looked slowly across the group, meeting their eyes unflinchingly. "Including all of you here. I grieve when it is extinguished so abruptly. This man took many lives including his own. I mourn not only for those that were lost but for those who were left behind. There was no other choice but to intervene and stop him, to standby and do nothing would have been unconscionable."

"A neighborhood was destroyed in Mumbai, many are wondering, who you and others like you are accountable to? As a follow-up, with all of your powers, should you be registered like a gun-owner must be?"

Guardian refrained from glancing at Petrov and chose her words carefully. "We are all subject to the laws of the nation in which we find ourselves—and again, I can understand the concerns that some might have. But for those that strive for right action it is unnecessary for those who don't, like Ravana, their compliance would be unlikely."

"Mr. President, what measures is your government taking to protect ordinary citizens from the threats metahumans represent?"

Petrov gestured as he spoke. "As it is in all nations, the laws of the state will be respected by all citizens and visitors, and steps will be taken to ensure this."

Other reporters began to ask follow-up questions about the same thing Guardian wondered, *what steps?*

Petrov had his communication secretary and security detail shut the conference down. He stood up and buttoned his suit jacket. "Well, I have a cabinet dinner to discuss recent events so here we must part."

"But Mr. President—"

"Yes of course, your questions. I haven't forgotten. Someone will be along to assist you." He shook her hand before departing with his entourage.

###

Minutes later, feeling used and snubbed, Guardian was escorted out of the Kremlin to the office of deputy minister of Emergency Situations, Ivan Grekov.

The sixty-something senior mandarin was paunchy, thick-jowled and balding. His paneled office smelled of tea, stale tobacco smoke, and cologne. Three steaming glasses of tea in silver podstakanniks, and a polished silver samovar rested upon his desk. A rather severe-looking woman stood to his left and behind him.

Lieutenant Colonel Anna Akulova wore the gray dress uniform of the ministry of internal affairs. Guardian estimated that she was in her mid-thirties. She tried to soften the woman's stony, unblinking gaze with a more neutral expression of her own.

"Thank you for taking this meeting, I have some questions that I hope you're able to answer."

Grekov leaned forward amiably. "Please…we can get to that in a moment, first I would like to begin by discussing your work. We're very impressed by it."

Guardian wondered if he had consulted with the colonel on this blanket statement, but responded cordially. "Your emergency services did the lion's share."

"Your efforts with the meteorites are greatly appreciated but I'm referring to your aid work." He opened a thick manila folder. "Fifteen countries since 1970 or is it sixteen now?

Wondering what all was in the folder, she kept her tone even. "I try to do my part."

"You are too modest. Neurosurgery, trauma surgery, expert in tropical pathologies and pandemics, pediatrics, orthopedics, so many listed here…." He tapped the section he was reading.

"When you're the only doctor present, you do what is necessary."

"You've never worked in Russia however." Grekov set the folder down.

"Not since the reign of Alexander the Second."

"That explains the aristocratic accent." The colonel sniped.

Guardian ignored the attempt at a slight and instead regarded the bureaucrat with good-natured amusement. "Is this a recruiting session, sir?"

"You shouldn't be surprised that we would make the most of this opportunity."

"How did you come to compile such a thick file?"

"Our embassies, but that isn't nearly as important as the positions we could offer you such as chief of staff at the Russian Children's Hospital or dean at our best medical school, The Moscow Medical Academy."

"Two august institutions, I'm flattered."

"Not flattery at all. A doctor of your experience and skill could improve the skills of hundreds if not thousands of doctors."

"Don't underestimate the dedication or skills of your countrymen."

"And you're a skilled diplomat," Grekov said.

"Perhaps now that she is a superhero, medicine is too mundane." The colonel sneered.

Guardian turned her full attention to the security officer. "I'm a damn good surgeon, colonel and I go where the need is the greatest."

Grekov's eyes widened. "Ladies," he stammered, "let's keep this a cordial meeting—"

"I understand you're working at NASA under someone named—"

Guardian's heart froze. "Who's been telling tales, Colonel?"

"Roscosmos has liaisons within NASA and they—we, are quite happy you protected our cosmonaut." Grekov interjected.

"You just couldn't stay away from your dark appetites for long, eh?"

Grekov tried to interject a second time. "NASA is a very prestigious—"

Irked, Guardian cut him off. "My apologies, Mr. Grekov. Colonel Akulova, I'm very concerned about you."

"Oh? Why is that?" The brunette folded her arms across her chest.

"You seem a little pale, regular meals are important for good health and agreeableness."

"My dining habits are of no concern to you."

"Nor should mine be to you."

"Ladies...." Grekov attempted to intervene again. "We can have something sent in if you're feeling peckish."

"I'm fine thank you, Mr. Grekov, but...." Guardian's brow furrowed.

"I doubt she would find our food to her tastes," Akulova said derisively.

Guardian's nose prickled, detecting a more pronounced scent of tobacco smoke in the air. Something was amiss. "Do you smoke, Colonel?"

"No, why?" she asked.

Guardian turned her gaze to the bureaucrat. "Do you, Mr. Grekov?"

"I? No, my doctor convinced me to quit," he said sheepishly.

"Then...." Guardian's voice trailed off, her expression puzzled.

"What is it, Miss Guardian?" Grekov leaned forward.

Extending her senses as she had in Chicago and in Mumbai, Guardian's answer came in an instant. She left her chair in a blur. "This must be the smoker." She halted next to Akulova and reached out in the space beside the woman. She felt a man's shirt. A grunt and shout ensued, then just as quickly, her hand grasped at thin air. "How?" She looked around, puzzled.

"Hello, Legs," a middle-aged man appeared on the far side of Grekov's desk. He grinned at Guardian through a thick, well-kempt beard.

"Master Sergeant Semenov!" The colonel barked.

"You can turn invisible *and* teleport?" Guardian asked, mystified.

"I haven't reenlisted yet, Colonel," the bearded man responded first to the colonel before turning to grin at Guardian. "And yes, I no longer need a car; it makes my commute much faster."

Guardian began to piece things together. "If you're not calling for security, he must—"

"I am security," Semenov declared.

Guardian raised an eyebrow skeptically and gestured to the double row of buttons of Semenov's white coat. "You look like a chef."

"One can't be a paratrooper forever, Legs. Welcome to Russia, Sergei Semenov at your service." He offered his hand.

Guardian took his hand, noting that he surrounded hers in both of his and lingered a moment. "And how did you come to be changed, Mr. Semenov?"

"Call me Sergei."

"Only if you refrain from calling me, Legs."

"Very well. I have no family in Moscow so when the asteroid came, I went to my allotment; it's very beautiful."

"That's enough, sergeant," Akulova warned.

The chef ignored the officer, continuing to smile wolfishly. "Would you come to my garden? I would like to show you to my roses."

Guardian recognized the bit of poetry and clucked with amusement. "Just how often do you quote Sheridan, Sergei?"

"Often enough to avoid starvation." He winked.

"I don't think you're to her taste, sergeant," Akulova said.

Semenov frowned. "Why do you say that, Colonel?"

Guardian turned from Sergei to regard the other two. "How many more have you recruited?"

"That's a matter of national security," the colonel said firmly.

"So, these offers of work were a means to an end?"

"You are a nuclear bomb that needs to be monitored," Akulova said.

"I think the term you want is bombshell, Colonel," Sergei interjected.

"Quiet!" the colonel snapped.

Guardian felt a chill of dread. "You're recruiting a team, aren't you?"

"The Americans are fools. The next war will be fought by the likes of you," Akulova said.

"There are no others like me."

"Different manufacturer, same effect."

"Rubbish; I'm not a weapon."

"I'm sure that beast in India would agree," Akulova said sarcastically.

Ignoring the insult, Guardian turned to Grekov. "Sir, I came here today to ask Russia's help in obtaining a piece of that asteroid to cure those afflicted by this event." She gestured to Sergei.

"I am not afflicted. I..." Sergei protested.

Guardian turned her attention back to the chef. "Sergei once trained you would be the perfect spy, the perfect saboteur, the perfect assassin. Is that what you want?"

"It is the sergeant's privilege to serve his country in whatever legal capacity that is required."

"Slavery was legal, apartheid was legal, the Holocaust legal. If you think forming a group of metahumans to intimidate political opponents or international rivals is legal, you will find me standing in your way."

Grekov shook his head regretfully. "I'm afraid the genie is out of the bottle."

"A Russian genie that will do its country's bidding." Akulova raised her chin haughtily.

Guardian leaned on the desk with her knuckles. "I don't care a whit about nationality. If a metahuman abuses their powers, they will be dealing with me—even someone doing the bidding of a government."

"Russia is a sovereign state, you cannot dictate policy here."

Guardian's tone hardened. "I will do whatever is necessary, Colonel."

"I've heard enough. We're done," Akulova turned to Sergei, "Semenov, take us out of here."

"All right, Boss." He stepped behind the desk to place his hands on the officer and the bureaucrat and in a blink, they were gone.

"Bloody hell," Guardian cursed. She reached out with her cosmic sense but she could not detect them. She turned towards the door.

"Enough of those Piz'duk, eh?" A voice asked from behind her.

"Sergei." A wry smile, creased Guardian's lips. She looked over her shoulder. "Are you going behind their backs?"

"I'm about to."

"What are you playing at?"

"A very dangerous game, if we are caught."

"You have something to tell me?" she asked.

"Not here. I was thinking...my place, over dinner."

"My breakfast is still settling."

"A drink then." He smiled.

"One drink."

He held out his hand for her to take.

"I'm not sure if this will work on me."

His hand closed over hers. "It will."

###

Guardian did not have time to respond. They reappeared inside a disheveled apartment. The previous day's newspaper along with an empty vodka bottle and a dirty ash tray covered the coffee table. A black and white chef's coat was draped over the back of an arm chair.

"We're here." Sergei stepped over then picked up a pair of shoes from the floor. He tossed them to a mat in the entry way.

Guardian's hands rose to rest on her hips as she looked around. The contrast in the furnishings was quite striking. In the kitchen, she saw gleaming, stainless steel appliances. They appeared to be German manufactured. The entertainment center in the living room featured the latest in Japanese electronics. The remainder of the furnishings including the well-worn area rug beneath their feet could best be described as Soviet-era antiques.

Did they give you an enormous salary with your position or did you come by these things by other means?"

"The mafia paid for them."

"I beg your pardon?"

"Come see." Sergei opened the door to a bedroom to reveal bales of cash, vacuum sealed in plastic and stacked shoulder high. Each bale of rubles, dollars, pounds, or euros bore a label with amounts contained within.

Guardian's hand rose to her cheek. She looked at him wide-eyed. "Sergei, there must be millions here—tens of millions."

"That scum won't miss it. And I took fifty-bottles from their cellar too." He chuckled.

"And what do you plan to do with it all?"

"Well, one bottle I intend to share with you and—"

"I meant the money."

"I will buy a house in the country with a big kitchen and a big vegetable garden, and perhaps an orchard. I also gave ten million rubles to the animal shelters and another ten million to the War Veterans Committee, and ten million to each of the orphanages in Moscow—I had no idea so many children lacked families to take care of them."

Guardian became sympathetic. "Yes, it seems to be a problem everywhere and it also seems you've become a sort of a modern-day Robin of Loxley, haven't you?" Seeing his puzzled expression, she quickly added, "Robin Hood."

"Just doing what I thought you would do."

Her eyes softened. "What a kind thing to say and do."

"Come...let's get that drink, then I want to show you something else." He led the way into kitchen and delved into the depths of the new refrigerator. "What do we have...let me see..."

Elizabeth heard the clink of bottles.

"This—this will do." He drew forth a green bottle.

Guardian's brows rose as she read the label, a 1959 Dom Perignon Rosé. A single bottle could auction for as much as the cost of a new automobile. "Are you a sommelier too, Sergei?"

"A good chef knows the right wine for each dish and a good host knows the right drink for every occasion."

"Then I'm flattered." She watched as he popped the cork and poured out two glasses.

He handed her one and raised his to touch it. "Za Vstrechu."

"And so, begins a friendship." She sipped from her glass, feeling the bubbles tickle her nose.

He touched her glass again and held her gaze. "And to the beautiful lady present."

"Thank you. What did you want to show me?"

"The wall of heroes." Thrusting the bottle into an ice bucket, he led her towards a collection of framed photographs. "My grandfather fought in the Great Patriotic War, my father in Afghanistan, and that one is of my brother and me."

Taking a sip of her drink she noted that Sergei had but one medal compared to his well-decorated relatives. "What was your medal for?"

"One more moment." He left her to disappear into the apartment's master bedroom and returned after a moment to hand her the medal in a frame. "Shooting." He chuckled. "There aren't many feats of bravery inside army kitchens. But now I can do great things."

"I'm sure you've made a difference to people long before you came to be able to move around with a thought."

"Not that I can remember, but now everyone will remember me."

Guardian kept feelings of pity from her face. "May we sit?"

"Anywhere you like."

Guardian sank into the sofa and well aware of his attention, crossed her legs. She watched him sit down next to her with scarcely less than half an arm's length between them. She felt his gaze rise to her face. Sweeping her hair back, she exposed her neck and smiled at him. "Sergei, tell me…"

"What? What can I tell you?" He smiled wolfishly.

"Just how many has Colonel Akulova recruited to the team?"

"Ah." He tilted his head back and chuckled. "Six, so far…"

"And what can they do?"

"One is like you, strong, bulletproof and he can fly, another one can fly and can create fire out of thin air, another one can turn into animals. All of us are different."

"Do you know if they found any pieces of the asteroid, Russia received more hits than any other."

He shrugged. "I don't know. Sorry."

"Sergei, I need your help with something."

"Name it." He leaned closer.

"Not everyone who gained powers wants what you want. Some don't want to have powers at all."

"Are they crazy? It's the best thing that could happen to anyone."

"Not everyone shares your view. Some want to be normal again."

"I'm not sure I can help with that."

Tilting her head, she regarded him for a moment, calculating what it would take to change his mind.

"Tell me," he began, "do you have a husband?"

She noted his lack of wedding ring. "Not for a long time."

"But you do like men? Don't you?" He sipped his champagne.

"Of course, I do!" She laughed. "Men are lovely, or I mean, noble and charming, and very helpful when one wishes to dance."

"Did I mention I'm an excellent dancer?"

"I thought you might be." She tittered.

"Shall we put on some music?" He lifted a remote. "I have satellite radio, anything you like."

"Classical." She picked something she felt might be safe and instantly cringed as the dulcet notes of Saint-Saens' Mon coeur s'ouvre a ta voix, filled the room. The aria was from the opera, *Samson and Delilah*, a story of how Delilah strove to gain the secret to Samson's strength. Despite her misgivings, a second look at his thick black hair, give her an idea.

"May I refill your drink?" Sergei lifted the bottle in offering.

"Thank you," she held out her glass, and watched him first refill hers, then his own. They toasted again before she set her glass down. "Sergei, will you excuse me a moment?"

"Of course." He watched her. "Perhaps we'll dance when you return."

She turned to smile over her shoulder. "Perhaps."

"Do you mind if I put something else on?"

"Not at all." She kept walking for the bathroom.

In contrast to the rest of the apartment, the bathroom was mid-twentieth century Soviet era in its fixtures: simple, serviceable, and plain. Guardian turned on the faucets to cover the sounds of her search as she looked for a hair brush, a tooth brush or a razor that would have traces of Sergei's cells and thus his DNA. She planned to abscond with one of them, reasoning he could easily replace it without more than a moment's inconvenience. There was nothing on the sink but a new bar of soap. The only item on the bathroom's single shelf was a neatly folded hand towel. She frowned, finding it odd.

Her index finger rose to her lips to tap them contemplatively.

Guardian re-emerged into the living room but did not see her host. The champagne glasses and ice bucket were missing from the coffee table and the beautiful melodic figures of Ravel's Bolero filled the apartment. "Sergei?" she called out.

"In here." His voice carried from the bedroom.

Guardian pushed open the door and beheld Sergei in bed. His chest bared, he lay propped up on one elbow, his lower half covered by a sheet. Groaning inwardly, she folded her arms across her chest and leaned against the doorframe. "Well, isn't this a sight?"

"Thank you. But you haven't seen the most impressive sight of all." He patted the space beside him, "Shall we dance?"

Guardian scoffed and tilted her head to one side. "You know, I'm not offended by sex, just by your presumption of it."

He gave her the same wry smile he had in Grekov's office. "Not offended? That's a beginning."

Guardian's chest rose and fell as she released a great sigh. "I must admit this began as quite a neat plan on your part, playing on my sympathies, orphans, elders, stray animals. The exquisite champagne, the family angle, but this was a set up, wasn't it? Where are the cameras?" She craned her neck looking at the dresser and the clock radio. "I just cannot believe—"

"All of those pictures are real. As is my medal."

"And which agency do you work for? Never mind, we're done." She threw up her hands in exasperation and turned on her heel to go.

Sergei appeared before her, holding up his hands in supplication. "Please...."

Guardian glanced down at his naked, half-risen form and groaned. "Sergei, I may be a physician but this isn't a clinic. Cover yourself."

Sergei blinked out and back in the expanse of two seconds. When he reappeared, he was tying a sheet around his waist.

"Come back. We can help one another. I have things you want and you have things that I want." He reached out to take her wrist.

Guardian's eyes flashed with anger. "Mind yourself, Sergei, before I dip *your* bottle in that ice bucket."

Sergei's hand jerked back. "All right."

"You know, I've dealt with plots and schemes long before Ivan the Terrible, and you were doing well but expecting me to share your bed so soon? Poorly played, Sergeant Semenov—if that even really is your name."

"It's Major. And what can I do to convey my sincerest apologies?"

"That room full of money? Donate it. All of it. Give it to the orphans, and the elders, and the strays."

"And if I do this?"

"The world will be a better place."

"And how will you feel about me?"

"This is only supposed to be one drink and you've had it. Goodbye, Sergei Semenov." She pushed past him.

"You're wrong about me."

Gripping the door's knob, she hesitated for a moment. "Then prove it. Good afternoon." She exited the apartment and headed for the stairs to the roof.

10:55 AM, The Russell Building, Washington DC

Over the centuries Elizabeth learned, no matter where you were, if you looked and acted like you belonged, people would assume you did. The blonde sat on a bench across from the Russell Building, feigning a telephone conversation on her mobile while watching visitors enter and exit from its main entrance. She wore a navy-blue skirt suit, matching pumps, frameless glasses, and had pulled her hair back and folded into a barrette. The one crucial item she was missing was a lobbyist identification badge. They hung from clips on visitors' breast pockets or from lanyards.

After spending many moments scrutinizing the details of the critical item, a lanyard formed around her neck. Picking up her purse and attaché case, she crossed the street to breeze through security and onward towards her destination.

Her heels clicked a purposeful, staccato beat on the corridor's gray and white marble floor before coming to a halt at the door of Rupert Longstreet's outer office. The entrance was flanked by the flags of the United States and Louisiana. Turning its brass knob, she stepped inside and caught the tail-end of a conversation.

"It's all right mama—no, it's no trouble I'll pick up your chemo meds on my way home but I've got to go…that's right, work. Goodbye Mama…love you too," the young secretary said patiently into the telephone before hanging up.

Elizabeth felt genuine sympathy for the young woman ensconced behind the office's counter. Assuming a cordial expression, she spoke as she advanced upon her, reading the desk placard as she did. She set her case down at her feet. "Good morning, I'm here to see Senator Longstreet."

"I don't recall seeing an appointment scheduled this morning but let me have a look," Shannon Kerr, as identified by her own Senate ID, said. She turned to her computer clicking her mouse to negotiate to Longstreet's schedule. "What was the name, ma'am?" Shannon glanced upwards.

"One moment, allow me to get you my card," Elizabeth sank down out of sight, to remove her glasses, fix her hair and commanded the symbiote to revert to her uniform. She stood back up and smiled. "Then again, perhaps I won't need it?"

Shannon's hand rose to her mouth. "Oh my gosh! I never imagined...it—it's you!" she stammered then laughed.

"It's lovely to make your acquaintance, Shannon." Guardian smiled congenially and offered her hand.

The secretary gasped, accepting Guardian's handshake, lingering in duration. "How did you know my name...?" Her wide-eyed expression morphed into a sheepish cringe. She opened one eye, tentatively. "My placard?"

"It's terribly convenient," Guardian quipped. "I do apologize for arriving unannounced but fame makes moving about discretely rather difficult."

"No need to!" Shannon beamed. "This is just such a surprise—an honor!

"The honor is mine."

"Sorry for gabbing on. You're here to see the senator, aren't you?"

"If I might?"

"Just...just wait right there." She held up finger in a momentary gesture. "Just wait right there, please. I'll be right back." Not taking her eyes from Guardian, she inched her way backwards, finding the knob to the inner office door before disappearing behind it.

Guardian examined her surroundings as she waited. Besides the reception desk, there were two other desks in the outer office along with a copier and a pair of comfortable leather sofas for visitors. Helping herself to one of Shannon's business cards, she frowned upon hearing Longstreet voice through the wall. He was barking a rebuke.

"What the hell were you thinking!" Longstreet demanded. "You're putting your job and your mama's health in jeopardy Blondie—and after I pulled some strings to get her on your health plan too!"

"I'm sorry, sir—"

"Sorry, sir—sorry, sir," he mocked in a sing-song voice. "You better shape up, girlie, or you'll be out on the curb."

"It won't happen again, sir."

"You're goddamn right it won't. Now smile like me." He beamed in a way that could only be described as plastic.

Shannon hesitated.

"Smile," he growled softly, never losing the grin.

Shannon pasted on a similar expression.

"Good. Now get her in here."

Shannon returned to the outer office to hold the door open. "Senator Longstreet can see you now."

Guardian noted the subdued expression on the other woman's face as she passed her. "I'm so sorry," she whispered softly.

Rupert Longstreet rose from behind his desk, an ebullient expression upon his face. "Bridgette! How long as it been?"

Not long enough. "I haven't been Bridgette for quite a few years now."

"But you're still lovely as ever! You've lost that charming Irish lilt, though." He crossed the office, his arms opened to embrace her.

Guardian retreated half a step and guided his outstretched arms down into a handshake. "Hello, Rupert," she said politely. She found his emotional transformation from fury to joy, disconcerting but kept it from her face.

"'Hello Rupert' she says. I'm hurt. Kiss it better?" Still

holding her hand, he leaned in.

She turned her face at the last moment to avoid his lips.

"No? Then how about an obscene prescription?"

How about a course of Cyproterone to reduce that libido? "I would prefer to keep this on a friendly basis, thank you."

A look of irritation briefly crossed his face before vanishing just as quickly. "Mm...." He sniffed the air. "You still wear rosewater. I'll never forget waking up to that."

Recalling only dinner and a walk on the beach, Elizabeth decided not to challenge his recollection. "I've been reading about you in the newspapers."

His eyes glittered as he looked her over, "And I've been seeing you everywhere. I have to say...." He shook a finger at her. "I'm a little jealous of all the attention you've been getting. That was a nice shtick with those two little Black kids—but pro-tip, don't do it when the news cycle is going to shift. The whole story gets lost in the fuss."

Guardian kept her annoyance from her face at his cynicism. "You mustn't be so modest, Rupert. What do they call you? Senator Hollywood?" She gestured to the wall covered in photos, framed awards, and plagues of frosted glass or wood. "A lifetime of accomplishments."

"This one I'm particularly proud of," he strode to the wall and tapped a black wood plaque inlaid with gold. "The United States Film Critics Award, for acting."

Feigning interest, Guardian leaned in to examine it a little closer before stepping back. "Congratulations and there are so many others here. INB's Newsmaker of the Year...I wonder who will win it this year?"

"Probably not someone who cavorts with the Russians, you need to demonstrate more discretion."

"I am nothing if not discrete."

Longstreet gestured to her cape and sneered. "Yes, very

discrete."

Mildly peeved at herself for leaving him an opening she carried on. "To respond to your concern, I intend to meet with all the political leaders of the world. Were you hoping to be my first?"

"I know there were quite a few before you got to me."

Guardian frowned. "Let's keep our discussion in good taste, shall we?"

"What were you talking about with that Russkie anyway?"

"Current events." She turned her attention back to the awards. "The Louisana's Chamber of Commerce Award of Appreciation, six Senator of the year awards—congratulations! And seven Grey & Steele, Protector of America awards—"

"Eleven, there are a few more down here," he tapped the wall below her waist.

"Grey and Steele. You were executive vice president of research and development for them, weren't you?"

"You've been doing your homework."

"I told you. I've been reading." Her eyes softened. "I was so sorry to learn about your wife, Eleanor."

Longstreet frowned. "We only talk about her when I want to talk about her. Now what do you want?"

She gave him a penetrating look. "I've been watching the news and I want you to stop this thing you've started. This...this campaign of fear."

A flush of heated color appeared on the Senator's cheeks. "I suppose if you're bulletproof it's not much of a concern but these freaks—"

"People," she interjected.

"You and your bleeding heart," he spat. "Did you forget about what happened in Chicago? That cop has a wife and kids."

"I haven't forgotten Rupert, nor have I forgotten the

teenager I met yesterday whose home has been vandalized, or another girl who would have likely been killed because of irrational prejudices—prejudices that you're helping to propagate."

He strode to his desk to rest a hand atop his computer's monitor. "Two you say? I've got thousands—no tens of thousands of letters demanding something be done."

She straightened up. "The Earth is under my protection, Rupert. If there's an—"

"Is it now? You're doing a piss-poor job at it, China Doll."

Guardian recognized his old pet name for her. "You lost the privilege to call me that, decades ago."

"And you're rapidly losing the privilege to be in my office."

Guardian sighed and touched the tip of her tongue to her upper lip in thought. "All those years ago and what happened...it would haunt anyone."

"And if you—"

"Rupert...." She looked him in the eye. "I'm asking you to be the person you needed when you were hurt, not the person who hurt you. Act from your heart, not from your pain."

Longstreet stared straight at her for a few seconds before throwing his head back and laughing derisively. After several seconds his expression hardened. "You think you're the good guy? Come on, Blondie, how many could you have saved when you decided not to..." He held his fingers up in air quotations, "'Act from your heart'? What a bunch of clap trap."

Elizabeth felt her argument slipping away. "I see it now...you're using this issue, like you use people, to advance your own ends. It's no secret that you want to be president."

"Will be president, you ditzy blonde."

Guardian's face puckered with annoyance. "People are not like...like..." She glanced about and spied an award from the Coal Alliance of America and plucked the chunk of polished coal glued to its surface. "Are not like this lump of coal, something to be used up for your ends." Guardian closed her hand around the black rock. It crackled. Her hand tensed then shook. "They're like diamonds, each of them wondrous and beautiful." Her hand opened to reveal an opaque, rough white diamond.

"Is that supposed to intimidate me?"

Guardian groaned with frustration. "I'm trying to reach you, Rupert. These are real people, with real families. Don't you dare try to hurt them."

"Or else what?"

Guardian strode towards Longstreet.

He moved to put his desk between them.

"Or else..." She closed her fist over the diamond. It crackled. Sparkling white dust hissed through the bottom of her fist to form a tiny pile on edge of his desk. "I'll stop you."

Longstreet bristled. "I can have you arrested for that."

"For littering?"

"For threatening a United States senator."

She leaned across the desk. "Halt this poisonous campaign, Rupert."

"It's Senator. Whatever we had is dead and buried. Now get out!"

"This isn't over, *Senator*." She started for the door.

"I'll see every one of you alien freaks locked up!" He thundered.

"Well at least I know your game now."

"Get out!"

Pulling the door shut behind her, Guardian paused and pressed her back to its surface. She drew a calming breath. *So much for kindness.*

Shannon looked at her with concern.

"He's rather difficult, isn't he?" Guardian said wryly.

"He's under a lot of stress."

"That's hardly an excuse." Guardian walked around to stand before Shannon's desk. "But I am so very sorry about what happened earlier."

"It's all right."

"It's not all right, not one bit, and I'd like to help you."

"Help me?" She nervously glanced at Longstreet's door.

Guardian rested her gloved hands on the countertop. "There are situations in life we will endure out of love that we would otherwise refuse to be part of."

Shannon gave her a look of puzzlement. "I'm not sure I follow, ma'am?"

"I must apologize, but I overheard the last bit of your telephone conversation with your mother and I'd like to offer a second opinion—without charge of course."

Shannon's eyes fluttered. "Oh! But my mother has a good oncologist."

"I'm sure they're competent but there are options that she might not be aware of—options far superior to chemotherapy, such as immunotherapies, checkpoint inhibitors, medicine that can be tailored specifically to your mother's genetic makeup and the makeup of her cancer. If..." an image of Rudy came to mind.

"If, ma'am?"

"I'm sorry; I was thinking of another patient that these therapies might help. But to my original proposition, do you think your mother would be amenable to a second opinion?"

"Well..." Her gazed darted to the inner office door again. "I think she'd be thrilled to meet you. Could you come for dinner? It's chicken night."

"Chicken sounds delightful."

"This is so exciting!" Shannon scribbled on the back of one of her business cards and handed it to Guardian. "This is my address and my cell in case you have an emergency and can't make it. Is seven o'clock, all right?"

"Seven o'clock. I'll bring the wine."

11:15 AM, New York City

Disappointed but not surprised by Longstreet's rejection of her request, Guardian flew for Boston and Jennifer. She wondered what the scientist would think of checkpoint inhibitors in the case of Rudy. Jennifer wasn't an immunologist but she might have some thoughts on using Rudy's immune system to heal him—if it still functioned in a conventional fashion.

As she flew, she checked Harold's program for any metahuman related emergencies. There was a text message from Ruth Atkinson, with a number and a message to call her. Finding a rooftop where she would be out of the wind, she waited to be connected.

"I have some bad news for you," Ruth Atkinson began to say.

Guardian felt a pinprick of fear. "Is Melanie all right?"

"We've been in contact with the public defender in Shasta County. Melanie wasn't booked at the sheriff's station; she was immediately taken into custody by the military."

She recalled Longstreet's declaration about jailing metahumans and the pin prick became an icy dagger, as she imagined the happy-go-lucky coed imprisoned and alone, in a cold, gray, cell. "They must have already been in the area looking for her. I should have stayed."

"You couldn't have known."

She cursed herself. "I should have anticipated. I'm frightened for her. You've got to get her out."

"Just try to remain calm," Ruth said in a voice long practiced in soothing clients, "we've filed a writ of habeas corpus in federal court."

"I could fly out there right now."

"I don't think it would help. The judge is still in deliberations, but if she is deemed a national security threat, it could be denied."

Guardian's face flushed with anger. "National security threat? What nonsense! She's sweet, selfless, girl."

"I understand how you feel, but if our writ is denied because of jurisdictional issues, we'll go before the Judge Advocate General. In the mean time, she does have a right to counsel, we'll get in to check on her and start building her defence."

"It's just such nonsense."

"Obviously the military feels it's something more."

Guardian's whole body clenched right down to her toes in frustration. "I'm not even sure her parents know where she is."

Ruth scribbled a note to herself as she talked. "We should be able to track them down."

"Thank you." Guardian's eyes flitted from side to side as she considered where Melanie could be. "The Army Medical Research Institute and the Air Force Office of Special Investigations were the lead agencies in Chicago."

"We'll bear that in mind." Ruth made more notes.

"Please advise me the moment you know anything— anything at all."

"Of course. On an unrelated note, I have some news for you about a publicist." Ruth read the front of a business card. "His name is Geoff Joel, but he prefers to be called Gee-off."

"Gee-off?"

"Yes, he operates the Front Row Talent Agency." She continued with his contact details.

"How do you know him?"

"We got him and two of his clients off with misdemeanors after they were arrested at an Occupy Wall Street protest. He's an acquired taste, but he does an enormous number of charity functions and represents quite a list of A-list celebrities. He's expecting you."

"I just care that he's competent and ethical."

"I understand. He's all of that and he's quite media savvy."

"I wonder if he could raise the media profile of Melanie's case."

"With you as her advocate, I think that would be child's play."

The frosted glass of the talent agency's door rattled as Guardian closed it behind her. Geoff Joel's waiting room was tastefully furnished with brown leather sofas, a coffee bar and silver screen movie posters in Art Deco frames. At the reception desk, half hidden by a trio of computer monitors, a receptionist clattered away at a keyboard.

The receptionist, Kelton Campbell, bronzed, fit and sharply dressed was identified by his desk's name plate.

The hardwood floor creaked softly beneath the track carpet as she approached him.

Seemingly unaware of her presence, the receptionist carried on with his keystrokes.

Perplexed at what was so engrossing, Guardian glanced at the monitors but they were covered in black privacy screens that prevented anyone but the person sitting in front of them from reading the content. Unwilling to wait any longer she began to speak up. "Good morning, I'm here to see Gee-off." Inwardly she hoped she had the pronunciation correct.

Kelton halted his work and turned to look her over. "We don't represent impersonators." His chair creaked as he turned to continue his typing.

Mildly annoyed, Guardian kept her expression congenial. "I'm not an impersonator." She paused to pinch the lip of his desk to raise it several inches off the floor before lowering it again. "And I believe Gee-off is expecting me."

"Excuse me," Kelton rose from his desk. "I'll see if he's available," he muttered, rose from his chair and moved towards the inner office.

"Thank you kindly." Guardian watched him go into the inner office without knocking.

Cocking an ear she heard a second voice hastily end a telephone call followed by an admonishment about knocking first.

Muffled footfalls on a carpet signaled someone was approaching the door and then it opened.

Perfectly tanned, slightly less than average in height, and in his mid-thirties, Geoff Joel's Irish linen suit was without a wrinkle and accented with a turquoise tie, pocket handkerchief, and spectacle frames.

"Ruth told me to expect you and I'm delighted—no, thrilled to finally meet you." Geoff beamed. "Kelton, send three dozen white teacup roses over to Atkinson, Marble and Woolfolk and have them write on the card...." He raised a halting finger. "On second thought, I'll take care of it."

Kelton stepped past them without a glance.

"Come in! Come in!" Geoff warmly slipped a hand into the crook of her arm to escort her inward. "I love this look, love the cape, love the boots, love the tights—but most of all, I love what you do!"

Amused by the contrast of the two men, Guardian allowed him to guide her inside.

"I read you worked at the free clinic in Harlem."

"By the stars, that was during the civil rights era."

"Well, people are still talking about it—and no publicity is bad publicity. We were so impressed Front Row Talent sent a cheque off this morning—well I did at least." Geoff pushed the door shut with his heel. "By the way, did Kelton offer you anything? Mineral water? Cappuccino? Latte?"

"We never spoke quite long enough to get to that, but I'm fine." She glanced over her shoulder. "He seems quite reserved for a receptionist."

"You're very kind, but my Pygmalion is really just one step shy of being rude."

"Your Pygmalion...?"

"My latest project. Do you know the story of Pygmalion? It's like My Fair Lady..."

In the interests of time she decided not to bring up the differences in the stories. "I'm familiar, yes. But you're trying to—"

"Trying to make a silk purse out of a software engineer."

Guardian gave him a puzzled smile. "If you don't mind me asking—"

"Why the attempt at alchemy? It's a long story but let's just say the three of us have more than just Ruth in common. We share an outlook on standing up for the underdog and have been bitten for it." Geoff ushered her to a guest chair before walking around his desk to take his own.

"Ruth did mention a brush with the courts."

"More like a flick—at least for me. They were a little harder on Kel." Geoff lowered his voice conspiratorially. "He exposed some muckety-mucks by hacking them but on the upside, thanks to Kelton, it's never happened to us—or any of our clients."

Guardian's eyebrows rose with alarm. "Did he hurt anyone?"

"Oh, he didn't embezzle funds or anything. He just hijacked their emails to send some mass messages."

"What sort of messages?"

"The embarrassing type about misdeeds, personal and professional—mostly professional. That said, he's been an absolute vault of discretion when it comes to our clients." Geoff made a zipper motion across his lips.

"I'm glad I don't have email."

"Yes, I saw on the news you said you don't have a web presence—at least not one of your own."

"What do you mean 'one of my own'?"

"Darling, Google your name, the hits are in the millions—if not billions. But you have no control over the message, that's where I come in."

"I'm not really comfortable with any of this but may we discuss something more pressing?"

Geoff propped his elbows up on the desk and knitted his fingers together in a bridge to rest his chin upon. "How can I make your life better?"

"Hate, Gee-off." She saw his expression of concern and continued on, "Fear and ignorance are germinating it in the media and I want your help to nip it in the bud."

"Yes," he said sympathetically. "Disinformation works because it creates an impression and accuracy doesn't matter. Then reporting on the disinformation spreads the impression. And even debunking can spread the impression. We in the media have to find a way not to be accomplices. So far...." He grimaced, his shoulders rising and falling as he sighed deeply.

"It's not your fault and it's not the first time I've had to deal with rumors and speculation Geoff—forgive me, Gee-off. But I'm referring to the people who are already struggling with suddenly becoming metahumans. They are also becoming the subjects of unprovoked hate. With the exception of a few cases..." She recalled an unpleasant image of Ravana. "It is completely unwarranted."

"Yes, we need to humanize them—and you as well."

"Humanize is exactly it. I want to help these people, return them to normal, return life on this planet to what it was before." Her mind went to Issa and Juma, "And get back to my life."

"You're going to leave us?"

"Well not leave you, I'll still be here; I just won't be flying around in this cape." She paused to fluff it, "You see, I have patients that need me."

"Patients? I mean—" His shoulders sank as he sighed. "I don't want anyone to be sick but you can't do that. You can't go. We need you." Geoff came around his desk, to take the chair beside her.

"I'm sorry but the world managed to muddle through before it knew about me, it will manage again."

Geoff paled visibly "But..." Gritting his teeth, he threw up his hands and shook his head as if to clear it. "No. No you can't— you absolutely can't."

"Geoff—Gee-off, once this matter is settled, I—"

Geoff latched onto her forearms with both hands. "Don't you realize the difference you make? Even when you're not there to see it? You're an example for us—for all of us. You inspire us to be our best selves—to stand up in the face of the storm when all we want to do is run. To not look the other way but reach out, to lift someone up, to do what's right. The world is a better place because you're in it. You bring out the hero in people. We need you."

Guardian trembled at the warmth bubbling up in her heart. Unable to withstand his look of desperation, she turned her gaze toward the window until her vision began to blur. Dabbing her eyes, she took a ragged breath and swallowed the lump in her throat. "Thank you, Geoff—Gee-off. That's very kind of you to say."

"Then you'll stay?"

"You've given me more to consider."

His expression became one of elation. "That's all I ask!" He glanced down at his hands and released her arm, giving it one final pat. "Now let's get to work on your media campaign." He held up his hands like he was framing a placard. "A Campaign of Courage."

"My campaign of courage?" She wrinkled her nose and shook her head with displeasure. "No, that doesn't sound quite right."

"A campaign of heart, that sounds better and still sends a message of courage."

"Yes.," She nodded. "I quite like that."

"Leave it to me!" He enthused. "We'll get you on all the late-night talk shows, the two Jimmys, Seth, Conan, Stephen—Graham over in the UK..." He reached to pull his keyboard across the desk to type his ideas onto an open word processor document.

"Talk shows?" she asked dubiously.

"I work with the producers all the time! The host says a couple of nice things, tells a couple of good-natured jokes, you spread your message, and bing-bam-boom, it's over in eight minutes."

"Well..."

"Don't worry, I'll handle everything, a website, a hashtag—"

"Hashtag?" She asked warily. Ever since the invention of the camera she had managed to stay out of their lenses and now within one week she was about to become some sort of media diva.

His blue eyes were almost feverish. "Just leave it to me and we'll adjust it any way you want."

"As long as it doesn't take me away from more important things. Speaking of which..." She reached for her mobile device to check Harold's program. As the device found a signal, it vibrated in her hand. "I have a message, my apologies but I should find out what this is." She brushed the hair back and lifted the phone to her ear.

"Of course, darling," Geoff rose from the chair and returned to his desk.

It was a message from Kate Tekakwitha. As she listened, Kate's words thundered in her head. Chilled to the marrow and blanched white, she trembled as she rose.

Geoff stood up, his face filled with concern. "What's wrong?"

"Everything." She ran to the window and threw up the sash. The entire building shook as she roared off into the sky.

Sean Ramos was in the lobby of the Cumberland Foundation.

11:35 AM Offices of the Cumberland Foundation, New York City

Standing in front of a restroom mirror one floor above the offices of the Cumberland Foundation, Elizabeth's complexion changed from ghostly white to volcanic red as increasingly frightening scenarios played out in her mind. She imagined the ratings hungry media descending on aid camps, destroying decades of good work, or worse children being kidnapped from the camps for the purpose of revenge or extortion.

Her human half was taking over; like a mother bear she was ready to devour Ramos for threatening her cubs. She clenched her fists so intensely that cracking of her knuckles sounded like the collision of billiard balls. It was enough to shake her from her ruminations.

She caught sight of herself, the feral expression looking back at her was far too intense to convincingly play the role of the jet-setting dilettante, Charlotte Cumberland. She needed to put on the performance of a lifetime.

The reporter had appeared in the lobby of the Cumberland Foundation claiming financial irregularities with the charity's finances. Under the threat to expose them to the Internal Revenue Service and the world in his article, he asked for comment before he handed the story in to his editor.

Granted an interview with Kate, he was unsatisfied with her response and demanded to speak with a member of the Cumberland family. As Charlotte was the only member of the family Kate had access to, an urgent and apologetic call had been placed and 'Charlotte' responded.

Now with her hair in a neat bun and wearing a designer navy-blue wrap dress, Elizabeth took several deep breaths to get into the persona of Charlotte. If Ramos was astute enough to track her down, it was probable he would detect her fear and it would be like blood to a shark, confirming his suspicions and inspiring a feeding frenzy from every news outlet in the world—not to mention how much it would delight Rupert Longstreet. She quaked at the thought of what he would do with such information.

Compartmentalizing her emotions like she would before a major surgery, Elizabeth lifted a pair of frameless glasses to her face and left the restroom for the charity's office.

Sober-faced, Elaine extended a greeting to Elizabeth before directing her attention to Ramos' presence.

The reporter sat in one of the lobby's chairs, his ankle crossed over his opposite knee. He wore a summer-weight sports coat over a button-down shirt and blue jeans. Hearing Elaine's greeting, he turned his gaze from the lobby television to Elizabeth.

Elizabeth forced a pleasant expression. *En-garde. No. To hell with it, the gloves* are *off. He had better be prepared for brass knuckles.* She began to cross the room.

Ramos' eyes glittered as he rose from his chair to buttonhole her. "We meet again."

"Have we met, sir?" she asked with feigned innocence.

He smiled with the confidence of a cat in the presence of a canary. "We have."

"It would seem you have the advantage of me."

"That's no small feat."

"Indeed."

"I'm Sean Ramos, the reporter from The Spoiler?" He offered his hand.

She kept her objections from her face and shook it in a perfunctory manner. "Why would you ever wish to assume such a nefarious title or vocation, Mr. Ramos?"

"Nefarious isn't the word I would use. But I'm not here to discuss my occupation but yours, more particularly…I'm here to ask you some questions about this foundation and about your role in its front-line operations."

"Front-line operations, Mr. Ramos?"

"Were you aware that, according to my research, the superhero known as Guardian has been involved in projects funded by this Foundation?"

"Well, how fortuitous, but at any given time my family's foundation funds dozens of community aid projects around the world—including some right here in America."

"Yes, like Ark of Hope—the same place she took that homeless man." He leaned in and murmured, "I know who you are."

"Do you now?" she said with thinly veiled annoyance, "so, few can truthfully make that claim."

He kept his voice low. "The steps you've taken to conceal things are nothing short of impressive."

Elizabeth's eyes flicked over him. "The right to be let alone is indeed the beginning of all freedom. Do you know who said that, Mr. Ramos?"

He shook his head. "No, I'm afraid I don't."

"Justice William Douglas."

"Well, I'll do you one better with Scott Howard Phillips, and I quote: 'You can't pick and choose which types of freedom you want to defend. You must defend all of it or be against all of it.'"

Her expression hardened. "Yes, and?"

"Are you against the freedom of the press?" He glanced at Elaine. "Or the people's right to know, *Ms. Cumberland*?"

She resented the arrogance and sarcasm in his tone. "It would all depend upon if it was both the truth and that in knowing that something would be so essential that causing great harm to defenseless innocents would be justifiable."

"Defenseless innocents?"

She resisted the urge to poke him in the chest for emphasis.

"Look around you…." She gestured to the poster-sized pictures of the beneficiaries of the foundation's grants. "Is what you allege greater than this? Potable drinking water? Medical care? Children receiving an education?" She interrupted his rebuttal. "Take a few moments to consider your answer, Mr. Ramos." She began to turn away.

"Where are you going?"

"The foundation's executive director requested a meeting."

"Oh, damage control." He nodded.

"There's no need for melodrama, Mr. Ramos. I'll speak with you, if there's time, on my way out. Please make yourself comfortable." She gestured to the glossy brochures neatly arranged on the lobby end tables. "Elaine will get you a beverage while you read."

He called after her, "Don't be too long, *Ms. Cumberland*, I have a deadline to meet." Giving Elaine a subdued look, his eyes flicked over the bright pictures of grinning children from around the world. "Yep, I'll just wait right here," he murmured. The wooden frame of his guest chair creaked as he resumed his seat and stared after her.

Kate met Elizabeth at her office door and ushered her inward. "I just don't understand the source of this reporter's allegations, Charlotte, that's why I contacted you but I didn't expect for you to come in. I'm sorry if there was a misunderstanding."

Elizabeth's hands came to rest on the back of a guest chair. She resisted the urge to grip it out of fear she would inadvertently destroy it. "His allegations are a ruse, Kate. He's here about my involvement with the aid projects we sponsor."

Kate went around to the other side of her desk but remained standing. She looked at her employer with puzzlement. "But your family sponsors our grants, not just you."

"This is about my personal involvement in our work."

"I wasn't aware you were down in the trenches but isn't that a good thing?"

"I fear that it isn't any more—or will be ever again." Elizabeth's last admission crushed her heart. She trembled and swallowed the lump in her throat. "May I use your ensuite?"

"Of course." Kate watched Elizabeth disappear into the washroom's interior. "But why do you say that? Never being able to work on our projects again?"

Stepping in and turning on the light, Elizabeth left the door open as she looked at herself in the mirror. Coming to a decision she removed the pair of cosmetic glasses and released her hair from its bonds. With a thought, the business dress morphed into the white uniform. "It seems he's matched the reports in the media of my involvement with the aid projects and traced the common link to all of them, this foundation's sponsorship."

"There were reports in the media? I didn't see them. What did they say?"

"We'll get to that in a moment. First allow me to say how much I truly appreciate all of what you've accomplished here; it's a testament to the skill and knowledge you've brought to the position. But what I admire most about you is your integrity...your trustworthiness."

Kate raised her voice to project it across the room. "Thank you, Charlotte; but is there anything I should know about?"

Elizabeth noted the doubt creeping into the administrator's voice. Her shoulders rose and fell in a sigh as she contemplated what she was about to do. "More than that can be explained in mere words."

"Can you tell me anything?"

Guardian switched from the aristocratic mid-Atlantic accent of American old money to the regal, received pronunciation that the world had come to know. "Saving this foundation will depend as much upon you as it will me."

"Saving the—" Kate's speech became a gasp as Guardian stepped into the office space. "Oh my God!"

The blonde felt a pang of conscience. "I'm so sorry for the

deception, Kate."

The administrator's hand rose to her neck. "This is…this is unbelievable."

"Please sit down."

"So, all this time…." The administrator sank down into her executive chair.

"I owe you an expRuthtion—and you shall have it, but at this moment, I need your help."

"My help?" Kate blinked.

"That reporter out there," she paused to point towards the general direction of the lobby, "is convinced he has the story of the century and if we fail, he just might. He believes he has deduced that Charlotte Cumberland and Guardian are one and the same person and—"

"But that's the truth, isn't it?"

"It is, but I cannot be associated with this foundation or any of its staff because someone could attempt to get to me through you. I would close down the foundation before I allowed that to happen. So, will you help me preserve what this foundation has created?"

Kate pressed her lips together and remained silent for a moment before nodding. "What do you need me to do?"

"Thank you," Guardian said with an expression of relief. She paced towards the center of the room. "I've been making this plan up for about the last nine minutes so I've not yet settled on all of the details."

"What do you have so far?" Kate swallowed, folding her hands in a tight ball atop her desk.

"I think if he saw me in two places at once, it would convince him his deductions are in error."

"Can you do that?" Kate asked in amazement.

"I believe that with your help, I can." Guardian moved to stand behind the desk with Kate.

"What would you have me do?"

"He has to think that Charlotte is in a meeting with you

while he sees Guardian on the news. Can you pull up the web browser and find a well-publicized breaking story—one with television cameras and witnesses.”

Kate turned to her computer. “Let me search breaking news.”

“And I’ll check your television.” Guardian began to move to the flat screen angled across one of the room’s corners.

“Here’s the remote, if you like.” Kate took it from a desk drawer and offered it.

Accepting the remote with a word of thanks, Guardian flicked on the set and began surfing the channels for news. On a twenty-four hour news channel, she found flickering images of black smoke, white police cars and a distressed reporter. At the bottom of the broadcast, a red and yellow ticker read ‘LIVE: Active Shooter Albuquerque, New Mexico.’ Guardian tensed and turned up the volume.

Clutching a microphone, an African-American reporter stood with her back to a white news van. “We are live at a police standoff near The Bulls-Eye Gun Shop in Albuquerque, New Mexico. It is alleged members of the infamous street gang Las Roja Lobos, or in English, The Red Wolves, attempted to rob the store and were interrupted by officers of the Albuquerque Police Department. Moments ago, a police SWAT team attempted to end the siege by breaching the front door. They were repelled when their armored car was struck by some kind of rocket or anti-vehicle type weapon. While police have the getaway driver in custody, it is believed there are two active shooters holed up inside along with one victim, who has been tentatively identified as Mr. George Miller, the shop’s owner.”

Guardian hit mute and dropped the remote on the desk. “I’m going out there—even if I don’t make it on the television.”

“I’ll make sure Elaine has the lobby on this channel.”

“Keep everyone out of your office until I return.”

Kate watched Guardian open one of her office’s windows. “I

will. Good luck."

"Thank you. I'll be back as soon as I can—and again I'm terribly sorry to involve you in all of this," she said before launching herself through the opening and rocketing for space.

9:55 AM, local time, The Bulls-Eye Gun Shop, Albuquerque, New Mexico

Guardian quickly found the scene of the stand-off. News helicopters circled the neighborhood like dragonflies flitting about a swamp. Dozens of police cars, some riddled with bullet holes, jammed the street. The armored car she had seen on the news only moments before was now fully engulfed in flame. To its rear, she could see a trail of blood smeared on the asphalt from someone being dragged free of the wreckage.

The muzzle flashes of a sustained salvo from the gun shop sent her speeding into the midst of the firefight with the suddenness of a thunderclap.

The ground shook and pavement cracked as she landed. Squaring her shoulders, she interposed herself between the hail of bullets and a police SUV. Rounds ricocheted off her body. A mental command unfurled her cape; blocking any that missed her as easily as an umbrella would repel raindrops.

The gunmen cursed from their hiding places, and poured on the fire. For a split second, Guardian regarded them with a kind of pity, wondering about the terrible circumstances that could have molded the pair into such casual killers. Disgust and revulsion quickly replaced it. Ignoring the bullets as easily as they were bits of lint, she gave them a steely look and reached out with her cosmic sense.

She felt three vibrations, one of which was very faint. Recalling the strife between the police scene commander and the Air Force commandos in Chicago, she didn't bother to seek out the officer in charge.

Anyone present who blinked would have missed the white streak that collided with the shop's barricaded door.

Torn from its hinges, the door sailed through the interior of the shop and slammed against the opposite wall with a crash.

Guardian skidded to a halt just inside the entrance. Fists clenched, she glowered at the hoods with a righteous fury.

They had ransacked the shop. Piles of automatic weapons, along with the casings of hundreds of expended rounds and the spent green fiberglass tube of an anti-tank weapon lay at their feet. They wore bulletproof vests purloined from the store's inventory. One had long, black hair that flowed over his shoulders, the other was bald his thick arms covered in gang tattoos. Behind the counter, the stocky, middle-aged shop owner lay bleeding and unconscious on the floor.

The robbers hesitated for a split second before the long-haired one shouted, "Kill the puta!"

The world slowed down. The acrid stench of cordite and unwashed bodies hung in the air. She saw their fingers twitch at their triggers, and heard the weapons' firing pins draw back. In the blink of an eye, Guardian was between them. The tips of her fingers slapped down on the crowns of their heads. Their guns gave one brief thunderous report before the pair tumbled to the floor as if they had been struck by lightning.

Leaning down, she grabbed them each by a heel and dragged them through the entrance to drop them, not ungently, onto the sunbaked sidewalk. "I need the paramedics, stat!" she bellowed before speeding back to the side of their victim.

A shove sent the counter screeching across the tile floor and out of the way. All of her other concerns, even the ones she left in New York, were set aside. It was all about this single patient. Dropping to a crouch, she leaned in close to the wounded man's face. "George, I'm Dr. Welkin. I'm going to take care of you."

Pulling back to assess him, the blonde's sympathetic expression became sober, and clinical. Miller's state of unconsciousness, his blue lips, his ghastly complexion, and the crimson blotches on his plaid shirt were enough for her to conclude a diagnosis of hypovolemic shock. A deft flick of her fingers tore open his shirt and revealed a pair of wounds.

Her hand came down to seal a sickly red puncture to his upper right chest. He was tachycardic, she could feel his heart racing like a baby bird's. The bullet had collapsed his lung. Left untreated, the pressure from the air filling the chest cavity would collapse the healthy left lung and induce a heart attack.

Her other hand pressed down to cover the wound on the left side of his belly. Experience told her the bullet had struck the spleen. The injury was filling his abdomen with blood. He needed a transfusion and surgery or he would bleed to death.

Miller coughed; blood splashed from his mouth to dribble down the corners of his lips.

"Hold on George, I've got you." She turned her head and bellowed a second time for the paramedics. Outside she saw SWAT officers in their olive drab uniforms handcuffing the unconscious gunmen. She considered how much she could heal George without arousing suspicion.

In response to her shout, SWAT officers streamed into the shop with their weapons raised. To her frustration, they ignored her as they checked the aisles, delved into centers of clothing racks, and explored the shop's storage room all the while aggressively shouting 'police' when they entered an area and 'clear' as they left it.

Watching them, she reiterated her demand. "There's no one else here; now please send me the paramedics."

A SWAT officer came up behind her with two others in tow. "Keep your shirt on. No one comes in here until we know it's safe."

Guardian bit back an impatient retort and glanced up at officer. His olive drab clothing had become soaked from the morning's heat and the stress of a firefight. He was middle-aged; leather faced, and bore an ornery expression.

"Officer—"

"Sergeant," he said, curtly.

"Sergeant have you ever had to do a sudden death visit? Because you're going to if this man doesn't get advanced life support immediately."

"You had no trouble flying into my crime scene, why don't you just fly him out?"

Bloody hell. "Because moving him before he's stabilized would risk opening any clots he's formed and he would bleed out."

The SWAT leader motioned to an officer at the door. "Send them in."

She felt a sense of relief at the sight of the two paramedics. The wheels of their stretcher rattled across the threshold. They guided it around the vandalism of the store's interior to the counter area. After depositing their equipment bags on the floor, they crouched down at George's side opposite to her. She began to rhyme off her initial diagnosis.

"This is George Miller, he's approximately fifty years of age. He has a right pneumothorax and probable splenic trauma that is hemorrhaging into his abdominal cavity. He's tachycardic and in hypovolemic shock. I'm also concerned about possible head and spine trauma from his fall."

"Are you a doctor?" Paramedic Maria Córdova asked as she began to set up a monitor to measure his vital signs.

"Surgeon," Guardian said simply, as she looked the pair over. Both Latino, she guessed them to both be in their middle twenties and seasoned by the way they remained unfazed by the scene or her presence at it.

"Licensed in this state?" the other paramedic, identified as Dom Chavez by his engraved name tag.

"I don't think that's his greatest concern at the moment and neither should it be for you." She ignored the wary look they exchanged. "Dom, bolus a liter of ringers lactate, and push 1 gram of TXA, please and thank you." She used the abbreviation for the clotting agent, tranexamic acid.

She turned back to Maria who had finished fitting Miller's arm with a blood pressure cuff and his finger with a pulse oxygen monitor.

"Pulse one-thirty, pulse ox…eighty-one," Córodova reported.

"Let's see if we can get his saturation over ninety. Start him on fifteen liters of oxygen."

"Are you going to do a thoracostomy?" Dom asked, hanging the clear bag of ringers lactate on the stretcher's IV pole to free up his hands.

"We'll do an Asherman seal and leave the chest tube to the trauma team."

"What about your gloves? They're not sterile are they?" The police sergeant interjected over Guardian's shoulder.

Guardian watched the paramedics work as she continued to cover Miller's wounds. "Sergeant, I take the Polonius approach to disease."

"Felonious?" the cop asked suspiciously.

For a brief instant the corners of Guardian's lips twitched upward in mirth. "Polonius."

"From Hamlet? Dom asked, peeling the backing off an Asherman seal.

"Well done, Dom, you're a lifesaver and a scholar."

"He wants to be a doctor." Maria glanced at the monitor. "Pressure eighty-five over fifty-three."

Guardian lifted her hand for Dom to apply the seal. "I think you'll find the calling of being a physician very rewarding."

"What about Hamlet?" the police commander asked.

"Yes, of course." She watched Dom place the escape valve over the hole in Miller's chest and smooth down the adhesive. The valve hissed softly releasing the air trapped in Miller's chest cavity. "The Polonius approach to illness. Neither a borrower nor a lender be. I don't get sick and neither do I pass illnesses along."

"That's a neat trick," the cop commented.

"I'm glad for it, and so are my patients." She focused her attention back on the paramedics. "Once he's stable, I want him at the hospital within five minutes." She looked over their medical bags. "Let's get a pressure bandage on his abdomen."

"Five minutes?" Dom asked.

"And on the table in fifteen."

Maria handed Dom a compression bandage. "U-N-M is about a twelve-minute drive from here—minimum." She used the abbreviation for the University of New Mexico's hospital.

Guardian watched as Dom tore the vacuum sealed wrapper from a pressure bandage and pressed its gauze pad across the wound. "Does the stretcher lock into the ambulance?"

Dom frowned. "Yes, why?"

There was a crackling sound as Guardian leaned down and reached beneath Miller's body. Her arm cut a furrow in the floor to retrieve the bandage's tail from Dom and pass it back over Miller's abdomen. "Not too tight," she cautioned, "just snug."

"Why do you want to know if the stretcher locks?" Maria watched Dom finish the bandaging.

"We'll be flying. Let's get him collared and splinted." She motioned for the collar in one of the bags.

"Do you know how much trouble we could get into?" Dom asked.

Guardian assisted Maria fitting the collar around their patient's neck. "He's in danger of developing a tension pneumothorax and going into cardiac arrest. We're flying."

Maria glanced at the monitor. "He's stabilizing. Blood pressure is coming up, ninety over sixty, pulse is one hundred."

Time for a little insurance. Guardian took hold of George's hand. Concealed from those around her, the palm of her glove receded. For a few precious seconds her life force flowed into her patient, strengthening clots and giving him the equivalent of several hours of recuperation. She watched his blood pressure rise five points closer to normalcy. "George you're doing wonderfully, we're going to strap you into a splint and take you to the hospital." She released his hand with a pat.

Maria wore an expression of amazement as she glanced from the monitor then back to Guardian.

Guardian ignored Maria's look of question and watched Dom pump air into the flexible body splint. A French invention, the splint was quickly replacing backboards as the option of choice for suspected spinal and pelvic injuries. Filled with tiny beads, the mattress was designed to be wrapped around the patient and then deflated, creating a rigid, form-fitting splint.

Under Guardian's direction, the three caregivers along with the police officer worked as one to roll George onto his side. They checked for exit wounds and after finding none, slid the thin polymer mattress beneath their patient. They completed the process by deflating the split and strapping George into its confines. In moments, the front of Miller's semi-cocooned body was crisscrossed with the splint's nylon belts.

After loading George into the back of the ambulance, Dom appeared at its back door. "I'm driving him in."

"There's no time, Dom," Guardian countered. "If you're nervous about flying then you can ride in with the police but we're flying."

Dom bristled. "I'm not leaving the truck."

"Then buckle your seatbelt." She grasped the ambulance's rear bumper and lifted its backend a few inches to make her point.

Dom's face hardened as he turned to take a seat in the back of the truck next to Maria and pull the four-point restraints over his shoulders.

Getting directions to the hospital from the SWAT commander, the blue and white ambulance creaked as Guardian carefully lifted it over her head. Finding the point of balance, she took off, rising above traffic lights, overhead wires and the city's rooftops. Desert breezes began to buffet the ambulance's cabin-like rear, threatening to blow it from her grasp. She pressed her fingers into the truck's steel chassis and increased her speed.

The heroine's passage overhead drew looks of bewilderment from down below. People stopped to point, gawk, and raise their mobile phone cameras into the air to record the fantastic spectacle. Despite the urgency of her task, she welcomed the attention, hoping for as much of it as possible. The irony of that desire was not lost upon her. Fighting the media by using the media might just save the foundation.

UNM was the state's only level one trauma center. A teaching hospital, a patient could expect to receive the care and attention of multiple doctors. Guided to the complex by the enormous H painted onto the rooftop helipad, she winged downwards to the ambulance bay. A trauma team dressed in blue hospital scrubs and pale-yellow gowns waited just outside the doors. They scrambled to the rear of the ambulance as she set it down.

As George was wheeled into the ER, Guardian conferred with the lead trauma surgeon all the way into the trauma bay before stepping back to the Emergency Room's desk. Despite the gravity of the entire situation, she felt a momentary sense of satisfaction. It felt good to practice medicine and to be among her professional colleagues. Her mind strayed back to Kenya and the thought of returning there. The feeling vanished as she glanced at the clock. Twenty-five minutes had passed and she was unsure how long Sean Ramos would linger in the foundation's offices, it was time to go.

Through the ER's bay glass doors, she could see that the media had taken no time in tracking them down. Cameras pointed over the shoulders of hospital security while journalists attempted to wave her over for comment. She wondered if she could she ever practice medicine again if she was pursued and hounded wherever she worked. Dom's voice interrupted her thoughts.

"Do you have any idea how much shit we're in?" He sat next to Maria filling out paperwork in the nursing station.

Guardian paused to lean across the station's counter and regard the male paramedic with gentle amusement, "Dom, the fifteen minutes of fame you're about to get from this call will likely keep you out of the trouble you're so desperately worried about."

"If you hadn't butted in—"

Maria cut him off. "If she hadn't butted in we'd be writing a different report."

Guardian looked from one to the other, "You're both good street doctors, I'm grateful for your help saving George's life. But...." She looked up at the staff and patients pausing in their travels to stop and stare. "I'm creating an unnecessary disturbance here."

"You got that right," Dom spat.

"Dom!" Maria scolded.

"Vaya con Dios—and good luck in your studies Domingo." Guardian gave them a parting smile before turning to quickly find the stairwell and from there; she flew to the roof and onto New York.

12:40 PM, local time, The Cumberland Foundation, New York City

Feeling a tightness in her chest, Guardian flew, feet first through the window to Kate's office. "How did we do? Please tell me he's still in the lobby."

Kate did a double take from the television back to her boss. "I don't know but you're—you're still on the TV."

Guardian gave the screen a glance and nodded in satisfaction. "I just need a moment to put myself together." Guardian stepped back into the washroom to begin quickly fixing her hair back into a bun.

"Charlotte—Guardian...what should I call you?" Kate stood next to her desk and fidgeted.

Elizabeth talked while she watched herself in the mirror. "When I'm in the white uniform, Guardian, otherwise—"

"Charlotte."

"Hopefully for a long time to come," the blonde muttered, holding her bobby pins between her teeth while her hands moved too fast to be seen fixing her hair back into a bun.

"Where did you hide your clothes? I went in there and I didn't see them."

"A fair question. I wish I could give you a fair answer." Elizabeth strode back into the office, wearing the blue wrap dress.

Kate frowned. "How about another question, then?"

Elizabeth glanced the door. "Of course?"

"Is your grandmother like you?"

"My grandmother?"

"I met her seven years ago when I was hired?"

"Oh yes; I'm sorry. She was an actress, quite a good one in her time. She was struggling on social security. I offered to take care of all of her expenses in exchange for her posing as the

Cumberland matriarch. Sadly, she passed away last year."

"I'm sorry." Kate pressed her lips together. "What about the reporter's allegations about our financial situation and offshore shell corporations?"

"Another necessary deception I'm afraid but the wealth is legally obtained."

"If you don't mind me asking..."

"There's a white dwarf star about fifty light years from here, known as Lucy. Her core is a diamond a little larger than the sun."

"You're a diamond merchant?"

"There's quite a treasure trove of elements in the Earth's neighborhood. I extract and sell about a few tons or so to the appropriate processor who in turn sells them in the commodities markets. That's how we make our budget."

"Like gold?"

"Gold, platinum, rhodium, others. It's lucrative." Elizabeth replaced her glasses and started for the office door. "You deserve more answers, Kate. If our ruse has been successful, I'll take you to dinner at Eleven Madison and try to provide them. But right now, we must hurry."

"I can wait."

"I hope he's still out there, I haven't had time to conceive of a plan B."

Elizabeth's impromptu performance had a greater effect than she or Kate anticipated, much of the office's staff was paying more attention to the special report on the overhead televisions than their work. They began to retreat to their desks at the sight of both the executive director and Charlotte emerging from Kate's office. The pair of women shook hands, going through the motions of the conclusion of a meeting.

Ramos stood in the lobby, looking up at its television. His smug expression had vanished, but his expression was neither one of defiance nor even embarrassment.

Unsure if their attempt at deception had any effect, she worriedly murmured to Kate, "Wish me luck."

Ramos turned his gaze from the screen to Elizabeth as she approached him.

"What is on the television that you are watching so intently Mr. Ramos?"

He pointed at the screen where an image of Guardian dragging a pair of hoods out of the gun shop was being replayed. "I was just remembering a Saturday morning when I was nine, my brothers and sisters and I were eating our cereal and watching cartoons on TV when my parents came in to see us. My mom was sobbing inconsolably, and I'd never seen a look like that on my dad's face before, kind of confused and like he'd been punched in the gut. It was scary." He paused and sighed. "My dad broke the news that the night before, my uncle had been working at his job on the midnight shift at a gas station. Someone robbed it and shot and killed him—just like they tried to do to this guy."

Elizabeth's face fell with sympathetic sorrow. "Oh, I'm so sorry."

"I believe you are."

"That must have been terrible for you and your family."

"My uncle didn't have someone like Guardian to swoop down out of the sky and save him."

"I believe she would have if she had known."

"I have no doubt about that. Anyway, I'm just going to go." He turned to retrieve his satchel.

Elizabeth trailed after him. "Mr. Ramos? Are you all right?"

"You don't have to worry; I'm not turning in my article. The world needs y—" He halted his speech. "I mean, the world needs Guardian more than I need a story."

Feeling breathless it was all she could do to keep her

shoulders from sagging in relief. Watching him prepare to go, an idea struck her. "Mr. Ramos do you have a card?"

"Why?" he asked, lifting his satchel across his body.

"I travel a great deal and there's no telling when I might come across a story that is worthy of a journalist as sagacious as you."

Ramos shook his head and gave her a smile of amazement as he fished a business card from his pocket.

She held the card up to read it. "It seems to me that your talents could be better suited writing about things other than aliens and Elvis sightings."

"You're unbelievable—you really are."

"Oh, I'm not so sure about that."

"I am."

She began to walk with him towards the elevator. "Well, I suppose they do say that seeing is believing—or not believing?"

"Well, I believe in her." Ramos smiled as the elevator doors closed.

Elizabeth kept her smile until the door rumbled shut. Her hand rose to the wall to steady herself as her vision began to blur.

12:50 PM, New York City

From atop the Boise Building, Guardian grimly stared down at the streets below. A storm had broken; the deluge that accompanied it threatened to fill up the gutters. New Yorkers without umbrellas sought shelter, scurrying past those who had them. She had done good work, so much very good work. Now, no matter how many ways she turned it over in her mind, her ability to continue the work was slipping away like the water rushing into the sewers below. Her heart felt as leaden as the skies above.

Blinking back the rain dripping into her eyes, she swallowed the lump in her throat. Sean Ramos' decision not to publish his article was the only silver lining of his visit. She would have to distance herself from her foundation and most depressingly, as she thought of the children, its projects. Its operating budget could continue but a committed day-to-day role seemed all but impossible.

Sighing deeply and fighting the urge to retreat to Avalon, Guardian reached for her mobile device to check Harold's program. The top headline in the feed shocked her from her grief.

Bio-Terror Plot Foiled in Boston

Below the headline was a picture of the biology building.

Fear threatened to overwhelm her. How had they been found out? Where were her friends? In custody? Bound for some black site military prison? Leaping into the air, she flew for Boston, the sonic boom of her mad haste attributed by startled bystanders to the overhead thunderclouds.

In the seconds-long flight, she changed her uniform from white to slate gray to match the ominous atmosphere. Over

Boston, she hovered and frantically pored over the campus and its surrounding neighborhood. Lightning leapt between the clouds and moisture beaded on her clothing; she saw blue and white police cars blocking every entrance to the campus and black JLTVs, like those she had encountered in Chicago, surrounding the biology building. Airmen dressed in orange biohazard suits used carts to push crates marked with biohazard trilliums from the building's main doors to a black, windowless bus, also like the one she saw in Chicago.

Checking her mobile device again, there was no word about Bernard or Jennifer. Dreading they shared Melanie's fate, Guardian moved to land quickly and covertly in a tree lined alley a few blocks from the campus. Adding a hip-length, forest green raincoat to the disguise she had worn to travel the roads in China, she set off for the campus at a run.

A crowd of reporters milled about on the adjacent sidewalk of Vassar Street. Four Boston police officers kept them from getting any closer. Changing her accent to something between the highbrow Brahmin accent of John F. Kennedy and the Southie, working class accent of South Boston, she approached a heavy-set camera man who sported a graying crew cut and a yellow raincoat.

He looked her over. "How are ya'? School's out for today."

"What's going on?" She craned her neck as if to see.

"They caught some kook scientist making a germ warfare bomb."

Assuming an appropriately startled expression she asked rhetorically, "A bomb?"

"Scary as shit, isn't it?"

"Did they arrest him?"

"Her, and I don't know but they've got cops rolling all over this part of town." He nodded towards a Boston Blue and White rolling past them at a reduced speed.

"Just the one? No one else?"

"One's enough. I hope they get that bitch soon." He gave her a decidedly unbiased look of anger. "Boston doesn't need any more shit like this."

"Well, I guess I'd better get out of here then." She turned away to look up the house address Jennifer had given her on Google maps. It was past noon; they might have gotten Jennifer while she was at home eating lunch and what about Bernard?

Elizabeth started running for Jennifer's home on Tufts Street. At the best of times, she found a human's running pace agonizingly slow, her feelings of desperation made the trip excruciating. As she sprinted through the soggy, residential neighborhood, she tried to call the school and connect with Bernard but after three hang-ups she was convinced that the school's telephone system was now locked down too.

Rounding the corner, she saw a Boston Blue and White blocking the top of the street. She slowed her pace, directing the symbiote to unlace one of her shoes. Coming loose, the laces clicked on the wet sidewalk. She stopped and crouched down between two puddles to through the motions of retying it while listening in to the police radios.

Through the car's glass, she heard a radio squawk, "Bravo nine-eighty, any signs of the suspect?"

Out of the corner of her eye, she watched the officer in the passenger seat lift the microphone. "This is Bravo nine-eighty, negative."

The information brought only a modicum of relief. She tried to think of where else Jennifer might be. In hiding on the campus? At Bernard's home? If she was there, how long would it take them to find her? *Where else?* Pressing her lips together in thought, she recalled everything Jennifer had ever said to her or around her and came up with another possible answer: The Boxcar Theatre.

Google Maps lead her to the small, one screen theatre. It was a converted storefront with a small box office and lobby. Elizabeth paid for a ticket and bypassed the popcorn stand to step inside.

With only three minutes to the start of the one o'clock matinee, the theatre was sparsely populated. In its center a pair of retirees chatted amiably. Off to the left a single man was crunching handfuls of popcorn into his mouth and in the back right corner, slumped down in her seat, was Jennifer.

She practically jumped out of her chair when Elizabeth called to her in a whisper. Her eyes rimmed red from tears, the scientist looked her over in terror before recognizing the blonde behind the glasses.

Elizabeth lifted a tub of untouched popcorn from the seat beside Jennifer and slid into it. She laid her hand atop Jennifer's and squeezed empathetically. "Jennifer, I'm so sorry. I was warned about interfering in human affairs and now I've cocked up your life."

"I am so fucked. F-U-C-K-fucked. What am I going to do? They're at my house, they're at the school. I'm beyond fired. They think—"

Anxiously glancing around at the other movie goers, "And what they think is wrong."

"That doesn't matter."

"I promise I will use all my resources to restore your name and your station."

"Where am I going to live? I can't go home. I can't go to my mom's. I can't..." Jennifer's voice trailed off forlornly.

Elizabeth's eyes fluttered as she reached a decision. "You'll...you'll come home with me."

# # #

1:20 PM, Avalon, Maine

Guardian stood at her kitchen's island as Jennifer cooed while petting Butler and Delilah. She watched the scientist with concern; it had been a stress-filled day for both of them. The pair of canines seemed the best medicine for the chaos she knew was lurking within Jennifer. She wished that something so simple could solve the chaos *her* day had become.

They won the race with the thunderstorm that rattled the windows and drummed a rat-a-tat beat on the steel roof by mere moments. Behind the dogs, and set neatly to one side, was a hastily purchased scuba tank and respirator, it made Jennifer's underwater journey possible. Safely cocooned inside her cape, Jennifer had seen neither the trip out over the ocean nor the trip under it to the secret passage to the little red barn across Avalon's meadow.

"Good girl." Jennifer stroked Delilah's ears back with one hand while hugging Butler around the neck with the other.

"Yes, I am!" Delilah gave a short yap of agreement and lapped Jennifer's cheek enthusiastically.

Butler woofed.

Jennifer drew back in alarm. "Did I do something wrong?"

Guardian came around the kitchen's island. "Butler, no! She does not have to kiss you! I'm sorry—"

"He wants a kiss? Awww...." Jennifer planted a kiss squarely atop his head. "Mmmwah! And one for you!" She did likewise to Delilah. "What a couple of sweeties." She went back to scratching their ears.

"Yes, I am," Delilah yapped again.

Butler's eyes became contented slits, the storm outside forgotten.

"By the stars! You two go lay down," Guardian said in exasperation.

Seeing the dogs ignore the blonde's directive, Jennifer continued to scritch their ears. "Where did you get them?"

"They were rescues."

"Just like me."

"*You* are a valued guest. Now, may I get you something? Coffee? Tea? Lemonade?" She regretted the need to take her away from the comfort of the dogs.

Jennifer's mood grew more serious. "Do you have orange pop? Or better yet, orange pop with vodka?"

"I'll be sure to purchase you some."

Jennifer gave the dogs a final pet and joined the blonde at the broad counter. "I just don't understand what happened. I didn't tell *anyone* about what we were doing. I swear I didn't."

"I believe you," Guardian said, quietly.

"I locked the lab, and went home for lunch—and to make your tattoos. On my way back I was just turning the corner when I saw them rolling up on my house. It was crazy. Lights, sirens, men with guns, I just ran. And now we've lost everything. I am so sorry."

"I'm most concerned about the two of you, luv. The rest of it can be replaced. But do you know where Bernard might be?"

"I..." Jennifer's face creased with consternation. "I don't know—his house? I mean I don't normally see him outside of work. Sometimes he eats his lunch on one of the benches in the common areas but do you think they got him?"

Guardian frowned. "I hope they haven't. When I go out, I'll make a few calls."

"Do you have a TV? We could check the news."

"Capital idea. The media center is in the basement. This way..." She opened the basement door and flicked on the lights.

"Can the dogs come?" Jennifer looked back at the pair, panting and anxiously wagging their tails in the mudroom's doorway.

Guardian leaned on the doorknob. "The queen of England may allow her dogs the run of her homes but the queen of Avalon does not. You'll see why when we get around to a tour."

"Gotcha." Jennifer turned back around to the dogs. "Sorry doggies." She gave them a shrug of regret. "I tried."

The pair of dogs groaned softly in disappointment and slunk off to lie down.

"Oh, the drama!" Guardian looked to the heavens as if hoping to receive some blessing of strength.

She led the way down the broad stone steps into the basement. "While I'm thinking of it, we should probably go over a few things. First, since you're going to be living here, call me Elizabeth or Betty, Guardian is for the media and the public."

"Thank you, Betty."

"You're welcome. Second, don't stray too far from the house, the dogs may love you but the animals and the birds around it are very protective of my home."

"What? Like wolves?"

"There is a pack out there but just the birds and bees would make things very unpleasant long before you made it to the trees."

"Wowzers; okay."

"Third, and this is even more important. In order for Avalon to remain hidden and for you to remain safe, there is absolutely no outgoing communication from Avalon, not a telephone call, or a text, or an email, or a visit to a personal website—nothing."

"But what about my mom?" Jennifer protested. "She's going to be going crazy."

Guardian's features became sympathetic. "I understand, I'll get you some paper to write a note to her and I'll deliver it for you, moreover, tonight I'll go by your house and pick up your things."

Jennifer's face filled with doubt. "Are you sure that's safe?"

"If I can borrow your key, they won't notice anything missing until at least tomorrow morning," she said matter-of-factly. "Then we'll let them wonder." She gave the redhead a conspiratorial smile.

"Hah! Sure," the redhead fished her key ring from her purse. "It's that one." She held it up and handed them over.

"You know, this is kind of like being on a space ship, hostile environment outside, no communication with the world," Jennifer mused.

"I've been in a few space ships, Avalon is much nicer and I'm sure you'll find the hospitality far better as well." She smiled sweetly.

Guardian led the way past long, neat lines of crates, barrels and boxes, giving a mini tour as they passed the wine cellar, the power wall for Avalon's electricity storage and her library of thirty-five millimeter movies. She paused to point out Close Encounters of the Third Kind and brought a smile to Jennifer's face.

"We'll have a movie night when things are more settled," she promised.

"Have you ever tried popcorn and Milk Duds?" Jennifer took hold of the blonde's arm in earnest. "They're the best for watching movies."

"I'm not familiar with that confection."

"Chocolate covered caramel mixed into hot buttered popcorn, yum!"

"I'll add them to the list." Guardian halted at a granite wall in an alcove. "Here we are." She stripped off her glove and pressed her hand to a gray granite block. "Open." The command was followed by the sounds of a heavy bolts releasing and the hum of electrical motors operating the door hinges.

Jennifer stepped back as the wall opened to a landing and a second set of broad steps. "You have a secret door!" Jennifer exclaimed. "That is so cool."

"Avalon was a station on the Underground Railroad. I used to hide runaway slaves down here. You're the first person to see the subbasement since 1866—truth be told you're my first house guest since 1866."

"Wow, thank you, but slavery ended in 1865."

"Well two gentlemen lingered for a time."

"Gentlemen? As in plural?"

"They arrived barefoot and ragged and left well dressed, well-spoken and on horseback," she said with an air of pride.

"Wait a minute; I'm still digesting the plural part."

Guardian tittered. "Come on; we have to find Bernard."

"Is that all you're going to say?"

"For now."

Jennifer grinned. "Are you being serious? Come on, mama needs details! You know I'm going to keep needling you until you spill."

"I thought we had already established I'm needle proof."

"I'll find out, just give me time."

"Right, well here we are," Guardian opened the vault-like door to the subbasement.

"Look at this place!" Jennifer stood in the door, surveying the expansive room. "This is so cool!"

"Allow me to give you the two-pence tour." The blonde led her further inside. "My vault—because banks require identification and addresses, my workshop, my laboratory, and lavatory—please don't mix them up!" She giggled. "And my media center."

"What's that?" Jennifer pointed to what appeared to be a shower stall in the corner of the workshop.

"Oh, that's my aerosol bronzer, it gives me some color whenever I vacation someplace warm."

"Yes, you are pretty white."

"Blindingly so in bathing costume." Guardian looked at the media center and recalled what she had seen on the news concerning her friend. "Erm, perhaps to speed things up, I could check for news of Bernard while you write a note to your mother and a list of what you need to get things started again."

"You mean other than a sample?"

Guardian grimaced. "Yes, quite. I'll find another donor."

"Once you do, we'll need a sequencer."

Guardian retrieved a pen and stationery from the media desk and handed them to the scientist.

"Cambridge Genetics has the fastest, the Nanopore-3Gen, but they cost about a million bucks."

"Money isn't an issue. How quickly can it do a complete sequence?"

"About twenty-six hours."

"First class! That's the best news I've heard today. Get started on your notes." She pointed to the lab. "All the cupboards and drawers are labeled. I'll look into Bernard's situation."

"On it." Writing materials in hand, Jennifer went to find a lab stool to get to work.

Guardian gave her friend one final cautious glance before turning on the monitors. She set the volume at level one, too low for a human to hear without pressing an ear to the speaker and frowned as she watched the screens for several minutes. They had Jennifer's picture from her school ID on every monitor. They were calling her a bioterrorist and talking about prison terms of twenty years to life. The American president spoke briefly about getting to the bottom of the matter and deploying federal resources to assist. Talking head analysts were offering up opinions that were without merit or basis. There was no mention of Bernard. She was unsure whether to take it as good news that he was not considered a suspect or that it was very bad news and he was already in custody and took him away like they had poor Melanie.

"This is quite a lab," Jennifer called from across the room.

Guardian didn't take her eyes off the screens. "Thank you. For the most part I use it for diagnosing pathogens for aid work. That reminds me, I have a house call to make at seven this evening, but I will look into rescheduling it."

Jennifer looked up from her list-making. "I should be okay—especially after you find Bernie. Is there anything on the news about him?"

"Nothing, which I hope is good news." Guardian clicked the mouse to power down the computers and the disturbing broadcasts.

"Here's what I need." Jennifer handed the hastily compiled list over. "I wrote down the companies that sell them but I didn't have enough time to get addresses. I could do that on the computer." She glanced at the media center.

Guardian quickly scanned the page. "All of this is in the lab but the sequencer. I'll purchase one after I get Bernard. Don't trouble yourself with an internet search, I can find it on my mobile device and call around."

"All right, I'll start poking around the cupboards and get set up. And this is for my mom." She handed her a page that had been folded over twice with the address printed on the outside.

Guardian held it up. "I'll visit her first then I'll find Bernard." *Perhaps then we can get some answers.*

"Good luck."

2:00 PM Fremont, Ohio

The delivery of Jennifer's note was relatively easy. From her vantage point in the sky, Guardian spotted a pair of unmarked police cars in front of the Novak residence. Their out of place presence on the quiet suburban street tipped her off immediately.

She stealthily avoided their surveillance by landing at the rear of the home and took further steps to blend in by changing her clothing during her descent to shorts and a t-shirt. To her dismay, Ms. Novak's car was missing from the garage. A quick check with her cosmic sense revealed only the family cat was inside the house. Guardian resorted to taking a slender finishing nail from the garage's workbench to nail Jennifer's note to the backdoor with a gentle tap of her finger. With the message of reassurance delivered, she was on her way to Boston.

Desperate to find Bernard, she realized she would have to do it discretely, that meant no cape, no flying, and no use of her fame. An internet search for all the Bernard or simply 'B' Ropers in Boston yielded three results.

She settled on using taxi cabs as the most practical and inconspicuous option to move between locations. An added feature to her taxi cab odyssey was conversing about the events of the day with the cabbies. She found it a curious but informative exercise to discuss herself in the third person with the unaware drivers. They wondered where Guardian was in the face of the local crisis, something she dared not offer an opinion about. Their thoughts on Jennifer demanded nothing less than advocacy for her friend and the presumption of innocence, a demand that was met with disbelief and mild derision.

The first 'B' Roper she spoke with was a senior in a

retirement village. The elderly woman was so happy to have a visitor that Elizabeth had to regretfully turn down an invitation to stay for a visit with tea and cookies. The second Roper's young wife peevishly wondered why a pretty blonde woman was at their door. Cringing inwardly, she begged off with an apology and a true admission of a mistake.

The third B Roper lived in the South Boston neighborhood in which she now found herself.

Rain drizzled down and spattered off Elizabeth's newly purchased umbrella. Dressed in her jogger disguise, Elizabeth walked along the broken sidewalk, glancing from her mobile device's map up at the apartment address numbers with disbelief. The neighborhood was not what she was expecting.

The brown-brick apartments and store fronts seemed to be at least pre-World War Two construction. Flies buzzed around curbside trash bags, most of the parked cars were more than ten years old. Groups of listless young men hung around stoops smoking, listening to rap music, and taking notice of her. To her relief, there didn't appear to be any unmarked police cars anywhere in sight.

Mounting the steps of a brown-brick housing project, she found the outer door unlocked, it swung inward with the gentlest push. She paused at the address panel, to find Bernard's name among those listed and discovered a B Roper in apartment 312. She began to devise a way inside when the exterior door swung open behind her.

"Hey, you dropped something."

Elizabeth glanced at the floor then up at the speaker. He was Black. His hair was styled in cornrows and pulled tight to his scalp. He wore a white tank top that revealed a wiry, otter-like body, beneath.

"I was kidding; I just wanted to get your name."

She tilted her head and gave him a tight-lipped smile. "Cute."

"Talk to me." He extended his hand. "I'm Anton Valentine..."

You need to give more thought to names. "Your last name is Valentine?" She shook his hand out of social convention.

"That's right. You're very beautiful," Anton purred in a smooth baritone.

Well, you're quite a rake, aren't you? "Thank you."

"I like your smile."

"Thanks, what do you want?"

"Where are you from?" he asked.

"The Valley—in California."

"Oh, a California girl."

"I sure am," she declared, proudly.

"So why are you here?"

"Visiting a friend."

"Oh, a boyfriend? He wouldn't mind me talking to you, would he?"

"I talk to who I like."

"Oh, so you like me?" He smiled as she giggled. "You know I've got a crib, upstairs, room 207. We could drink some wine, get to know each other. Why don't you come up? What's your name?"

My, aren't you quick? "Callie. Your place, is it neat? You know...put together?"

He laughed. "Callie from the Valley's got standards."

"Yup."

"Classy and beautiful, I like that. You just give me five minutes to make things immaculate." He took her hand and kissed it.

Despite it all, she felt a kind of psychic rush. "Okay, five minutes." She watched as he unlocked the interior door and then stepped through at his invitation.

"You gonna wait right there?"

"I'll text my friend I'm going to be late." She held up her

mobile device. *Sorry luv, but I'm sure you'll tell your friends outside something better than it would have been anyway.*

"You do that." He grinned.

As Anton briskly ascended the staircase on her left, Elizabeth took in the rest of her surroundings. The lack of air conditioning left the interior of the building dank and reeking of the nostril curling stenches of stale tobacco smoke and burnt food. Scuffed and stained, the olive-green linoleum floor looked at least three decades past need of replacing. To her right was an open half door marked 'Superintendant.' From the unit's confines, the smell of buttered cabbage wafted outward. Looking a little closer, she saw a desk, stacked with papers and a ring of keys. Anxious to find Bernard, it was all she could do to stop herself from flying. She mounted the stairs, taking them two at a time.

The third-floor corridor was clamorous with the sounds of apartment life. She heard television sets turned to daytime soap operas, a baby crying, and a woman laughing, seemingly on the telephone.

Reaching the door, she knocked and waited. After a moment with no response, she reached out to sense the life force of anyone inside. She knew his quite specifically but did not feel it. Nibbling her lip, she seized the doorknob and considering pushing it in before recalling the ring of keys on the superintendent's desk.

A breeze, the rustle of papers, and the soft clink of keys being pressed together was the only evidence of her passage in and out of the superintendent's office. Back in front of apartment 312's door, her hand became a blur as she cycled through the keys, trying each one until she heard a satisfying click and she was quickly inside.

She looked around anxiously, both fearing and hoping that this was not Bernard's home, that the apartment belonged to someone who merely shared his first initial and last name. To her right was a small kitchen with breakfast dishes still in the sink. Straight on, the room opened into a family room. Books stacked knee high surrounded an arm chair and filled the seats of a sofa. Her heart sank as she spotted a wedding portrait hung behind the chair. Bernard looked to be about thirty, his wife a few years younger. Elizabeth nibbled her bottom lip, wondering what had landed him in these circumstances and what happened to his marriage.

On the kitchen table was a toaster-sized television, stacks of newspapers, including to her chagrin, multiple issues of The Spoiler. Among the crumbs, bits of dehydrated peas, and a smear of mustard were bills and promotions to various casinos in the state. Elizabeth frowned with disappointment. She leafed through the bills, all of which were at least a month overdue, telephone, credit cards, and rent. She sighed with sadness, pondering what she could do after she found him. First pay off his debts, she had enough money on her to take care of every bill on the table. Second, when circumstances would allow it, buy him a luxurious condominium; he deserved something for all of his help and a lifetime of work. She tapped a finger to her chin, wondering where he might be.

She looked around for a computer to check a list of favorites, or a browser history but there was none of any description to be found. A quick check yielded no notes on his refrigerator, but there was an address book underneath an old landline telephone next to the arm chair. Picking it up, she flipped through it, the entries were sparse, a couple of dentists, a family physician, and a few numbers that had been erased with a pencil rubber. Examining the answering machine next to the telephone, she shrugged to herself. "In for a penny...."

She twisted the switch. The initial answer with Bernard's voice rumbled along in a monotone. The tape began to play the first saved message.

"Dr. Roper this is Alicia Lindberg, I'm Mr. Grey's personal assistant. Mr. Grey and Mr. Steele are looking forward to meeting you and learning about your new discovery. Our corporate jet will be waiting for you at Terminal Five of Logan Airport at one PM. If you have any questions, please contact me at my number..."

Elizabeth ceased to listen. Feeling like her insides had been kicked out, she slumped into one of the kitchen chairs. Recalling his talk of money, she moaned sorrowfully, "Oh Bernard, what have you done?"

4:30 PM Avalon, Maine

Guardian left Bernard's apartment in a fog of turmoil and disbelief. She flew north for Avalon on a kind of mental autopilot. A lightning bolt arcing between two clouds struck her in an explosion of sparks and blinding light, shaking her from her stupor. The realization she was halfway across New Hampshire sent her veering out over the storm-tossed Atlantic for the final leg home.

Stepping inside from the rumbling, gloom, she noted immediately that Delilah and Butler were not there to leap up and greet her. She called out, there was no response. Through the open basement door, she heard the chatter of the twenty-four hours news cycle mentioning Jennifer's name. She groaned in realization.

The scientist sat upon the floor, her back leaned against the end of the L-shaped media desk. The biting tang of alcohol hung in the air. A green wine bottle and a glass with a minuscule pool of wine in its bowl rested near the lip of the desk above her head. Jennifer's face was blotchy and red. She looked up, her puffy eyes filled with desperation.

Guardian recognized an old adversary. She wasn't sure how much experience Jennifer had with grief but losing one's position and reputation without cause was an invitation for him to visit. She resolved to do all she could to keep him from staying.

Butler and Delilah lay next to Jennifer and lifted their heads from her lap. "Help, sad." They whined plaintively.

"I'm here," she said softly motioning for the dogs to rise. "Go to the mudroom," she murmured. They paused to give Jennifer one last lick of sympathy before shuffling off for the stairs. Guardian leaned down to give them a reassuring pat as they passed by. "Good dogs."

The blonde turned to the media center. "I think we've heard quite enough of that." She powered down the system with a click of the mouse and absentmindedly lifted the bottle to read its label: Château Margaux 1787. At a quarter of a million dollars per bottle, she mused Jennifer knew how to pick a great wine. Setting the bottle down, she pondered restoring her friend to clear-eyed sobriety with a touch but in the end, decided against invading Jennifer's dubious sanctuary of inebriation.

"Hello you," she said, gently.

Jennifer's voice trembled. "Did you see my mom?"

"I'm sorry darling, she wasn't at home, but I did deliver your note. I'll check on her later before I go to retrieve your things."

"She probably went to my grandma's. Oh my God, I hope they're not watching the news—my poor babcia!"

"I shouldn't worry too much about your grandma, Jennifer. We old ladies are tougher than we look." She tried to give her a smile of reassurance.

"What about Bernie? You didn't find him?"

"No. Did he...did Bernard ever show any signs of a gambling issue?"

"No, why!" Jennifer shouted than clapped a hand over her mouth. "Sorry. Loud."

"To put it rather plainly, it would seem, Bernard made an expedient, yet...." Her voice changed, charged with frustration and anger. "Bloody foolish decision. He—"

"He told someone didn't he?"

"Yes," she said, tersely, "yes he did, all for what it would seem, is a financial payoff."

"From who!" The red in Jennifer's cheeks intensified.

"From what little I could gather, multinational conglomerate called Grey and Steele—"

"What the hell? I get called a terrorist while he gets a big pay off? Can't you do something?"

Guardian shared her frustration. "Believe me, it took every ounce of my willpower not to go after him, but if I had, it would have only made matters worse."

"But he already makes over two hundred thousand a year, isn't that enough?"

"It's not fair, it's not right, and it won't stand."

"Won't stand?" Jennifer glared up at her. "What are you going to do about it, super lady?"

"We are going to solve this medical mystery, restore your name, and cure some people. But," she added quietly as she sank to the floor to sit beside her, "not today. Today we're going to take care of us." Her arm slipped around Jennifer's shoulders. "That will be enough."

"This is so effed." Jennifer leaned her head onto Guardian's shoulder.

"It certainly is." She gently stroked the scientist's hair and wondered if Rupert Longstreet had a hand in what happened.

Jennifer sat forward abruptly. "I didn't do anything wrong did I? I don't think I did."

"Not a thing." *I failed at least two friends though.*

They sat in silence, alone with their thoughts for many moments. Guardian ruminated, wondering if she had missed some sign of Bernard's desperate financial state and the stress he must have been under. She berated herself for not sitting down to really catch up with him, wondering if he might have revealed something had she stopped long enough to listen. If she had been a better friend, it was likely they would not be in the situation they found themselves.

Jennifer turned and grabbed Guardian's wrist. "The dogs aren't in trouble, are they? It's my fault they were down here."

Guardian smiled kindly. "No luv, not at all, to tell the truth, that's my prescription for a dreadful day: pet two dogs as needed…just not in the house proper, please."

"Okay, gotcha." Jennifer gave her a sad, apologetic smile.

They sat in silence for a few moments before Jennifer spoke up again. "I like your outfit. It's pretty."

"Thank you."

She turned her head. "You didn't want slacks?"

"I've worn slacks almost every day for the last fifty years and before that, I endured more than seven hundred years of floor length skirts and shamed prudery. I'll wear what I like—and I like my uniform."

"Am I talking too much? Because I'm not drunk you know? I'm just like this—and not because I've drank a lot of wine."

Guardian smiled with quiet amusement. "How did you find the vintage?"

"It was good and I'm hot." She freed herself from Guardian's arm and after a few moments of struggle and muted snarls of frustration, the white lab coat as well. "There, that's better!" She triumphantly spiked the inside-out garment to the floor. Her expression became subdued. "Question…"

"Yes darling?" Guardian felt a kind of mirth bubbling up despite the day's events.

"How do you hide your boots?" She pointed to the white swashbuckler footwear and their neat mid-calf folds. "When you're not… you know…dressed like that?"

"Well, luvie, would you like to see?"

Jennifer gave her a sideways look. "You're not about to get naked, are you? I can't take that level of perfection today."

"Perfection? You're beautiful Jennifer," she said sincerely. "Intelligent, kind, and beautiful."

"Please don't matronize me."

"I'm not doing anything of the sort. How do you stay so willowy?"

"Does eye rolling count? Because I do that about three

hundred and sixty-eight times a day."

"No." The blonde shook her head, giggling with amusement. "No, it does not."

Jennifer sighed exasperatedly. "Okay....Every day I eat my vegetables do my squats, wear red lipstick, and don't let the boys be mean to me. By the way, what shade is that?" She gazed at Guardian's lips.

"All sensible practices and this one is called Cramoisie, I'll purchase you a few tubes when I pick up the Joie de Vivre."

"That's very generous of you."

"It's my pleasure."

"So, are you going to get naked or what?"

Guardian tittered. "I'll put that remark down to the wine."

"Down some more wine? On it!" Jennifer seized the bottle and drank the remaining few ounces in one pull. "It's been a long day." She wiped the corners of her mouth and peered longingly into the bottle for signs of more.

"Jennifer..." Guardian looked at her with concern.

The redhead cringed. "I'm sorry, I didn't offer you any."

"I don't normally drink wine."

"Why do you have so many bottles of it?"

"On occasion I have need of a bottle but otherwise, I keep it more as a legacy of human achievement and joie de vivre."

"Then what gets you buzzing?"

"I like to sing, dance, laugh—"

"Sex!"

Elizabeth chortled. After decades of teaching sexual education and enjoying the act herself, the raunchy and the ribald did not faze her. "Yes, I quite like sex. I know some people don't approve—"

Jennifer's eyes flashed with anger. "Well fuck those people!"

Elizabeth's blinked with disbelief. "Jennifer?"

"Fuck those prigs and trolls. If you're lucky enough to find someone you like and they like you, who cares if it lasts for one night or forever?"

Elizabeth chuckled, grateful for the support. "Thank you. Eight hundred years has afforded me the opportunities for my share of...buzzing."

Jennifer's anger vanished in an instant to be replaced by a triumphant grin. "Woo! Exactly! Buzz! Buzz! Buzz!"

Guardian smiled despite herself. "Indubitably. Now, are you ready?"

"Show me what you got! Hit me!" She slammed a hand down on the desk and pulled herself up on the furniture's edge to sit and watch.

Prepare to be knocked over with a feather. "Very well, one...two...three!" Guardian's vestments began to shimmer and morph. As Jennifer gasped and shouted with surprise, Guardian's cape melted into the body of the leotard, a circle skirt dropped like a curtain from her waist to her knees, her gloves withdrew and her sleeves shortened into puff sleeves on her shoulders, white fabric darkened to powdered blue and the symbol on her chest disappeared into a row of black buttons that ran down below her bust line. Using her imagination issuing a mental command, the body suit and cape were now a circle dress, her boots, had become black pumps.

"Oh my God!" Jennifer slid off the edge of the desk, pausing to steady herself. "That's amazing, how..." She stared. "How does it work?"

"My mother made it for me. She—"

"Can I touch it?" Jennifer pinched the hem of its skirt and ran it through her fingers. "It's so soft—like silk! And it's so cute! You're like a Little Suzie Homemaker—no, a Little Betty Homemaker, right out of the 50s!"

Elizabeth smiled with amusement. "I believe she made it out of primordial matter and energy—dark matter and dark energy, but no I don't think she—"

"Have you put it under the microscope?"

"I have," she said remembering the battery of tests she subjected it to.

Jennifer straightened up. "And?"

"The closest comparison would be stem cells."

"Wowzers! That might explain how it changes. But it's alive?"

"However not particularly sentient." Elizabeth smoothed her dress's skirt.

"You won't hurt its feelings saying that will you?"

Elizabeth's tresses bounced as she shook her head with amusement. "No...not at all. The dogs are better conversationalists and they only know a few hundred words. It just responds to images of what I want."

"Can I try it on then? I mean once you have something..." She glanced around and retrieved the discarded lab coat. "You could wear this."

"Erm, sorry—"

"Sorry, that was rude. I'm a little drunk." The redhead set the lab coat aside.

"I would let you but—"

"I'm not the right size? I mean you've got boobs; I mean you've got *boobs*! And I've got..." Jennifer glanced down at her chest and pulled on her top. "Acorns."

"Please stop. I won't stand for anyone saying such a disparaging thing about a friend, even if it's that friend that is saying it."

"But it's true. I—"

"Jennifer, if you're not on your side, who will be?"

Suddenly choked up, Jennifer lifted her glasses to run a hand across her eyes. "Thank you for being so nice to me."

"You're very welcome and remember what I said. Now, the

reason I can't let you try it on is that it would leave you in a coma."

"What? Why?"

"My clothing needs energy to change—even to maintain its shape. Humans possess only the tiniest fraction of what it would require to do something even as simple as change the color of one button."

"Wowzers! Then how much energy do you have?"

"Quite a lot."

"Is that twice as much as me? Five times as much? Ten times?"

"More than all of you, combined."

"All people?"

"The entire history of humanity and their predecessors."

"That's insane."

She recalled broken tools and door latches. "It did take some time and practice to pass as human."

"But that's how you fly and do pretty much everything?"

"Yes, with primordial energy—but by human standards, I'm a newborn, still inhaling my first breath as it were."

Jennifer chortled incredulously. "How long until you're considered a grown up?"

"In Earth time? A billion Earth years, perhaps a little more. By then I won't be able to hold onto this form. Anyway, we were talking about clothing, weren't we?"

"Right." Jennifer folded her arms and began to walk around the blonde, eyeing the garment with fascination. "And it can change into anything you can think of?"

Guardian turned her head to follow the scientist. "Anything so far."

"So you can do telepathy? What am I thinking now? No—I mean say something into my brain. Hit me with it!" She goaded, beckoning with her hands.

Elizabeth giggled good-naturedly. "No-no, it only works with the suit."

"Hmm..." Jennifer cradled her chin in her hand in thought. "There's something I want to ask you but I can't think of it." She lifted her hand to speak then frowned. "Nope, it's gone."

"I'm sure it will come to you."

"Oh, well." Jennifer frowned. "I have something to show you too!" Jennifer skipped to the desk and pulled a manila folder from her handbag. "Ta-da! Your tattoos!" She proudly thrust the folder into Elizabeth's hands. "I even put a queen's crown in the middle!"

Elizabeth opened the folder and flipped through the contents, her eyebrows raised in astonishment.

Inside were pages of tattoos of the continent of Africa, blacked in with two narrow borders of silver and white piping and a stylized white crown at the center. There were different sizes, some as large as a playing card, others as small as a quarter. The final page was filled with two columns of Marcus' name in stylized cursive. She mentally counted them, arriving at a total of twenty-eight.

"Marcus' name? For my shoulder? I told you I didn't want anything on my arms."

"Of course not! Those are for over your spasm chasm!" Jennifer grinned wickedly.

Elizabeth blinked, imagining it. "Have you taken leave of your senses! I can't do that. What sort of message would that send?"

"The kind that'll make him crazy—but, you're probably right, maybe not on the first date. But you could do one of the small ones on your left boob over your heart."

Envisioning the stares, she shook her head reflexively. "I don't think so."

"Okay...maybe one for your ankle? Very sexy."

Elizabeth wrinkled her nose and shook her head again. "Perhaps not."

"All right, then can you wear something backless? Something less goody-goody?" She giggled.

"But why?"

"Because I'm puttin' one on you right now."

"Are you sure you're steady enough for that?"

"I'll be fine. I'll just use the page to make sure the line is straight."

Elizabeth squelched her objection about straight lines still being quite capable of being on an angle. "Very well, allow me to think, won't you? Everything must be in contact, no bikinis, no bare legs with shoes—at least not symbiote shoes."

"Fine, just hurry up!" Jennifer waved her hand urgently.

"How about something more...urban?"

"Let's see it babe!" She swatted Elizabeth's backside.

"Calm down!" Elizabeth laughed with disbelief. *Betty homemaker, eh?* A mental command turned her dress into a backless halter top and high-waisted jean shorts. Her black pumps became Lucite mules. Only her tights remained the same.

"Woo! Urban sheik meets southern belle."

Elizabeth's face fell. "Truly?" She sighed. "I was attempting bawdy lass."

"More like sexpot!" Jennifer laughed.

"Sexpot? By the stars you're a silly goose!"

Jennifer reached behind Elizabeth to pulse a handful of the blonde's bottom. "Honk! Honk! Do you have scissors and a damp cloth?"

She pointed. "Try the drawers in the lavatory vanity." Elizabeth watched her go, hoping that the distraction would defuse Jennifer's state of upset.

Jennifer quickly returned with the needed items and took up

a position behind the blonde. "Now hold still and prepare to live a little," she murmured.

"I heard that and I've lived plenty." She felt like she was back at Sehemu Nzuri, putting her trust in one of the children to style her hair. The thought brought a brief surge of amusement and a twinge of pain.

"This is going to look so hot. Next we'll do your cutieous maximus!" she cackled.

The blonde turned her face to speak over her shoulder. "My cutieous is anything but maximus. You can bounce a quarter off of it."

"You can bounce a bullet off it." Jennifer gave Elizabeth's backside a swat for emphasis.

"I cannot fly around showing even the slightest bit of tattoo, the point of this...body art is a disguise, remember?"

"Okay, well maybe we'll save it for before your date."

Elizabeth didn't bother to argue the point. She stood by patiently, feeling Jennifer use the cloth to gently press and smooth the tattoo to her skin.

"This tattoo will give your skin some character," Jennifer declared.

"You're a character."

"Yep, and you're very white."

"Hence the tanning stall."

Jennifer's head ducked around as her fingers traced Elizabeth's skin. "Do you even have a blemish? I mean, *anywhere?*"

Only the kind you can't see. Guardian spoke over her shoulder. "I'm hardly perfect."

"Don't move."

"Sorry."

"So are you wearing this tomorrow night?" Jennifer continued to smooth down the tattoo.

Elizabeth chortled with disbelief. "I don't bloody think so. Perhaps on our second date."

"Hah!" Jennifer scoffed.

"Truthfully," Elizabeth spoke over her shoulder, "I think I've narrowed it down to a dozen."

"Only a dozen?"

"I do believe I have the perfect jewelry; I have an Africa charm for my anklet and another for a necklace or a choker."

"Choker...we'll put your hair up, it will look so hot."

"I'm placing myself in your capable hands."

"So...tell me about your experiences being a Bettilicious sandwich."

"I beg your pardon?"

"You know? Those two Black guys you lived with? One in the front and one in the—"

"I take your meaning!" Elizabeth smiled self-consciously.

"Well spill it!" She completed her dabbing and patting with the damp cloth. "Tell me about being a spit roast!"

"Such colorful terminology; are you quite done?"

"I'm just getting started!" Jennifer grinned.

Elizabeth shook her head, sighed, and took her friend by the hand. "Come along."

Jennifer followed, using the stairs' handrail to steady herself. "Don't you want to see it? I gave you one of the big ones."

"In a moment, first I must show *you* something." The soles of her mules clicking on the granite stairs, Elizabeth led Jennifer upwards.

Figuring it was better to have her boisterous and lascivious rather than angry and blue, Elizabeth allowed Jennifer to continue her jabbering and teasing all the way to the main floor. Her jibes abated as she beheld the parlor.

Jennifer gasped. "You weren't kidding about being a queen!"

Elizabeth looked down at her outfit and spoke in sotto voce.

"Yes, a queen in hot pants and five-inch heels."

"And one that rules from a branch of Buckingham Palace."

Elizabeth felt a kind of amused pride as her friend's expression changed from one of buffoonery to one of fascination. She watched as Jennifer's gaze flitted from the Persian rug beneath their feet, to the wainscoting and molding around the doors and ceiling to the antique furnishings and magnificent art.

"Is that a da Vinci?" She pointed to a painting in a gilded frame.

"Yes, and with all respect to your genius, he was the most brilliant person I've ever met."

Jennifer folded her arms across her chest and looked Elizabeth over. "Mona Betty."

"I think I have better cheek bones than Lisa."

"You have better everything bones than Mona Lisa, you'r more like Mona Aphrodite."

"And which goddess are you?"

"Probably one of the virgin ones, Athena maybe."

"A wise choice and forgive me for asking but you've...I mean...haven't you?"

"Not lately babe. I'm as tall as a twelve-year-old and mutually boring conversations doesn't make for the best aphrodisiac."

Elizabeth frowned with sympathy. "I'm sorry. Would you mind too terribly if I—"

Jennifer's eyes lit up. "Set me up with someone? Like a hunky astronaut? Maybe I should make you a list?"

Elizabeth smiled. "I'll see what I can do."

"No, we need someone for *me* to do." Jennifer waggled her brows.

Elizabeth chuckled. "By your command, Athena."

Jennifer's gazed wandered further, her expression became

awestruck. "That's a Van Gogh."

"Yes, and there are two more of his, upstairs."

The scientist took a few steps, "And that's a Picasso." She pointed to a proto-Cubist painting. "I'm going to have to sit and look at these when I'm not as blurry."

And I will have to check the angle of the tattoo. "He was a rake in word and deed."

"A rake, huh? Did you two ever?" Jennifer stirred a finger into her opposite palm. "Mix paint?"

Elizabeth lifted a hand to her mouth to stifle her laugh, "I was his patron not his muse."

"Not your type?"

"It's more about charm, wit, an ability to dance—"

"And fuck!"

We must get you a boyfriend soon. "Well, to one degree or another but with some very subtle tutoring—when necessary, an average or even above average night becomes—"

"A night of hair-pulling, sheet-ripping, ass-smacking, fun?"

Elizabeth chortled at Jennifer's fascination. "I'm certain any of their future partners will appreciate the improvements, I know I did." She smiled in memory. "Now, are you quite done?"

"Never!"

Elizabeth sighed. "Jennifer, you must understand, those men were just fun and—"

"Fellatio?"

Elizabeth's eyes slid shut momentarily as she shook her head in amused disbelief. "Play, mutually agreed upon adult play, like sharing a ride on a roller coaster with a stranger. There's excitement—"

"And vomiting."

Elizabeth regarded Jennifer with patient amusement. "I was about to say, that it's novel, thrilling, and most of all, you know where it ends. A relationship is like sharing a long journey by car, despite detours and disasters, you're with them, both of you committed to the journey, going in the same direction, even if there is an occasional bout of car sickness. One is frivolity, the other is love."

"And Marcus?" Jennifer grinned.

Elizabeth couldn't help but smile at the mention of his name. "He's more than fun—at least I hope." Seeing she had at least temporarily cowed Jennifer's antics, she turned towards the opposite wall, "Now would you like to meet, in a manner of speaking, the two fellows who showed up at my door one cool April morning?"

"The two runaway slaves?"

"The very two."

"Story time!" Jennifer rubbed her hands together.

"Come on, you." Elizabeth surrounded Jennifer's shoulders and gently guided her towards a portrait of her between two, handsome, smiling Black men. "Allow me to introduce you to two of my husbands, George, and Benjamin."

"You weren't teasing. But how did it work? Did they get jealous?"

"George and Benjamin were as close as brothers and were the best of friends long before I met them. When they arrived, Benjamin had pneumonia and needed to be nursed back to health. While he convalesced, it was clear to all of us that there was something between all of us. Once Benjamin recovered, we had a very direct conversation in this very room."

"What did you say?"

"I told them that I knew how they felt about me and that I would not come between them."

"But then you did!" Jennifer cackled.

Elizabeth rolled her eyes and sighed good-naturedly. "Needless to say, we had a very adult understanding that if they were to remain, I would not favor one over the other, and we would be together as husbands and wife." She shrugged, "They were agreeable."

"I bet they were."

Elizabeth shook her head with amusement. "We didn't spend all of our time making love. Our days were chores, lessons—they were both brilliant men, quick studies who, I think if their circumstances were different, could have been professionals. But after lessons, there was lunch, and reading, or music, or walks in the woods or fishing down by the sea. It was..." Her expression became wistful. "Quite wonderful."

"And hot."

Recollecting them in vivid detail, Elizabeth tipped her head back as her hand rose to her throat. "Oh, by the stars I loved those men! When we were together, it was like...gelignite."

Jennifer cackled. "That intense?"

"They were vigorous, assertive..." Elizabeth took a deep breath in an attempt to calm herself and banish the rosy flush that kissed her cheeks. "And they were good husbands—even if we weren't legally married."

"No, not that! I mean, did they leave you waddling and aching?"

"Well darling, to put it indelicately, our first time I thought I was going to split!"

Jennifer clapped her hands together triumphantly. "Now that's the kind of story I'm talking about!"

Elizabeth smiled, feeling a touch of melancholy. "I miss them." Her gaze traced the length of the line of portraits. "They take a piece of you when they go, but they leave a piece of themselves too..."

Jennifer's expression sobered. "I suppose that's true, isn't it? That must be so hard for you. Is that why you only stay in one place for a short time? So, you don't have to see us...go?"

Elizabeth regarded her thoughtfully. "Well, you're never

truly gone."

"I know, as long as we're remembered, but still..."

"As I said, there is more to you than stardust, Jennifer Novak." She gave the other woman a penetrating look.

Jennifer's brow crinkled.

"Now..." She directed the redhead's attention to the mantle clock. "The afternoon grows late and I have that house call this evening that includes a dinner invitation but before I go, I will fix you anything you like for supper."

Jennifer's eyes fluttered; she lifted a hand to stifle a yawn. "I'm sorry. I think the thing I need most right now is a nap." She yawned again and apologized again.

Elizabeth stifled a reflexive yawn of her own and led the way towards the hallway staircase. "Well, let's get you a room and I will prepare...what was it...?Hawaiian pizza that you prefer?"

"With orange pop?"

"I wouldn't think of serving it with anything else."

Jennifer halted their progress to look at the blonde in earnest. "Now I remember what I was going to ask. Elizabeth, why did this happen?"

The blonde regarded the other woman with sympathy. "I can say with certainty, darling, that it wasn't to hurt you, as for the rest, does it matter? All that matters is what we're going to do about it."

6:50 PM, Leesburg, West Virginia

Elizabeth left Jennifer contently chewing pizza in her kitchen while in the mudroom, Delilah and Butler licked their chops, hanging on every bite. The symbiote, now a summer dress, fluttered about her calves as she stepped around puddles on the sidewalk in front of Shannon's home. She carried a bouquet of flowers for Shannon's mother and a carpet bag containing her medical equipment and two softly clinking bottles of sauvignon blanc. Looking forward to using her skills to help someone in desperate need, Elizabeth could not help but smile. Raising a finger to ring the bell, she heard the seal of the front window to her right crackle as it was cranked open to a narrow slit. A middle-aged woman, wearing a blue scarf atop her head and a surgical mask over her face, glared at her through the glass.

"Ms. Kerr? How do you do? I'm—"

"Y'all get the hell away from our house! We don't need any of your Ebola-AIDS here! And stay away from my Shannon too!" she hissed in a thick West Virginia accent.

Stunned, Elizabeth stepped out onto the cement walkway to face her. "I believe there's been some sort of mistake. I don't—"

"You're trespassing. Now get to walkin' or I'm gonna call the police." She held up a telephone receiver.

"Ms. Kerr, I—"

"Now get!" She continued to glare.

Deciding not to exacerbate the situation further, Elizabeth bade her goodbye and walked back down the empty driveway to the sidewalk and around a neighbor's privacy hedge to call Shannon.

It rang three times before Shannon picked up and after determining who it was, immediately began to apologize. "I'm sorry I didn't know how to contact you. The senator asked me to come along to dinner at the Watergate and I couldn't say no."

Rupert. A feeling of protective anger began to rise in Elizabeth's breast. "Asked or told? What I mean is, would there be consequences if you said no?"

"These are good opportunities for me, I learn a lot at these dinners—just a moment please."

Elizabeth listened through Shannon's hand covering the mobile device's microphone. Longstreet approached Shannon in the hotel's lobby. "Shannon, I've got to go. You show Adrian a good time tonight."

"Sir? Shannon asked.

"Order anything you like; the meal is on him. Give my regards to your mother."

"Yes, sir." She removed her hand from over the mobile device's microphone.

"I guess I've got to go and keep Adrian company."

"Shannon, wait." Guardian spoke quickly, "I realize it's none of my affair but this situation sounds rather untoward. If you're not comfortable, you can excuse yourself and leave."

"I have to roll out the welcome mat all the time at the office for the Senator's guests, ma'am."

"But this isn't the office and you haven't known Rupert as long or as well as I have."

"This isn't my first time having dinner with a man."

"Of course, but I must advise caution."

"Thank you for your concern, ma'am, but I shouldn't keep him waiting."

"Shannon, wait please." Guardian thought quickly. "Would you mind too terribly if I called you in an hour to check on you?"

"A rescue call?"

Guardian pondered the term for a split second. "Yes, a

rescue call."

"If it makes you feel better then that would be fine, ma'am."

"I will call you in one hour then."

"Perfect. Don't worry, and again, I'm sorry about my mother."

"I'm sorry I wasn't able to help her."

"I'll talk to her but I've got to go, bye."

Elizabeth glanced down at her bag and looked back in the direction of the Kerr home and frowned with frustration. She could have helped Shannon's mother and taken away Longstreet's leverage in the process. She checked Harold's app for incidents involving metahumans in the news. There was nothing pressing, no emergencies to respond to, but that did not mean there were not others who needed help.

She started with a telephone call to Ruth Atkinson who informed her that Melanie was in the custody of the Army Medical Research Institute, and they were attempting to get access.

"We'll file a writ of habeas corpus but it may take time for a federal judge to decide," Ruth explained.

Expressing her appreciation, Guardian ended the call and set off for people who wanted and needed her help while carefully avoiding the complications of Boston.

In Philadelphia, she swooped to the rescue just in time to catch a reporter plummeting from a news helicopter that had become ensnared in its skyscraper's landing pad's stabilizer cables. She followed it up by catching the helicopter after the cable gave way, safely carrying both the befuddled reporter and the helicopter back to the rooftop. On Interstate-95 freeway, she rescued a tractor-trailer driver. She tore the door off his burning rig then ripped away his jammed seatbelt as easily as if it were a cobweb, freeing him. In Miami, she stopped a car-jacking in progress. None of it was surgery, but saving lives and the heartfelt thank-yous were fulfilling—particularly after the kind of day it had been.

Hoping Shannon had already fled from her conscripted dinner, Guardian placed her call precisely one hour later. On the third ring, Shannon picked up. "Hello, Shannon, how—"

"Hi mama. It's pretty noisy here, hold on a second."

Guardian heard the clink of silverware and the soft din of conversation in the background, it faded after a moment.

"Shannon, it's Guardian."

"I know I'm sorry, but I couldn't say hello to you on the phone without tipping him off."

"How are you faring?"

"He's getting really flirty and hinting at dessert in his room."

Guardian felt a surge of anger. Pandering was a low she did not think Longstreet capable of. She was disappointed to be wrong. "Shannon that is beyond—"

"I know, but I need this job."

"But at what cost?"

"I know but—"

"Do you need me to come there?"

"You can't, you absolutely can't. You know how the senator feels about you. I'm just trying to think of something. Maybe I could fake being sick?"

I know I'm feeling a little nauseous. Guardian thought of her own past. "Or you could try this...." She quickly began to detail a plan.

"Are you sure this will work?"

"For the sort of company Rupert Longstreet keeps? I'm certain he won't be expecting it in the least."

"Could you maybe call back in say twenty minutes?"

"I'll be overhead if you need me before then."

"Thank you, ma'am, wish me luck." Shannon hung up.

Guardian found the address of the hotel and flew for its rooftop.

Shannon negotiated her way through the Watergate's bustling dining room back to her seat. "Sorry about that." She smiled brightly.

"I was beginning to think you'd run off with another handsome stranger." Adrian Crowley smirked.

"That was just my mom."

"Let me guess..." His eyes narrowed. "She's sick."

"Just the opposite actually, she was ecstatic for me when I told her I had met the man of my dreams, and she wanted to come along."

Crowley began to grin. "She wants to come along? Does she look like you?"

"You're so funny!" She giggled. "When you elope it's supposed to be just the bride and groom."

Adrian's expression changed to one of bewilderment. "I beg your pardon? Elope?"

"Of course; and then we'll have..." She raised her hands and simulated air quotations. "Dessert upstairs afterwards. But first we need to find a chapel. I never thought it would happen this way but it's such a dream come true!" She beamed at him.

Crowley's face screwed up. He looked at her wine glass. "Just how much of that have you had?"

"I'm not drunk, silly! Should we talk about children now or wait until after the ceremony?" She grabbed his hand to squeeze it.

"Wait a minute..." He assumed a wry grin. "Are you fooling with me? Was that Chuck White on the phone? Did he put you up to this?"

"Of course not, sweetie, it's not the kind of thing you discuss with your boss. I just can't believe you felt the same way. But it all makes sense now, the way you always stop to say hello, the compliments, the way you look at me when you think I don't see!"

"You're serious?"

"Uh-huh. Aren't you?"

"Does Senator Longstreet know you're like this?"

"A big sappy, romantic? It's never really come up...but I'm so happy that—"

"I think you've got the wrong idea and we should just leave it right here." He freed himself from her clutching hand and stood up.

"But Adrian—"

He waved to their server. "I'll take care of the check. You...you just keep your distance."

"But Adrian...." she pleaded.

His expression hardened. "Get help." He strode past her in a rush to the cashier.

Pressing her cambric napkin to her face to cover her grin, Shannon feigned heartbreak and scurried for the restroom.

Guardian carried Shannon and her car all the way back to Leesburg before setting her down in her driveway. They paused on the patio outside the backdoor.

"That was amazing, if anyone had asked me if I would be flying home from work...well, thank you. I guess as a superhero you hear that a lot."

There was that appellation again. "You're welcome. Could you answer a question for me?"

"Of course, ma'am?"

"Can you tell me why you wasted this gorgeous cocktail dress on that bounder?" She gestured to the young woman's garment.

Shannon looked down at her clothing and snickered softly.

"Thank you, but it's just one I keep in the office for nights like tonight. But I have to admit, before he ran out of there, I was absolutely terrified that he might actually take me up on your idea."

Guardian frowned. "Birds of a feather flock together, if he's a friend of Rupert Longstreet, he's not the type."

"But Senator Longstreet was married before, and hasn't remarried because he says he can't imagine ever being with anyone else."

Guardian's face soured. "Well, that's utter rubbish. He attempted to make me into an 'anyone else' and that was only six months after he married."

"Are you sure?"

"Quite sure."

"That's awful!" Shannon's fist rose to her mouth, a look of pain marring her pretty features.

"To be perfectly honest, I'm rather surprised that you're not more upset with him for putting you in that position."

"I know," Shannon said apologetically, "but what can I do? I need this job to keep my insurance to take care of mama."

And he gets to extort you with it. "And that is precisely why I wanted to help your mother, to take away his leverage."

"Requesting that I stay to have dinner with his favorite lobbyist isn't exactly the worst thing."

She decided not to press the issue of Longstreet's procuring ways. "Who was this lobbyist anyway?"

"His name is Adrian Crowley; he represents Grey and Steele."

Guardian's nose wrinkled with distaste. "He has quite a few ties with them, doesn't he?"

"Yes, he worked there for a time and the two of them talk and email every day—the law requires a lobbyist as a go between for things related to business."

"What sort of things—if you can say?"

Shannon shrugged. "The kinds of things you'd expect: consideration for contracts, legislative benefits, cuts to regulations, that sort of thing."

"Influence peddling and graft then."

Shannon sighed. "It's the way things work in Washington."

Guardian began to turn ideas over in her head. "Yes, but that doesn't make it right." She turned her attention to the backdoor. "Do you think your mother might be more amenable to meeting me if you were present?"

"I don't really know a lot about what you mentioned earlier today, but she should at least hear about them."

"She did threaten to call the police on me when we spoke earlier."

"Oh my God, I'm so sorry!" Shannon's brow creased, "But it's my house and you're my guest so you can come in and at least say your piece."

"I wouldn't wish to cause any difficulties between the two of you."

"You're trying to save her life. I'll take that kind of difficulty any day ma'am. Come on in."

Guardian followed Shannon through the backdoor into a small kitchen. The strong scent of tobacco smoke wrinkled her nose

"Mama, I'm home!" Shannon called towards the front of the house.

"What happened? Why are you home so early from your date?"

"It wasn't a date, Mama, it was a dinner meeting."

There was a squeak of upholstery springs releasing. The older woman's voice approached the kitchen. "Honestly Shannon, do you think your looks will last forever? The Senator goes to the trouble of matching you up and—" She stopped short in the doorway, her annoyed expression becoming one of contempt. "What is she doing here? Get away from Shannon, before you make her sick!" She strode across the kitchen floor to grab her daughter's wrist and pull.

Shannon twisted free of her mother's grip. "I invited her, Mama."

"Shannon, she's got Ebola-AIDS! She's slept with every monkey in Africa!"

"Mama!" Shannon admonished.
Regarding the sallow-skinned woman as she barked and snarled insults, Guardian felt more pity than anger. "Ms. Kerr, I am a carrier of many things, memories, secrets, responsibilities, but not diseases."

"Don't you lie to me, Typhoid Mary! And don't you hurt my Shannon! Now get out! Get! Now!" She snatched up a tea towel from the counter to cover her mouth and nose, muffling her speech.

Shannon's jaw dropped open. She looked at her guest. "Oh my God! I am so sorry!" She looked back to her mother. "You apologize, Mama."

"No." Mrs. Kerr glared overtop the kitchen towel. "I read all about it in the paper and on the interweb." She held up a copy of The Spoiler from the kitchen table.

"Mama, I told you to stop looking at that trash! She helped me get away from a creep tonight!"

"Helped you? Probably cost you your job and if you don't have a job, then I ain't getting no medicine. She's killed me, Shannon. She's killed your poor mama. You gotta call the Senator right now. Tell him—tell him this Jezebel used some kind of mind power on you." She reached for the telephone on the wall and staggered. The towel fell from her hand. "Do whatever...needs to be...what he says..." Dorothy's words slurred, she lurched forward and began to fall to the floor.

"Mama!" Shannon lunged for her mother.

A sudden stiff breeze temporarily filled the kitchen. "I have her." Guardian halted Dorothy's fall, lifting the ailing woman up in the cradle of her arms. "Where is her room?"

Teary-eyed, her face filled with terror, Shannon grasped first at Guardian then at her mother. "Mama! Please help her!"

"Where is her room?" Guardian repeated herself.

"Down—down here." Shannon quickly led the way through the living room and down a short corridor to a smallish bedroom.

Guardian followed, laying her patient out on the bed. She removed a glove to press two fingers to the side of Dorothy's neck to feel for a pulse.

"Is she—is she having a heart attack?"

"Likely a CVA—a stroke."

"A stroke! Please don't let her die!" Shannon wailed.

Guardian pressed her hand to Dorothy's forehead. "She's going to be fine."

"I'm going to call 911." Shannon frantically found her mobile phone.

"Shannon...." Guardian's voice became soft and soothing. A halo of golden light shone forth from her face and filled the room. "I have her."

Shannon looked up from her frantic dialing and gasped. "What's happening?"

Guardian watched as the lines of pain and anger disappeared from Dorothy's features and a healthy glow returned to her complexion. Dorothy's breathing became soft and easy. Guardian looked back up at the young woman with a tranquil smile.

Shannon stared back at the blonde. "Oh my God, are you an—"

Dorothy murmured and her eyes began to flutter open.

"Not a word." Guardian raised a finger to her lips in a shushing gesture as the halo disappeared as if by a light switch.

As Dorothy's eyes opened completely, they hardened like bullets as she beheld Guardian. She retreated across the bed, pulling the coverlet up protectively to her chest. "What the hell are you doing here? Get out of my room! Get out of my house! I'm—" She looked around frantically and spied the bedside telephone. "I'm going to call the police!"

"Mama, no!" Shannon grabbed it up and hugged it away from her mother.

"Shannon," Guardian waved her off, "I think it would be best if I were to go."

"But...you just—" Shannon sputtered.

"Shannon! You give me that damn phone right now!" Dorothy demanded.

Guardian paused at the door to give the Kerr matron a look of pity. "Goodbye, Dorothy. Good night, Shannon."

"But Mama, she helped you."

"Helped make me sicker."

"Wait! Don't go!" Shannon paused to unplug the telephone from its jack and hurried after Guardian.

"Shannon, you just let that hussy go and get back here and help me find my cigarettes!" Dorothy shouted.

Shannon caught up to Guardian in the kitchen. "Can you just wait a minute? Please?"

Guardian's cape swirled about her as she turned and found herself swept into a vice-like hug.

"Thank you!" Shannon sobbed. "Thank you for my mother, thank you for my family. Thank you for coming to help us."

Her heart was touched by the outpouring of emotion, Guardian wrapped her arms about the young woman. "I'm glad I could, luv," Guardian murmured.

"I'm so sorry about my mama...I can't believe you helped her after all the things she said." Shannon sniffled, releasing Guardian to retrieve a tissue from a box on the kitchen counter.

"Your mother needed a piece of my heart more than she needed a piece of my mind. How long has she been in pain?"

Shannon dabbed at her eyes and sniffled. "Umm...she was diagnosed with cancer about ten months ago."

"And the addiction to nicotine?"

"Right after my daddy died, she went from a casual party smoker to two packs a day."

Guardian's features softened with sympathy. "I'm so sorry about your father. Losing a loved one can be quite traumatic, and addiction is often a response to trauma."

Shannon swallowed a lump in her throat. "But what can we—or at least what can I, do to thank you?"

"Well, you could get out from under Rupert Longstreet's thumb, so I don't have to worry about you." Guardian's eyes twinkled with warmth.

"First thing tomorrow, I'm going to do that." Shannon's expression became pensive. "But..."

Guardian tilted her head. "But?"

"What will happen to the next girl?"

Guardian regarded her thoughtfully. "Yes. What indeed?"

Shannon's eyes flitted from side to side. "And if he runs for president and wins? Oh my God, for him to have that much power..."

Guardian tapped her chin with her index finger. "Then we'll have to do something before then, won't we?"

"We? I mean you could fly him to the moon, but what can I do? He's not just a senator, he's *the* Senator, the leader of the majority."

An image of the proposed solution brought a brief crease of amusement to Guardian's lips. "There will be no flying him to the moon. He's already convinced enough people that I'm dangerous, that would most certainly confirm it."

"Then what?" Shannon lifted her hands in a shrug.

"Do you know who he meets with? Who he calls? Who he emails?"

"Of course; I do all of his scheduling—and everything else until most of the staff get back next week."

"Well, that doesn't leave us a very big window. Would you mind doing something a little shifty?"

Shannon stood in silence for a moment. She turned her gaze towards her mother's room before looking back at Guardian. "What do I have to do?"

4:30 AM Sehemur Nzuri, Kenya

Leaving Shannon, Guardian turned her mind to her own family. Floating high above Sehemur Nzuri, the peace of the sleeping camp contrasted with the turmoil she felt. She would miss the companionship of these friends, the singing and dancing, the telling of jokes and stories. Leaving all of them without expRuthtion was bloody unfair—heartbreakingly so.

They needed her, especially the orphans. She, more than any other staff, answered their never-ending questions, cared for their bumps and bruises, held them when they felt sad or scared. She read to them, sang to them, and kissed them goodnight. They were alone in the world; she knew about that. Equally frustrating, there was no where to direct her anger. A rock from space? A journalist doing what probably a thousand others were also doing?

Reminded of Sean Ramos, she looked down for signs of journalists and wondered how long it would have taken to discover her association with the camp. She knew the nuns would be discrete but other aid staff might not be able to contain the urge to brag about sharing even a casual acquaintance with her. Sharing that information through an email or telephone call home would likely speed the world to the camp's gates. She had to go, but not without telling at least one person why.

She was relieved to spy a long rectangle of light stretching out across the hardpacked road outside the camp director's office. A single shadow flitted across its expanse. Ever the early riser, Ayana was awake.

Changing the symbiote to her customary camp clothes, a cotton blouse and khaki slacks, she landed nearby and approached the door, with all the solemnity and gnawing sorrow of a death notification. Inhaling deeply, she set her shoulders back and rapped gently.

"Yes?" Ayana opened the door, her face broke into a broad smile of recognition. She threw her arms around her friend. "Elizabeth! What a wonderful surprise! It is so very good to see you!"

Ayana's hug was a balm. Elizabeth held on for many moments, finding solace in its warmth. "I'm glad to see you too." Struggling to keep her expression even and friendly, she wondered when she would see her again after tonight.

"Please..." Ayana stepped back to bid her to enter. "Come inside." She stepped to one side to allowing passage while waving mosquitos away from the door.

Elizabeth's boots softly scraped the tiled floor as she stepped into the middle of the room. A wheeled linen cart sat next to Ayana's desk, neat stacks of towels and pillow cases atop it indicated she was using it as an improvised laundry table.

Ayana plucked up a fresh towel from the cart as she followed after the blonde. "We have you to thank for this."

Elizabeth regarded her friend with puzzlement. "I'm not sure I understand?" She picked a towel from the cart to assist in the folding.

"Guardian."She threw up her hands in mock exasperation. "*Everyone* wants to be Guardian." She began to fold the towel. "The children have been taking the towels and linens from the hospital to wear as capes!" Ayana smiled with amusement.

"By the stars..." Elizabeth said in a mystified whisper. She felt a warmth wrestle with the melancholy that afflicted her heart

Ayana chuckled. "The sisters are now posting a guard so that we will have enough for the hospital."

Ayana folded the towel first in half and then into three even sections. "They have seen you on the internet and it is been a good thing. The children are better behaved in school and we are never short of little helpers these days. All of them—even the boys, want to be you, brave, kind, helping people. Even when you are not here, you are making things better; you are quite an example. Why, if I were to go out and tell them—"

Elizabeth swallowed the sudden lump in her throat, while raising her hand in a halting gesture. "Please don't—I mean I do so badly want to see them—all of them, but—"

Ayana ceased her folding and fixed the blonde with a look of concern. "But why not?"

"Have any reporters come here to talk with you about me?"

"No, should we be expecting someone?"

Only mildly relieved by the news, she pressed on with an air of urgency. "What about that documentary crew from France? Are they still here? Do they know about me?"

"They left for home as soon as the news came about the asteroid, but I think, thanks to you, they all got to see their families. Why do you not you want to see everyone?"

"There was this reporter..." Elizabeth began to recount Ramos' visit and the events of the day, how the Russian government had looked into her past aid work.

Ayana listened quietly, her expression changing to one of sympathy as Elizabeth's emotions played out. At the end of the blonde's account she set aside her laundry and surrounded Elizabeth shoulders in a hug. "I see, so you have come to say goodbye."

"I don't want to go." She released a sigh that stretched right down to her toes. "But I can't remain if it puts all of you in danger. Honestly, I'm not sure if I can even be a doctor anywhere, anymore." She struggled to contain fresh tears.

"I am sorry," Ayana said softly.

Elizabeth held onto her for many long moments. Her friend's warmth tempered the weariness and sense of loss that threatened to overwhelm her.

Ayana drew back and brushed a strand of hair from Elizabeth's eyes. "I want to show you something." She walked around her desk to retrieve a folder from a side drawer, flipping through it she smiled and withdrew a sheet of paper. "I do not get nearly as many pictures drawn by the children as you do but I think this one will interest you."

Elizabeth took the crayon drawing from her. It was a brightly colored butterfly, its wings were orange and trimmed with yellow. The child who drew it had given the insect a smiling face.

"It's so cute," Elizabeth murmured.

"You are like a caterpillar that becomes a butterfly, living in the garden until it is time to change, but once it leaves its cocoon, it cannot go back, it must fly and be what it is. You cannot hide away in the forgotten corners of the world anymore, Elizabeth. The world needs you to be who you really are. The world needs Guardian."

Looking from her friend to the picture and back, Elizabeth's emotions were a tangle of confusion. "But I'm needed here."

"I know you do not wish to go, but this patient is thriving. The food-forests, the hospital and sanitation system, the school, and even the lamps over the roads." Ayana gestured towards the window. "The world is your patient now, she has many wounds that need tending. She—they, need you."

It was a bitter medicine to take. She wished her friend had, instead, come up with the solution to her conundrum. Elizabeth found herself unable to speak.

"You have said more than once that we are The Good Place not because of the work of any one of us but because of the work of all of us. Your work here is done, you have succeeded, that is something to celebrate and be glad about."

Ayana placed her hands on Elizabeth's shoulders. "We love

you and you will always be welcome here but the world needs Guardian. It would be selfish for us to keep her to ourselves. Also, as you said, you want us to be safe."

Elizabeth accepted another hug and swallowed another lump in her throat. "You remembered that part of my blathering?"

Ayana laughed softly. "I heard every word." Ayana released Elizabeth enough to give her a smile of gentle warmth. "Elizabeth, you are my friend, you are my sister, and you are *my* hero, you have my permission—our permission, to go—and go without worry or guilt about us."

Elizabeth drew a shuddering breath. In her heart, her friend's permission felt more like rejection but she knew it was not the case."I'm not certain if I will be able to manage the worry part."

"Do you trust us to continue on?"

"Of course, but—"

"Then do not worry. You have set an example for all of us to follow. And..." Ayana smiled with gratitude, "Thank you for choosing this camp. You have taught me so much about being a director."

Elizabeth snuffled and laughed with surprise. "I did?"

"Most certainly."

"Well," Elizabeth took a tissue from Ayana's desk to dab at her eyes, "I suppose I have picked up a few ideas here and there."

"The best of ideas, and we are all the better for it. Now..." Ayana turned to gesture to an electric kettle. "Can I make you a cup of tea?"

Despite her desperate desire for its comfort and an excuse to remain, she knew the answer. "I so dearly want to but..."

Ayana nodded. "There is so much to do."

"I'm sorry." Elizabeth grimaced.

"I'm not. I'm happy you will be all of who you are—even if it interrupts our tea."

"I should...I should get my things from my room."

"Of course." Ayana hugged her again.

"I wish this wasn't goodbye."

"It isn't. Wherever else you are, you are always here in my heart."

Elizabeth swallowed the lump in her throat. "Did I ever tell you that I love you?"

Ayana smiled. "Everytime we talk."

Ayana hugged her again. "And you are always welcome here—whenever you wish," Ayana whispered.

"I hope often." Releasing her, Elizabeth started for the door then paused and turned to gaze at the half-filled hamper with a critical eye. Her movements became a blur of activity.

Ayana clasped her hands together and lifted them to her cheek, grinning as she watched, in the span of seconds, the contents of the laundry bin emptied out, grow into neatly folded stacks on her desk and then quickly reappear in the hamper, ready to be returned to the hospital's shelves. "Wonderful! Thank you!" she gushed.

Surveying her handy-work, Elizabeth gave a satisfied nod. "And thank you—I would tell you to look after them for me but I know that you already do."

###

Working in the dark, Elizabeth finished packing her few belongings and turned to the art pinned her on walls. Every artist always received a hug and a kiss of genuine gratitude. These daily heartfelt gifts were among the things she would miss most of all.

The sound of crunching gravel and the flicker of a flashlight on the door caused her to tense, other than under the framed bed, there was no place to hide.

"Who's outta bed?" Sal's voice enquired in a tone that was almost playful. Holding a folder in one hand and a flashlight in the other, he stepped into the doorway and shone the light about.

"It's only me."

Startled, he swore softly, "Jesus!"

"I'm sorry," she apologized.

He gestured to the half-stuffed duffle bag and typewriter case on the bed. "So, you've had enough of us huh? The Singing Surgeon is packin' it in and takin' the show on the road?"

Elizabeth felt a rush of anger at his flippant remark. "How could you say that?"

"Hey! Whoa! I was just jokin'. What's goin' on? And why are you here in the dark?"

"I'm sorry Salvador but I won't be here to be the target of your philanderous overtures anymore."

"Target?" he asked defensively. "And what do you mean philanderous overtures?"

"Please, will you just allow me to do this in peace?"

"Hey..." His expression became one of concern. "What's goin' on with you?"

She spoke to him in terse tones. "A side effect of living a consequential life is consequences. I had no choice other than to push that asteroid aside, and I had no choice other than to help in its aftermath. The consequences of my choices are that in order to keep all of you safe, I must leave."

"Wait a minute...there's a lot goin' on in that sentence. Safe from who?"

She halted her work to glare at him. "Haven't you seen the news? The world. They're relentless, they'll come here looking for me and stories about me. Some won't be just curious, some will be malicious." Her expression changed to one of sorrow.

"And so you see," her voice trembled, "I must go and that as they say, is that." Feeling her emotions welling up again, she turned back to her task.

Sal grimaced with sympathy. "I'm sorry, I didn't know." He watched her for several minutes, holding up the light and shining it where she was working. "Is there anything I can do?"

Not taking her eyes from her work she said, "Could you please turn that torch off? I don't think I could weather explaining things to the entire camp."

"Sure." He clicked off the light. "I guess that's one of your super-powers, huh? Seeing in the dark?"

Elizabeth kept focused on her work, increasing the pace. "You've been taking care of the children?"

"I told you I would."

"Yes, you did." She turned her head long enough to give him a sad smile. "Thank you."

"Were you worried?"

"Not about your ability." She resumed her careful work, plucking out pins and stacking the crayon-artwork in a neat pile.

Sal's expression changed from concern to thoughtfulness. "You know when it comes to kids, you're like my mother. She loves being a mom—in fact she's after all of us for grandkids—or more grandkids." He chuckled.

"I wish you well."

"You don't see what I'm gettin' at, let me finish."

"All right." The emotions the pictures evoked were piling up on her as the artwork likewise piled up. No longer needing to conceal her abilities, she increased her pace beyond what was humanly possible. "I'm listening."

He paused to watch her. "That's freaking amazing."

"You were saying?" She continued to work without a pause.

"Oh yeah—sorry. When I was just a kid my father got hurt at

work—he was a construction worker. After the insurance ran out, my mother had to get a job working at the hospital, cleanin' up rooms and messes. She wanted to be home for us—I mean she *really* wanted to. And my dad was proud; he didn't want her working either. We used to hear them fighting at night."

"I'm sorry, that must have been difficult."

"What I'm tryin' to say is that sometimes you've got to do what you got to do, even when you don't like it."

"I don't like it." She released a shuddering sigh and finished stacking the pictures on her table.

"Got some more for you." Sal put the folder on the table and flicked on the flashlight to illuminate its contents.

Elizabeth lifted the top picture to examine it. It was a crayon drawing of her, in white uniform, sitting on the stoop in New York with Mannie. She lifted the next one it was of her carrying the ambulance on her back in New Mexico.

He pointed over the top of the second drawing. "World's first self-propelled air ambulance."

A smile tugged at her lips.

"You're not gonna bench yourself, are you? I mean, you're the best cutter I've ever seen. You've got to teach what you know."

"Thank you, you're the second one to suggest that today."

"Well, it's true. Where did you learn to cut like that anyway? Some kind of space medical school?"

Elizabeth clucked softly in mirth despite herself. "No, not a space medical school."

"Then where?"

"I will tell you this in confidence, Salvador."

"All right, just between us. Shoot."

"I graduated from Johns Hopkins with a degree in medicine and general surgery in 1907. From there I went on and completed a neurosurgery fellowship at the Mayo Clinic in nineteen-fifty."

"Get outta town." He scoffed, "My great-grandmother was born in 1907."

The corners of her lips twitched upward. "Where? I might have delivered her."

"You're not foolin' with me, are you?"

She shook her head.

"You mean all this time..."

"Yes." She regarded him with amusement. "You seem to have an attraction to much older women."

"And here I thought...you must think I'm a Goddamned pup."

Elizabeth shook her head and spoke to him in cordial tones. "Not at all. You came to a place to help people who could never possibly pay you back. I think that's very noble and mature."

"Thanks, but they pay me back—every day, in fact. You're not the only one around here with a fan club, I get art too."

Elizabeth's smile made it all the way to her eyes. "That doesn't surprise me."

Salvador glanced over at the high, neat stack of medical journals on the table. "You ever get published in one of these?"

"No, but you may have them, I've finished reading them."

"And you remember everything in 'em, right?"

"Well...." She vacillated not wishing to brag. "Yes."

"Tsk," he scoffed out a chuckle. "Figures, another super power. You want for me to get my prescription pad and write it out for you? Teach two semesters and call me in the spring?"

"Thank you for the consultation, doctor." She laughed softly and then looked at him directly. "Will you tell me why do you do that?"

"Do what?"

"Talk in such...." She paused to consider a diplomatic phrase. "In such a downtown manner? You're an educated man. New

York University is an excellent school."

"I'm Brooklyn proud, but you're one to talk, Uptown Girl."

"I beg your pardon?"

"Best doctor in the world *and* you can even..." He made a swooping gesture with his hand. "You've been hidin' out and playin' for the farm team. You've been here too long Betts, time to get in the game, play in the big leagues."

Feeling chastised, she grimaced in acknowledgement. "Touché."

He shifted his weight from one foot to the other. "So uh...we're never gonna have that picnic are we?"

"Erm..." She looked at him sympathetically and gestured to the chair. "Please."

He took a seat and regarded her warily. "I don't like that look."

I don't like giving it. Elizabeth's bed creaked softly as she sat down on its edge. She lamented inwardly that she should be the world's best at the talk that she was about to give but she suffered right along with whomever received it—every time. She wanted for them to be all right afterwards—especially the good ones. "Salvador, what's your favorite fruit?"

His face screwed up. "What's that got to do with anything?"

"Please...." She looked at him imploringly. "Indulge me?"

He shrugged. "All right, grapes. So what?"

"Why? Why are grapes your favorite?"

"What does it matter?"

"Please?" She reached out to gently touch the back of his wrist.

Sal glanced down at her hand. "All right. Well, because of my grandfather, I guess. He has a little vineyard in his backyard on Long Island. He's the one who gave me that bottle of wine. Anyway, when we were kids, we would sit out there Sunday afternoons eatin' them in the shade while he told us stories about the Old Country. Then my grandmother would come out and give him hell for ruining our appetites before dinner." He chuckled in recollection.

"They sound delicious. My favorite fruit are mangosteens."

"What's that?"

"They're from south-east Asia. They have a tough outer rind with a sweet fragrant fruit inside."

"Sounds like somebody I know."

Elizabeth regarded him gentle patience. "Salvador, I will always be a second-rate grape for you and you deserve the best there is."

He grinned impishly. "I could learn to be a mangosteen."

"No...." Elizabeth shook her head good-naturedly. "I see you going back to America, having a thriving practice and being married with three or four children. Or you might meet someone here."

"Thought I had."

She took the rebuff in stride. "You're a good man and I'm flattered, but I can't give you what you want. You deserve someone with whom you can make a great vintage with...someone you can age gracefully with."

"Still a no on the picnic, huh?"

"I'm sorry."

"Well...." He frowned. "I'm sure a lotta guys hear that from you."

It was the truth. She sighed. "I burn men down. I don't want to—I desperately don't want to. They want me to be someone I can't be and they tend to get hurt."

"That's part of the risk Betts, win big, lose big. You can't half-ass your way through life. Now I've got a question for you."

Elizabeth's eyes fluttered as she contemplated giving him carte blanche. What would he ask her? Well, she could always refuse to answer if the question was untoward. She looked at him warily. "All right?"

"I want to know, when was the last time you were with someone?"

Elizabeth's brow furrowed, she looked at him sideways. "I beg your pardon?"

"Don't go gettin' your panties in a bunch. I didn't mean it like that. What I meant was when was the last time you let someone love you? Not a kid who loves you like their aunt or someone on staff who loves you like a sister, but the way a man loves a woman?"

Elizabeth pressed her lips together, considering whether to answer him. "It's been…it's been some time."

"Then I want you to do me a favor."

"What are you driving at?"

"Let somebody love you. Somebody good. Somebody who appreciates who you are and treats you right. Because that guy…." He licked his lips and looked away. "Because that guy will worship the ground you walk on and slay any dragon for you."

Elizabeth felt her heart clutch.

"Doctor's orders," he murmured.

"Doctors," she scoffed softly, "they think they know everything."

"Just the important stuff." He gathered up the artwork on the table and thrust it towards her. "Here, better not forget these."

Feeling his eyes upon her, she rose and took the artwork from him to carefully place it in the duffle. "And I won't forget you either, Salvador, I promise."

"That would be impossible; I'm unforgettable in every way."

"That's how you'll stay." She hefted the typewriter and duffle. "Thank you for taking care of the children."

"No problem, now… will you get outta here? Go on! Go find a

mangosteen, teach, stop movin' around and put down some roots. Maybe even save the world while you're at it."

She gently leaned in to press her lips to his cheek and whisper in his ear. "Thank you, and do take very good care of yourself, Sal."

Friday 10:30 AM, The Russell Building, Washington DC

Longstreet gazed out his office window at the cliques of tourists moving about the Upper Senate Park across the road. He listened through the telephone as Adrian Crowley explained the events of the previous evening.

"I don't know what to tell you my boy, maybe it was some kind of hormonal episode, makes them all crazy. But if you want another shot—"

"I don't think she understands how things work, Senator, she's been around right?" Adrian Crowley asked.

"That peach has been plucked for sure. I think she was just testing you."

"I want a make-up exam."

I'll bet you do. "I can arrange it but what have you been arranging for me? Let's talk about that other crazy blonde."

"The Typhoid Mary shtick is going over well but we need more."

"Yeah...let me think a moment..." Longstreet lowered the telephone to his chest and turned his attention to the park. He watched a toddler drop his recently-purchased hot dog onto the sidewalk and reach to pick it up. The little boy burst into tears as his mother grabbed it away before he could cram it into his mouth. The Senator smirked as the child's tears became a tantrum.

Turning his chair back towards his desk, he lifted the receiver back to his mouth, "I think I've got it. Is the bio-warfare lab still up and running?"

"Your baby has been very useful in creating new vaccinations to sell."

"What about the other part of it?"

"They're there too."

"People need to see how dangerous these 'morphs are—and

how dangerous she is."

"What did you have in mind, sir?"

"There's no telling what diseases she's been passing around. I think Grey and Steele needs to do a good deed and bring in anyone she's been around for a complete check-up—just to be sure that they haven't contracted anything. That bum in New York would be a good one to check."

"What about that TV reporter, he definitely seemed convinced he was in danger."

"Boothman? Yeah, he'd be another." He grinned wickedly into the receiver.

"And that cop in Chicago?"

"No, no cops, they get enough risk." He flicked a glance at his lurking chief of staff. "And they ask too many questions."

"No problem, I'll look into getting a list made. What about those two Black kids in Texas?"

"I'll have Barnes add them to his pickups, nothing like a couple of dead kids to drive a movement."

"You'll have the list by the middle of the afternoon."

"Good, we need to act quickly, my boy."

"I'll get on it, sir. And Shannon...?"

"You take care of that; I'll take care of her." Longstreet looked to Chuck and motioned with his head towards the outer office.

White nodded and moved off as Longstreet said his goodbyes.

Chuck positioned himself at the entrance of Shannon's wraparound desk. "You know who was just on the phone?"

Shannon looked up at him, her expression fearful.

He jabbed a thumb towards the inner office door. "Adrian Crowley. He said something...something so fucked I can't even believe it. He said you wanted to elope? What are you? Some kind of psycho?"

Shannon's skin flushed red. "No Chuck. I mean, I—"

"Sir. After the boss, I'm the most powerful, mother-fucking man in this building."

"Yes, sir."

"You may be blonde but do I have to fucking spell it out for you? Why do you think you were hired for this job? Your telephone skills? If a computer could give a good blowjob you'd be out on the street."

Shannon's eyes began to well.

"The next time the boss tells you to show someone a good time, you do it, or you'll never work in this town again. Are we clear?"

"Yes, sir."

"Now get in there and apologize—and don't you dare fucking cry."

"Yes, sir."

"And undo a couple of buttons. You're not a fucking schoolmarm."

She looked down and fumbled with the top button of her blouse, loosening it open.

"And another." Chuck watched her comply before allowing her to rise and move past him to the inner office's broad, wooden door.

Shannon paused and swallowed the lump in her throat before going in.

Longstreet looked up from his desk, noting with a smile, the way her creamy flesh peaked out from between the folds of her blouse. "Shannon! Come around here." He motioned with a wave of his hand. "Right around here behind the desk."

Trembling, the blonde moved to comply, going around to the back of his desk, lingering at its corner.

"A little closer now." He motioned again.

Shannon took a half a step forward.

"Come on, I won't bite. I want to see you." He opened his knees, watching her step closer.

"Yes, sir?" Her voice quavered.

Good girl. "You gave poor Adrian quite a start last night, but I have got to tell you that's one of the funnier jokes I've heard in a while. Elope? You had him all wound up. Good for you."

The corners of Shannon's lips creased upwards in a grimace. "Yes, sir—thank you, sir. It was a joke."

"A naughty one though, eh?"

"I guess, yes, sir."

"Seems to me, that as of late, you've been the naughtiest you've ever been. What would your poor mother think? I'll tell you what she'd think. She'd wonder what had gotten into her daughter who has always done everything that's been asked of her up to this point."

"I do my best, sir."

"Well, I'm just going to put it down to stress, after all you're the only one besides Chuck here right now and it has been a crazy week. So I'm going to give you a chance to make it up to me."

"Make it up—yes, sir."

"Turn around for me."

"Sir?"

"Go on, you just stay in place and do an about turn for me."

"Yes, sir." Shannon turned and glanced over her shoulder.

Longstreet rose from his chair and took hold of the curves of her hips, enjoying the softness. "You're a good-looking woman, Shannon."

Shannon trembled. "Th-thank you, sir."

He leaned into her and spoke in low tones. "You're going out with Crowley tomorrow night, and you're going to enjoy yourself, you hear?"

Shannon's breath caught. "Y-y-yes, sir."

"Do whatever you have to do to get all prettied up and if the dessert doesn't appeal to you, just close your eyes and think of this moment." His grip tightened. "Because if I get another phone call about you not staying for dessert, you won't work in this town ever again and you can go home and explain that to your dear old mama! Are we clear?"

She nodded vigorously.

His voice and mood brightened. "Good." His hand clapped against the under curve of her bottom. "Now get back to work and do me proud."

Her eyes wide, Shannon stumbled forward. She turned her face briefly towards him. "Yes, sir."

Longstreet watched her exit, admiring her backside all the way to the door before retaking his seat. *After tomorrow night, everything will fall into place.*

Friday morning, 8:45 AM, Avalon, Maine

Elizabeth's morning began with a news alert in the Caribbean via Harold's application. She flew straight away to prevent a floundering freighter from running aground on a coral reef.

Returning home, she began to prepare breakfast and looked up to see a bleary-eyed Jennifer lurch into the kitchen. Her guest wore red jeans, a Cincinnati baseball shirt that was so long on her slight frame that it could be a dress and, much to Elizabeth's pronounced amusement, a pair of gray, overstuffed, alien slippers.

Jennifer squinted against the sunshine that streamed through the window over the sink. "Oh my God, that's bright."

Elizabeth halted her breakfast preparations. "Good morning. How did you sleep?"

Jennifer cringed, covering her ears. "Ugh...not so loud. The sleeping was fine, it's the waking up that is the hard part. And I smell coffee." She looked around until her eyes came to rest on the Moka pot atop the electric range. "May I have some?"

"You may have all of it. I prefer tea." Elizabeth held up her steaming cup for emphasis.

"Thank you, thank you, thank you." Jennifer scurried to the stove top and began to look for a cup until Elizabeth handed her one. "Thank you."

Elizabeth watched with astonishment as the redhead poured herself a cup of the aromatic beverage, added a liberal amount of steamed milk, and drained it in one swallow.

"Oh, that's better," she murmured. "I have far too much alcohol in my coffee stream right now." She groaned again and poured herself another. "And thank you for getting my clothes and everything."

"Think nothing of it; the police parked in front didn't even stir a bit."

"Did you get to talk to my mom?" She took another long pull of coffee.

"I'm sorry there was a police presence, and I didn't wish to risk it. I'll look for another opportunity."

"That's okay, I'm sure the note was enough…" A wince of pain overtook her. "…oh my head."

"Can I offer you some relief?"

Jennifer groaned again. "Do you have a Tylenol the size of a Volkswagen?"

Elizabeth chuckled softly. "Nothing so weighty." The blonde set her cup down. "May I have your hand?"

"You can have all of me if you can stop my head from pounding." Wearing a pained expression, she held out her limb.

"There's a pressure point right here." Elizabeth gently pinched the web of flesh between Jennifer's thumb and forefinger. "This should give you some relief." Desperately needing the scientist in good health, she took the acupressure point to a whole new level, releasing some of her own energy into the other woman's body.

Jennifer blinked rapidly. Her grimace became a grin. "Wowzers! That's much better."

Elizabeth released her. "That meridian point is called He Gu, the Union of the Valley. Now, would you care for some breakfast? I have crepes, fruit, yogurt, and eggs."

"Some of everything please, I'm famished."

Elizabeth drizzled lemon juice over a crepe following it with a sprinkling of sugar for her guest. "It seems you enjoyed my pizza recipe."

"It was the best I've ever had."

"Thank you. The pineapple was fresh from Hawaii. The remainder is in a dish in the refrigerator if you would like a snack later."

"That sounds awesome thank you. Would you happen to

have a juicer and a spare ice cube tray?"

"The juicer is in the cupboard at your knees and you may empty one of the trays in the freezer. What are you concocting?"

"I would like to make juice cubes to put in water. They're better for me than drinking this stuff." She held up her coffee cup. "...or pop."

"A healthier practice to be sure." Elizabeth slid a plate containing crepes, eggs and a generous helping of berries, across the kitchen island to her. "I wondered if we might talk about yesterday."

"Oh...." Jennifer cringed. "How much of an ass did I make of myself?"

"I prefer the term cuteous maximus."

Jennifer blushed and sighed deeply. "Oh God, I am so sorry, I don't normally drink like that. In fact, I haven't been drunk in years. That's probably why my headache was so excruciating."

"Indubitably."

"You don't have to worry about your wine cellar, it's safe."

"Excellent. While you were sleeping, I was in England, obtaining that gene sequencer.

"The Nanopore-3Gen?" Jennifer asked.

"The 4Gen."

"There's a 4Gen? How much faster is it?"

"The four-hour 4Gen."

"That's insane!" the redhead marveled.

"It's a prototype. My publicist is working out the details of the endorsement campaign that I agreed upon to get it."

Jennifer cringed. "Endorsement campaign?"

"I know, but the situation is dire and I want you to have all that you need to discover the cause of these transformations."

"And clear my name."

Elizabeth felt the burden of responsibility weighing upon

her. "Most assuredly."

Jennifer and Elizabeth spent the day setting up the gene sequencer and preparing the laboratory to be ready for a new sample. As they worked, the scientist recounted what she gleaned from her initial analysis of Huan's blood.

"I mean I can't explain how he's even alive. Silicon, aluminum, sodium, calcium, all present in levels that should be toxic. And, there was one element I couldn't even identify; it's one percent of the sample, lighter than hydrogen—less than one mole per gram. I have that same problem with the metal sample you gave us of Rudy's, the spectroscopic output indicates an unknown element. And there were pluripotent stem cells present in the sample as well."

Elizabeth took a seat on a lab stool. "If you could have seen Stone Tiger change from a man into a living statue, you could see why the elements of granite are present."

"I think whatever was in that asteroid has to be element X. Is there any chance of getting a sample to analyze?"

"Marcus is helping me but it remains a work in progress."

Jennifer glanced at the clock on the wall. "Speaking of Marcus, shouldn't we be getting you ready for the ball, Cinderella?"

"Cinderella? I have no intention of being home by midnight."

"I hope you'll come waddling home after dawn. But I need time to weave my magic." She waved her hands like a mesmerist.

Elizabeth wondered who was more enthusiastic about this date, Jennifer, or her. "Well, Fairy Godmother, I did promise to put myself in your hands."

"And you won't regret it."

###

"What do you think of this one?" Her hair already done in an updo, Elizabeth stepped from behind the vintage dressing screen wearing a sugar-pink halter dress with a plunging neckline and box pleats that were well above her knees.

"I think he'll love it but if you're going dancing, your girls might come out to join you." Jennifer shook her shoulders for emphasis.

Elizabeth glanced downward. "*That* might draw some undo attention." She disappeared back behind the screen for a few seconds before reappearing in a black tank dress.

"Oh, that's very pretty and I like how it contrasts with your hair but it's summer, wear it after Labor Day."

"All right, thank you." She ducked back again behind the screen to order the symbiote to alter its appearance again. She reappeared in a filmy red dress cut high in the hemline and held up by a pair of spaghetti straps. "What do you think?"

"Wowzers, that's hot." Jennifer's hand came up to fan her face for emphasis. "But, if you wear that, you probably won't make it to dinner."

Elizabeth rolled her eyes mischievously. "Well, the thought had occurred...but since Marcus did go through the trouble of planning an evening, let's try something else."

"It must be fun having an unlimited wardrobe." Jennifer sat up on the end of Elizabeth's bed. "And a body to wear it," she murmured.

"Sometimes it's a hindrance. How about this?" she asked, stepping out in a cobalt blue skater dress. Cap sleeved, scooped low in the bodice and even lower in the back, its flirty hemline showed off her legs.

"Oh, that's it!" Jennifer clapped her hands together. "It's sweet, and sexy, and I love the white stockings and stilettos." She pointed to Elizabeth's four-inch heels.

"He likes my tights, and I think hosiery offers a bit of polish and sophistication."

"And its makeup for your legs—not that you need it."

"Yes...makeup. I think this dress is the one; are you ready for me?" Elizabeth smiled encouragingly and took her seat on the purple velvet pillow of her vanity's stool.

Digging into a makeup kit atop a tea cart, Jennifer began to apply primer. "I'm going to make your eyes pop and give you all-night lips."

"All-night lips?"

"It won't matter how much you drink or how many times you...kiss." Jennifer giggled. "It's guaranteed to stay."

"Well, he is a good kisser."

"And what else is he?" Jennifer waggled her brows.

"Brave."

Jennifer's smile vanished. "I didn't expect you to say that."

"He's the first one who has ever known about me and he's not treating me differently—at least, I don't get the impression he is."

"Unless he's acting at not being affected."

"No." Elizabeth resisted the urge to shake her head while Jennifer worked. "He's very assertive, confident, and straight-forward. I think he has too much integrity to deceive himself or me in that manner."

"He's sounding more and more like a keeper."

"Which frightens and thrills me in equal measure."

"For those of us not going out tonight, thrills and chills sounds like a fun evening."

"I'm sorry."

"It's okay. Now let's see... outfit, hair, tattoos—"

"Which I'm still getting used to."

"Oh come on, admit it, they look hot. But I didn't get to see the one you did yourself."

She took a second to glance in the direction of her ankle and smiled. "They do bring a certain feeling of naughtiness—and that last one is just for him." She recalled looking at herself in her closet's three-sided mirror and finding the look and the anticipation of Marcus' reaction, rather exciting.

"See? I said you would like them. Now where was I?"

"Tattoos?"

"Right, what else? Accessories, doing your makeup now, and… last, birth control."

"If he wants to wear something, I won't object."

"Bareback? For real?"

By the stars… "I should be going. I have to fly to Baltimore and hail a cab."

"Ok, have fun, be bad."

Elizabeth gave her a conspiratorial smile.

6:55 La Carroza Ristorante Baltimore, Maryland

As the yellow taxicab slowed, Elizabeth checked Harold's application one last time. No emergency alerts were popping up. That bit of good news did little to settle the butterflies in her stomach. Through the windshield, she spied Marcus standing on the curb. Smartly dressed, he wore a deep purple sports jacket over a black silk shirt and slacks. She saw him smile at her through the window. Her butterflies flew away, and a red bird fluttered in.

As she paid the cabbie, Marcus opened her door and extended his hand to assist her. She swung her legs out, hoping that he would see the anklet and accompanying tattoo.

"Hello, Mansa," Elizabeth purred sensually. "How do I look?"

"Like a woman who wants to kiss me."

"An astute diagnosis, Dr. Jackson." She giggled, then shrieked with surprise as Marcus lifted her from her feet, spun her in place and kissed her deeply. Setting her down, he examined the Africa pendant of Elizabeth's choker on the pad of his finger. "I like your charm, Your Majesty."

Feeling dazed, she nodded struggling to compose herself. "Thank you. I have one on my anklet too." She pointed but noticed he continued to gaze into her eyes.

"And I like your disguise," he murmured into her ear. "I like your earrings." He gently brushed the generous hoops. "I like your hair up...." He balanced her chin on the top of his hand, using his thumb to caress her bottom lip. "And I like the glasses...very sexy."

"Thank you." She captured his thumb with her lips and while gazing deeply into his eyes, gave it a languid kiss. "I hope it's enough."

"I'm not worried." His hand encircled her hip, turning her towards the restaurant. "Are you hungry?"

The musky amber of his cologne caressed her senses; she felt like melting into him. Giving him a grin she hoped wasn't too feral, she said, "Absolutely ravenous."

The ambiance of La Carozza, washed over them in a wave of warmth and hospitality. Three interconnected dining cars made up the restaurant, the first served as a reception area and kitchen, the remaining pair were appointed in an old-world aristocratic fashion, mahogany molding with booths upholstered in polished green leather, and tables draped in white linen.

Amid the murmur of friendly conversation, forks scrapped on china plates, stemware rang with toasts, and the scents of warm olive oil, fresh baked bread, and roasted garlic tempted their taste buds.

Holding Marcus' hand as he walked ahead of her, Elizabeth's eyes flitted to each diner they passed as the tuxedoed maître d' lead them down the narrow path between the booths and small tables. She listened to the comments that followed.

"Did you see that trampy tattoo? No wonder she's out with him."

"I'm surprised they let them in here."

"Her parents must be so ashamed."

Disappointed by the remarks, Elizabeth wondered if such a little thing as a bit of pigmentation could provoke such vitriol, what Longstreet's influence could foment by comparison. As they drew closer to their table, she heard a remark that encouraged her.

"That's the future of America right there, Black and white in harmony."

Shortly after they were seated, their server appeared.

Marcus snapped his menu shut. "The polenta with roasted tomatoes is so good here you'll want to order it for the appetizer and the main course." He gestured for emphasis.

"That sounds lovely and for the wine...."

Marcus surreptitiously winked at the waiter. "A bottle of wine? Are you trying to get me drunk again?" he asked with an air of suspicion.

Elizabeth caught the tone in his voice. "Well, the thought had occurred."

"I never know what she's going to try next," Marcus explained to their grinning server. "You want me to tell him about that time you got me drunk and—"

"You said we would never speak of that again," Elizabeth sniffed, playing the game.

"We did have fun though, didn't we?"

She gave him a mock look of warning. "Maybe we should just order some wine?"

"All right, but I'm not bailing you out this time."

Elizabeth sighed theatrically. "I promise it won't happen again."

Marcus raised a hand in a gesture of resignation. "Order then."

Elizabeth flipped through the wine menu. "The Chianti Classico 2009, please."

Clearly amused, their waiter murmured approval and finished taking their orders before disappearing down the aisle.

Red-faced, Elizabeth burst into giggles. "You need to behave."

Marcus took her hand, intertwining his fingers with hers. "Me?"

"Well, you mustn't expect me to—after all, apparently I'm so easily inebriated I have no recollection of the time I needed to be bailed out of a police cell."

"That was the least naughty thing we did that night."

"Oh? Please...jog my memory." Elizabeth tilted her head.

"That ink." He nodded towards her. "Getting you marked made me so proud. That is some fine art."

Elizabeth felt a thrill at the implication. "I think it's very evocative."

Marcus looked at her directly. "Its message couldn't be clearer."

Feeling her heart race, Elizabeth caught herself lowering her eyes demurely and looked up to see his intensity had not abated.

"Excuse me, I don't mean to interrupt your dinner folks, but could I get an autograph?" a male voice inquired.

Elizabeth's heart seized with panic. *Please no.* She glanced from the speaker to potential exits.

A Caucasian man stood over them. He had a butch haircut and wore a navy blue business suit. In one hand he held a gold-plated ballpoint pen and in the opposite, a scrap of paper. "I can't believe you're here. It's a huge honor to meet you."

Elizabeth's eyes flicked to Marcus and back to the interloper. "I—"

The stranger offered the pen and paper to Marcus. "If it's not too much trouble, Mr. Carter? I'm a huge Axeman fan."

Marcus' expressions quickly morphed from wary to puzzled, to amused and apologetic. "Sorry man, Terrell and I play the same position but I never went pro."

The stranger winced. "Well, this is embarrassing? Sorry to have disturbed you and your beautiful date." He paused to look directly at Elizabeth. "Sorry, miss."

"We all make mistakes," Elizabeth said congenially.

After the autograph seeker had apologized once again and disappeared, Elizabeth turned back to Marcus with a profound sense of relief. "Leading a double-life?" she teased.

"It makes it hard to go out, you never know when you're going to be recognized—and how's your heart?" Marcus snickered sympathetically.

Elizabeth brought a hand to her throat. "Now I know what a myocardial infarction feels like."

"Got your blood pumping, did he?" Marcus continued to chuckle, turning in his seat to glance down the aisle as the man returned to his table.

She inhaled deeply and blew out the breath. "Not in a good way."

"Leave that to me."

Her date's remark evoked a feeling of solace that grew into optimistic hope through dinner, and by the time they departed, she was feeling positively ebullient.

The inner-city avenue bustled with the soft rumble of passing cars and people out strolling under the evening's burnt sienna sky. Marcus parked his Cadillac in front of a brightly-lit bodega before going around to assist Elizabeth onto the broken sidewalk. The big man slid his hand around her back to corral her hip as they began to walk to their destination.

"I was thinking, Mansa, that if we're going to have the perfect, wild, fantasy date in our past..." Elizabeth reached down to squeeze the hand on her hip. "We should probably establish a few key events in our narrative."

"Nah, more fun to create something as we go."

Elizabeth's eyes sparkled. "That could be enjoyable, too."

He gave her hip an extra squeeze and nodded toward their destination. "A couple of my friends own this place."

The cinder block dancehall was painted azure blue. Above the steel door entrance, a blue neon aardvark played a brilliant yellow trumpet seemingly fashioned out of its snout. Beneath it, an immense, heavily muscled Black man sat on the stool. He wore a yellow t-shirt that read 'Jamaica 10' and a leather Rasta crown that did little to contain a cascade of thick dreadlocks. He grinned and stood up as they drew near.

"Wagwan brethren, who's the pretty lady that cast a spell on you? I got a bad mind on ya man." He clasped Marcus' outstretched hand and pulled him to him in an embrace.

"Eddie, my brother!" Marcus' laugh boomed out over the reggae music that flooded through the open door.

Elizabeth smiled and waited for the two men to part. "I'm Betty." The blonde congenially offered up her hand.

"Welcome, Betty. It is an honor to have you here with us tonight." Eddie shook her hand. "Do you have some ID with ya, girl?"

"Eddie...." Marcus frowned.

"I've got to check them all, man. The boss is a real slave driver about it." Eddie chuckled.

"Well, I wouldn't want you to get into trouble." Elizabeth produced a blue auto license from a tiny, leather pocketbook. Believing him to be a good-natured flirt, she took a liking to him immediately.

The doorman accepted the piece of plastic and examined it. Bringing a hand to his chin he murmured in thought. He held it up next to Elizabeth's face. "Nope."

"Nope?" Marcus puzzled.

Elizabeth glanced from Eddie to Marcus and back again. "Is there anything wrong?"

"Yes. This picture doesn't do you justice. It doesn't capture your presence."

Marcus chuckled. "Smooth, brother. Smooth."

Elizabeth giggled. Accepting her card back, the sight of the ring on Eddie's thick pinkie raised her brows.

The ring featured an old English gold 'E' set in black jet. It was the ring of the Embassy Club, an international society of hedonists and libertines. She occasionally encountered its members on her resort vacations. She reasoned it could only be a ring and a complete coincidence. She glanced at Marcus. He seemed either oblivious or unconcerned as Eddie pulled her back to the present.

"I think my accent is tripping her up," Eddie said to Marcus.

Elizabeth's eyes fluttered. "I'm sorry, I beg your pardon?"

"Will you save me a dance, Betty?"

"Well...." Her eyes twinkled with mischief as she decided to bait the hook. "Is he a good dancer, Mansa?"

"Mansa?" Eddie interrupted his friend's response, "Marcus is your mansa?" His eyes gleamed.

She cozied up to her date and beamed at him. "Yes, he is."

"I like the sound of that." He reached out to shake his friend's hand.

"And she's my queen." Marcus accepted the handshake while squeezing the blonde's hip to him with his other.

Eddie lowered his head to look Elizabeth in the eye. "I look forward to our dance."

"Sounds like fun." She maintained her congenial semblance while feeling confident about her deduction.

"All right smooth operator, because you're my best friend, one dance—if you can keep up with her." Marcus laughed and took Elizabeth's hand.

"We'll flap a wing." His gaze lingered a moment on Elizabeth before turning his attention to another approaching couple.

Inside, a wave of offbeat rhythms and brass horns washed over them. Spotlights of strawberry red, Kelly green and lemon yellow reflected off a disco ball, and down onto a dance floor filled with revelers. On the stage, a DJ, wearing a slouchy beanie, exchanged a wave with Marcus. A long and very busy bar, backlit in neon blue, occupied an entire wall. Along the opposite wall, was a mixture of tables and booths. Elizabeth detected Caribbean accents from seven different countries mixed in with the local Baltimore accent. She felt a sense of relief Eddie remained oblivious to her alter ego and hoped the music and flashing lights would help keep her secret.

Marcus leaned into her ear to talk over the music. "Where did you get the fake ID?"

"I have my sources. How would you like to be Terrell Carter?"

He scoffed with amusement. "I'm out with Jane Bond."

"Licensed to heal." She smiled and seized on the pause. "How long have you known Eddie?"

"Since we were fifteen but don't take his flirting too seriously. He flirts with all the women and lays the accent on thick for the prettiest ones. Let's show you around." He took her wrist and led her toward the bar.

She followed and watched him strut, with the swagger of a cock-of-the-walk. His pride sent a thrill through her, and their passage through the singles and cliques of partiers, drew attention and comments.

"Looks like Barbie's here," a female voice jeered.

"Marcus got himself a white girl!" another voice accused.

"Jacks is the man!"

"Come on over here and love me white girl," someone said in a grating, smoker's voice. A burst of cackles followed.

She scoffed with amusement and added a little more sway to her hips, and got a hoot of approval in response.

"That girl's been Africanized!" A mocking laugh followed.

She glanced up at Marcus, a smile played upon his lips. She realized he was enjoying this.

"That girl is F-I-N-E, fine!"

A woman harrumphed. "You get your eyes back in your head!" The scold was followed by a cuffing sound and an exclamation of pain.

"Mm, face down ass up all night, baby."

"I'd pipe that down and pass it around." The clinking of multiple glasses followed.

Drink and the anonymity of crowds seemed to be universal in effect. She had heard similar remarks in taverns and royal courts going back centuries, and found it impossible not be swept away by the moment. *I am a radiant goddess, thank you for noticing.* Marcus interrupted her musings.

"What are you smiling about?" he growled.

Unable to contain her feelings, she laughed. "Just the things they're saying!"

"I know," he murmured.

The provocative banter and jeers continued without a single hint of recognition. She saw only grins, smiles, and the occasional scowl from a female party-goer. Halfway down the bar, a particular bit of lewd bravado gained her attention.

"Damn! That body was built to work. I'd turn that out and make bank."

Elizabeth's amused confidence became a sense of revulsion, she began to turn to confront the speaker but Marcus was already responding.

In his thirties, the speaker wore an emerald green gabardine suit and enough gold to be mistaken for a jewelry store. His curly black hair was wound into cornrows and pulled back tight to his scalp.

Marcus jammed two fingers into the speaker's chest hard enough to push him back on his heels. "No, man, you wouldn't."

Startled, the speaker grunted and lifted his hands apologetically. "Hey I was just—"

Marcus, a full head taller than the speaker, growled ferociously. "You were just leavin'."

"My bad—my bad, I was just playin'!" He looked past Marcus to Elizabeth. "I'm sorry. You're beautiful. I was just playin'."

Marcus' eyes burned into the would-be pimp's. "Play

someplace else. *Be* someplace else."

Elizabeth anxiously glanced about as a crowd begin to encircle them. She tugged at her date's arm. "Marcus...."

The speaker picked up his bottle of malt liquor. "All right...all right. Ain't no thing. I'll just finish this—"

Marcus snatched the bottle from his hand. "You're finished now."

The crowd murmured and hooted.

"Okay-okay, just be cool, man." He lifted his hands defensively and turned to wind his way through the crowd.

"Marcus, you didn't need to—"

Hard-faced, Marcus turned to her. "I did, and I will every time."

Swooning at his gallantry, the blonde's eyes shone with desire. Her finger rose to trace her choker. She leaned up to whisper in his ear. "You have no idea how much I want you right now."

Marcus' hand clapped against her bottom. "You just hold onto that feeling. I'm going to make sure he finds his way out." He lifted her onto the vacated bar stool. "Leroy, get her anything she wants," he said to the bartender and slapped a twenty-dollar bill on the bar.

"You got it, Magic!" the barman responded.

"Be careful!" Elizabeth watched Marcus go, nibbling her bottom lip.

Leroy leaned across the bar. "What will you have?"

Elizabeth watched Marcus for a moment, struggling against the urge to go with him. Finally, she addressed the barman. "Hello," she began cordially, "how do you make your pink ladies?"

"The only way, gin, apple brandy, lemon, grenadine and egg white."

"That would be perfect." Ignoring the music and the many

male gazes, Elizabeth crossed her legs to watch Marcus slowly pursuing her masher. The cad anxiously glanced back at the big man as Marcus herded him towards the door.

"A lady for the lady." Leroy pushed a drink across the bar.

She turned to retrieve her drink and happily accept the compliment when she noted the scents of two different colognes. She was no longer alone.

"I haven't seen you around, but I have seen you before," a smooth male voice said.

Elizabeth felt a stab of icy fear. Unsure if she had been discovered or it was a line, she turned to regard the speaker and his companion.

Both African American, they looked to be amateur bodybuilders, and barely into their twenties. She noted one had the block letter X tattooed on his exposed shoulder.

Keeping her composure, she regarded them neutrally. *En garde.* "I was a girl on some bus stop ads," she lied with the ease of a seasoned spy.

"Damn! And we thought you were a movie star." He thumped his chest with a fist and gestured to his companion. "I'm Darnel, this is my boy, X."

"You have a letter for a name?" She asked with feigned disbelief, taking a sip of her drink.

Darnel glanced at his friend. "Yeah, he's cool like that."

"So, you like reggae?" X asked in a voice so deep and definite, it might have been a croak.

"I love it." Elizabeth balanced her glass daintily in her hand.

"Ever been to Jamaica?" X's hand came up to rest on the bar behind her.

"Love it too."

"You ever danced with two men at once?" X continued his questions.

"If she's been to Jamaica, you know she has." Darnell

interrupted her response.

"It sounds like you two have something in mind?" she asked, keeping her Manhattan accent.

Darnel tapped his friend's meaty bicep. "My man's got moves that will make your back arch all night."

Elizabeth shifted in her seat, pushing her shoulders back, continuing the thrust and parry. "Oh? And what do you do?"

He licked his lips and grinned. "Me? I'm on diet and replenishment, can't have you dehydrating. But you got to look me in the eye and show me respect."

"Well…" she began to speak, aware they were hanging on every word and gesture, she reached down to casually smooth her calf, "that's quite an image."

X moved closer. "If you can see it, you can believe it."

Darnell nodded. "That's right man, just like coach always said, if you can view it, you can do it."

"Oh! You have a coach?" It was all she could do not to laugh in their faces.

"Nah, but we got a crew, if you really want to get freak nasty." Darnel turned his shoulder to one side.

Elizabeth spotted a table of four other young men, all looking back at her with a kind of voracious hunger and impertinent certainty.

X leaned in to rumble into her ear, "Airtight, all night, baby."

She decided it was time to stifle their boorish advance and salt the wound. "Well gentlemen." She absentmindedly stirred her drink with its cherry garnish. "It's not that I never have…it's just that I never will with you. My dance card is full."

"Ohhh!" a chorus of onlookers grinned and laughed mockingly.

"Aw, why you gotta be like that?" Darnell complained.

"I might ask the same." Her question elicited another chorus of taunts and laughs from the crowd listening in. She watched them turn to retreat and called after them. "Remember gentlemen, condoms are cheaper than diapers!"

Like a queen holding court, she began to chat with the small crowd that had formed while she waited for Marcus to return. Turned on her barstool and laughing at a joke, Elizabeth heard an indignant voice almost shout at the back of her head.

A voluptuous Black woman had pushed her way to the front of the crowd to glower at her. "Well look here. It's lil' miss 'I'm blacked and I'm proud.'"

Elizabeth regarded her with bewilderment. "I beg your pardon?"

"Skinny white bitch. Come in here showin' off that ink!" the woman snarled.

"Diamond! You just cool it or you'll be outside," Leroy warned from behind the bar.

"Shut-up Leroy! Barbie and I are just getting acquainted. So, what corner he find you on? Hmm?" Diamond pressed the back of a wrist to her hip and sucked her teeth.

Elizabeth met the other woman's brimstone anger, with unflinching silence.

"Oh, I'm sorry, was that rude? Are you gonna cry?"

"Diamond…." Leroy warned.

"It's all right, Leroy," Elizabeth said over her shoulder before regarding the newcomer cordially. "Diamond, such a pretty name. I like your shoes. They're perfect with that dress, so lovely."

"Don't try and smooth talk me!" She glowered. "All these fools buzzing around you like flies on shit!"

"Diamond. You have—"

Diamond's eyes budged with indignation. "What? What do I have? I ain't got nothin'! You got 'em all!"

"You're welcome to any of them but my king." Elizabeth gestured to the men surrounding her.

A chorus of upset and dejection came from the throng of admirers.

"You've all been so sweet gentleman, but I'm leaving with the man I came with."

"Do you even remember what he looked like?" Diamond taunted.

Elizabeth ignored the jab and directed the onlookers to regard the other woman. "Look at this queen. Do you think we just roll out of bed looking this amazing?"

"She looks like she just rolled in—" one barfly began to say.

"Hush! Don't' be a wag." Elizabeth shot the speaker a glance of annoyance.

"Look at her, her hair, her jewels, her makeup...this just doesn't happen." Elizabeth looked to Diamond whose anger was shifting to confusion.

"Yeah, and they don't notice!"

"You deserve a king."

"King, huh? Well, where's yours at?" Another shamed barfly scoffed.

"My Mansa—"

"Massa? What is that? Some kind of S&M shit?" The barfly continued to taunt.

"Not at all. He gives me the freedom to be who I truly am *and* he's standing right there behind you."

"Hello, brother." Marcus clapped him on the shoulder.

"I was just—"

"You were just going over there." Marcus jerked a thumb over his shoulder.

"I hope you find your king, Diamond," Elizabeth set her glass on the bar and slid from the stool.

"Excuse us." Marcus took his date's hand to lead her out of the circle.

"Nice to have met all of you," Elizabeth said graciously.

Elizabeth glanced in the direction of the door and leaned up to Marcus' ear. "You didn't thrash that fellow, did you?"

Marcus frowned. "That lime lollipop? Punk's lucky I didn't use him as a cocktail garnish."

"But you didn't, did you?" She looked at him in earnest.

Marcus chuckled. "You are so sweet, but nah, I didn't."

"Thank you." Elizabeth's shoulders relaxed. "Then are we dancing?" Elizabeth asked, feeling the music begin to take her.

"Not yet baby, there's some folks I want you to meet first."

Marcus led her into the lights and music of the party on the dance floor. They met Eddie coming the other way.

The club owner leaned in and quipped, "Are you two out for a walk or are you gonna dance?"

Marcus chuckled. "I'm taking her over to meet everyone, man."

"I'll do that. Go get some drinks while we talk."

"If he offers you a job, make sure he gives you the rest of the night off," Marcus quipped.

"Why? You got plans?" Eddie laughed heartily.

"You take good care of my girl and I'll see you over there." Marcus gave Elizabeth a buss on the lips and gave a brief look in the direction of the opposite wall.

"You ready for that dance?" Eddie grinned.

Elizabeth cast a glance at the back of a retreating Marcus. "Love to."

Eddie's catcher's mitt-sized hands gently came to rest at the juncture of her hips and waist. Leaning down, he murmured in her ear. "Are you having a good time?"

"Yes, thank you. I'm so glad we came."

"I heard you roasted a couple of little birds at the bar."

Groaning in memory, she leaned up to speak into his ear. "I think I may have used too much salt—but is that all you heard?"

"I heard something that is either a nasty rumor or a beautiful truth."

"Which do you think he will think it is?" she asked though she already knew the answer. She had given up being mortified and indignant about what some imagined her being part of their personal 'beautiful truth.' It was a waste of energy and moreover, though she rarely did it consciously, the mere fantasy of enjoying her company was enough to open doors and minds. Frankly she preferred to be a beautiful truth rather than something far more disparaging.

Eddie lifted his hand from her hip. "See this ring?" he held the golden jewelry up before her eyes. "It means I'm the president of the Baltimore Embassy Club. We're grown folks who regularly enjoy beautiful truth."

"And Marcus is a member?

Eddie laughed and shook his head. "No, but maybe you can help with that."

"Wishful thinking?" she challenged, an image taking shape in her mind, one that at least included Marcus.

Eddie's joviality vanished. "My first thought is for my best friend to have a quality lady in his life. He deserves it. And I want to get to know you better."

She regarded him skeptically. "Better? In what way?"

"Do you hear yourself, girl? Marcus hasn't looked at anyone the way he looks at you since Melissa."

Elizabeth's features softened. "He told me about what happened. It's so sad."

Eddie's expression became thoughtful. "He never talks about them to anyone."

"You really are like brothers, aren't you?"

"From different mothers. Now don't you worry about Marcus, I can tell, he likes you—a lot. Come on, I'll introduce you to everyone." With a jab of his chin towards their destination, Eddie ceased their dance and began to lead the way through the crowd.

Imagining what would happen to Marcus if their budding relationship became common knowledge, Elizabeth's chest tightened. "Have they heard?"

"Discretion, Betty-girl, discretion."

Her mind a jumble, Elizabeth followed him through the dancers and up two steps leading to the tables surrounding the dance floor.

"Here we are." He gestured to a horseshoe shaped booth where three Black men looked back at her appreciatively, while a fourth, who had been sitting on a chair in the aisle, stood to receive them.

"Gentlemen, this is Marcus' girl, Betty." He gestured to her with flourish.

Elizabeth flushed with pleasure at Eddie's announcement and noted that the expressions of the men at the table were cordial and welcoming.

"Well, we knew she wasn't with you!" someone sniped good-naturedly.

"Marcus' girl, the super-model," another said as the others made their initial hellos.

Eddie chuckled and made introductions. "The one in the three-piece suit, here on the aisle, is Ezekiel."

Ezekiel shook her hand. "A pleasure, Betty. I see you have some beautiful ink, but it doesn't compare to the canvas."

Eddie continued his introductions. "And from left to right are Ty, Ridley, and Bumpy."

Elizabeth noted among Marcus' other friends, the smartly dressed Ty also wore an Embassy Club ring.

"Come on in here, Betty," Bumpy shifted and motioned for her to sit next to him. He wore a pale-yellow Hawaiian shirt. White curls peaked out from beneath his straw fedora.

Elizabeth sank onto the leather seat of the booth's curved bench and sidled up next to Bumpy. Eddie slid in next to her. Cozily ensconced, she detected the scents of alcohol, tobacco, cannabis, and the musky scent of men.

Ty watched his guest as she got situated. "We don't get too many models in here."

"Did Marcus tell you I was a model?" she asked, wearing an expression of puzzlement.

"Just the rumor going around the club," Ty said.

Among others. "Well, I'm very flattered, Ty, but I'm an engineer. I met Marcus consulting at his work." It was not exactly a lie she told herself.

"If you're an engineer, I'm gonna start riding the train more," Ridley said.

"Ridley's an engineer too—a domestic engineer." Eddie snickered.

Elizabeth's eyes brightened. "Oh, you're a custodian?"

"Yes ma'am," Ridley replied.

Elizabeth shifted to regard him. "That's a very important job, Ridley."

"Sure is. Everything at that school just shines," Eddie added.

"Well...." She cast a sideways glance at Eddie. "How surprised would you be to learn that half the reason life expectancy has grown so much is due to improved sanitation and hygiene?" She reached to pat the wiry man's forearm and watched him puff up with pride.

"That's right, man, what I do is important." Ridley gave a single emphatic nod.

"What do you do for fun when you're not engineering with Marcus?" Bumpy asked.

"Well, I love to sing, and dance, and laugh."

"What do you sing?" Ty asked.

"Oh, the standards, jazz, rock, folk, opera—"

"Opera?" Ty stopped her short. "What's a classy lady like you doing in a place like this?"

Elizabeth looked around at the happy people, the flashing lights, the snapshots of regulars tacked to the wall. "I like this place."

"Good." Ty nodded curtly. "Because I own it."

"Oh, you're Eddie's partner?"

"Yeah, but I do all the work." Ty chuckled at the instant retort from Eddie.

She looked across the table. "And what do you do, Ezekiel, that has you dressed so sharply?"

"Ezekiel Washington, attorney at law." He presented his card with practiced ease.

She accepted the card and examined it. "Oh! I was reading about you the in the paper. You're the lawyer suing that slumlord on behalf of the tenants?"

"Until the Attorney General gets involved, I'm all they've got."

"I think that's a very noble thing you're doing, Ezekiel."

"How long have you been Marcus' girl, anyway?" Eddie interrupted.

"There are times when I think I've known him all my life." The admission surprised her.

"Marcus has found himself a charming lady," Bumpy said.

Grateful for the interruption, Elizabeth turned to the elderly gentlemen to her right. "Thank you Bumpy—they say people judge you by the company you keep and going by that, Marcus is an outstanding gentleman." She beamed and looked at all of them.

"Cheers to that, and to you." Ty raised his glass and led a toast.

"Very charming," Bumpy added and sipped his rum and cola.

She tilted her head to regard the elder. "Thank you again,

Bumpy—and why do they call you that?"

"If you've ever seen him dance, you'd know why." Eddie laughed.

The elderly gentlemen shook a finger at Eddie. "You just mind yourself or next time you're in for a beard trim I just might slip."

The table burst into laughter.

Elizabeth waited for the good-natured ribbing to die down. "So, you're the one who keeps all these gentlemen looking so handsome?"

"It takes all forty-seven years of my experience and skill to do it too!" He taunted his tablemates.

A chorus of laughing retorts followed.

"Aw...man!"

"Forget you!"

"Do you believe this guy?"

Elizabeth squeezed Bumpy's thick forearm. "I don't believe you're a bad dancer at all, Bumpy. In fact, I think they're playing our song."

Bumpy cocked an ear. "What? Bob Marley? I mean...yeah, I do believe they are."

"Please excuse us, gentlemen." Elizabeth began to shift, prompting Eddie to exit the booth. She took Bumpy's gnarled hand in hers and led the way to the edge of the dance floor. The blonde turned to the old barber whose hands quickly found her waist. Draping a wrist over his shoulder, her hips began to gently rock. She leaned in far enough to be heard over the music and the crowd. "How long have you known Marcus?"

"Ever since he moved to Baltimore with his mom, almost thirty years ago now."

"A longtime customer."

"A lot more than that young lady. You see, a Black barbershop is a trust of knowledge; a place where young Black men who may not have guidance, can get it. When his daddy was killed, the men in the shop took an angry boy under their wing and kept him goin' straight."

"You must be so proud of him."

"So must you. But how has it been though? Dating a Black man? I'm old enough to remember when the two of you couldn't walk down the street together."

Elizabeth's face fell in memory. "There have been some comments, some good, some not."

"Well don't you two worry about the hate. Once people get to understand that there's nothing to be afraid of, they tend to get more acceptin'. You just hold onto each other and things will be fine."

"I hope so," Elizabeth murmured as much to herself as to him.

Marcus reappeared behind the barber. "You trying to steal my girl, Bumpy?"

The older man smiled. "Just keepin' the players away from her for you, Young Blood."

"He's a good dancer." Elizabeth smoothed the barber's shoulder.

"You take good care of this lady, Marcus." Bumpy took her hand and patted it.

"That's what I intend to do," Marcus said.

Impulsively, Elizabeth hugged the old barber. "Lovely to have met you, Bumpy. Thank you for the dance."

"My pleasure. I'll take those." Bumpy took the drinks from Marcus. "And you take her."

Elizabeth cast a warm look in Bumpy's direction as she reached up to wrap her wrists around Marcus' neck. "He loves you a lot."

"Bumpy's like a father figure to a lot of people in this neighborhood," Marcus intoned as his hands found her hips.

"How are you doing?"

"Hopefully there isn't a jail cell in my future tonight." She giggled.

"Maybe we'll get you more ink," he growled suggestively.

"I already have four."

"Four? I only saw two."

Elizabeth tittered coquettishly.

Marcus' eyes gleamed as he looked her over. "You know what people have been saying behind your back?"

Unsure if he was referring to the rumor about her encounter at the bar, she decided test the waters. "That I'm a movie star or a model?"

"No."

Her breath caught. "What then?"

"Nice ass."

Elizabeth resisted the urge to lift a hand to her heart and gasped with mock indignation. "And just who have you been talking to?" She glanced up at Marcus' friends and noted they were being watched.

"Myself."

She giggled some more and turned to grind against him. "I'm sensing a fixation." She groaned.

"Fixation—the action of making something firm or stable. Yeah, that's a good description." He gripped her hips, swiveling them in time with his.

Feeling her excitement build, she trembled. "I thought it was the action of concentrating the eyes directly on something."

"That too," Marcus murmured in her ear.

As the evening went on, Marcus' large hands matched the music in their movements. When the music was soft, they gently caressing the flat of her stomach and roamed over the taut curves of her bottom. When it was raucous; they gripped the saucy flare of her hips or glided over her sleek thighs.

Between heated kisses to her neck, he murmured words in her ear that had her gasping in shock, laughing in delight, or both. She felt a sense of relief that Marcus might not have heard about what Eddie described as a 'beautiful truth'.

As if reading her thoughts, Eddie appeared and caught them sharing a kiss and snapped their picture with his mobile phone's camera. He stayed to dance. "Show us that beautiful truth," he rumbled, taking her hips. Marcus' hands rose to under cup her breasts.

Now tucked between them and musing it was only a dance; she lost herself in their rhythm. Reaching back she held Marcus' hip and turned her face to kiss him while hooking her other hand over Eddie's shoulder. The Jamaican thrummed his hips, egging her on. "Get it girl, get that beautiful truth."

The liquid warmth percolating in her belly was ready to boil over by the time Eddie left and Marcus seemed to sense it.

Marcus growled into her ear. "Let's go back to my place and watch porn on my flat screen mirror."

"On? Oh!" Her body aflame, Elizabeth choked on a laugh. "Will I be shocked?"

"Girl, it will reset your DNA." Marcus took her hand.

###

Traffic on the street and the sidewalk had thinned considerably. Elizabeth felt Marcus' hand slide around her hip as their impatient footfalls clicked and scraped on their path back to the car.

"Girl you've got some moves! Where'd you learn to dance like that?" Marcus asked.

"Africa...." Her eyes glowed in memory. "But, did I tone it down enough? I was trying to avoid drawing too much attention." She wrinkled her nose playfully.

"Not drawing attention? That's what that was?" He goosed

her bottom.

"Mansa!" She jumped and gave him a look of mock reproach.

His eyes shone. He slid his hand back up to her hip to continue their walk.

"Marcus…" Elizabeth began nonchalantly.

"Yes, Queen?" he murmured.

"Our last dance…."

Marcus murmured in the affirmative. "I heard about what happened at the bar."

Her heart leapt into her throat.

He halted their progress and turned into her path. "But I'm not upset."

Elizabeth swallowed a lump in her throat. "Are you quite sure?" She searched his face for signs of disappointment or anger.

He brushed an errant strand of hair from her face. "Elizabeth, we're not kids. We've both…travelled."

"But I don't want to be Jane Bond anymore, Marcus. Travelling here and there."

Marcus shrugged. "Why be her? When you can be Elizabeth? I like Elizabeth." He squeezed her to him and punctuated his words with affectionate kisses. "She's beautiful…kind…brilliant…and sexy."

Her shoulders sagged. "Thank you. I can't tell you how relieved I am to hear you say that."

He regarded her tenderly. "It's been a stressful night for you, hasn't it?"

"A rollercoaster, but I'm so glad that I came—and I liked meeting your friends. And…." She drew in a breath. "Eddie wants us to join the Embassy Club."

Marcus' head tilted back as he burst into throaty laughter. Calming down, he shook his head. "I'd be surprised if he didn't want you in, but I think he's going to have to settle for that dance."

"And, could you imagine the scandal?" She giggled, her sense of relief only growing.

He chuckled in kind. "'I don't even want to consider it."

Resuming their walk, they had scarcely taken twenty steps when Elizabeth's ears perked up to a group of recently familiar voices. She murmured sideways, "We're being followed, and they're coming quickly."

"Oh man, someone's about to have a really bad night."

"And I believe I know who. Shall we turn? It will be brief, I promise."

"*This* I've got to see," Marcus murmured.

Elizabeth recognized their pursuers. Keeping her irritation from her voice, she addressed them cordially. "Hello Darnell, X, gentlemen. Walking home?"

Darnell lifted his chin and looked down his nose at Marcus. "You know brother, your ho is a gangbang slut, so why don't you share the love?"

Marcus' hands balled up he took a step toward the gang. "What the fuck did your punk-ass just say?"

Elizabeth gripped Marcus' arm firmly enough to halt his advance and spoke to Marcus in a low tone. "There are six of them, please allow me to deal with this." She felt Marcus' momentum ease. Her mind raced for a strategy before quickly settling on one, more salt.

"Well, where do you think we're going? I would invite you but as I said, my dance card is full and I couldn't possibly accommodate one more."

"You'll be *accommodatin'* six more, Snowflake. You ain't gonna be able to walk when we're done with you."

Peeved, it was all she could do to keep an even tone. "Darnell, your personality is your strongest form of birth control."

The thug scoffed and glanced to his companions. "Ain't gonna be no birth control—"

"Not, for him." She glanced at Marcus. She wasn't sure if she was more inflamed or appalled by her crude admission.

"Bitch, we're gonna make you scream." Darnell snarled.

"Like this?" She took one step forward. The sonic blast was little more than a split second chirp, like a police siren flicked on and off in an instant, but as the night air rippled, the effect was instantaneous. They began to sway, struggling to stand. Their knees buckled and they collapsed clutching their heads and bellies. They fell to the sidewalk, retching up the contents of their stomachs.

Marcus winced and grunted at the spectacle. "That was badass—and gross." Marcus grimaced. "What'd you do to them?"

Elizabeth surveyed the crew as they groaned and cursed on their knees. Not seeing any blood, she turned back to him. "I irritated the fluid in their inner ears."

"Their inner ears?" Marcus looked at her for a moment then burst into laughter, clapping his hands together. "Damn! You made them seasick."

Impressed by Marcus' skills of deduction, she gave him a nod of admiration. "Well, they got what they wanted, after a fashion."

Marcus tilted his head in question.

"Now that I'm done with them, they're not able to walk." She saw Marcus' shoulders shake with amusement. "As it stands," she purred, "I can't wait to see the movie you told me about, I heard the star can make a girl's back arch."

"That's why they call him Magic." Marcus' hand slipped down to rest on her bottom for the remainder of the short walk to the car. He held her door for her before going around and moving them into traffic.

After driving a few minutes, they halted at a stoplight. He turned to her and chuckled. "You told him we were going to an orgy?"

She looked at him apologetically. "I'm sorry. That was rather dishonest of me, wasn't' it?" She paused and deadpanned. "Unless we are?"

"Nah, I want you all to myself."

"Good answer—I mean, thank you, Mansa."

He leaned to kiss her. "You're welcome…." Marcus murmured as their lips parted. He stepped on the accelerator and reached over to press his hand to her abdomen. "About that talk back there about not wearing something?"

She trembled. "I don't want anything between us. I want you to take me…." She licked her lips. "Bareback." She felt a thrill as she said it.

Marcus' eyes gleamed hungrily. "Are we safe?"

"Other than developing an addiction? Yes."

"Addiction huh?" Marcus slid his dark hand up her thigh. "Then this is what your *pusherman* wants, everything off but the stockings and heels."

It was a perfect night for sleeping. An ocean breeze fluttered the open sheers of the bedroom. Gruff taunts, paroxysmal mews, and the steady clap of flesh broke the still. The moon's silvery light reflected off the dresser's mirror, illuminating two figures in the throes of passion.

The drone's operator grinned wickedly, capturing it all.

Saturday, 9:15 AM, Avalon, Maine

The next morning, Avalon seemed to have changed. The air seemed sweeter. The birds seemed to be singing an Ode to Joy and the flowers in the meadow seemed to cheer her arrival. Butler and Delilah however, behaved as if completely oblivious to it all. The pair looked up from their breakfasts only long enough to wag their tales before going back to eating. Unperturbed, Elizabeth floated like a feather borne on a soft breeze across the meadow and up onto the porch, only then did her feet finally touch down.

Jennifer was dining al fresco on the back porch. As her friend came around the side of the house, she put down her cutlery and grinned. "Hey sweetie, so how was your night?"

Elizabeth's eyes slid shut in blissful memory. "Wonderful. Perfect. Beyond—beyond."

"And how was the sex? Or need I ask?" The redhead tittered.

"Vigorous, rigorous, and...so...mmmmmm." She closed her eyes and smiled with contentment. "Just beyond—beyond..." She shrugged her shoulders and threw back her head and sighed again. "Just beyond."

"Eee! I'm so happy for you."

Elizabeth beamed. "Thank you, I'm...just..." She sighed deeply.

Jennifer giggled. "I get it, your brain has gone beyond—beyond." She gave the blonde a mischievous, sideways look. "So...any waddling to speak of?"

"All the way to the vagus nerve." Elizabeth shivered in memory.

"I think he's still there." Jennifer grinned.

Elizabeth stretched to the sky and groaned blissfully. "For as long as he wants to be."

"And what about the tattoos?"

"Hmm?"

"Earth to Betty. Did he like the tattoos?"

"Oh, my tattoos?" Elizabeth paused long enough to focus. "Oh yes, he loved them—and they were a good distraction, no one even knew it was me. Thank you."

"So, are we putting his name on you?"

"Mansa?"

"I can do a Mansa tattoo if you want, or Mansa Marcus...?" Jennifer stood up and waved a hand across her friend's field of vision.

"I'm sorry, I'm just so...ooo!" Elizabeth's shoulders jerked upwards in another shiver.

"I hope I can find someone like that."

"Me too!" Elizabeth beamed, genially.

"But do you want his name on you?"

"Do I want...? Yes, right where you suggested. I'll have to remove the one that's there now."

"What?" Jennifer gasped. "That is so hot! I can integrate one with the other."

Elizabeth's regained some focus. "I think he'll love that as much as what's there. But at the moment, I need you to take the one off my bottom."

"Are you sure? I mean will it really show?"

"Quite sure, I checked in the mirror this morning and a part of it did peek out."

"Do you have scotch tape or rubbing alcohol?"

"The tape is in the lavatory...I mean the alcohol...by the stars I've lost my mind." Her hand rose to her throat.

Jennifer watched Elizabeth half-walk, half-float past her for the backdoor. Jennifer shook her head and smiled wryly. "I definitely will have to help you. Someone who's had their mind blown shouldn't be left on their own—and besides I want to hear everything." She giggled.

"That's probably a good idea. And if you could do my makeup again, please? I have someplace else to go."

"Freshening up for a little matinee?" Jennifer waggled her brows.

"No." Elizabeth said with a note of disappointment. "It's something serious."

"Oh, superhero stuff, no problem." The screen door creaked as Jennifer held it open for her friend. "So did he wear something?"

"Yes, a nice jacket and slacks."

"You are so out of it. I meant *after* dinner."

"Oh." Elizabeth's eyes playfully rolled upwards as she tingled in memory.

"He didn't, did he?"

"Well...no."

"Eee! Elizabeth you're addicted!" Jennifer hugged her.

"Oh yes, completely..." she murmured dreamily, "completely...."

Elizabeth's heels clicked a sharp, staccato rhythm as she walked towards Shannon's perch, a bench in the Upper Senate Park. Their expressions could not be more different, Elizabeth, still glowing from the previous night, could barely keep from smiling. Shannon's face was drawn and strained. She furtively glanced around at the throngs of tourists who walked past. Both women wore summer dresses, floppy sun hats, and oversized, identity-hiding, sunglasses.

"Well, hey cousin, y'all lookin' for me?" Elizabeth asked in a thick accent lifted from Savannah, Georgia.

"Oh geez!" Shannon's hand slapped against her chest.

"Sorry, sugar, I didn't mean to frighten you." Elizabeth took a seat next to the other blonde and lifted a rattan handbag onto her lap.

"Hi, Betty-Lou." Shannon wriggled back from the edge of the bench to join the other blonde.

"So, how's Aunt Dorothy doin'?"

Shannon's face lit up; she twisted her body to lean in to squeeze Elizabeth. "Perfect, thank you, again. She doesn't suspect a thing. She thinks it was a miracle-but it was, wasn't it? I mean you're not really an—"

"Sug' this is not the time or the place for this conversation. We have business to attend to." Elizabeth looked beyond the grassy expanse of the park's lawns and across Delaware Avenue to the Russell Building.

Shannon followed her gaze and her smile vanished. "I'm so nervous right now I could pee myself."

Elizabeth lowered her glasses enough to look the other woman in the eye. "Shannon, you are stronger than you realize."

"I don't know..."

"I do. You've put up with that man's nonsense for far longer than I ever could—that takes some fortitude." Elizabeth smiled grimly and pushed her glasses back up her nose.

Shannon's expression remained drawn and pensive. "But how are they not going to see it's you? Your face is everywhere."

Elizabeth's voice became breathy and bubbled up with giggles. "My friend Norma Jean gave me a lesson on how to be a distraction and I never forgot it. They'll be so busy looking at what's in front of them that'll they forget to think about *who's* in front of them. Come on." Elizabeth doffed her head towards their target. She stood up, pushed her shoulders back and began to walk with a shimmying sway in her gait.

Shannon scurried to catch up with her. "Every guy around

here is looking at you."

Elizabeth spared a smile for a balloon vendor as they passed him. "But not seeing me, Sugar. Now do you remember the plan we talked about on the phone?"

"You're my cousin Betty-Lou Collins, and you're up from Georgia to see the sites but I have some copying to do for the Senator for Monday."

"The sheets are here in my bag." Elizabeth paused in her speech to flash a smile and wave to the drivers who stopped to conspicuously watch them strut across the busy avenue.

"I must be crazy," Shannon said as they reached the opposite sidewalk and the main doors of the Russell building.

"You just leave the talking to me. This is your last day with that man, so be happy about it. Now giggle."

"Giggle?"

Elizabeth demonstrated. "We're out seeing the sites, not going to a funeral."

"I'll try." Shannon followed her friend inside.

Elizabeth led them into the cool, dim interior of the Russell Building's marble rotunda. A solitary, middle-aged, police sergeant sat at the entrance desk. Spotting the pair of comely blondes entering the foyer, he rose from his chair.

Elizabeth passed through the metal detector without it uttering a peep, while Shannon paused for her purse to pass through the airport-style x-ray machine.

"Hey there, officer." Elizabeth fluttered her fingers in a wave to the cop before continuing on past him. "Down here?" she pointed down one of the broad corridors and glanced back at Shannon.

"Hold on, ma'am," the sergeant interrupted. "Can you step back here, please?"

Elizabeth's fingertips rose to her mouth. "Oh? Did I do something wrong? You're not going to slap the cuffs on me are you?"

The cop chuckled. "No, I just need to see your ID."

"Oh good. I thought I was in trouble."

"Only if you brought trouble with you."

"Thank you for being so friendly. In fact, everyone here in Washington has been so friendly, why Shannon and I were just crossing the street and every car stopped to let us cross." She glanced at the other blonde who nodded and smiled.

The cop studied her. "I bet, but I still need to see some ID," the officer demanded.

Shannon already had her official identification out and ready which he scanned with a mere glance.

"And yours?" The policeman looked Elizabeth over.

"I need one of those?" She pointed a finger daintily at Shannon's plastic badge.

"Yes ma'am, but if you don't have one and since she's a staff member, we can get you a visitor's pass." The officer clearly struggled to keep his eyes from drifting to Elizabeth's décolleté. "I just need to see some ID and have you sign in."

"Of course, officer." Elizabeth fished an overstuffed wallet from the hand bag and produced a Georgia driver's license. "I like your hat." She pointed as she handed it to the officer. "It's very distinguished."

The cop's face began to bloom red. "Thank you."

The blonde kept a frown from her face at the sight of the copy of The Spoiler on the desk. There was a picture of her in uniform accompanied by a particularly disconcerting headline: $250,000 REWARD Show Us Where Guardian Lives.

He glanced at the ID but didn't scrutinize it too closely; choosing instead to gaze upon its owner.

"She's my cousin." Shannon interjected, casting a glance at Elizabeth.

"A Georgia Peach if I ever saw one." The cop leaned forward

on the counter.

"Why I sure am!" Elizabeth's eyes flared open playfully.

The cop handed back her license. "Do you ever get to Atlanta to see a ball game?"

"With a Hammers Dog and a frozen lemonade? I can't think of a better way to spend a Saturday afternoon." Elizabeth wrinkled up her nose endearingly.

The officer grinned as his shade of red deepened. "Well uh…just sign here Miss Collins and this is your pass."

"Thank you ever so." Batting her eyes, Elizabeth signed and hung the visitor pass around her neck.

"This way Betty-Lou." Shannon ushered her 'cousin' away from the desk, as the officer watched them depart.

"So big in here." Elizabeth marveled, gawking at the rotunda as the pair walked the distance to Longstreet's office.

Shannon pressed the office door closed with her back and laughed. "Oh my God! That was crazy! I think his ears were sweating! Your friend must turn men inside out!"

"She did but they never really saw her—at least not most of them," Elizabeth said soberly.

"But I never expected something like that from you."

"Be thankful you live in a time when you count for more than just your figure." She frowned at Longstreet's portrait. "At least for most. Shall we get started?"

"Yes." Shannon led the way into Longstreet's inner office and sounded off the password as she typed it. "PRESIDENTLONGSTREET—all in capital letters."

"Ambitious, isn't he?"

Shannon groaned and rolled her eyes. "You have no idea. He plans to scare his way into the White House."

"Not if we can help it." Elizabeth put a flash drive as long as a finger on the desk and unfolded a copy of The Post to reveal a stack of printed off articles from various news sources. "These are for you."

Shannon took the pages and flipped through them. "The news stories about you?"

"Yes, some of them are so slanted that they might be criminal." She smiled grimly.

Shannon glanced at the door. "How long will it take?"

Elizabeth pressed the flash drive into the computer's hard drive. "Until it's done, Sugar."

"What do you hope to find?"

"For starters, some explanation as to how a man that only makes two hundred thousand dollars a year has a fortune in excess of thirty million, but whatever I find, his time in politics will be up, the rest depends on the courts and the lawyers. You had better—"

They were interrupted by the soft click and the clunk of a lock's deadbolt being turned.

Shannon glanced towards the outer office. "Someone's coming! The cop!" Shannon hissed and dashed for the door to outer office. "Go out the window! I'll stall!"

Shannon thundered up to her desk. Unable to make it around to the chair, she slapped down the sheaf of printed articles and looked up to see her boss step from behind the open door.

"My, my, this is a pleasant surprise," he drawled.

"You scared me, sir!" She smiled timidly. "I thought I would get a start on these." She held up some of the articles in demonstration. "With the bill you're writing I thought you would want some articles for the co-sponsors to read."

"Let's see what you have." Longstreet moved to stand beside her and examine the pages.

"What about your golf game today, sir?"

"I cancelled it. Did you see The Spoiler? Two-hundred-fifty-thousand to the one that can tell us where she lives! Once we get her, we get them all!"

"That's a lot, sir."

Longstreet took her arm and muttered into her ear conspiratorially, "Might be the best two-hundred-fifty ever invested."

Shannon stiffened. "Invested sir?"

"Hush now." He looked down at the printed off articles and began to sift through them. "I like these," he picked out the bits most egregiously slanted against Guardian. "Shred the rest."

"Yes, sir." She took the stack from him.

He leaned in to look her over. "I must admit you're turning into a real team player." His hand snaked around her back to rest on her hip.

Shannon swallowed. "Thank you, sir."

"Picked out something nice to wear tonight for Adrian?"

The corners of Shannon's lips creased upwards in a grimace. "Yes, sir—thank you, sir."

"A little naughty?"

"I guess, yes, sir."

"Good. I'm glad you took our little discussion to heart."

She nodded vigorously.

His voice and mood brightened. "Good." He reached behind her and clapped his hand against the curve of her bottom. "And remember to take precautions. Your health care plan doesn't make allowances for mistakes."

Glassy-eyed, Shannon nodded. "Yes, sir."

"That's a good girl." His mobile phone vibrated audibly in his pocket. Answering it, he began to traipse towards his office.

Shannon licked her lips. "Can I get you any coffee or anything, sir?"

"No, I won't be here long enough to drink it." He turned his attention from her to the call. "Hello Chuck," he said opening the door to his office.

Above him, pressed to the ceiling and concealed by the symbiote, Elizabeth listened and seethed. By her command, the versatile garment had stretched out to all four corners of the ceiling, matching its color and its texture. She hoped he didn't notice the height of the ceiling had shrunk by a foot.

Longstreet leaned back in his chair, talking into his phone. "You found him, Chuck?"

"Yes sir, and some useful idiots to bring it together." Chuck White's voice sounded vaguely metallic through the mobile phone's speaker.

"When do you plan on taking care of this?"

"We'll meet this afternoon around two and if things come together, then we'll do it tonight."

"Good, so you'll be able to fly back tomorrow with what we need?" Longstreet turned in his chair to regard the activity across the street in Upper Senate Park.

"Yes sir, that's what I had planned."

"I want this ready to go Monday, give the news cycle a whole week to chew it over."

"Then when the hoi polloi are all worked up you'll be there with your very reasonable bill to protect them."

"You're a man of vision, Chuck," Longstreet said.

"I think you'll be happy, even surprised with what I have to show you, sir."

"Call me tonight when it's done."

Elizabeth listened as Longstreet ended the call and rummaged around at his desk for a moment before his chair squeaked and his footfalls softly rustled across the carpet. There was the sound of the door opening and latching shut followed by a brief conversation with Shannon and the outer office door opening and closing.

She waited a moment, continuing to listen. Shannon burst into the room and ran to the windows to look out.

"I'm behind you, Sugar." Already redressed, Elizabeth dropped from the ceiling to quickly embrace the other woman in apology. "I heard what he said and I'm so very sorry, sweetheart. You did nothing to deserve that."

"I just wanted to run." Shannon gripped the other woman by her arms.

"But are you all right?" Elizabeth asked.

"I will be, once we get that bastard," Shannon spat.

Elizabeth released her and nodded. "Then let's do that. For you, for me, and for everyone else he's hurt."

"I think he funded that tabloid doxxing scheme in The Spoiler."

Elizabeth touched the top of the monitor. "Do you think there's any email record of it?"

"Maybe, but Chuck White—that's his chief of staff, he normally handles that sort of thing."

"This Charles White…he knows all his secrets? And what sort of mischief is he into in Louisiana?"

"I'm not sure but he'll be calling here in a minute for me to book everything for him, flight, hotel…car—everything."

"Can you provide that information to me? Because I think I'm going to the Pelican State." She nibbled her lower lip in thought. "And one other thing, do you have plans for the rest of the day? I know someone in New York that can parse through this data and perhaps organize it for us but your help translating it would be invaluable."

"I'm free for as long as you need me."

"I hope not too long but all the same, we'll go by your house so you can pack a bag."

"And I'll get that information for you." Shannon departed for the outer office.

What is Rupert scheming now? Elizabeth restarted the computer, once she was in, she began the data transfer. As she watched its progress, she placed a call.

"How can I make your day better?" Geoff Joel asked.

1:30 PM La Jolie, Louisiana

Two miles outside the small town of La Jolie, Louisiana, a group of cars lined the gravel laneway of a seemingly innocent white clapboard house. Besides the home owner's white Cadillac and his wife's white subcompact, there was also a full-sized black sedan, a dusty, yellow tow truck with the words Stuart's Service and Towing on the door, and a green panel van with the logo of a business called La Jolie Extermination and Taxidermy. Inside, a group of conspirators huddled around a coffee table hatching a scheme.

Ron Lynch, blonde and mustachioed, turned from his guests to shout to his wife. "Kayla, take your pretty little butt to the market and buy us ribs with all the fixings and stop at the liquor store and pick up beer and Number Seven Bourbon. Get enough for probably a dozen."

She came to the door of the living room, her face bright with anticipation. "Are we havin' a party? I'll invite—"

"No, you idiot, we're having an emergency meeting of the Society. Now get going, y'all got a lot of peach cobbler to make this afternoon—and don't be picking up any of those fool tabloids. That blonde hussy you're always going on about is a Jezebel, an angel of light, and has got no place—not even a mention in this house. Now bring yourself here and get some money." Ron dug a fold of bills from the pocket of his linen suit and peeled off five hundred dollars.

"I'll be home as quick as I can, honey." Her eyes turned downward, Kayla put the money in her purse and left the house.

Chuck regarded the glad-handing dandy with skepticism. "You're positive you can get at least a dozen for tonight, Ron?"

"Hell, I can get ya at least ten, probably a dozen. I'm a Grand Knight of the High Table, they'll come if I tell 'em to be here."

Cletus Tybalt interjected, jabbing a thumb to his chest before taking a swig from the sweaty can of beer he held tight in his pudgy hand.

White regarded the exterminator and thought he more closely resembled a knight of the buffet table. "Are these men patriots? Ready to do what's necessary to protect America?"

"Sho'nuff, Mr. White, don't you fret none. Everyone of 'em's a loyal man, experienced in keeping the natural order of things around here—just like our daddies and grand daddies did." Jeb Stuart, the local garage owner took a swig of sweet tea from his glass. He had three days' worth of beard stubble and wore a grease-stained, neon-orange t-shirt.

"Mr. White, you called the right people, we're ready to defend this country and our homes against this Godforsaken menace. All of the Southern Sons feel that way." Ron looked at his compatriots and got nods of agreement.

"Uh, who gets Dixon Station once we've taken care of him?" Cletus asked. The leather sofa creaked as he shifted his bulk.

Jeb leaned forward to regard the other men. "I thought we were just gonna get rid of all of it."

"That's a good business, no way Dooley Burnes deserves it. Old man Dixon should have—"

"Sold it to you, Cletus?" Ron chuckled, setting his drink down.

"Didn't he call the sheriff on you one time out there?" Jeb grinned and scratched his beard with a grease-stained fingernail.

"Damn coon wouldn't have missed one—I wanted it for my collection," Cletus spat.

"Now you want 'em all," Ron said.

"Nobody will care, hell even his own kind won't go near him."

"His Grandma might care, once he's gone, she'll probably get the title," Ron said.

"Not if you sweet talk her into signing it over—I bet the old bat can barely see." Cletus grinned at Ron.

"What's in it for me?" Ron asked.

"Well, what do y'all want?"

"One a month—and not one of those old stringy ones either, two-year olds, nice and tender." Ron pointed at Cletus.

"Done." The pair of men leaned forward and shook hands over the length of the table.

White silenced them with a look. "The Senator doesn't care about what happens to the property." He lifted a stainless-steel case onto the coffee table and snapped it open to reveal a digital camcorder. "Any of you know how to use one of these?"

"I do. I record all ma' boy's football games," Cletus spoke up.

"When you're not pointing that thing at the cheerleaders." Ron guffawed, receiving a lewd grin from Cletus in response.

"Let me see you operate it then." Chuck handed the case to Cletus.

"This is nice." The big-bellied man pulled the camera from its foam packing and snapped it open. "Hey, it's got night vision too—shouldn't be too hard to use even with my hood on." He held it up and swept the room, the lens auto-focused as the subject depth changed.

"You won't be wearing your hoods for this job, boys, none of you will." Chuck looked at each of them in turn.
"Why not?" Jeb's brow furrowed.

"The story is, boys, is that you were just part of a group hunting alligators on the bayou when you were attacked; so you've got to look it."

"I'm not sure if I want to be seen on TV," Cletus said.

"Idiot you'll be holding the camera!" Ron cut him off. "But what about the rest of us? We normally like to keep things on the sly."

"It'll be edited before it's released." *And I'll have the original as an insurance policy.*

"You think people will believe it?" Jeb asked.

"Ron's in advertising, he'll tell you, something doesn't have to be true to be believed." Chuck gave them a knowing look, eliciting nods and chuckles. *And when I get done, it will scare the shit out of anyone who's not convinced.* "You sure he's gonna take the bait and come out?" Jeb rubbed his chin in thought.

"If'n when you shoot a few of them 'gators, that'll get him riled up fo'sure." Cletus looked up from the camera for a moment before going back to playing with its features.

"Do we have an expense account-in case, you know, something comes up?" Ron asked, a grin appearing from beneath his chevron mustache.

"Yeah, in case something comes up." Cletus looked up from the camera again.

Predictable, but cheap. Chuck pulled a fat brown envelope from the inner pocket of his jacket. "There's a thousand for each of you, plus five hundred more for Ron taking care of the meal." The hundred-dollar bills crinkled softly as White dealt four stacks like he was laying down cards. He pushed two in the direction of their host and one each in the direction of Cletus and Jeb. "They'll be two thousand more each when it's done and I get the footage."

As the gang of misanthropes continued to plot and boast, a patch in the tall willow outside the living room window began to shift and alter. The symbiote reverted from long stalks of leaves to Guardian's now world-famous white uniform. Finally, the heroine's face emerged as a mask of revulsion. She left the tree's crown to ascend into the afternoon sky, and from there, onto Dixon Station.

2:00 PM Dixon Station, Verte Parish, near La Jolie, Louisiana

A narrow, gravel isthmus stretched for a hundred yards from the road through the olive-colored waters of the bayou to Dixon Station. A billboard at the laneway's entrance featured a friendly cartoon alligator licking its chops along with the words:

Dixon's Station
Home of Dixon's Delectables

It, along with other signs warning about live alligators and trespassing, were holed by bullets and streaked with egg yolks. Guardian frowned at the vandalism and quickly bounded over the gate.

The heat and humidity of the afternoon hung over the landscape like a wet blanket. A high chain link fence lined the laneway on both sides. Bottle-blue dragonflies flitted about, finding prey in the clouds of whining mosquitoes that lingered and lazed over the swamp. Alligators drifted silently, watching her intently with amber eyes.

Dixon Station's compound consisted of a series of faded red barns and a one-storey home up on stilts. An enormous alligator lazed next to a gravel-filled crater. He lifted his head and rumbled a warning that sounded like a broken muffler. The corners of Guardian's lips creased upwards with mild amusement as she drew closer.

"You know who I am, now hush." She leaned down to pat the top of the reptile's head like he was an overexcited terrier.

A heavily muscled Black man burst through the door of the nearest barn and charged towards her. "Y'all cooyons lady? Get away from him before he eats ya!"

He wore an alligator skin cowboy hat, a yellow rubber

apron, bib overalls, and the sheen of his labor. What was most striking about him were his amber eyes. The pupils were black slits. The back of his head and neck were squamous with deep-brown scales.

Keeping her sense of alarm from her face, Guardian spoke to him, "Thank you, Sir. I assure you that I am quite in command of my faculties." The blonde stepped past the reptile and continued towards the speaker. "However, I do offer you my regrets if my actions have caused you any consternation. I'm looking for a man called Dooley Burnes."

The speaker looked from her to the placated alligator with a dumbfounded expression. "How did y'all do that? Are y'all from the circus or somethin'?"

The blonde's hands rose to her abdomen as she glanced down at her clothing. "Oh, my uniform, yes, it is a little showy, isn't it? But no, I'm not."

"Then why y'all dressed like that?"

She halted a few steps from him. "It's what I wear while I'm working. Are you Mr. Dooley Burnes?"

He cocked his head to one side. "Who's asking?"

"You may call me, Guardian."

"And who's guardian are y'all?"

"Today? Yours."

He looked her over and scoffed. "So y'all are here to protect me, huh? I ain't even gonna ask from who."

"Perhaps you should. May we talk, Mr. Burnes?"

"I don't have time for whatever it is y'all want."

"I'm quite serious, Mr. Burnes."

"I am too. Y'all ever tried to do the work of seven people by yourself? The gate's that way." He extended his arm and pointed down the lane. Turning, he began to retrace his steps back to the barn.

Guardian glanced at the two refrigerated trucks backed up

to the loading dock. She was beside and walking with him in an instant. "I've done the work of more than seven. If I lend you a hand, may we talk afterwards?"

"Lady—"

"Guardian." She regarded him patiently.

"Have y'all ever held a knife to do anything more than to butter bread?"

Guardian's eyes twinkled with mischief. "Indeed, I have. Show me what to do and once we're done, then may we talk?"

"Lady—"

"Guardian."

"Whatever. This is a serious business and I don't got time for no foolishness."

"Well, that makes two of us, now shall we proceed? Time, as they say, is money and I don't see anyone else volunteering to assist you."

Stepping into the shade of an overhang, Dooley opened the barn's door. "I'll leave this open so once you see what needs to be done you can have a clear path out of here."

Guardian smiled and helped herself to a rubber apron from a hook on the wall. "Shall we get to work, Mr. Burnes?"

"Laud have mercy. I ain't never seen anything like that—'cept maybe in the movies." Burnes smiled a big, white, toothy grin. "Twenty minutes to do a month's work? Y'all have something happen to you too?"

Guardian sat on Burnes' sofa in his air conditioned, and modestly furnished, living room. The placed seemed to be a gallery of wrestling memorabilia and trophies. Some of it was Burnes' from high school and from his time in the army, the remainder consisted of garish posters of popular professional wrestlers. "It was five minutes. You spent fifteen explaining what it is you wished for me to do—and to answer your question, no I was like this long before what happened to you."

"Is that what y'all came here to talk about?"

"In part, yes. How are you feeling? About the change I mean."

"I hate it."

"What happened—specifically?"

"Sunday morning, I was up putting up a new satellite dish on account the other one was busted and I finally had time to do it and there was this sound like a tornado and a boom. It knocked me clear off the roof and out cold. When I woke up I was like this." He pointed to his eyes before turning to remove his hat and show off a row of thick scales that began at the base of his skull and disappeared under his clothing. "I was going to go in to see the doctor but he's closed on Sundays and come Monday morning, my crew came in to work, took one look at me and lit out of here like they was on fire—and I can't say that I blame 'em."

Guardian felt her heart squeeze painfully. "I'm so sorry, you didn't deserve that or, for that matter, what's coming your way."

"Huh? What's coming?"

"I told you earlier I came to guard you."

"And you never said from what."

"Do you know anyone called Ron, Jeb, or Cletus?"

"Cletus Tybalt? If that cracker ever shows his face around here again, he's gator food!"

"So you've met. Well, he intends on coming here tonight with a group of the Southern Sons."

"They what!" Dooley launched himself up from his chair. Balling his hands into fists, he began to stalk about the room. "Well, that's just fine. I got six hundred gators that need feedin'."

"Dooley, I find the Triple S repugnant too, but I think another way, a less carnivorous way, is preferable."

"I prefer to turn all of 'em into gator shit."

"Dooley..." She rose and tried to coax him from his fury. "That's no way to treat your animals...You'll give them indigestion."

"Yeah, and it's still too good for them motherfuckers," he snarled.

Guardian regarded him patiently. "I heard their plan, let's make one of our own—a moral one."

"But they ain't got no morals."

"Yes, and that's what separates us from them. Don't you see? They want to provoke you, create an incident, prove that you're a monster, and in doing so, make it easier to persecute anyone else affected by the asteroid." She grimaced sympathetically. "A friend of mine once remarked that returning hate for hate multiplies hate. I'm not going to join them in their darkness and I hope you won't either."

He folded his arms across his barrel-like chest. "So what do y'all say we should do?"

"I thought of a few things on the way up your lane, let's go back outside and discuss them. Afterwards, we can talk about curing your condition."

Dooley's look of anger became one of fevered desperation. "What? Why didn't y'all say there's a cure? Why can't we do that right now?"

"I'm sorry, that was a poor choice of words on my part. A cure is being worked towards."

"But there's doctors working on one?"

"Yes, when I'm not wearing this...." She gripped the edges of her cape. "I'm one of them—and we need your help."

"What do I have to do?"

Saturday, 7:15 PM Avalon, Maine

Guardian felt both a sense of relief and cautious optimism as she handed Jennifer the vacutainer containing Dooley's blood. The scientist went right to work with her pipettes and enzymes, microvials and centrifuge, readying the sample for sequencing. With nothing more to do, Guardian wished her luck and left Avalon for Dixon Station.

Dooley and Guardian spent the afternoon on a plan to turn the tables on White and his lackeys. After several rehearsals, and calculating the Triple S would keep to their more than century-old practice of attacking in the dark of night, Guardian anxiously returned to Avalon to receive Jennifer's initial findings.

The scientist met her in the lab. Sitting on a lab stool, her lips were pinched and her expression one of bewilderment.

Guardian felt her enthusiasm slip away to be replaced with apprehension, "What's wrong? What did you find?"

"I'm not sure…" she began tentatively. "Can you tell me *exactly* what happened when you were up there moving the asteroid?"

Guardian's brows knitted. She looked at her friend sideways. "Jennifer?"

"I need more information—and please don't leave anything out."

Deciding that acquiescing would speed the imparting of information, Guardian stood across from the other woman, gesturing as she recounted her experience starting with the moment she saw the colossal rock.

Deep in thought, Jennifer listened intently while pressing her fist to her lips. She maintained the posture long after Guardian finished speaking.

"Jennifer? What is it?"

The redhead slowly and repeatedly dragged her upper teeth over her bottom lip.

"Whatever it is, I can't help if you won't tell me."

"It's...." She spun on the stool tapped a few keys on the sequencer. "It will be easier to explain with more screens." She slid off her seat and led the way to the communication center.

She pointed to the monitor on the left side of the desk where a three-dimensional model of the human genome slowly turned on the display. "A normal human genome, twenty-three pairs of chromosomes, totaling approximately twenty-one thousand genes. Here in the middle...." She shifted her gaze to the display of an incomplete genome with quadruple the rungs of a normal gene.

Guardian gasped. "By the stars..."

"A whole galaxy of them," Jennifer said. "The count should have been completed about an hour ago. It's still on the fourth chromosome. And look here." She pointed to the screen on the right. "This rung on the genome is homo sapiens, the one adjacent contains elements of Alligator mississippiensis, American alligator. But the computer has no classification for what the remaining three are. But from what I can tell, there are five different species in the sample he provided."

Staring at the screen, Guardian's hand rose to her mouth. The color drained from her face.

Jennifer regarded her friend with concern. "Are you all right?"

"No...no, I'm not."

"You know something, what is it?"

"How? How is this bloody possible?"

"What do you know?" Jennifer pressed.

Guardian licked her lips and turned from the screens. "Ten years ago, after the technology advanced enough, I tested myself, and my symbiote."

Jennifer glanced at the screen then back at her. "You're saying...."

"But how?" the blonde asked plaintively. "And what about this other section?" She pointed out a section Jennifer had designated "Z".

"This is a hypothesis—and only a hypothesis." Jennifer bit her bottom lip. "What if...what if...when that missile struck you, you became a transgenic vector? Propelling some of your genetic material, and some of your symbiote's genetic material into the asteroid and...what if...what if the asteroid wasn't a rock but a star ship and the meteorites were a lifeform?

Guardian's hand rose to her forehead. "By the stars...I was told not to interfere. Now I have to tell her...Perhaps...." Her eyes flitted from side to side in thought. "I'm sorry but I must go." Guardian started for the door.

"Betty, wait!" Jennifer called after her. "Go where?"

"To ask for help."

A stiff gale sent the scientist's notes fluttering into the air.

7:55 PM, Miles Above Dixon Station, Louisiana

From her vantage point, Guardian could see both Dixon Station and the Lynch home. At the former, the rays of the setting sun shone through the branches of the swamp's cypress trees, casting long shadows across the farm's waters. At the latter, she could see a gathering of angry, flush-faced men seated in a circle of lawn chairs engaged in overly animated rhetoric.

Dreading the conversation she was about to initiate, she took a few breaths, blowing each out through her lips the way a human would. Her heart pounded like a human's would. Her thoughts raced as a human's would. Swallowing, she looked to the stars above and sent a thought across the universe.

"Mother?"

"What is it child?"

"May we speak?"

"You are troubled."

Guardian moistened her lips. *"Something...something has happened...."* For many moments, she recounted the arrival of the asteroid, the appearance of metahumans, and Jennifer's discovery. *"Could you relieve them of my mistake?"*

"I am sorry, but I cannot."

"But—"

"When you chose to remain here, child, I told you there would be hard lessons, this is one of them. And for me to do as you ask I would only be compounding your error by doing the very thing I told you not to."

"Mother, when you love something, you protect it."

"As I tried to protect you."

Guardian felt a flush of heat. *"So you will not help them?"*

"I cannot."

"Then I must. They need me more than ever."

"With every effort on your part, you risk causing further

complications—further harm," her mother said patiently.

"Complications are the risk of any decision, mother. This world is, despite my mistakes, a better place because of my efforts and I'm going to keep doing all I can for them because they are evolving just as I am evolving, by learning from my mistakes, and becoming wiser."

"It seems you have learned something from your time here."

"The lessons have been difficult." She looked down at Dixon Station and smiled. *"But to use the words of someone dear, I got this."*

9:30 PM Dixon Station, Verte Parish, Louisiana

Guardian reflected on her dispute with her mother. If Jennifer's hypothesis proved correct, then her mother was not wrong, her interference had caused harm. She looked over at Dooley, glumly thinking of him and of Rudy, and of Dr. Nakahara's experience with the worm, and the soldiers in India. There were the successes, however, successes stretching back centuries, where a kind word, a coin, or some unseen favor had made someone's life better. She resolved to do her best to ameliorate what went wrong and learn from it. There was still a possibility that Jennifer's hypothesis was incorrect or that if it was correct, a treatment could be created. That would have to wait.

From her overhead vantage, Guardian watched the convoy of cars and jacked-up pickup trucks swerve and weave along the otherwise deserted country road leading to Dixon Station. Ron Lynch's big, white sedan led the brood. It skidded to a stop outside of the farm.

"Are you ready, Dooley?" She asked over the hoots and bravado of the Triple S as they dismounted their vehicles.

Neck deep in the bayou, surrounded by his livestock, Dooley bobbed as he tread water. "I can't see y'all but we gonna whip 'em."

Her uniform now completely black, Guardian moved to hover over the laneway. She saw guns, and smelled the gasoline of Molotov cocktails fashioned from whiskey bottles. Flashlights flickered like strobes through the trees as the descendants of Verte Parish's slave catchers gathered to hear Ron Lynch speak from the payload of a pickup truck.

"You men have defended our ways for your entire lives. Tonight, we will do that again against the biggest threat to ever darken our land. The devil himself is in our midst!" He waited and nodded as the gang around him shouted in affirmation. "We knew this war was coming and now it's here! Tonight, one of you…." He pointed, sweeping an arm over the dozen assembled in front of him. "One of you will fire the shot that will be heard around the world. The first shot in a war for this parish, this country, and this planet. Tonight, the South rises again!" He listened as a chorus of shouts of confirmed it.

"Follow me!" Ron jumped down from the truck and entered the lane of Dixon Station.

As the crowd moved off to begin breaking down the farm's wooden gate, Cletus and Jeb used bolt cutters to cut a hole in the chain link fence that surrounded the property. Working together, they pushed a flat-hulled boat through the opening and into the bayou. Jeb glanced about anxiously as Cletus clambered into the boat. He gave the vessel a final push into the water. Once it was in and Cletus had the small electric motor humming, Jeb scampered back through the hole to find his gun and flashlight to rejoin the others.

Emboldened by numbers and strong drink, the mob invaded the farm. A bilious stream of shouted taunts, threats, and epithets formed their opening salvo. Advancing up the lane, they shone their lights along the path and out onto the water in search of targets.

Halfway across the bayou, Cletus piloted the boat running parallel to the gang. He gripped the digital recorder in one hand while steering the outboard motor with the other.

As Cletus passed him, Dooley swam breaststroke across the blackened water. Dripping wet and hidden by the darkness, he glanced cautiously at the mob as he knelt on the narrow bank along the fence line and began to carefully lift the brass padlocks from gates' latches. Each recently oiled gate swung silently open. Finishing his task, he slipped back into the water to begin to emit soft chumpfs, a cough-like purr that female alligators used to signal the desire to mate. His alligators responded, crowding up on the lane's embankment.

The resounding boom of a shotgun blast added to the ever increasing volume of the mob's taunts and epithets.

"Hey gator-boy! Get your Black ass out here!" One of them shouted.

A rifle cracked. The bullet thudded into Dooley's darkened house.

Guardian had seen enough. The night became as bright as midday. She hovered over them at the center of the brilliant display.

The mob halted, wincing and averting their eyes in pain.

"I see you..." she hissed in a voice that stood their hair on end.

"She-it!" One man shouted in alarm, turning to run back the way they came. Another was about to join him before Jeb grabbed him with a shaking hand and held fast.

Light shone forth from her eyes. "Disarm yourselves or I will do it for you."

From trembling hands, guns clattered to the ground, save from one.

"From—from m-my c-c-cold d-dead h-hands," a grizzled, Southern Son said through chattering teeth. In his hands he clutched a Kalashnikov rifle.

She floated over the landscape, advancing on the bigot like a specter. Her eyes bored into his until he could no longer meet her gaze.

"No one here is dying tonight." She snatched the rifle from him. With a twitch of her hand, all present heard the crunch of disintegrating metal and the cracking of wood. The weapon fell into the dust, broken at the breach.

The subject of her demonstration glanced down at what remained of his property and breathed an oath of disbelief.

"You may be strong, but we know what you are, Jezebel!" Ron Lynch screwed up his courage enough to speak.

She turned her face towards the dandy. "Ronald Lynch...imagine what good you could do with your gifts of persuasion rather than using anger to cook fear and ignorance into hate? And, by the by...did you arrange for the same payment of three thousand dollars for each of your co-conspirators or was that just for you, Cletus and Jebediah?"

"Three thousand bucks! What three thousand bucks!?" One of the members of the mob demanded to know. His voice was quickly joined by others accusing him of double dealing.

Guardian watched for a moment as Ron raised his hands in an attempt to calm the belligerent mob enough for him to speak. She did not give him a chance to rebut instead she rose up over their heads and began to speak, her voice loud, commanding and growing in volume with each passing word.

"In coming here, you sowed the wind but are you prepared to reap the whirlwind?" Like a roar of a hurricane her voice rose with each syllable uttered. "I know who all of you are. If anything should ever happen to Dooley Burnes or his family... You. Will. Know. WRATH!"

Her final word echoed over the parish. Dogs whimpered and cowered, cats hid and stared, animals of every type sought out places to cover themselves.

Terrible and resplendent in her fury, she rose above them. "March yourselves out of here! The Triple S of Jolie Verte, are finished!"

As the group turned to flee, Guardian's hands clapped down on the shoulders of two of them, lifting them from their feet and spinning them to face the compound once again. "Ronald and Jebediah, you're staying—along with the guns."

Trembling, Ron and Jeb looked at each other and back at her.

"Cletus Tybalt...." She turned her face towards the exterminator where he lurked beneath a bald cypress tree in his boat. "Why don't you come join us—" She was cut short by the scene unfolding before them.

"Y'all don't let us go I'll put one in his skull." Cletus had put the camera down and pressed a pump shotgun to the side of Dooley's head.

Guardian regarded him coolly. "I don't believe you've thought your actions through to their logical conclusion. Look around you. If you shoot him, the recoil will send you out of the boat and into the water. I doubt that even I could get to you in time before they had bitten through several of your arteries. Now put down that gun and come over here."

Cletus hesitated and glanced back at the water behind him. In the low light he could see the rough shapes of lurking alligators. He looked back to Dooley and found only a ripple; the big man had disappeared under the water. "Where the hell...." Cletus looked around frantically.

Dooley seized the long, narrow launch by the stern, and heeled it over in the direction of the lane. Cletus tumbled backwards and dropped to the boat's deck with a thump. White foam formed at the boat's bow as Dooley propelled it onto the bank with a hull-breaking crack. Cletus pitched forward, smashing his face against a cross-thwart.

Dooley erupted from the water to lift Tybalt from his boat by his belt and snatch the camera away in the same instant. "Y'all an idiot, now move your fat ass before I have one of my gators bite it off!"

Caught in Dooley's grip and wide-eyed with fear, the exterminator stumbled up to where Guardian had his compatriots corralled. "What are you going to do to us?" Cletus shook as Dooley handed her the camera.

"It's not what I'm going to do to you; it's what you're going to do for me." She dimmed her light so that they might look into her face without squinting.

Ron jutted out his chin. "Do for you? We ain't doin' nothin' for you, whore of Satan."

The blonde held up a hand to halt Dooley from cuffing the back of Ron's head. Her eyes narrowed and she took a step towards the ad-man. "Oh yes you will, because if you don't, I'll drop you into a hole, so dark, and so deep, and for so long that when I let you out, you'll be so old that even *you* won't remember who you are."

"Ron, shut the hell up, ya windbag." Jeb pushed Ron aside and glanced at Cletus before looking back at her. In a low, subdued tone, he asked, "What uh...what do y'all want?"

"Your unadulterated confession about what you planned to do here tonight, and Charles White's role in it. I want him, but, if you'd rather, I'll take the three of you."

That was all the convincing the trio needed. Using the camera, Guardian stood on the lane, pointing it into the faces of each of the co-conspirators in turn. They gave long-winded expRuthtions about what had been planned, each emphasizing White's role while Dooley lurked behind them like a brooding executioner.

10:18 PM, La Jolie, Verte Parish, Louisiana

The motor lodge at the interstate off-ramp offered travelers clean rooms, a restaurant, and a service station. Guardian examined it from above and noted how sparsely populated the parking lot was. Reaching out with her cosmic sense, she discovered only five of the rooms were occupied, four on the main floor with multiple occupants and one on the second floor with only a single occupant. Beneath the window of that particular room was Chuck White's rented black sedan.

Quickly inside, a press of Guardian's hand snapped the suite's door from its hinges. It fell to the floor with a thump. She strode across it like a gangplank and into a rather unremarkable hotel room. A clean bathroom, brown carpeting, curtains and bedspreads—one of which was ruffled from having been laid on, a dresser, a suitcase stand with an open suitcase and in the corner, lounging at a simple round table, was Charles White.

"She's here, sir," he said into his phone.

"Now you listen to me, Chuck, you get the hell out of there, now!" Longstreet bellowed through the receiver.

"I'm not worried, sir, and neither should you be. I'll talk to you soon." Smirking, his eyes flicked over the heroine as he ended the conversation with a press of his thumb.

Having never met Chuck White, Guardian quickly sized him up as she crossed the room. Despite it being well into the evening, White's suit was pressed, his tie was straight, and his shoes were polished. What struck her most about him, were his eyes. There was a gleam there; not one of warmth or mirth, but a secretive, malicious, arrogant gleam, calculating and unfeeling. She knew the type. Her hands rose to her hips as she stood looking down on him. "You seem quite confident for a man who's facing down a conspiracy to commit murder charge."

"As I just said, I'm not worried." He took a sip of brown liquor from a tumbler.

Guardian cocked an eyebrow. "Is that so? I have a recording of your gang of bigots perpetrating the crime, the recorded confessions from three of your co-conspirators, as well as the weapons and—"

White set down his drink and held up his mobile device with the screen outwards to her. "And look what I have here, a little Black on blonde action. Go ahead and look." He waved it at her in offering. "It's not the only copy."

Guardian's brows knitted. She took the mobile telephone from him and turned away to examine what had him so fearless.

"Be sure to swipe right," he taunted.

It was a gut punch. Her scalp prickled and her ears rang as she struggled to comprehend it. It was them, she and Marcus, in flagrante delicto. The picture was so clear she could make out the details of her tattoo through the veil of her stocking. She took an open mouth breath at the next. It was her, face locked in ecstasy, her tattoos on full display.

The idea that he had been watching them left her stomach roiling with nausea. Staving off the instinct to crush both him and the telephone in revulsion, she kept her face turned away, lest an expression of alarm crack her mask of general disdain.

"For an alien you sure are one hot piece of ass. He found that out what...four times? Eight? I could only really get one angle. But I've got t hand it to him, after all your antics in the press, he took charge. Imagine what all those little boys and girls who look up to you will think when this gets out? Face it, you're *our* bitch now."

As he gloated, Guardian's mind raced. What would people think? She would have to get to Marcus first. Their little tattoo scheme had failed where it would count the most, or had it? *My tattoos...* She turned on her heel back to him. "I'm not quite sure who this couple is, you peeping pervert, but this young woman has tattoos, and *I* do not."

"You know I wondered about that—for about two seconds. With your bulletproof skin and all, but then I remembered that tattoos can be painted on."

She dropped her chin and gave him a sideways look. "Painted on?"

"Any tattoo parlor can do it." He smiled smugly. "Gotcha."

"*Really?*" Her voice dripped with sarcasm.

"And I have enough there for four movies—maybe five. Honestly, I've never seen anyone fuck for so long, but you're a real pro, aren't you?"

You bastard. She looked at him like he had lost his mind. "So, you honestly believe that *I*, someone who suddenly finds herself to be the *most* famous person on the planet went to some artist, dropped her knickers and said paint me? And yet no one is tattling to some rag about it."

"I'm sure you paid very well and I don't begrudge someone their hard-earned cash when opportunity knocks."

"You bloody imbecile, you pustulant toad. Do you—"

"Just think of what this will do to your reputation. And once it's on the internet—" His triumphant grin became a gurgle.

Guardian seized him by the neck of his shirt and lifted him into the air. "Come on." Guardian carried him in front of the dresser's mirror.

"Wait! Wait! Wait!" he rasped.

She turned her back to the glass and lifted him high enough to look over her shoulder. "What do you see?" She used her free hand to draw back her cape like a curtain and expose the curve of her hip. The sight through the artificial tan of her tights was only flesh. "Do you see tattoos?"

"Let me go!" He grunted and pawed fruitlessly at her wrist.

The bed's springs squeaked in protest as she flung him to it.

"Extortion and manipulation by picture and recording? Those are Longstreet's methods? With you as the procurer? How much more of this do you have? How many people does Longstreet have under his thumb?" A thought struck her. "And what do you have on *him*?"

White sat up, leaning on his elbows. "Why would I have anything—"

"Come now, you cunning little scrub, you undoubtedly have a get-out-of-jail-free card."

"A what?"

"Longstreet will throw anyone under the bus but not you." She folded her arms across her chest. "I want what you have on him—all of it. It is, as you Yanks say, independence day for— I'm sure are far too many people. Where is it? Where are you keeping it? Tell me."

"What are you going to do? Kill me? Oh yeah, that's right, you don't do that, do you?" He smirked anew.

"There are fates worse than death, Mr. White. Such as being a hundred light years from home—and the only human in an interstellar detention facility. Your trial would be dizzyingly quick." She felt a sense of grim satisfaction as he paled. "Now...." She lifted him from the bed. "Where is it?"

###

A single bare bulb illuminated the steel Quonset hut in rural West Virginia. Guardian flipped a workbench aside as easily as if it was a child's toy. Its contents clattered across the shed's concrete floor. She had his mobile device already, permanently accessible by forcing his thumb onto its biometric screen lock and altering the security options. As he stood by glowering at her, she moved to exhume his mother lode of extortion.

Chuck White frowned. "You could have just pushed it out of the way."

"And you could have saved yourself all of this by not getting involved with a snake like Rupert Longstreet." *But like attracts like.* She crouched down to toss a pair of paving stones aside. They shattered like chalk. From the hole beneath, she lifted a trunk-sized waterproof case—much like the type she used to transport groceries to Avalon with. Its padlock crumbled in her hand.

"Let's see what we have." She ignored White's displeasure and began to flip through files contained within.

It was a treasure trove of what the Russians would call kompromat. Pocket file folders contained transcripts, video tapes and audio tapes going back decades, data sticks, and envelopes of photographs—including the negatives, reams of financial records, tax records, illicit transactions and ledgers. Each of the scores of dossiers was neatly labeled by name, including one for her, one for Marcus, one for Shannon, one for Bill Boothman and multiple folders for Rupert Longstreet.

Too disgusted to feel any sense of elation, she fixed him with a look of utter disdain. "Well, this is quite a collection." She held up her own file which a quick glance through revealed preliminary notes on past aid projects she had worked, and real and alleged lovers and the resorts where trysts, real and alleged, took place as well as a small black case containing a digital camera's memory card.

"I'm sure all of these people will be relieved to have these back in their possession, all except Rupert of course and..." her gaze came to rest on a white panel van parked nearby. She pointed a gloved finger. "What do you have in there?"

Chuck White's frown deepened.

"Is it open or must I create an opening?"

White fished his key ring from his pocket and singled one

out.

She took the key from him. "Now you see? You *can* be reasonable when you make an effort."

Opening the rear of the vehicle, she found what appeared to be the interior of a news van, monitors over a control board, microwave and digital transmission equipment, cameras—including one mounted on a drone, and multiple computer hard drives. Standing in the van's door she mused aloud, "Well, this should make for some distasteful viewing."

"All you're doing is weakening this country and this planet," Chuck snarled.

Guardian's eyes flashed with annoyance. "You obtuse troll of a man. An alien is someone from the *outside*. You live in *my* galaxy. And this may come as a surprise to you but some of your galactic neighbors are very interested in this planet, for food, for slaves, for...genetic material. To put it plainly, you would not be here without me."

"Well thank you very much," he said sarcastically. "But you sure as hell did a piss-poor job of protecting Mrs. Longstreet and the Longstreets' unborn baby."

Guardian's brows pressed together. "I beg your pardon?"

"Do you want to know how the Senator and I met? When he was a congressman, his wife got taken by what we think were the Grays and I was assigned to work the case by the Air Force. She was pregnant and then she wasn't. They took the baby. Where the hell were you for that?"

Guardian gasped. Her expression became sorrowful. "By the stars...poor Rupert."

"Oh yeah," he snarled. "You didn't save her or their baby now did you, *Guardian*?"

Holding onto the image of it, she felt a heaviness in her chest that left her breathless. Her heart ached for them. "I...I was not aware of this."

"He's got good cause—we've got good cause, to want you gone."

"I shall have to apologize to him and get whatever justice for them I can," she said, more to herself than to White.

"And what are you going to do about the rest of your alien friends?"

Guardian's eyes hardened in response to the demand. "What you should be concerned with is what I'm going to do about you."

11:20 PM Marcus Jackson's Home, Baltimore, Maryland

With Chuck White safely marooned where he could do no harm, Guardian turned her attention to a task that left her chest feeling tight and her stomach feeling nauseous: informing Marcus about what White had done.

She dropped from the sky and into the darkness of Marcus' backyard to be greeted by the chirping of crickets. His house was unlit. His car sat in the driveway. In the distance, traffic rumbled softly. As she approached the backdoor, it seemed askew. The frame was splintered at the lock. Her pulse quickened.

With the press of her hand the door swung silently inward. "Marcus?" she asked tentatively.

Getting no response, she flew through the house. The living room that was as neat as a barracks when she left that morning, was in disarray, the coffee table shoved against the sofa which was also at an odd angle, as if it too had been shoved aside.

His bedroom lay empty. Her eyes flitted from the disheveled sheets of the king-sized bed, to his keys and wallet on the dresser before they came to rest on multiple pairs of boot prints on the carpet. She inhaled sharply as her alarm deepened. Her mind raced in an effort to piece together who might have him and where he might be.

She paced in mid-air for a moment before recalling Chuck White's file on Marcus and his sneer when she entered his hotel room. She could still hear Longstreet bellowing through the mobile phone for him to flee.

A flush of anger rose up her neck. "Rupert," she spat.

She grabbed for her phone, certain that if anyone would know where to find him, Shannon would. Standing in the open window, listening to the call ring through, a peculiarity in the stars drew her attention. Some of them were missing. Looking closely, she saw a ship so great in size that it blotted out a swath of the heavens.

The color that burned her cheeks only a moment before drained. Her stomach clenched. She cast one regretful glance back at the bedroom. "I'm so sorry, Marcus," she whispered. Tucking her phone away, she flew forth to challenge the interloper.

11:26 PM Near Earth's Moon

Grim-faced, fists at her sides, Guardian streaked through the heavens towards the ship. The asteroid of days before was a mere pebble by comparison. Matte black and vaguely bat-shaped, it was an Everest in height and the size of a small country. The notion it contained millions or perhaps tens of millions of invaders terrified her. Another thought struck her, what if the ship's complement were sky-scrapping giants capable of striding across continents as easily as a human could walk the length of a football pitch? Certain the arrival of the ship so quickly after the asteroid was no coincidence, she remained on her guard, hoping to parley but preparing to do whatever was necessary to ward it away.

Her eyes widened as weapons sprouted from its massive hull like mushrooms. Ball-shaped, the turrets swiveled and began to fire, crisscrossing her flight path with a blinding latticework of neon-red beams. Swerving and dipping to avoid the rays, she immediately noted they matched the color of the asteroid's fragments.

Veering to avoid a beam coming straight for her, Guardian's vision exploded in a flash of pain. A searing bolt of light spun her around. The vacuum of space swallowed up her yelp.

As her uniform closed up its wound, Guardian cried out again as a second bolt struck her flank. Her body spasmed and arched. Instinctively her hand went to the site of the attack. She felt a welt rising up on her flesh and clenched her teeth, struggling to ignore the pain.

She spared a split second to glare at the ship with enmity. The blonde stretched out her fists before her and put on speed, jinking and jiving, corkscrewing towards her quarry.

The crisscrossing beams quickly became a veritable glowing wall of red light as more guns joined in the barrage.

###

"Two hits, Lord Draask," the tactical officer announced.

"And yet it advances. Impressive," the overseer rumbled. He watched the white dot on the holographic projection continue on. "A few more should overwhelm it then it will only be a matter of sending a shuttle. Is the retrieval crew ready?"

"They were aboard and ready the moment we arrived in this system," Z-Tek said.

"Give the order to launch. This shouldn't take much longer."

"Acknowledged, Overseer." Z-Tek motioned to the communications officer to relay the directive.

###

Flinty-eyed with rancor, Guardian slammed into one of the turrets like a torpedo into the hull of a battleship. The impact sent a shower of debris exploding inward.

The ship's atmosphere whistled past her through the gash in the turret. Her head swiveled in search of an operator. The capsule was empty, devoid of even a control panel to fire the weapon. Reaching out with her cosmic sense she detected no signs of organic life and wondered if the ship was operated by artificial intelligence.

###

The bulky tactical officer cursed in its native tongue. "We've been boarded, Overseer."

"Show me," Draask commanded.

The tactical officer keyed up a three-dimensional hologram of the gun turret's interior, replacing the holographic image of the Earth at the front of the bridge.

The projection drew a derisive snort. "It took on the Terran beasts' appearance. What an appalling insult to me and its kind."

"Its affection for them is incomprehensible, Overseer," Z-Tek said.

"Affection..." The overseer murmured and paused to watch Guardian in the passage.

The tactical officer began to stand. A shoulder cannon rose from his armor with a soft whine. "I will take three units of—"

"Maintain your station, First Tactical. This triumph will be mine alone." Draask's own shoulder mounted cannon deployed.

"Overseer, this foe is like nothing you've ever fought," Z-Tek cautioned.

The ship's commander regarded his second officer with a penetrating stare. "You forget yourself, Second."

Z-Tek's expression remained emotionless. "My sincere apologies, Overseer. No offence was intended, I only seek to advise caution. The entity is—"

"I am not a fool, Second. I will set the conditions of battle and best it personally." He watched the image for a moment more and rasped, "This should be stimulating."

Determined to find the ship's commander, Guardian punched the turret's maintenance hatch and launched it across the adjacent access corridor. It crashed against the opposite wall and fell to the deck with a clang. Grim-faced, she floated through the smoke and arcing scarlet lighting of the wrecked turret and into the ship.

In the passage beyond, the overhead piping ominously thrummed a steady tom-tom cadence. The shadowy gloom was pierced by a scattering of lights that glowed like red-hot coals. A clammy mist hung in the air, beading on her uniform, and concentrated on the deck, where it swirled in tendrils of concealing black fog.

She startled as the turret's emergency hatch slammed down behind her with a hiss and a boom, sealing her in. Turning towards the fuselage, she cautiously ventured into the darkness in search of its commander.

"It is moving, Overseer." Z-Tek pointed to a three-dimensional projection of the ship's passageway.

"Seal all hatches, but these." He pointed to the holographic projection of the deck. "And guide it to this section here."

"Sealing them now Overseer." Z-Tek's spindly fingers danced across the controls.

Moments passed. Z-Tek watched Guardian's progress. "It is following the path."

The overseer's eyes gleamed. "Powerful but inexperienced. Send three units of sentinels to assist me." The S-Ga commander vanished into the darkness, leaving only a puff of shadowy mist and a thin, tarry residue on the deck to mark his departure.

Flying down the center of the passageway, a series of metallic booms from ahead of her caused her to halt her flight and listen. *Someone is moving around.* She emerged from the maintenance passage to a junction as wide as a freeway and whose height she guessed could best be measured in stories. Only one of the intersection's three enormous bulkhead doors remained open.

Her lips twisted into a wary grimace. She recalled the banners containing Sun-Tzu's axioms hanging on the walls of Huan's kwoon. "The clever combatant imposes his will on the enemy, but does not allow the enemy's will to be imposed on him."

She considered going back outside the ship and risking the barrage but dismissed the idea and followed the offered path for a few thousand yards while noting the presence of other hatches, large and small in the bulkheads to the left and the right.

Hoping to sow some chaos, she ducked right, slamming into a small hatch to burst through, leaving a jagged hole in her wake.

Z-Tek spoke into his communicator, "It left the passageway and found its way into a hold, my lord."

"It will quickly find out how tough trotium bulkheads are and return to the course I have set for it. Nevertheless, keep me apprised."

The overseer resumed his lookout at his chosen ambush site. Around, above and below him, were three score of heavily armed and armored robot drones.

Gun-metal gray with four segmented arms, each drone mounted a shoulder canon and a panel of stout spikes across its thick, oblong body. Partially concealed by the passage's misty atmosphere, they hovered motionlessly with only the single, pulsing, vertical light of their optic sensors giving away their presence.

What Guardian beheld inside the vast hold, left her first dumbstruck, then appalled. A sickly green light glimmered off the transparent covers of millions upon millions of stasis tubes. Stacked up like doll boxes in a department store, they stretched from the deck to the overhead in row after row that went on for miles.

Her hands clenched in rage. She flew like a bullet for the overhead compartment and bounced off.

Wincing, she tentatively rubbed her head and regarded the ceiling with a squinting, baleful look. Undeterred, she growled deep in her throat and stretched out her arms to the overhead, pressing her fists together, she began to spin like a drill. Sparks, filings and droplets of molten metal showered the deck below as she ground her way through the dense alloy.

Moments later, Guardian spun out of a smoking molehill of filings and emerged into another hold also filled with stasis tubes. Her fury growing, she repeated the process, moving upwards, flying from the previous borehole to randomly zigzag and create another, miles distant from its predecessor, intent on finding the bridge while keeping whoever was commanding the ship, off balance.

Using his armor's flight system, Draask hovered beneath a freshly drilled tunnel in a hold's overhead. He ran a gauntleted hand over the opening's sharp edge and frowned. "Where is it now, Second?"

A holographic projector in the Overseer's armor displayed Z-Tek's head and shoulders in the front of the captain. "It is two decks above you Overseer, and moving quickly. We have traced a rough pattern and have three probable points of intercept." The image changed from Z-Tek to deck plans.

Draask quickly studied the holographic schematics. "Send three units of sentinels to each location but have them remain in the outer passageways. I have just the thing to slow it down—and prepare to initiate the signal; I want to begin the harvest once I have it."

"As you command." Z-Tek terminated the transmission.

###

Estimating she had travelled a hundred miles inwards, and at least the height of two Empire State buildings upwards, Guardian arrived in a smaller hold, one filled with alloyed crates and cylinders. Neatly stacked but maze-like, she could hear movement among them.

Cautiously she floated forward. Rounding the stacks, she gasped in shock. The source of the movement was human.

Pale, draped in rags, and lean to the point of being sinewy, a young man and a young woman moved about carrying crates in their arms. Their hair was long and unkempt. The young man's shaggy beard covered his neck. Their shoulders were slumped and their eyes half-lidded as if in a daze.

Shocked and wide-eyed with concern, she flew into the path of the young woman, a redhead she estimated to be no more than twenty. "Hello. Are you all right? I'm called Guardian. I'm going to get you home as quickly as I can."

The redheaded young woman stared at her without recognition and immediately moved to go past her.

Worried by the lack of response, Guardian took the crate from the redhead and set it aside. *What have they done to you?* "Can you hear me? Do you understand what I'm saying?" Guardian gently but firmly took the woman by her shoulders and shook her. "Can you tell me your name or where you're from?"

The redhead continued to stare blankly.

"By the stars," Guardian murmured. Commanding the symbiote to open the palm of her glove, she pressed her hand to the young woman's neck, expecting the stupor to clear.

The redhead's demeanor did not alter.

Guardian frowned in realization. "They've exposed you to one of those damned crystals, haven't they?"

She released the young woman and watched as she

immediately resumed her labors.

The sound of metal clicking on metal interrupted her investigation. She turned to see a robot scuttle towards her. Gray and vaguely resembling a headless scorpion, it was the size and height of a coffee table. It carried itself on six, scimitar-shaped legs. A segmented tail balanced over its back. Scarlet lights resembling two pairs of eyes stared back at her from the top of its thorax.

Keeping her ire over the stasis tubes in check, Guardian kept her expression neutral. "Greetings, I am called Guardian. I come from Earth. Is this your ship?"

The quiet was only broken by the sound of whirring servos as the robot's legs extended to lift its body upward.

Unsure if she was talking to the equivalent of a robot custodian, Guardian repeated herself.

The robot lowered itself back to its crouch and launched itself into the air with a malevolent hoot that sounded like a combination of siren and diabolical cackle. "Woo-Hoo-Hoo-Hoo-Hoooo!"

Guardian caught the thing in mid-air as its front legs hooked over her shoulders.

A pair of cables launched from beneath the robot's body to encircle Guardian's neck. Its whip-like tail jabbed at Guardian's face, hissing out a scarlet gas.

"Ugh!" Guardian twisted her face away in revulsion and ripped the cords free. She flung the robot into a stack of crates, toppling them.

The robot, tucked its legs to its body to roll to the deck before righting itself and beginning to skitter forward to launch its attack again.

Ready for it, Guardian caught the robot in mid-air. Its alloyed body screeched as she rent it asunder and tossed the pieces aside.

Uncertain if the contraption had some sort of transmitter and had relayed her presence, Guardian began to turn her attention back to the stupefied victims when the hold's hatch slid open.

The compartment's overhead lights glinted off metal. Two by two, bulky ellipsoid shapes trooped inward and formed a rough horseshoe shape around her. From two of their four arms, heavy, claw-like pinchers emerged. On their left shoulders, stubby, coaxially-mounted cannons whined softly as they shifted and took aim.

Glancing in the direction of the recently-discovered humans, the blonde retreated, determined to keep the threat in front of her and away from the man and woman behind her.

She looked from left to right at the hovering robots and extended a warding hand. "Stay back."

The air rang with the sound of metal striking metal. The cadence was one of heavy, unhurried footfalls.

"How presumptuous of you to give orders on *my* ship."

The hissing rasp in the speaker's voice raised the hair on the back of Guardian's neck. She watched in disbelief as the owner of the voice stepped into the space between the lines of crates.

What struck her first was his size. Broad and powerfully built, the speaker possessed four, stout arms and was at least twice her height. The alien's scaly visage and armor were as black as onyx. Tiny webbed flaps lined his jowls. A comb formed a crest atop his head that ran down the back of his neck and disappeared into his armor. Bone ridges protruded over both eyes, his squat head resembled a dragon's. Tendrils of inky black smoke wafted out of his broad nostrils and the corners of his even broader mouth. He grinned at her, revealing rows of sharp, bullet-shaped teeth.

The Overseer paused and spared a glance at the pieces of broken robot scattered about the deck. "I suppose it's to be expected, I take some of your pets and you retaliate by destroying one of mine."

Guardian glared at him indignation. "They're not pets! They're people!"

The Overseer hissed out a mocking chuckle. "*People?* People are civilized and sentient. These...." He gestured. "I've heard a great deal about. They are pitiful and mindless, constantly fighting with, and killing each other over the most trivial things. If they were intelligent enough, they would thank me for rescuing them from their wretched existence. I have brought order, oneness, sameness, purpose to their insignificance. Very soon all of them will partake in my benevolence."

Her mind recoiled. "I don't know who you think you are but—"

"I am Draask, known to many as The Devourer. I am overseer of this ship and soon, I shall be Grand Overseer of the S-Ga Empire. Now, I have a question for you. Why do you hover over this insignificant speck? What value does it have to one such as you? You see, I know what you are," he gloated.

Guardian's head snapped back, wondering for an instant how that was possible before recovering her defiant demeanor. "If you truly don't understand why, then you don't know what I am."

Draask hissed out a mirthless chuckle. "The archives of the ancients and the stories told by your enemies provided more than enough information."

Guardian lifted off the deck to look the alien captain in the eye. "I saw the stasis tubes. Whatever it is you think you have planned, ends here. You are not welcome. The beings that inhabit this planet—"

"They are at best an afterthought, a modest benefit. There are far more useful species in greater numbers closer to my home. Nevertheless, the S-Ga empire could not exist without them—and those like them."

Catching the look in his glittering, black eyes, she felt like a fly in the presence of a spider. "Then what do you want?"

Draask hissed out a laugh. "You truly are a youngling, aren't you? I'm here for the only thing of value on this pitiful little planet, you of course—"

"What!" Guardian's head craned forward in disbelief.

"For my amusement...my appreciation...my...elevation."

"I'm afraid you're about to be disappointed. I am no one's—"

"Not nearly afraid enough and I grow tired of your incessant chatter." He flicked a finger at Guardian. "Take it."

The spikes of the sentinels' armor launched in an explosion of pops, like strands of fire crackers. A cacophony like the whine of mosquito wings filled the air. The projectiles broke into two sections, unspooling broad straps of flexible, shimmering, metal between them. Like a swarm of angry hornets, they sped towards her.

Not about to cooperate in her own capture, Guardian thrust out her fists and launched herself at Draask.

The S-Ga commander extended the palms of his armored hands outward to form an improvised shield.

A thunder-like crack split the air. Guardian bounced off Draask's hands. Stunned and flailing backwards, she struggled to regain her equilibrium.

The swarm fell upon her.

Wending and winding, the miniature drones crisscrossed through the air, wrapping their target over and over again in bands of flexible, trotium metal.

Guardian experienced a moment of panic as her sight was taken from her. The taste and scent of metal was on her lips and its scent, in her nostrils. The incessant whining of the drones became muffled. The bonds pinched. She floundered in mid-air, mummified. A heavy blow rocked her. She grunted pancaking to the deck and wincing in pain.

"That was easier than I thought it would be," Draask mused. He advanced and reached for the neatly trussed package squirming at his feet.

Guardian growled in the back of her throat. Straining against her bonds, the trotium cocoon bulged then twanged as she tore through it. First her elbows then her hands burst forth. Quickly she ripped away the straps obscuring her vision and covering her mouth. Wearing a mask of fury, she finished shredding the alloy cocoon and rose to confront a retreating Draask.

"So, there is more to you," he guffawed in his hissing voice.

"More than you and your flying dustbins can handle."

Draask pointed at Guardian as she began to regain her feet. "Capture it!"

Heavy trotium claws grabbed at her limbs, at her body, at her neck, ripping holes in the symbiote as she thrashed about, pulling off robotic arms and sending robot heads pinballing off the surrounding cargo.

One seized her arms from behind, its servos whining as it tried to keep its hold.

Guardian reached across her body to free herself and groaned as another turned her head with a hard cuff to her face.

Kicking up her feet she flew straight backwards, smashing the mechanical monstrosity that held her, against the bulkhead and leaving it in pieces.

The sentinels charged her, shooting and grabbing at her with their claws, attempting to smother her with numbers.

A straight kick to the body of one directly in front of her sent it, and the two behind it, flying across the hold. She jammed her hands into another, lifted it over her head, and hurled it into another trio, knocking them to the deck.

Undeterred, they pressed in on three sides.

The resulting clamor resembled a chain-reaction mass car pileup. She waded through them, leaving a trail of torn and twisted metal in her wake. Slamming the final minion to the deck, she looked up at their reptilian master.

In one of Draask's outstretched hands he held up the lanky, young man by his neck, in another hand was the petite redhead. "Which should I devour first?" He opened his maw wide to clack his jaws together menacingly. Tilting his head back, he alternated between dipping the feet of the stupefied pair into his open mouth.

Horrified, she reached out with her hand in desperation. "No! Please, no. Just wait a moment."

Still holding the pair aloft, Draask straightened up. "Wait? Why should I wait? What will you give me to spare their lives? What will you give me to spare their planet?" He snapped his jaws menacingly.

Guardian's heart and mind raced, her eyes flitted from one captive to the other. Images of Marcus, Ayana, the children and countless other friends turned into automatons and stuffed into the stasis tubes filled her mind. Swallowing, she straightened up. "I cannot trust your word. I—"

Two teardrops of light, accompanied by the high-pitched whine of a weapon discharge, illuminated the hold in flashes of red light.

Guardian's back arched. She shouted in pain. The first shot felled her to her knees. The second took the light from her eyes. She dropped to the deck in a smoldering heap.

Draask cocked his head to one side and examined his vanquished prize. "Such a baby, perceptive, but not perceptive enough."

The cannon on Z-Tek's left shoulder folded down as a power line detached itself from one of the hold's power conduits and spooled back into the rear of his armor. The second in command advanced on his commander and the fallen heroine. "I set the power to one higher than we used to injure it earlier."

"A tactic worthy of a S-Ga warrior, Second. Well done." Draask's python-sized tongue shot out of his mouth to seize the little redhead and coil about her. Fully wrapped, he snapped her back into his mouth. His neck bulged for an instant and she quickly disappeared down his gullet.

Z-Tek waited and watched the young man share the redhead's fate.

Draask licked his chops. "A little snack before our victory feast, are you sure you will not partake? They taste better than they look and truly I find your diet of protein supplements and plants to be repulsive. Live food is best."

"It serves my needs, Overseer. But, in the matter of the conquest—"

"It was unsuccessful."

"Yes, the entity, it must have intercepted—"

"As I expected it would."

Draask used his tongue to pluck up his foe from the deck and snap her limp form back to his waiting hand. He held her up, his thick thumb and fingers nearly encircling her waist. Using his other hands to grip her legs and brace her lolling head, he paused to sniff at her face. "Not only does it look like one of them, but it tastes and smells like them as well."

"Overseer, the crew will expect—"

"Payment. And they shall have it—as will you and your brethren. You see, I anticipated this. Were some thralls created?"

"Not enough to even fill a small part of one hold."

"Very well, collect what we have and instruct First to inumbrate and modify the crin in the ship's drive to the Terran's frequency, we will use them to finish what we started."

"But what—"

"We will use the entity's energy. We will siphon it off to supplement the drive. This task is not beyond you and First Science, is it, Second?" Draask's eyes narrowed.

"It will be done, Overseer."

"I am pleased to hear it." Draask extended a finger and prodded his captive's body. "It's unfortunate that you plan to leave us, Second. You have been an asset to this ship."

"Your words are appreciated, Overseer."

Draask studied Guardian's form for a moment, turning her in his hands, inverting her before righting her again. "Perhaps, First Science can revert it to its true form."

"Every effort shall be made to achieve it. I will summon maintenance drones to dispose of this debris and—"

Carrying Guardian before him, Draask began to walk towards the hold's hatch. "No. This is a field of victory, a place to celebrate where I achieved my destiny. When I return home and become Grand Overseer, this ship will become an exhibition of my achievements."

"It will remain as you desire, Overseer."

"Now, alert First Science that we are bringing him a task."

"It will be done, Overseer." Z-Tek keyed a pad mounted on the wrist of his armor.

11:45 Site Q, A subterranean facility in the mountains of West Virginia

Bernard was in his element, a metallurgist in a metalline candy store. All around the lab were steel crates of samples, alloys of all ninety-one known metals. The Foundry Man, as they were calling Rudy, had provided them with wonders that left Bernard mystified and excited to the point of exhaustion. The alloys' tensile strength, impact strength, compression strength, and every other known method of measuring metals, exceeded all expectations. He discovered a pencil-thick strand of tungsten processed through the Foundry Man could bear the weight of over one hundred cars. His discoveries had kept him in the lab for sixteen hours for each of the past two days. He only stopped to sleep, drink coffee, and eat the occasional sandwich.

The scientist groaned and leaned back from the electron microscope. He lifted his glasses and rubbed his eyes. His elation and wonder matched a child's at Christmas but his body was ready for retirement. If he had stayed away from the ponies and the gaming tables he would be retired and would have missed out on this opportunity, no matter how it came about. The second half of his thought brought a slight sting to his conscience.

"Still here?" a male voice called from the doorway, "I admire your dedication."

Replacing his spectacles, Bernard turned to see his immediate supervisor, Grayson Weber. The scientist had twenty, maybe twenty-five years on the younger man whom, by his estimation, seemed more about money and less about knowledge. "I guess I'll see you Monday then?" Bernard began to gather his notes.

"Not Monday, tomorrow, bright and early, at nine o'clock."

"But tomorrow's Sunday."

"That's why they call them golden handcuffs, buddy. Corporate is licking its chops at the potential profits."

Bernard's hand rose to his chin. "I was so wrapped up in the research, I hadn't considered that."

"Bernie, buddy...that's the only consideration."

"They must be paying the Foundry Man like an all-star ball player."

Weber snickered. "Yeah."

"I'd like to meet him sometime."

"No-can-do, pal. He's in protective quarantine."

As Bernard's face fell with disappointment, Weber half-leaned out the doorway to look down the exterior corridor.

"Hey you want to see something?" He stepped back into the hall and motioned for the scientist to join him. "Hurry."

Bernard pushed himself off his seat and joined Weber at the door. "What is it?"

"Look." Weber pointed down the hall where four black-clad guards, their faces obscured by goggles and balaclavas, were escorting a shuffling hooded figure towards them. "That's one of the big Black brutes that was doing super slut last night." He laughed.

Alarmed, Bernard's face filled with question. "I don't understand."

"The super slut? The blonde in the cape?" Weber pointed to the shuffling figure, "He took her to a swinger's club last night. I guess she did two of them si-mul-taneously on the dance floor."

Bernard's face squinched. His description did not sound like his Claire, but then again, there were newspaper reports about her dalliances all over the world.

"I know, it's disgusting, but still, it's funny as hell." Weber cackled.

Bernard struggled to keep his emotions in check. "What are

they doing with him?"

Weber clapped Bernard on the shoulder. "Buddy you've got to get on the team and visit the communications center from time to time. You can't be a lab rat every second you're here."

Bernard winced at the impact of the unexpected gesture of camaraderie. "But what are they going to do with him?"

"Not our department but I guess super slut made off with some Senator's lieutenant and they think he might know where she took him."

Bernard's face distorted with distaste.

"Don't worry, I'm sure they'll get it out of him. Anyway...." Weber turned back to Bernard. "Shut her down and get some sleep. I'll see you in the morning." He turned and left in the direction of the prisoner and paramilitaries.

"See you tomorrow," Bernie said reflexively, watching as the shuffling figure and his escort disappeared inside a room down the corridor. He realized with a shudder that if Claire had been out with him on Friday, he could have been the one in the hood. Wearing a dark expression, he turned back to the lab intending to ensure he was set up for the morning before locking up for the night.

As the black hood was pulled off, Marcus murmured with discomfort and clenched his eyes shut at the blinding presence of the interrogation room's lights. One of the guards unfastened Marcus' shackles from the leather prisoner belt around his waist and left. As his eyes adjusted, the engineer immediately noted that he wasn't alone.

Standing across from him, separated by a polished steel table, was another man dressed in black battle dress like his guards. He had a crew cut and looked vaguely familiar but he couldn't quite place him.

"Can I have your autograph, Mr. Carter?" He sneered.

Marcus countered the smirk with a contemptuous glare. "Who the fuck are you?"

"With your cooperation? The cavalry."

"Like Custer's cavalry meeting Sitting Bull?"

The grin continued unabated. "History buff too huh? We'll have to add that to your file."

"Did you bring me here to write my biography?"

The interrogator scoffed. "No, but it helps to know who you're dealing with and after checking into you for a few days, I must say, you keep some very interesting company, Dr. Jackson."

"There's nobody in my life I don't want there with one exception." Marcus' eyes narrowed. "Now what the hell do you want?"

"To be at home pumpin' the wife and if you'll just answer a few questions, I'll be on my way."

"Don't worry about it. I'm sure someone's taking care of it."

The punch that followed swelled Marcus' lip. He spat a blood-flecked wad of saliva on his assailant's boots and looked up at him. "Is that your best shot, broke-dick? No wonder—"

The mercenary grabbed a handful of Marcus' bloody suit. "Where is she—"

"Your wife? Probably giving—"

The next punch turned Marcus' head.

Feeling his cheek tingle, Marcus resisted the compulsion to wince. "You're going to have to be a little more specific."

"Who the fuck do you think, jarhead? That alien bitch, the space bimbo. Where'd she take him?"

Marcus returned his interrogator's glare. "Well, shithead, I don't know. Maybe if I had some more details, because I don't know what the fuck you're talking about. Where'd she take who?"

"That doesn't matter, where does she go?"

"If you're looking for a missing person, I suggest you call the FBI, not NASA."

"Think you're smart, do you?"

"Which one of us here is the rocket scientist?"

"Last chance, rocket scientist. Where. Would. She. Take. Someone?" he asked through gritted teeth.

"I don't know what your boy did to get on her radar but I know who's next and God help you when she shows up."

The interrogator shook his head. "Well, I tried to do it the nice way. It seems you need to be introduced to Dr. Payne."

Marcus snorted derisively. "And who the hell came up with that name? You?"

"Oh that is his name. He was a dentist before he came to work for us. I'm sure he'll enjoy your time together." The interrogator turned and shouted for the guards. "We'll see how you feel about talking in a few hours—if you can still talk."

"Finally! Fucking amateur hour is over."

Four guards pounded into the room to pull the black hood back over Marcus' head and wrench him from his chair.

As he was led away, he hoped they didn't kill him before she found them.

Sunday 12:00 AM S-Ga Ship, Science Lab One

With the Earth's only defence neutralized, the great black ship flew on, unchallenged. Despite the approaching moment of triumph, Z-Tek remained indifferent. He entered the main laboratory to check on his brethren's progress. He remained unaffected as he walked through the ship's expansive biobank, a ghoulish gallery of amoral desperation and appalling violence.

Set out in long rows, each of the hundreds of stasis tubes glowed with a bilious green light that illuminated their gruesome and tragic contents: species snatched from their worlds across multiple galaxies and preserved in various states of dissection.

Some were bisected with their internal organs on display. Others were completely eviscerated, staring with unseeing eyes through the tubes' covers. To date, none of the hapless specimens had provided a solution to the Zetas' impeding extinction.

At the end of the biobank, Z-Tek entered a brightly illuminated examination area. Under the glare of white spotlights, Guardian resembled a butterfly caught in a web. Still unconscious, she lay stretched out on a saltire, her limbs ensconced up to her knees and elbows in gleaming trotium cylinders.

Overhead, surgical instruments hung menacingly from articulated power cables. A stout, box-shaped, cannon projected scarlet beams onto Guardian. Nearby, a stasis tube stood open. Lit with the same eerie green light as the others, it was hooked up to the piping overhead and ready for occupation.

Z-Tek found the lead scientist, Azyn, working in shadows. Like all Zeta-Reticulans, they shared an identical appearance.

He spoke to his compatriot telepathically *"It remains neutralized."*

The scientist did not look up from his brightly lit console. *"By unexpected means. While attempting a standard examination, I made a noteworthy discovery, fluctuating energy levels."*

"Elaborate."

"Its garments proved too resilient to remove conventionally. I experimented with the broad beam neutralizer to remove them but they continued to regenerate and reform."

"A molecular technology?"

"That was my initial hypothesis, but after taking a specimen, I determined its covering to be a living organism." Azyn approached another backlit station where a stoppered jar contained a gray blob. It pressed against the container's transparent surface in Guardian's direction.

"It has a symbiotic relationship with the entity, feeding off its energy. I theorize that once the sample's analysis is complete, it will be possible to combine this organism with an inumbrated crin and create a hybrid that can be commanded to extract the entity's energy and power the ship."

"Probability of success?" Z-Tek asked.

"Barring unforeseen circumstances, certain."

"The Overseer will find this agreeable. Is there any danger of the entity regaining consciousness and escaping?"

"Unlikely. The symbiote's need to regenerate itself is a continuous drain on the entity's energy. With the beams in place, it will remain too weak to free itself. Once the conversion of its symbiote is complete, I will restore it to the entity, place it in stasis, and move them to the engine room for First to finalize the interface."

Z-Tek examined the control console and noted the low setting compared to what was required to bring their nemesis down. *"Were you able to complete an initial examination?"*

"No. Its physiology remains too durable for external scans to penetrate. Internal examination did yield some useful information."

"Expound," Z-Tek directed.

"Arthroscopic examination of its respiratory, digestive and reproductive systems indicate that it is structurally identical to Terran females."

"Were you able to obtain genetic specimens?"

"Attempts at excision of cellular matter were unsuccessful."

"Did you attempt to obtain material from its organic fluids?"

"Also unsuccessful, it seems the entity regenerates and does not discard cells however in taking fluid samples from its reproductive system I discovered a zygote." Azyn paused to look up at Guardian's form,

"Fascinating. Where you able to harvest it?"

"It is currently being scanned in the incubator."

Azyn keyed his panel and projected a hologram of a roughly spherical image of an otherwise unremarkable ovum containing a pair of pronuclei.

He watched with his fellow scientist as web-like microtubials inside the egg pulled the two sets of chromosomes together. *"As you can see, the genetic material is combining."*

Z-Tek's gaze turned toward their captive. *"Speculate. If it is capable of reproducing with Terrans, could it have offspring on Terra?"*

"Long distant scans from the observation post on the system's fourth planet have not recorded any. Compatibility may be impossible beyond initial fertilization, but our experiments on Terran reproductive processes may provide the necessary insights to obtain a viable outcome. Should the overseer be informed?"

Z-Tek turned his attention back to his compatriot. *"No. He has what was negotiated. Your discovery will remain with us for further analysis and development on Zeta-Prime."* The second officer prepared to go. *"Continue your efforts, I will inform the overseer of your promising outcome and recommend that the conversion signal be initiated."*

12:01 AM, Site Q

Marcus' head throbbed. He shivered. His eyes flew open in memory then clenched shut with a groan of pain. An overhead operatory light shone directly into his eyes. "What the hell?" Opening his eyes to a slit, he discovered his clothes had been taken from him and his limbs were held fast by broad leather straps.

"Ah, there you are," a male voice gloated. "No, don't close your eyes, we have work to do." The voice's owner cracked an ampoule of smelling salts and lifted it to his captive's nose.

The sharp tang of ammonia stabbed Marcus' nostrils. Wincing, he let out a wheezing cough and tried but failed to jerk his head back. His attempt at movement shook the chair. He discovered four rubber covered prongs held his skull in a vice-like grip. Fully awake, his heart renewed its racing beat and cold sweat dripped off the back of his scalp.

"You're not getting out of those. I made sure they were extra tight."

Marcus glared at the speaker as he stepped into view.

Graying at the temples and pasty-white beneath his surgical mask, Payne wore a black rubber apron that hung down to his knees. What struck Marcus most were his captor's eyes. As they gazed back at him from over the hem of the mask, he recognized the eyes—not specifically this man but the kind of person who possessed such eyes. He had seen eyes like them before among terrorist prisoners in Afghanistan, remorseless, and empty.

Marcus' gazed flicked left and right. He was strapped into some kind of stainless steel examination chair, his wrists and ankles buckled to it with bands of thick leather, with a further strap across his chest. Around him were a terrifying array of red tool boxes, trays of medical and dental instruments, a car battery with jumper cables, and an assortment of power tools.

"So, you're this morning's problem? The good news is that I'm a natural problem-solver."

Marcus' nostrils flared as he struggled to steady his breathing.

"Why won't you talk? Hmm? We already know some of it. That you two are fucking. That she turned down an orgy, wears a slave collar and calls you master. But then again, you are such a magnificent specimen."

"Fuck you," Marcus growled.

Payne chuckled malevolently. "Such spirit."

The disgraced dentist traced a gloved hand over Marcus' bare chest and continued on down past his waist. "I might just have to find out for myself *'cuz I just loves me some brown sugar.*"

Marcus bellowed as his testicles were seized and pain shot right through to the top of his brain. He strained at his bonds. Something hard and metallic-tasting filled his mouth and clacked against his teeth.

"Have I got your attention, boy?" Payne's eyes gleamed. He ratcheted the lever on the Jennings gag, forcing Marcus' mouth open.

Marcus huffed at the residual pain still pounding in his head and throbbing in his groin. He eyed Payne feeling the two bands of pencil-thick steel keeping his jaws pried apart.

"Now here's how this is going to go." Payne turned back to the bench behind him. A dental drill whined menacingly as he held the gleaming instrument up for Marcus to see. "We're going to drill a little then talk a little. How much, depends on you."

Marcus watched in horror as the tiny bur spun.

Payne leaned in, pressing a hand to his prisoner's forehead, gripping it tightly.

"I hon't knom anything," Marcus mumbled against the gag.

"We'll talk later, right now we're drilling."

Payne ground into a big molar. Bits of tooth and bloody mist mixed with the drill's whine and Marcus' pain-filled shouts.

The lights flicked off; the drill's whine died while Marcus' gasping groans continued.

"What the fuck has gone wrong now? Am I the only competent one in the entire place!" Payne snarled in the total darkness. "I just can't work like this!"

Klaxons joined the cacophony. Above the door, a cherry-red emergency light began to spin.

"Now what the hell is that all about?" Payne asked. Throwing down his tool he turned back to Marcus. "You just wait right there, I'll be back as soon as I can, and we'll start again." He gave Marcus a pat on the top of his head and left him to consider his answers.

A single bank of lights dimly lit the subterranean warehouse that served as Rudy's cell. An electromagnet held him pinned to the wall like a beetle in a taxidermist's diorama. It hummed from its steady vibration. Unable to even lift his head from the enormous disk's surface, Rudy stared at the distant door, his thoughts alternating between escaping, collecting his fiancée somewhere beyond the door, and getting the sons of bitches that held them in confinement. His anger grew with each passing day.

They were using him. In exchange for one look at Josephine at the distant door, he absorbed ingots of ordinary metal, turned them adamant-tough and poured them out into a mold for collection. That's what they were calling the newly-created metal, Adamant. He could wipe them out with a single cough but he feared what they would do to her.

His thoughts of revenge were interrupted. His head began to buzz. Strange images of unblinking reptilian eyes and garbled words threatened to overwhelm him. His face creased in a moue. Speculating their captors were behind this new torture, his anger grew.

Without warning the lights flicked out, the electromagnet holding him ceased its vibrations. He pitched forward, crashing to the concrete floor and sending forth a web of cracks. Compelled by a feeling he could not explain, Rudy lifted himself up and charged through the darkness for the warehouse's steel door. Red emergency lights clicked on. Klaxons began to blare.

Disregarding the commotion, Rudy arrived at the door and pressed his hands to its surface.

In seconds it melted away, absorbed into his body. The plastic biohazard sign on the exterior surface clattered to the floor. He stepped on it, shattering it as he passed into an outer corridor lined with doors similar to his own. Charging guards, already alerted to his escape from the magnet, shouted an order to return to his cell.

His response sounded like the roar of a blast furnace. "Get the fuck out of my head!"

The security officers took aim and opened fire. The bullets from their automatic rifles rang harmlessly off his body, ricocheting in every direction.

Rudy's arm elongated, stretching to the door across from his cell to absorb it. Never taking his eyes from the guards, he opened his mouth and sprayed the length of the corridor with darts of red-hot metal. The guards cursed and frantically dove to the floor before crawling away from the fusillade overhead.

Josephine's cell door melted before her eyes, and without hesitation, she burst forth, calling to her fiancé. Instinctively, she reached out with her hands to touch him before immediately yanking them back, the heat of his body an instant reminder of his dangerous state. Rudy turned his face to look at her for a fleeting moment. "Stay behind me Josie, we're goin' home."

Trembling, she cut short her response, nodded, and fell in behind him. "Okay, hon."

Rudy lifted up his hands, fanning them outward to form a shield that stretched from wall to wall and from the floor to as high as his neck. As he moved forward, he absorbed each cell's door as he came to it. Behind him other family members emerged from cells and scrambled to the cells opposite to reach for their loved ones in the same manner as Josephine had.

Some found their metahuman loved ones comatose, others were found curled up on the floor, trembling and whimpering, some gripped their heads in pain, and others ignored their families and moved out into the corridor to follow on Rudy's heels.

###

Bernie cowered beneath the workstation furthest from the laboratory's door. He clutched a titanium rod with shaking hands while hoping and praying he would not need it to defend himself. Outside, the crack and pop of automatic weapons mixed with panicked shouts and the incessant blare of klaxons. The ground shook violently, dust from the ceiling tiles floated downwards, filling the air and coating everything in a fine layer of particulate.

Bernard coughed and sneezed. A heavy metallic thump at the laboratory's door startled him, lifting him from the floor to bump his head on the counter's underside. Groaning and seeing stars, it took him a few seconds to realize the sounds of battle were all around him. His knuckles turned white around the makeshift club. Sweat trickled off his nose. He pushed himself as deeply as possible into the corner of his improvised bolt-hole.

His dentures felt like they were about to crack under the pressure of his clenching jaw. After several moments of terror, the sounds of battle faded and he dared a peek over the top of the counter.

He was alone and, most puzzlingly, the laboratory's door was missing, hinges and all.

Setting his questions about the missing door aside, he hooked a grasping hand over the top of the counter to find the telephone and pull it down to him. His hands were shaking so badly that he was grateful for the speed dial options on the telephone's panel. First, he tried to contact security, and the call went to voicemail after ten rings. The communication center yielded the same result. His mobile phone was at the security desk along with everyone else's who were in the bunker, a measure taken by the corporation to prevent industrial espionage.

His stomach dropped out with the realization he had been abandoned. He lingered for several moments before coming to a decision. He would have to extradite himself from his situation and walk all the way back to Boston if he had to.

Growing angrier, he pushed himself up from the floor and silenced the lab's alarm by bashing it off the wall with the rod. His state of upset unabated, he poked his head out the lab's door to observe the shadowy corridor. The nostril-stinging stench of cordite mixed with ozone hung in the air.

Leaving the lab, he carefully picked his way among the hundreds of brass bullet casings littering the floor. Further down the hall a guard lay in a heap, his weapon beside him. He concluded from the mark on the guard's jaw, not only was it broken but that he would be unconscious for some time. He considered taking the gun but he knew almost nothing about them and feared shooting himself should he attempt to use it.

As he moved up the corridor, he noted all of the doors were missing. Passing an entryway, he saw the top of the Black man's head. The one Weber had told him about earlier, the one who had taken Claire to the swinger's club, the one that had made an indecent spectacle of her. His fear forgotten, Bernie gripped the titanium rod and, red-faced with anger, stormed into the interrogation room.

"Why!" he began to demand, "why did you—"His voice cut off abruptly as he came to witness the scene fully. "Good God! What have they done to you?"

Blood dribbled down Marcus' lower lip. "Het me out of fefe hohhamheh ftwaff." Marcus' snarl became a mumble.

Nodding frantically, Bernie set the rod aside and began to pull at the broad strap binding the black man's wrist to the chair.

"Huwwy uf!"

"I'm trying." Bernie cursed his fingers struggling to get them to work, tugging the tongue out of the buckle and freeing it from its pin.

As soon as his first hand was free, Marcus leaned over to free its opposite. With some help from the elderly scientist, the gag and the remainder of his bonds were removed.

"Where are your clothes?" Bernie asked."

The big man rolled out of the chair. "First priority is to get the hell out of here."

"I was just doing that myself. But...." Bernie looked at Marcus' state of nakedness and took off his lab coat and offered it up. "Here."

Marcus looked over the garment for a split second and uttered a curse before tying the garment's arms around his waist and tucking its tail into the improvised belt to make shorts. Moving to the door he ducked his head out and back in to address the scientist. "Now, which way is out?"

"I'll show you. But I want you to know I didn't sign up for this. This isn't me."

"Hold on." Marcus jogged to where the felled guard lay and picked up the fallen man's rifle. He checked to see if the weapon was loaded and its magazine was full before turning back to ask, "Now, which way?"

"You believe me, don't you?" Bernie implored, "I didn't have anything to do with what they did to you."

Rudy stalked after Site Q's staff like a tiger pursuing sheep. The painful pounding in his head was exacerbated by the clank of his floor-cracking footfalls, the ricochets of bullets, and explosions of grenades and anti-tank rockets. His fury grew with each step.

The chase wended through the bunker's network of corridors. Along the way, the foundry worker absorbed every bit of metal he encountered, doors, alarm klaxons, even the housing of security cameras added to his bulk—and to his supply of ammunition.

Behind him, most of the metahumans, some of them walking with the help of their families, stayed tucked around corners to avoid the munitions flying through the air. The bulletproof Charlie Hill and the amazingly agile, pentathlete, Jessica Córdova followed on his heels, champing at the bit to exact some justice of their own.

Climbing the ramp leading up and out of the bunker, Rudy, Jessica, and Charlie emerged into the night air. They halted, stunned by what they beheld.

In Site Q's parking lot, a gleaming, scarab-shaped UFO rested atop the wreckage of crushed cars and trucks. A ramp extended down from under its fuselage, at its foot stood a spindly gray humanoid, flanked by four hovering, armored robots. Other robots were carrying trussed up and terrified Grey and Steele employees up the ship's ramp.

The alien raised a long digit and pointed at the emerging metahumans. A troop of metal marauders surged forward. Their metal claws stretched out and whirred menacingly. Capture drones launched from their chests and filled the air.

Rudy grumbled, "This just gets better and better. Come on you bastards!" Extending his arms like medieval lances, he charged to meet them.

They crashed together.

Rudy seized the first two robot attackers even as their capture drones began to truss him up with their metallic bands. The bands, along with the bodies of the robots, melted into his body like snowflakes on a hot summer day.

Feeling his strength surge, he paused to flex before putting his fist through another one of the sentinels. "Oh yeah!" he crowed.

Seeing the sentinels begin to fall, Z-Tek activated his armored suit's propulsion system and rocketed upwards towards the mother-ship. He spoke into his communicator as he flew. "Communications One, terminate the signal immediately. The thralls have been subverted."

Charlie Hill hoisted robots into the air and slamming them down to the parking lot's blacktop.

While Charlie bashed, Jessica caught one of the straps intended to mummify her and began using the drones carrying it like a flail. The Raven-haired athlete from Michigan whirled the drone overhead smashing other approaching drones. She leapt fifty feet straight up and came down with both feet on the head of a sentry.

Other metas joined in, Melanie threw up her own snares of thorny vines, wrapping up sentries for Rudy to absorb. Ray-

Anne, groggy from sedation, smashed drones together, breaking them open like eggs.

A shower of sparks, a flash of lightning, and a whip crack of thunder heralded a new arrival—from a cloud of acrid ozone stepped a statuesque young woman. Athletic in build, she wore a royal blue cyclist jacket, with matching leggings and high-top running shoes. The neon yellow laces of her shoes matched the piping on her jacket. Amber cycling goggles hid the color of her eyes. Her long, sand-colored hair was woven into a single braid. She began to speak when the sentries and their flying drones took note of her and attacked.

The new arrival seemed to vanish. Chains of lightning appeared from thin air, joining the metal marauders in a long strand of electrocution. As the last drone collapsed to the pavement spewing smoke, the newcomer reappeared. "Does anyone else have a headache?" she asked in a thick, Serbian accent.

"You have one too?" Melanie asked and introduced herself.

"It started a short time ago. It must be them," the newcomer said looking up at the ship blotting out the stars overhead. "I am Stephania Tesla," she added.

"Tesla? Like the car?" Melanie asked.

"Like my distant relative. We are both engineers. Is Guardian here?" She looked about.

"We haven't seen her. I hope she's all right," Melanie said.

"I'll check." Stephania vanished for a split second before reappearing. "I don't see her but there are people in there. They are tied up in those steel bands."

Ray-Anne scowled. "More like criminals."

"You move as fast as lightning?" Melanie asked.

"I—"

A series of explosions overhead lit up the landscape. The assembly looked up to see the remains of a flight of jet fighters falling like pieces of burning confetti.

Stephania pulled her gaze away from the spectacle to address the others. "Those fighters do not stand a chance. We must get up there."

"What about Guardian? Shouldn't we wait?" Melanie asked.

"We can't wait. We'll just have to do like she would." Ray-Anne turned her attention to the alien ship in their midst. "Let me try something,"

As the others watched, the end of the ramp began to rise off the ground. It began to shake and rattle. Her face screwed up in concentration. Perspiration beaded on her forehead. She groaned and began to tremble. After a moment, she emitted a wheezing, frustrated cry. "I'm sorry, y'all. It's too heavy and hooked on there too tight."

Rudy drew Ray-Anne's attention, "If I can build a platform can you lift us up there?"

The dancer turned superhero looked up at him and nodded resolutely. "Just make it as light as you can."

"You got it." Rudy rumbled like a furnace in acknowledgement. Now over eight feet tall and considerably bulkier than when he started his trek to the surface, Rudy stood like a Goliath among them. His hands stretched to the smoking shells of the sentry robots. In moments he turned them into a disc large enough to fit them all.

"What the hell do you think you're doing?" Bill Spellman spun his daughter around by her arm.

"Daddy..." Ray-Anne looked at her father's hand until he released it. "We're going up there. We're going to fight them."

"The hell you are!" Bill Spellman bellowed, "I've already lost your mother. I'm not losing you, too."

The young woman's features softened. "Daddy I'm sorry and I love you but if I don't go, we could lose everything."

"Y'all ain't no hero, that's Guardian's job." He jabbed a finger at her. "Did she put you up to this?"

Ray-Anne's eyes began to well with tears. "No Daddy, you did."

"What? The hell you say!" her father shouted.

"You always told me that when duty calls, that's when character counts. You raised me to have character. I have to go. I can't stand by and let them go into danger without me—not when I can help."

"But I just got you back." Bill smothered his daughter in a hug.

"I'll come back. I promise." Ray-Anne sobbed, kissing her father's cheek.

Meanwhile, the others, their hearts breaking with grief, were having similar conversations with their weeping, ashen-faced loved ones.

Saying their goodbyes, they gently extradited themselves from desperate embraces and turned to grimly march to the improvised elevator to ride it into the night sky and to war.

Science Lab, S-Ga Ship

Pain roused Guardian from her unconsciousness. She gasped sharply. Her body convulsed, and arched upwards. Her lips drew back in a guttural groan. From her neck to her knees, she felt as if she were draped in a blanket of stinging nettles. Seeking the source of her torment she peered through cringing eyes that quickly widened with shock.

Her symbiote was missing. Overhead, lasers blazed, turning her fair skin to an angry shade of sunburn-red that prickled and stung incessantly. Determined to be free, Guardian lifted her limbs, expecting to split the polished cylinders that held her as easily as if they were made of tissue. They held her fast her effort did not even net a tiny metallic creak of protest.

"Bloody hell," she cursed. She glared angrily at the bond trapping her right arm. Taking a deep breath, she reefed against the cylinder.

The results were immediate.

She cried out at the sharp stab of pain in her shoulder. As she lay there wincing and huffing, a sheen of perspiration broke over her skin.

Despite the throbbing in her injured joint, she tried a second time and stopped immediately as her shoulder stabbed her again in a sharp rebuke. As her chest heaved and a growing sense of dread churned in her belly, she stared at the bond in disbelief.

The metal was scarcely as thick as her finger, she couldn't fathom as to why it was so strong or why she was so weak. Still panting as much from fear as from the exertion, she twisted her head about, examining her surroundings and received another shock.

An alien stared at her with lifeless eyes. Haloed in green light, it floated, suspended in a stasis tube. Other deceased aliens were similarly displayed in tubes all around her. Nearby, off to her right, was another stasis tube, this one was empty its domed cover open and ready for an occupant. Trembling she turned her face from the horrors to encounter others.

Hanging from the pipes and wires in the overhead, were an array of gleaming, articulated, mechanical arms. Each of the nightmarish appendages was tipped with a perversion of a surgical instrument, laser scalpels, diagnostic scanners, regenerators, retractors fitted with claws.

She snarled in frustration and cast about for a solution. Looking down between her breasts her heart leapt into her throat.

A gangrel figure in polished armor emerged from behind a row of stasis tubes pushing a hovering cart carrying a canister.

The sight of the Zeta-Reticulan elicited a strangled cry of alarm. Her pulse pounded in her ears. Unpleasant memories of rescuing humans in the same situation flooded back to her. Heart racing, she began to shake.

After a moment, heart still pounding in her ears, she realized that he was either unaware or unconcerned with her conscious state. She turned her attention to what he was working on.

In a larger canister, a gray blob writhed and bubbled, pressing to its transparent surface in Guardian's direction. It was her symbiote.

Huffing anger winning out over fear she bellowed at him. "What are you doing! You let me off here you little, gray bastard!"

Much to her frustration, he did not even look up to acknowledge her and carried on with his work at the console.

The lasers burning her skin flared in intensity. It felt like red-hot rivets were being driven into her. She winced and writhed; her groans became shrill screams. "Stop! Stop! Stop!"

Azyn resumed his preparations to subvert the symbiote.

After several, excruciating moments, the intensity of the red light, and her pain, lessened.

Still panting, her eyes opened and quickly came to focus on the lasers' projectors. She cleared her throat, took a deep breath and screamed.

Her scream quickly became a screech and then a burning, wheezing cough. "What have you done to me?" she croaked, her throat raw. A second attempt became a fit of coughs before she could even raise her voice.

Azyn soon appeared at the edge of the spot light.

"You!" she gasped in recognition. Decades before she had prosecuted him before the Federacy's Adjudication Panel for abduction and experimentation on humans.

"Your interference has cost valuable time, but no longer. We will take what we need."

Tears flowed down her cheeks. "No...Please...spare them. Take me."

"You are Draask's." A cable unspooled from the rear of his armor. It clattered against the deck.

"No..." Her chest heaved. Her teeth clenched. She grunted, arching against the frame that held her.

The cord slithered to a power conduit. A stubby canon reared up on his shoulder like a cobra. It whined softly as it angled and drew a bead.

She turned her face in a vain effort to avoid the coming blast.

His body bowed sideways, the Zeta flew through the air. He struck the side of a stasis pod with a hard crack. It burst apart, spilling its gruesome contents over his unconscious form.

Guardian's head whipped around to discover the source of the assault.

"Legs!" Sergei bellowed. He stood in the passage between

the stasis tubes, gawking.

A second man stood near her outstretched feet. He was burly and a full head taller than Sergei. Both of them wore sealed environmental suits.

Guardian's eyes swept over them in confusion before hardening. "See anything you like?" she snapped.

"Not this way. Sorry." Sergei averted his gaze and scowled at his companion, "Boris, turn your face…"

"Thank you," she said as he complied. "Please…." She swallowed the lump in her throat. "Get me off this thing."

Sergei spoke to her sideways, his voice half-muffled by his internal respirator. "We wondered where you were. What happened—"

"Sergei, please…." She paused to huff out a breath.

"Right. Boris, break her out—but don't look."

She looked up at it and grunted in pain, "Watch out for the lasers."

Their gaze followed hers up to the overhead.

"Where is the switch for it?" Sergei glanced at her and then turned his face again.

"The console—"

The glare of the overhead lights blinked out replaced by the putrid green glow of specimen tanks. Boris floated over her, an arcing power line in his hand.

"He can fly," Sergei supplied.

"Thank you." She slumped back on the hard metal of the frame, feeling a profound sense of relief at the cessation of the assault on her skin.

"I will have you out in a moment." Boris dropped to the deck and seized the bond around her left leg.

The big man curled his fingers into the top of the cylinder, grunting, and then swearing as one hand became two. He braced his foot against the trotium frame and tore at it.

"Come on!" Sergei shouted, "You carried a submarine all the way from Russia and you can't—"

"Neither can I Sergei, whatever they did to me, I'm too weak." She watched as the big Russian stepped back, his face shield steamed up and reflecting the place's eerie green light.

"See if you can find a switch on that console," Guardian directed.

Sergei blinked from where he stood at the instrument panel. "I don't know what this says." He looked up and then looked away just as quickly.

"Dammit," Guardian cursed under her breath, pulling on her bonds again. She could feel her strength slowly returning but her dignity continued to be insulted by her predicament.

"I know what to do." Sergei reappeared at her head. "One second, Legs—don't' worry, I'm not looking—or trying not to." Sergei patted his way along the cylinder holding her arm until his hand finally met flesh.

"What are you going to do?"

"Teleport us back to the submarine. We can get you something to wear and—"

"No. Please wait, my clothes are here. If you could just relieve me of my predicament."

"Relieve you?" Sergei's expression became puzzled.

"Get me off this thing?" She continued to regard him, grateful his face was turned.

"I can do that. I'll try and catch you so you don't fall."

"Sergei, remember, I can fly too." She reminded him patiently.

"Right. Ready? One, two, three!"

The instant Guardian reappeared, she streaked for the privacy of the rear of the console while collecting the symbiote's canister along the way. Crouching on the floor, she unstoppered the lid. The symbiote exploded forth with the exuberance of a puppy. She grunted in shock as the life form washed over her, knocking her to the deck. "Oh! Ah!" A convulsion shook her body as the symbiote poured over her like molasses, drawing from her energy, reassembling into her uniform.

"Legs? Are you all right?" Sergei's head appeared over the top of the console.

"I will be." She lay flat on her back, looking up into his face. "In a moment."

"Let me help you up," he offered.

"Thank you, but...." With a groan she reached up to grip the corner of the instrument panel. "That won't be necessary." The panel crunched in her hand as she used it to stand. She panted for a moment, steadying herself.

"And thank you for coming to help me."

Sergei glanced to his comrade and then smiled back at her. "It was our pleasure and I want to say, I only saw for a second but you are the most—"

Her expression veered to one of warning. "We are not having this conversation, Sergei."

"But your tattoo, I never would have—"

"Yes, and you will never speak of it again—to anyone." She continued to huff, holding herself up by the console. "How did you find me?"

He turned to point to an immense, polished steel case next to Boris. "Bombs. We have to find places for eighteen of them—"

"Bombs?" She looked at him with alarm.

"Nine megatons each. Good thing we found you, we're going to turn this ship to ash."

She held up a hand. "Wait a moment, how did you get into space?"

"The ship is not in space; it is over eastern America."

"Then you absolutely cannot detonate those weapons. The power required to move a ship this size…" She frowned.

"It must be a lot."

"Detonating those bombs would…" She gestured for emphasis. "completely destroy the planet. They must be removed immediately."

"We have orders—" Boris interjected, his voice sounding hollow through his suit's face shield.

"Orders based on insufficient information. Now take that.…" She nodded to the steel box. "And any others you've placed, off the ship."

"What will you do?" Sergei asked.

Guardian quickly strode to Ayzn's slumped form, plucked him from the puddle of pickled offal, and pressed him down on the gantry she had so recently occupied. She looked from Boris to Sergei and laid a hand on the gray's shoulder. "He and I will be having a conversation."

S-Ga Ship, Science Lab One

Many moments later, Sergei reappeared in the lab to find Guardian had bound the gray to the saltire and was now questioning him. He looked on curiously before asking, "What is he saying?"

Guardian gave the gray a poke in the forehead rendering him unconscious again.

"It's bloody awful business, absolutely horrendous."

"What is?" Sergei asked.

"The asteroid, it was made up of a crystalline species called the crin. The commander of this ship used a wormhole—a kind of intergalactic shortcut through spacetime, to send it here. Each piece was intended to bond with and enslave Earth's adults by controlling their minds. I'm not even going to go into what they planned to do with the children." She shot the alien a look of fury.

"The bastards! But that explains the headaches."

"You have a headache?" Her expression changed to one of concern.

"It suddenly stopped; I don't know why."

She glanced at the alien. "That one told me about a signal sent to summon and control those exposed to the asteroid. Perhaps they turned it off. Incidentally, where is your friend?"

"Boris?" He glanced upwards. "He's outside with the others, fighting on top of the ship."

"Others?"

"Metas—lots of metas from all over *and* lots of robots plus a dragon-man."

Guardian fidgeted, rising off the floor and fighting the urge to go help. "How are they faring?"

"The robots are trash, but the big guy is tough. He's jumping around a lot. I think he can teleport like me."

The new information did not lend itself to a sense of optimism. "Have there been casualties?"

Sergei shrugged. "It's a battle. It's what happens."

The blonde let out a huff of frustration. "Damn. I should be out there but we have to take this opportunity to get his ship off the planet. We have to find the engine room."

"I think I know where it is."

"You do?"

"It is enormous and cold—even for a Russian, and has what look like reactors everywhere—a whole forest of them."

"Is it guarded? How many were working there?"

"We did not stay long enough to do a reconnaissance. But we did see robots flying around when we were hiding a bomb."

Still frowning, Guardian brought a hand to her chin in thought.

"Why not go to the bridge?" Sergei asked.

"It's likely heavily guarded and their weapons are quite formidable—but if this ship is like most of the ones I've been on, the engineering section will have rudimentary controls and all we need to do is command the ship to go up. I can take care of it once it's a few hundred thousand miles from the Earth. But we will need to get there without attracting attention."

"No problem. I can have us there in a blink of an eye." He began to reach for her.

She retreated beyond his outstretched hand. "I want to use that." She pointed to the empty stasis pod near the saltire.

"What is it?"

"According to that one." She scowled and inclined her head in the direction of the unconscious alien. "It was intended to be a matrix, a kind of conduit to subdue me by draining off my energy to power the ship, but it's about to become a Trojan Horse."

S-Ga Ship, Engineering Compartment

Her skin still crawling from the horror of Azin's revelations, it took a Herculean effort for Guardian to feign unconsciousness and not seek Draask out to deliver a comeuppance. She lay back in the form-fitting matrix. Tilted at an angle she resembled a kind of living bas-relief.

The pod's canopy was opaque from the inside and transparent from the outside. Her lack of sight only served to increase her feelings of anxiety.

The trotium shackles meant to hold her in place were laid over her wrists, arms, and ankles but not locked. The fat, insulated wires meant to leech away her energy hung loose, bait to draw the attention of a fastidious engineer.

She was alone, she had tasked a protesting Sergei with warning the force outside to be ready to evacuate. Before he left, the Russian had used the butt of his pistol to create a racket, tapping and rapping it against the deck plates to draw a response.

The reaction was not long in coming. Through the canopy, she heard the whir and hum of servos followed by the heavy clank of armored feet striking the deck. A series of S-Ga curses quickly followed. Maintaining the illusion of harmlessness, she kept her form limp as the matrix was jostled then lifted. Seconds later it thumped down and slid backwards for a short distance. One more hard shove shook the entire pod and it suddenly hummed to life. The pod's putrid green light shone down from over her head, illuminating it's interior. The canopy's hatch rose with a hiss.

Guardian's eyes flew open, startling the armored S-Ga engineer. She wasted no time, launching herself at the much bigger being. She tore off his shoulder canon and drove him back against the line of consoles behind him.

The panels and screens sparked and smoked with the impact. Her fist cracked against his toothy jaw. The dragon-man crumpled. She seized his armor's gorget and held him up, stunned by his seeming fragility compared to Draask. She touched the alien's jowl to heal him and rouse him from his stupor.

The engineer startled at the sight of her. "What? How?" he snarled, regaining his nature.

Maintenance drones beginning to hover in, crowding them. Metallic gray, they vaguely resembled octopi: ridged, mushroom-shaped heads topped by three heavy, dog-legged arms with grasping claws in the rear and three lighter, segmented arms in front that folded out a Swiss-army-knife variety of tools.

Guardian glanced at them before tersely ordering him to shut them down.

"The controls. They've come to—"

"Now!" she bellowed.

He spoke into the communicator on his gorget. "Maintenance drones, protocol one."

The demeanor of the hovering robots quickly changed. They extended narrow wand-like rods from each of their smaller arms that arced with red lightning. The claws of the heavier arms stretched open to grasp at her.

Guardian hissed a breath through her teeth at the sting of so many arcs of lightning. "Well, that was bloody foolish," she growled at him and wheeled to confront the mob.

Guardian tore into the impromptu security force, her shouts of battle mixed with the sounds of smashing and screeching metal. She finished by lifting a drone overhead and hurling at it three others when she suddenly found herself standing among the thick, black, silos of the reactors. The molten red light of the tank's narrow, oblong slit windows, reflected off Sergei's environmental suit.

Her fierce expression changed to one of astonishment. "By the stars, Sergei!"

The Russian gave her a frantic shushing gesture and motioned for her to peek around the edge of the reactor. Her nose rankled at the stench of burnt metal as her eyes fell upon Draask. She stifled a gasp, seeing the deck where she had been standing was now cratered and smoking.

"Where is it?" he demanded, looking first to the deck and then to his subordinate. "I did not have the weapon set high enough to disintegrate it."

The engineer stood at the edge of the crater examining it first it, then in every other direction, among the battered and destroyed drones, and up to the overhead, finally he looked to the towering reactors that contained the crin. Finishing his search, he turned back to his commander, "Do you think it can move as you do, My Lord?"

"It shouldn't be able to—not yet." Draask gestured to the row of computer panels. "Internal sensor sweep. Find it."

Guardian drew her head back and turned to Sergei, almost bumping into him. "Sergei, it's too dangerous for you here. You must leave immediately," she whispered frantically.

"We make a good team," he observed with a smile.

The blonde's eyes widened with disbelief. "I appreciate your help but didn't you hear them? They're initiating sensor sweeps. They'll find you. Go!" She hissed.

"They'll find you too," he countered.

"They're about to, now go." She pointed a hand in a direction she assumed was towards the outdoors.

 "All right, Boss." His voice reverberated through his respirator. He vanished from sight.

Relieved to have one less worry, Guardian readied herself to fight. Her heart in her throat she emerged from her hiding place in full flight aiming for Draask and his swiveling shoulder cannon. "You missed, and I'll have that!" She tore the weapon from Draask's shoulder, and twisted in mid-air to deliver a hard kick into the giant's back.

Recovering from his stumble, Draask growled and spun to face her.

Still airborne, she stung him with two quick punches.

Draask swiped at her with all four sets of claws.

Recalling hard won lessons from her fight with Ravana, she retreated but stayed on him, circling him, stalking the reptilian warlord like a mongoose would a cobra—darting in, turning his head with a flurry of blows and retreating beyond his reach.

The engineer reached for the computer panels where the remaining drones were rapidly making repairs. He keyed a panel and the narrow slits that ran the height of the reactor columns snapped shut, enveloping much of engineering in inky darkness.

Undaunted by the sudden blackout, and increasingly confident by the S-Ga warlord's inability to match her speed, Guardian pressed her attack only to be suddenly swinging at a black cloud.

Draask loomed from behind her. Grabbing her cape, he flung her into one of the silos.

She grunted and saw stars.

A leak sprang from the reactor. Coolant began to pour onto the deck, steaming as it met the relatively warmer atmosphere.

The reptilian brute was upon her. One of his clawed hands grabbed at her throat and squeezed. Her eyes bulged with alarm. All her martial arts training instinctively told her to sweep the arm away, but the strength of his grip was too great. She grabbed one of the fingers encircling her neck, struggling to pull it back as her legs kicked for his body without finding purchase. Seemingly in slow motion she watched his opposite hand draw back in a punch. She ordered the cape to plaster itself across his eyes. As it slapped into place, she jerked herself hard enough to the right to slip his blow.

Draask roared, keeping his hold on her throat with one hand and tearing the cape from his sight with another. His lower hands seized her waist in a vice-like grip.

Face screwed up in pain, she yowled, desperately clawing at his compressing hands.

Draask released her throat. Balling his upper hands into fists, he slammed them down onto her shoulders.

She shouted in pain, slumped over, and groaned.

Under-cupping her chin in a clawed hand, he lifted her up to gaze upon his prize and stare sadistically into her half-lidded eyes. "As entertaining as this has been. You have work to do. You see, you're going to play a significant part in my conquest by helping me destroy what you love most, *aeon*."

His declaration shook her. She labored to raise her chin. "No..." she moaned.

Draask scoffed contemptuously. "Now feast my minion, give me its strength," he said in a low, lethal, hiss.

An oily black spot appeared on Guardian's uniform. It expanded outward, growing, bubbling, roiling, staining and corrupting every bit of the symbiote.

Feeling her energy sapped, Guardian's heart raced with alarm. Tears of desperation streamed down her face. Her legs fluttered. Her hands clawed feebly at Draask's grip. Gurgling, she sent fruitless commands to her symbiote in a last-ditch attempt to get free.

Her skin crawled, feeling the clammy, rubbery, sulfurous membrane rise relentlessly upwards, swallowing her scream and capturing the outline of her comely face in an open-mouthed expression of horror. Her heart froze, realizing he had sealed her in completely.

Draask paused to admire his work before carrying her limp form from the forest of reactors to the engineering bay. "Is the matrix ready?" he asked his underling.

The engineer pointed a clawed finger at Guardian's statue-like, form. "It only needs to be restrained and I will complete the installation."

Draask quickly arranged her into the mold. He slid a digit over a touch panel. The trotium bonds snapped shut in a chorus of sharp, metallic clangs, trapping her in place. "Then proceed." He motioned to his first officer.

In short order, the engineer pressed heavy insulated cables into the symbiote's subverted form. Gauges and monitors adjacent to the matrix sprang to life. "It is done," the engineer said.

Draask stood back, his eyes glittering triumphantly. "Behold the greatest prize in the universe is mine."

"Hail, Grand Overseer Draask!" the engineer bellowed, crossing his wrists across his armored breast in salute.

Accepting the accolade, Draask turned his attention back to the reactors. "Have all of the crin been inumbrated and readied for release?"

"Soon my lord, the maintenance drones are repairing the damage it caused."

"Then I will dispose of the rest. Inform me the moment we can proceed."

"Of course, my lord...but your weapon?" The engineer looked to the shattered debris of his leader's cannon.

"I have others." A wispy black tendril drifted out of Draask's nostril.

"Of course." The engineer bowed his head. "Good hunting, my lord."

Draask's lips drew back to display his fearsome teeth. "It always is." The warlord disappeared into the shadows.

Closing the matrix, the engineer watched the drones speedily effect their repairs and noted on the monitors that one of the reactors was leaking. Directing one of the drones to follow him, he went to investigate.

Guardian felt as weak as a newborn kitten. So great was her fatigue that her mind lurched and stumbled through a pea-soup-like mental fog, struggling to conceive of a way to escape while fighting the urge to give in to sleep. Her body argued sleep would feel so good, even if it was for just a few moments…

Images swirled in her head: laughing with Ayana, performing surgery, playing with Delilah and Butler, cuddling Issa and Juma, kissing Marcus… Feeling herself slipping away, she jolted awake. She needed help.

Where was…what was his name again? Her mind tread water for many moments before the image of Sergei came to the fore. Was he here?

Struggling to concentrate, she reached out, desperately hoping that he was near.

What she detected brought new terror.

A void wraith.

Its bleakness and malice were all around her, leeching her strength and sowing its despair.

Her desperation overflowing, she knew of only one way to be rid of the foul creature.

Tensing in concentration, she drew upon the flickering spark at the center of her being.

A faint light, like a distant star, glinted on her skin.

The symbiote reacted punishingly. Growling audibly, it viciously squeezed her like a python, seeking to crush its rebellious slave.

Racked with pain, she persisted, turning her entire thoughts away from the torture. She fanned the spark, willing every bit of energy she still possessed to it.

The first spot of white appeared over her abdomen. It grew outward, a black wisp, like smoke wavered over the white spot. The spot grew further, reaching to her hips and up to the bottom point of her uniform's star.

Caught in a psychic tug of war, she groaned under the void wraith's crushing grip. The white spot began to shrink and darken. Guardian gritted her teeth.

The void wraith howled in pain as light pierced it. With one final screech, it evaporated into a black mist. The leads attached to her symbiote popped loose, expelled by the symbiote's instinct to clean itself.

Drenched in sweat, Guardian lay back against the cold metal of the mold, panting.

The thought of him brought renewed alarm. She tried the bonds, grunting against them, before relenting and laying back in desperation, mentally pleading for her strength to return.

Moments passed; the canopy began to rise.

She tensed.

"Hold on Legs," Sergei said. "I—"

He screamed in pain.

"Sergei!" she cried in alarm.

As the canopy rose, she beheld with horror the S-Ga engineer's toothy maw over the Russian's shoulder and chest. Blood poured from the S-Ga's jaws and rapidly began to pool on the floor.

"Legs...." Sergei gasped, reaching out in desperation, the color already draining from his face.

"Sergei!" Guardian screamed plaintively, straining at her bonds.

"Legs..." he groaned, his chin dropped to his chest.

The S-Ga engineer's eyes gleamed sadistically as he looked at her, still gripping his kill.

Sergei's eyes flickered; he lifted a trembling hand. It slid down the panel at the side of the matrix. The manacles snapped open.

Guardian sprang from the matrix, her face a mask of fury.

Frantically backing away, the engineer dropped Sergei. His body fell to the floor with a thud.

She bowled into the alien, knocking him backwards. His girth crushed the maintenance drones against the engineering console. She fell to the deck, the momentary burst of energy spent.

She looked over—Sergei's lifeless eyes stared back at her. Spurred by anger, she staggered to her feet as the engineer righted himself.

Clenching her fists, she seethed at him. "If you know what I am, then you know that the Void awaits you."

The engineer raised his hands in a fending manner.

Guardian leapt into the air, her hands jamming into the engineer's armor, peeling it back as easily as if she were peeling a grape. Red with anger, she grasped a handful of the S-Ga engineer's chest scales, eliciting a roar of agony.

"Get. This. Ship. Off. My. Planet," she snarled.

The S-Ga's eyes clenched shut, his body bowed towards her. "Just stop the pain," he rasped.

Guardian's hand came away from his chest. She spun him around and shoved him towards the console. "On with it!"

Anguish for Sergei and fury at the one who murdered him competed in her breast as she watched the engineer frantically work. She flexed her hands, feeling her strength returning.

"Why is the ship rising?" Draask's voice roared through the intercom on the console.

The engineer toggled the communicator. "My Lord—"

Guardian's fist smashed the console, stifling the response. "Now, for a place to put you—" She grabbed him by his mangled armor.

"Remove your hand from my engineer," Draask ordered.

Without taking her eyes from Draask, Guardian swatted the engineer once and sent him to the deck. "I know what you are, how many of you have taken control of this vessel?" She gestured to Draask.

"We are legion, aeon, and you will serve us...." A black cloud leapt from Draask's jaws, as if pushed by a gale it advanced towards her, hissing and snapping, emitting cackles of rapacious glee.

Clenching her fists, Guardian rose from the deck to face the black cloud head on. "Back to the Void with you!" Light as bright as the noonday sun radiated from her.

A chorus of howls and screams quickly ensued. The cloud convulsed before exploding into beads of black mist and dissipating completely.

"Now for the rest." With a battle cry, Guardian flew straight at Draask and seized his armor with both hands. Not stopping, she drove him backwards, using his body like a battering ram, exploding through reactor after reactor.

Draask's roars mixed with the heavy, hollow thuds of his impacts with the reactor silos and the crash of coolant splashing to the deck.

Guardian ducked his snapping jaws, and flailing limbs, keeping him off balance in a perpetually fall. She flew for the ship's hull.

A hellish red light from thousands of freed crin filled the section. Coolant formed a shallow pond on the deck. The crystalline aliens began to deteriorate and off-gas in the heat, filling the air with vapors.

The warlord slammed against the hull with a resounding clang. They fell into blows, trading punches, the thuds of their fists landing mixed with grunts of pain.

Guardian grasped the dragon-man by the throat and slammed him against the hull, stunning him. "You sought to destroy an entire planet, to turn its people into slaves, to render its flora and fauna extinct and subject its children unimaginable brutality, and use me to do it! For all of this, I will see you back in the Void!"

Draask licked a trickle of black blood from his lip and broke into hissing, mocking laughter. "How will you do that when you're too busy saving Terra?"

An explosion rocked the ship. She ducked her head. Recovering, she discovered Draask had vanished. Cursing she discovered the source of the blast.

The newly freed crin were detonating in the relative warmth of the engineering bay. The effects were readily apparent. Reactor casings were cracking open all over the section. Coolant flowed onto the deck as more and more crin were exposed to the heat.

An alarm chimed in a steady cadence. Warning lights flashed on every reactor column. An explosion rocked the ship. Its power supply faltering, it began to sputter and wobble threatening to fall from the sky.

Realizing she had to get the ship off the planet before the hull breached and the crin escaped—or worse the ship crashed to the Earth with catastrophic effect, she cast about for a solution. Her eyes came to rest on the matrix, now several miles distant. She was off in a flash.

She considered the device for a few seconds. The pod's wires hung where she left them. Trembling, she leaned back into the mold. Her mouth was dry as a desert. A melancholic sigh escaped her lips. Memories flashed through her mind's eye, family and friends long gone, new family and friends she would miss.

An explosion jolted her from her reverie.

She wiped a tear from her cheek and took a deep breath. She commanded the symbiote to allow the wires to do their work, she pressed them into the white fabric of the suit. Her body immediately convulsed, shaking as the matrix grabbed hold and began to draw from her. Her fingers dug into the metal that surrounded her. Her head felt like it was filled with bees. Her vision began to swim. Her eyes flickered. Then all was peaceful darkness.

S-Ga Ship, Engineering

The frigid cold of space permeated the engineering bay. Globules of reactor coolant drifted among the broken columns. The engineering consoles remained lit but the crin had departed, taking their brilliant crimson glow with them.

Guardian floated motionless over the S-Ga ship's deck. Her eyes shut, her limbs limp. Nearby, her symbiote, still tethered to the matrix, resembled a deflated gray balloon. A globe of golden light appeared in Guardian's mind, filling her vision. It grew outward, enveloping and swaddling her in warmth. A voice spoke directly into her mind.

"When I gifted you with your pet, child, I did not expect you to attempt to use it to self-extinguish. I trust you won't undertake such a reckless endeavor again?"

"Mother." Guardian's eyes opened.

"I am here."

An urgent thought struck her. *"Is the Earth...? Is the planet safe?"*

"It remains, as flawed and abused as it ever was."

"Then I was successful?"

"I struggle to understand your attachment."

"You don't have to mother, but it gives my existence meaning." Her eyes fell upon Sergei's lifeless form and creased with sadness. *"They are nobler than you believe."*

"One of them, saved you?"

"Without hesitation."

"The mysteries of free will never cease."

Guardian straightened her posture. *"I will not let his sacrifice be in vain."*

"You're making a simple decision very difficult."

"It is a simple one for me."

"You are being willful."

"I prefer certain." Guardian thought.

"And I am certain you will tire of this place."

"My stamina is legendary. I raised this ship off the planet, didn't I?"

"Do you plan on covering yourself before you return?"

"Yes, back to the planet…" she said, imagining the reaction of Sergei's family and friends, "It will not be a happy occasion for all."

"For all the things I can do, I am sorry I cannot take this sadness from you."

"Thank you, mother, but I should be sad. He was someone striving to become his best self. I must do likewise."

"No more misuse of your gifts."

"I will do better. Can you remain a moment?" Guardian snuggled into her mother's warmth.

"For as long as you need."

The Russell Building, Washington, DC

Along the first-floor corridor of the Russell Building, senators and their staffs loitered in office doorways. A collection of agents from various federal agencies, as well as Sean Ramos, stood grimly, outside Longstreet's office.

"Three minutes," the FBI agent said to Guardian and Marcus.

Guardian nodded. "That should be sufficient." She turned away from the gaggle with Marcus beside her. "Shall we, Dr. Jackson?"

Stone-faced, Marcus gave a curt nod and followed her into Rupert Longstreet's outer office.

"Madeline!" Longstreet barked from behind the inner office door. "Where the hell are you!"

Guardian breezed in to stand before the senator's desk. Marcus stalked in behind her. "Unfortunately, Rupert, she has been unexpectedly detained."

Sitting at his desk, the Senator's eyes bulged. "How the hell did you get in here! I—" His words choked in his throat at the sight of Marcus.

Guardian scoffed in disbelief at his reaction. It amazed her that despite who she was, Marcus was the more intimidating of the two of them. Or perhaps it was just his expression? She decided to rescue the poor fool and stepped into his line of sight.

Longstreet resumed his snarl. "Where the hell is my secretary? Or Chuck? Where's Chuck? What did you do to him?"

"Your very helpful chief of staff is convalescing in hospital."

"Did you torture him? Because if you—"

She frowned. "You would think that, wouldn't you?" After what Marcus told her, she believed nothing was beneath Longstreet.

"One thing I learned is your kind is capable of anything."

She ignored the barb. "Charles is in New Zealand."

"New Zealand!" Longstreet thundered.

"He didn't care for the island where I placed him and attempted to steal the boat sent to provision him. Its owner crowned him with a skillet—but he'll be fit for trial and prison in no time. By the by...." Sorrow touched her features. "He told me about Eleanor and your baby. I'm so very sorry. I will endeavor to obtain justice for your family."

Longstreet waved a finger at her. "Don't you even speak her name."

"Very well, let's talk about some other names then. Charles was quite forthcoming in our discussion."

"I've got my own list of names right here and they just keep coming in. How many of these sound familiar? Or do you even get their names?" He glanced in Marcus' direction before beginning to read. "Let's see...Abaeze Ab—"

Guardian's ears perked with familiarity and traversed the distance to Longstreet in the blink of an eye. She tore the page from his hand and retreated to scan it. Some of the names on it were legitimate. She looked at Marcus apprehensively.

Marcus' attention was on Longstreet. He advanced on the older man, his hand balling into a fist. "You're a grade A, asshole, *boy.*"

Longstreet's tanned face paled. "You touch me and—"

"Marcus!" Guardian called to her lover but did not move.

The big man's fist sent Longstreet and his chair crashing to the floor.

Guardian intervened, interposing herself between them. She placed a restraining hand on Marcus' chest. She was not one for schadenfreude but did not begrudge Marcus a few seconds of street justice.

Marcus stood over the older man glowering. "You're going

down. You and your corporate friends should be real comfy sharing a cell. We've got a long line of witnesses."

She stretched up to murmur in his ear. "You can't keep going around defending me like this or we'll never make it out of the bedroom."

Marcus smirked, his eyes aflame. "There are a dozen good hotels within ten minutes of this place."

Guardian ignored Longstreet's snort and smiled at Marcus. "Let's finish this bit of unpleasantness first, shall we? And please, no more punching."

Marcus stepped back and made a grand, sweeping gesture. "He's all yours."

Guardian righted Longstreet's chair before grabbing him by the lapels and setting him back in it. Standing over him she gave him a look of disapproval. "The real scandal has always been you, Rupert. With the help of your aide and his trunk of secrets, I've learned so very much about you. Tax evasion, insider trading, extortion, sexual assault, graft, as well as kidnapping if we can link you to Gray and Steele's crimes. You're going to be a media darling. In fact, I guarantee it, there's a journalist waiting outside waiting to take your picture and to know everything about what you've been doing these last forty-odd years."

Disheveled and holding his jaw, the Senator glowered at her. Before he could mumble a retort the door to the office flew open, a bevy of agents wearing windbreakers of their various agencies streamed in to begin arresting him.

"Goddamn you—all of you!" Longstreet snarled like a cornered cur as he was handcuffed. "All you did was make a country weaker."

Guardian and Marcus slipped out, while Longstreet continued to froth and curse. The blonde gave Ramos a friendly nod as they walked past him.

"You want to get some breakfast? Or..." Marcus lowered his voice to lean down and murmur in her ear, "Go back to bed?"

She shivered inwardly at his rumbling baritone, wanting to oblige him. "I'm sorry, darling. I can't." Her pretty face fell with a look of apology. "I must go to Moscow for the final arrangements for Sergei's funeral."

Marcus' demeanor altered on a dime. "I'll go with you if you want. I've got months of vacation days banked."

"I would like that but no. If this little escapade of Rupert's has taught me anything, it's that for us, keeping what we have on a low profile is safest. I have a few busy weeks ahead but after that I would love to show you some of my favorite places."

"For me, that's wherever we're together."

Guardian flushed and bit her lip. "Have I told you what a magnificent man you are?"

"To hell with a low profile," Marcus growled sweeping her up in an embrace.

Epilogue

First Saturday of September, 4:00 PM Fairland, Maryland

The jingle of the bell over the comic and game shop's door announced Harold and Guardian's arrival. She was there to kill two birds with one stone, making good on her promise to Harold for his emergency alert application and to set aside any doubts by his friends that she was indeed his friend.

The tail of her cape fluttered down to rest at the back of her knees as she took in her surroundings. It was an older building in an older part of the city with creaky hardwood floors and a ceiling that featured symmetrical patterns in the plaster. Roleplaying and board games lined an entire wall, and long display racks of colorful comic books formed corridors all the way to the back of the store.

The store's few occupants looked up. Their mouths gapped, and gasps quickly became smiles of wonder and disbelief.

"The lady's with me," Harold declared, staring them down protectively.

Guardian turned her face to roll her eyes at his caveman display. "Good afternoon, everyone, Harold invited me along to visit his favorite shop." She strode past the teen, and he fell in beside her.

Harold proudly introduced her to Chris, the shop's owner, and then to the shop's customers who immediately began requesting selfies and autographs. She posed with everyone and signed whatever was handed to her in her beautiful, flowing script. After her autographing was complete, he led her to the long, wooden tables at the back used for tabletop games.

"I'm looking forward to meeting your friends, when should we expect them?" She regarded him from across the table.

Harold checked the clock on his mobile device. "They should be here soon—I just wanted to ask you something first."

"Are you feeling all right, luv?" she asked, watching him take a puff from his inhaler.

Harold nodded, holding the medicine in for a few seconds. "I just wanted to ask...never mind."

"Harold, what is it you want to ask?" She watched his shoulders tighten up. "Come on, out with it." She reached across the table to squeeze his wrist affectionately.

Flushed red, he blurted it out. "I wanted to know if you would go to the Christmas semi-formal with me, but you'll probably say no." The last part of his sentence was a mumble as he averted his eyes to his lap in dread.

"Harold, I'm rather surprised at you." She looked at him with reproach.

"Sorry I—" Harold turned a deeper shade of red, starting to push his chair back.

"Harold...." She kept hold of his wrist and spoke in gentle tones, "I'm not angry, I'm just disappointed. You made my decision for me and you didn't believe enough in yourself to think I might say yes."

"Sorry. I just figured—"

She tilted her head to regard him. "I do understand your sense of hesitation. For centuries I made the same sort of assumption. I assumed I knew how people were going to react to me."

"But you're awesome."

"Thank you, but not everyone felt that way—or even feels that way even now. I was preoccupied with what people would think—just as you were concerned about asking me to your dance."

"You were nervous?"

"I was." She paused to look him in the eye. "Be the best you, Harold, and you'll be amazed at not only who you are but who will come into your life."

"You think so?"

"We're here talking together, aren't we? I think you're brilliant."

A light appeared in his eyes. "So, you'll go?"

"It sounds like great fun, but for me to accompany you, I think it would be more a matter of you saying yes to me—or my conditions."

"Really? You'll go?" He beamed as his emotions soared from the valley of despair.

"With some conditions."

"Name them! Whatever they are—yes!" He beamed.

The blonde was compelled to giggle good-naturedly at his enthusiasm. She held up a halting hand. "Allow me to finish."

"Okay, sure." He nodded, his demeanor becoming subdued.

"First, I don't want your Christmas dance being turned into a circus by the paparazzi." She thought of her experiences. "So you must be entirely discrete about this. Of course, you may talk with Dr. Jackson about it because I'm going to tell him anyway."

"Just Dr. Jackson, okay." He nodded in emphatic understanding, his eyes agog.

"Harold, please?" Guardian said, gently lifting his chin with the pads of her fingers.

"I wasn't...."

"I know. I just like to look into people's eyes when they're asking me on a...to go on an outing with them. Now to my second point, concerning Dr. Jackson. We're a couple so our night out would have to be as friends. Are you fine with that?"

"I—yes—I meant that in the first place."

"Good, I like being your friend." Her eyes twinkled. "Now third, about you, if you meet someone you would rather go with or someone asks you that you would rather go with. I want you to. My feelings won't be hurt."

"I—okay but I don't think I could do that to you."

"Harold, you're a darling, luv," she said with a smile, "but you haven't heard my fourth condition. An emergency could pull me away in an instant. If I'm called away before or during our night out, you won't hold it against me. Are you fine with that?"

"I understand." Harold nodded agreeably.

"Then I accept your invitation. Now come get a hug. You're worn to a frazzle and I just can't be the cause of that." Her button nose scrunched up as she rose, opening her arms to embrace him.

"Hey there, sorry to interrupt you guys."

The pair parted to regard a sweetly smiling blonde woman, in her thirties. She held a large translucent margarine box before her.

"Not at all," Guardian said. She politely shook the woman's hand as Harold introduced the newcomer as Chris' wife, Pauline.

"Chris called upstairs to say we had a special visitor, so I brought some sweets down for all of us." She opened the lid of the box to reveal a variety of homemade cookies and cupcakes.

"They look splendid!" Guardian remarked.

The words had barely left her mouth when Harold's friends arrived. All agog, they offered sheepish apologies to Harold.

Chris ambled up to embrace his wife's shoulders from behind. "I locked up early so you guys can talk without the media busting in from outside."

Grateful for the thoughtful gesture, Guardian joined the ensemble around the table. Selecting a chocolate cupcake to nibble on, she listened with good-natured humor as the teens competed to explain roleplaying games to her.

Avalon, 7 PM

Elizabeth's heart glowed as she nestled her head against Marcus' chest. The pair slowly swayed to Gaye and Terrell in Avalon's parlor. She was wearing the filmy crimson mini-dress that Jennifer told her would set Marcus ablaze. For the past week he had been on vacation, travelling the world with her and spending his nights at Avalon. The previous day, they visited Sehemu Nzuri where Jennifer had been volunteering while the red tape around her accusation was being unraveled and quashed. After meeting Issa and Juma, Marcus asked about sponsoring them, the shower of kisses that followed his question was the most affirmative answer she could give.

"You know it's after midnight in Kenya right now…" Elizabeth murmured.

"You think Jennifer…."

"Part of me hopes she picked one of them."

"My money is on Sal."

Elizabeth lifted her head from Marcus' chest to look at him. "You laid wagers?"

Marcus chuckled. "No baby, just an expression."

She simpered. "Doctors Mwangi and Wambui were equally charming candidates."

"Rooting for the home team?"

"I'm rooting for Jennifer to find someone as wonderful as you." Her eyes twinkled.

"Let's not get her hopes up that high." Marcus grinned.

Elizabeth giggled and rolled her eyes. She began to lay her head back on Marcus' chest when a thought struck her. "Harold asked me to his Christmas dance."

"He did what?" Marcus tilted his head and smiled incredulously.

She giggled in memory. "He was really sweet."

"I've got to stop teaching that boy how to talk to women—"

"You can keep teaching him. He's not quite the master you are."

"The master now…"

"Poor choice of words. "

"But you said yes."

"I adore Harold to the moon, so of course I did—with conditions."

"To the moon huh? But not over it?"

"There's only one man that I adore over the moon."

"And around the world?" His hands slid down to squeeze her bottom through the silky fabric. Elizabeth was forced to catch her breath and giggle at the sudden goose. "I'm in orbit every time I think of him."

Marcus grinned. "You're not wearing panties. Good girl." He gave her bottom a playful swat.

Elizabeth pouted. "I was attempting bad girl."

"That comes later." He grinned.

Elizabeth flushed. She felt her heart race. She had to slow this down before their dinner of prime rib was forgotten. "You know…" she said, as their dance halted, "I've been thinking about going to the moon with you—"

"Me too, all day." He grinned and pulled her in closer for a kiss.

Elizabeth struggled to keep herself from going where he was already and, after many seconds, breathlessly broke their kiss. "No, I mean…." She smiled giddily. "*Taking* you to the moon. We could construct a capsule and get a suit for you." She bit her lip, looking up at him.

"For real?" Marcus paused, the fire in his eyes became stars.

"Yes." She nodded. "I'm still not going to divulge the ins and outs of faster than light speeds but I thought you might enjoy experiencing it."

"But we would be there in a split second."

"Not Earth's moon, that's been done, I was thinking about something unique, just for you, like…Titan."

"Saturn?" His grin took on a quality of wonder.

"It would still be a short trip, minutes once we left Earth's atmosphere. I would wrap the capsule in my cape and pull it. We could go slower if you want to pause and make some observations along the way."

"I'm there. Let's do it!" Marcus lifted her in the air and spun her, listening to her laugh at his exuberant joy before setting her down to kiss her again.

She smiled up at him after their lips parted. "Can we have dinner first?"

"Whatever you want." Marcus beamed at her.

"I still have to make the salad and drizzle the cake."

"I can help with that. What are we drizzling? Chocolate?"

"No, it's a fruit glaze. Have you ever heard of mangosteens?"

Marcus looked at her sideways. "Have you been talking to my mom?"

"No…." She regarded him with a questioning smile. "Why?"

"When my dad was stationed in the Philippines, I would eat those things day and night. I couldn't get enough of them. Every year on my birthday, my mom makes me a mangosteen cobbler instead of cake."

"Truly?" Elizabeth's eyes sparkled.

"Yeah. Why are you looking at me like that?"

Squeezing his hand, she led him towards the kitchen.

Thank you

Thank you for reading my book. If you enjoyed the story, please consider leaving an honest review at the site of purchase.

About the Author

Born and raised in the rural community of Chatham-Kent in Ontario, Canada, and practically living in the classics section of the children's library, Lance began writing tales of adventure and heroism in the fourth grade. An old soul, he tries to sing, and dance, and play, a little each day. He has degrees in political science and psychology.

Check out his webpage: www.jlmeredith.com for announcements, contests, or to read his blog.

Facebook Page Address:
https://www.facebook.com/JLMWrites/

Join his mailing list to be eligible for exclusive, free stories at:

https://www.subscribepage.com/jlmeredithnewsletter

J L MEREDITH